The Ladies of Avanloch

(A Vienna LaFontaine Novel)

Juliana Andrew

Inquiries and Book Orders should be addressed to:

Great Writers Media
Email: info@greatwritersmedia.com
Phone: 877-600-5469

ISBN: 979-8-89175-018-0 (sc)
ISBN: 979-8-89175-021-0 (ebk)

Also By Juliana Andrew

Vienna
The Curse of the Infinity Bracelets
Seventh Crossing
The Arcadia Project
Beyond the Yellow Doors
November Queen

Acknowledgements

Special Thanks to:
My Ladies who posed for the cover
Cheryl Fofonoff, Kayla and Vienna Ferguson,
My friends, Karren Almstrom-Dixon
for her photography of the silhouettes
and author photograph
And
Peter Dixon for perceiving my vision
for the cover and bringing it to life

CHAPTER 1

Ava Lane

December 17, 1983

I had always visualized myself sitting on pillows of white billowy clouds as I ascended into heaven. It wasn't something I thought about often, but every now and then it would cross my mind, especially when I was flying, and today I was on route to Spring Valley via a cargo plane. I had closed my eyes as the scenery had become monotonous; nothing but trees and more trees. It was just as wearisome as flying over the ocean. I was suddenly aroused by an intense rocking of the plane. The pilot was telling us to buckle up as we were heading into a storm. The brilliant blue of the sky had been replaced by dark threatening clouds. I wondered how long I had been asleep. The plane was being battered by hurricane force winds and pellets of hail hammered against the windows. A flash of lightning zigzagged across the sky and I swear I saw a flock of geese fly dangerously close to the wing of the plane. The pilot came on the intercom and told us to prepare for a crash landing. "We are going to hit hard and fast people. If you have any influence with the Man upstairs this is the time to call in a favour."

No, no, no, this can't be happening…I must be dreaming. I put my head between my legs, covered my ears and prayed. A voice behind me called out for us to remain calm. What?

It was like awakening from a nightmare; the one where you dream that you are falling and if you can't wake yourself up, you'll die. Well, we had already fallen and the screaming had stopped so I must be dead. I slowly righted myself and was surprised to find myself still buckled up in my seat. I nervously looked out the tiny fogged up window. Droplets of water were streaming down. I wiped them away and gazed out upon a forest of massive trees heavily draped in wet snow. I hadn't imagined trees in heaven…wait; a faint voice was calling my name. Funny, because I didn't know anyone who had died? Just a minute, I did; the man who had adopted me and been my father for fourteen years. It must be Jeremy, but why was he calling me Miss Lane? I felt a hand on my shoulder and turned and looked into the dark eyes of a stranger. I brushed his hand off. "Get away from me!" I yelled. I closed my eyes and kept repeating under my breath. "There is no hell, there is no hell. Mama, you promised me, you promised me." Apparently I had spoken out loud for someone was answering me.

"Miss Lane, I need you to look at me and calm down! We are not in hell; do you hear me?"

It was the man with the black eyes; the voice that had told us to remain calm before the crash.

"Miss Lane, it's me Sali. Do you remember me? I was in the seat across from you?"

I looked past the man. "Yes, yes, of course. Wasn't there another woman with you? Oh, is she dead too?"

He was talking again. "You are not dead Miss Lane. We are all alive except for Grandfather Little Crow who probably died of a heart attack. However, the pilot is wounded and bleeding heavily and we require your help. Are you able to stand up or you injured also?"

He undid my seatbelt and I let him take hold of my arm and help me up. I didn't seem to have any pain except for a loud drumming in my ears. I asked why he thought I could help the pilot.

"Because you're a nurse, that's why!" He said rather curtly.

"I am not a nurse." I stated emphatically. "What on earth gave you the idea that I was?" I wanted to laugh because I was not at all convinced that I was still on planet earth.

"You are accompanying the medical supplies so you must be a nurse." Sali said. "A nurse always comes with the supplies."

Things were gradually starting to make sense. The plane had crashed, there was a casualty and the pilot was hurt and they thought I was a nurse. I had better explain.

"I'm sorry, but you are mistaken. I once worked for Malcolm Medical Supplies assembling the pharmaceutical kits for transport. I happened to be in the vicinity a few days ago so I stopped in to say hello and they asked me if I would give them a hand in assembling the supplies as their regular gal was off sick. Next thing I know I am asked to accompany the goods as the nurses who usually did called in sick also and I, out of guilt for having quit without notice several years earlier accepted. So here I am. I am sorry to say that I am not the nurse you thought I was."

The man stepped back and sighed. "So, you are no good to us then? Well isn't that just a fine kettle of fish; guess we are on our own Sal. We require bandages and drugs so I am going to have to open the cage that holds the supplies and the narcotic dispensary. I am quite sure it is locked so if you have a key I would appreciate you handing it over or else I am going to have to break into it. Do you have any idea what drugs are in there?"

"I told you I packed the crate and so I know everything that is in it. You will not have to break into it as I will give you the key just as soon as I see the patient." I asserted myself brusquely.

"Why do you want to see him? You just told us that you are not a nurse and can't help. Time is wasting; I need to find something to pry the cage open as it has fallen and the door is bent."

"Just a minute," I stopped him, "surely help will be here any minute and so we should just keep the patient comfortable until he can be assessed by professionals. I can see to that but I would not be comfortable giving him drugs…"

He cut me off. "I don't give a damn what you are comfortable with Miss Lane! I will take full responsibility and you need not worry that your good name will be tarnished." Then he laughed. "And just where do you think help is coming from? Darkness will be upon us in a few short hours and search planes do not fly at night. No help will be forthcoming today. We have just come through a blinding snow storm and our skilful pilot managed to land this disabled relic of a plane in a narrow gorge in a dense forest in the middle of nowhere, and with one exception saved our lives. I will do whatever it takes to keep him alive; have I made myself clear Miss Lane?"

He didn't wait for my response but took off for the rear of the plane telling Sali that she had better check on Ace with or without me.

"Who is that rude man?" I asked Sali.

She took my hand. "Come along, I will take you to Ace. That man is probably going to save us from freezing to death tonight. Do you not remember him getting on the plane? He was late and we had to wait for him?"

"Yes, I do remember. Didn't he have a dog with him?"

"Yes, Asta; she is outside running around. Nash is going to look after us, you will see."

I had no idea what she could possibly mean. The other passenger was a young woman whose name was Evie. She was sitting straight up in her seat with her hands clutching her neck. I asked her if she was hurt and she said that she had neck pain. I took the small pillow from her lap and placed it behind her neck and asked her to recline ever so slightly just so she was a bit more comfortable. I told her I would help her as soon as I checked out the pilot. I think I realized at that moment that I was the closest thing to a medic on board. I glanced in the direction where Grandfather Little Crow had been sitting. His lifeless body had been covered up with a blanket.

I found the pilot on the floor lying in the cockpit on what appeared to be a sleeping bag. He was clutching one of the small airline pillows to his abdomen under his coat. Another man, the co-pilot I assumed, was hunched over, still in his seat.

"Ace, here is the nurse to help you. She knows about these things don't you Miss Lane?"

"Hello Mr. Ace. The first thing I will tell you is that I am not a nurse. I have completed several comprehensive first aid classes and know the basics, but until I examine you I have no idea if I can be of any help to you. Do you understand?"

"I do, and may I say that you are the best looking non-nurse I have ever seen? Do I detect a Scottish brogue? Can you help my buddy Monty? See to him first will you? He is in terrible pain with that shoulder."

Ace's breathing was laboured and I was a little disconcerted about his lack of concern for his own condition. Sali informed me that the co-pilot's name was Melton Montgomery but that everyone called him Monty.

"Miss Lane," he said, "don't you be worrying about me, just fix Acerman up. Nash will throw me up against the wall and my shoulder will snap back right as rain."

I was busy assessing the scene to pay much attention to his preposterous suggestion.

"Mr. Acerman, before I take a look at your wound I need to know if we are safe here. Is there a possibility that this plane could catch fire? If you have any doubts then we are going to have to move you to a safer location."

"Nash said the plane is safe and there ain't no place to go but outside so here is good."

I knew that the first person on an accident scene set the emotional stage for the patient and the others so I would try my best to remain calm even though Sali and this Nash man had already tended to him. I didn't want to cause further injury and I needed to prevent contamination.

"If you remove your hand Mr. Acerman I will take a peek at your wound."

"Just call me Ace." He took a deep breath and released his hand from the pillow. I told him I would be quick. I gently eased the pillow off and saw that his shirt had been torn away and that there was what appeared to be a large pad over his wound. It was blood soaked. I looked at Sali.

"I had a sanitary napkin in my purse and thought it could double as a bandage."

"That was quick thinking Sali."

As careful as I could be I lifted the pad ever so slightly but I could not access how large or deep the wound was as there was too much blood. I covered it back up and replaced the pillow. I reached across his body and applied as much pressure to it as I could. I instructed Sali to remove the key from around my neck and take it to Mr. Nash so he could open the narcotic cabinet and to bring me the contents along with an assortment of bandaging kits. I told her to hurry.

"Mr. Ace, I am going to ask you a few questions while we are waiting for them to return. You don't have to talk if it is too painful, just nod or blink your eyes for no. Are you allergic to any medications?"

"Not that I know of Doc."

I smiled. "Do you know how you injured yourself?"

"Not sure. Was tossed out of my chair and I think I passed out for a second or so."

Monty pointed to a rusty old tool box on the floor. "He fell on that."

I took a deep breath. "Mr. Ace, have you had a tetanus shot recently?"

Both of them made bad attempts at laughter. I did not share their sense of humour. I asked him if he had pain anywhere else and he said it was hard to tell. I didn't find any more bleeding and did a quick check for broken bones. There didn't appear to be any. I asked him what his pain level was on the scale of 1 to 10. He said it was maybe a 7. He seemed to be breathing fairly well, but I figured it would become more laboured once I started probing. I was worried that the loss of blood and delay of treatment may cause him to go into shock.

"What do you want first, bandages or drugs?" Mr. Nash asked dropping half a dozen cartons on the floor beside me. I looked up at him and asked him if he would assist me as Sali was going to relieve me in applying pressure to the wound while I assembled everything.

"There is nothing I would rather do than assist you Miss Lane. Welcome to the team."

Our eyes met as he crouched on the floor beside me. "I'm sorry." I said.

"Sorry…for what?" His eyes were not black but radiated warmth and compassion.

"For thinking you were the devil."

Mr. Ace laughed. "You were right about that darlin. Don't let that little boy grin fool you."

"I would suggest that you save your strength for the surgery Ace. Now be a good boy and let this angel of mercy do her job." Mr. Nash said winking at me and grinning.

His remarks and blatant flirting caught me by surprise. "Surgery…there will be no surgery done here! We are just going to keep him comfortable and try and suppress the bleeding."

"Whatever you say Miss Lane; what do you require of me?"

"Inside those cloth wrapped bundles in that box," I said pointing to it, "you will find a disposable basin and bottles of sterile solutions, tweezers, forceps and scissors. Pour the solution over your hands and then Sali's and glove her and yourself. Then do the same for me as soon as Sali takes over for me in applying pressure to the wound."

He tore open two boxes, one large and one medium. He was quick and within minutes I was sanitized, gloved and had assembled everything I thought I might need. I was scared to death of what I might find. I wished my father was here.

I spoke in a fairly loud voice so that everyone could hear me. "I am not legally allowed to administer a narcotic without the supervision of a professional, but as Mr. Nash has pointed out to me, these are not ordinary circumstances. Seeing that you seem to be fully aware of your situation Mr. Acerman, I will leave the decision in your hands. Do you want me to inject you with a shot of Morphine for the pain?"

"I won't tell if you don't. Go ahead, hit me with it Doc." He said affirmatively.

"I wish you would quit calling me Doc, Mr. Acerman."

"And," he said, "I wish you would quit calling me Mr."

"All right then. I need to ask you a few more quick questions. Have you ever experienced breathing problems?" He shook his head. "Are you a drug user?" He replied with a definite no. "Have you ever had seizures, liver, heart, or kidney problems?"

"No, no, no, and no."

I was happy that he knew exactly how many questions I had asked him.

"One more thing, you may not consume any alcohol of any kind after the injection."

"You're kidding aren't you? I could use a good swig of whiskey right about now. What do you say Nash old man?"

"I say, "Carry on Miss Lane". I can guarantee you that there will be no libations of any kind offered up." Mr. Nash promised.

I relinquished my position over Mr. Ace to Sali and readied myself to inject him with the Morphine. I had administered needles dozens of times when I volunteered at the free clinic but that was over a year ago and always under the watchful eyes of a professional. My hands were shaking. Mr. Nash placed his hand on my shoulder and nodded for me to go ahead. He had already undid Mr. Ace's belt and pants and yanked them down just long enough for me to inject the needle. Mr. Ace flinched only slightly. I discarded the empty vial into one of the basins and asked Sali to slowly quit with the pressure. As soon as she had I pulled the pillow off and gently peeled the pad all the way off all the while preparing myself to replace it quickly if I needed to. Fortunately, there didn't appear to be any new bleeding.

"Good job Sali; the pad seems to have allowed the blood to clot. I need to get a closer look so I can clean up the wound. Can you tear a little more of the shirt? I'm afraid these scissors won't cut it. I would like to get his coat off but I don't dare move him and disturb the clot and beside that, it's providing warmth. Are you ready Mr. Nash? I will need lots of sterile cleaning solution and gauze. Fill several basins please and pass me the forceps. I wish I had more light…"

Monty told Sali that there was a large flashlight in the cabinet behind her. She retrieved it and held it up for me. I thanked her and asked Mr. Ace how he was holding up.

"Pretty good Doc; hardly feel a thing."

"I would like to give you Gravol but there is none in the supplies. I may have some in my purse which must be somewhere near my seat. Do you think you can find them for me Sali?"

"I don't get air sick Doc and I'm pretty sure I won't be flying today so why the Gravol?"

"Sometimes the Morphine makes a person nauseated and I certainly don't want you throwing up on top of everything else. It is just a precaution Mr. Ace and I don't even know if the tablets will help, but it's worth a try. The lesion is about fifteen millimeters wide and maybe six millimeters deep. I can't be sure of the depth without probing and I don't want to do that at this point. It should probably be sutured but I know I didn't pack any suture kits and I'm hoping a compression bandage will do the trick."

"I've got fishing line and Sali's got needles if it comes to that." Nash offered.

"Let's not get ahead of ourselves. Please pass me the Hibitane."

"What's Hibitane and can you translate into inches how deep the wound is?" Sali asked returning with the Gravol.

"Sorry, the wound is approximately six inches long and a quarter of an inch deep though I think it is deeper in places. The Hibitane is a skin cleanser and I am going to apply it liberally all around the site of the wound. It is added protection against bacteria and infections. An old doctor who volunteered at the clinic swore by it."

Sali handed the Gravol tablets to me. I asked Mr. Ace if he thought he could swallow and he nodded so I gave him two tablets with a small amount of water. I stated that we needed all the blankets that were on board as we needed to keep Mr. Ace as warm as possible and asked Sali if she could round them up.

"Never mind the blankets Sal, just grab another sleeping bag." Mr. Nash said taking the bottle of Hibitane from me and pouring it into a clean plastic basin. He soaked gauze sponges with the liquid and without missing a beat passed me a new one every time I discarded a used one. He had been just as quick with the sterile sponge solution.

Sali returned with the sleeping bag and said. "I think you two have worked together before."

"Whatever are you talking about Sali? Today is the first day I have ever laid eyes on Mr. Nash. In fact, we haven't even been formally introduced." I proclaimed.

"Well then let me introduce you; Ava Lane meet Colton Nash, Nash meet Ava Lane. I still say you two know each other from somewhere."

"Not in this life Sali." I declared.

She asked me if I believed in re-incarnation. "Sure, why not." I answered. "I believe in fairies and elves and witches and ghosts, so why not re-incarnation."

Mr. Ace had to offer his opinion to our weird conversation. He spoke in a wispy far away voice. "I think you've met your match there Nash man."

Colton Nash laughed. "Don't pay him any mind Honey; I think he's in a Morphine stupor."

"Quit being so damn polite you too! We're in Alaska you know, so quit with the formality;

enough with the Mr. and Miss thing." Ace advocated.

"What do you say Ava, can you call me Nash? And, by the way, we are nowhere near Alaska."

"Sali said your name was Colton so why do you go by your last name?"

He replied that he just did and passed me an abdominal pad which I laid over the wound. He seemed to anticipate exactly what I needed next and one by one handed me small strips of adhesive that I applied stingily. I sat back and waited for a couple of minutes to see if there was any new bleeding. There wasn't so I asked Nash for the pressure compress and laid it over the abdominal pad and then with his help wrapped a tensor bandage completely around his body and secured it. I had been working completely on instinct and had no idea if what I had done was right or enough to curtail the bleeding and prevent infection. We shed our gloves and Nash asked if we were up to one last task. I knew that meant adjusting Monty's shoulder and I hoped he knew what to do as I had no idea. I attempted to get up off my knees but was so wobbly that I collapsed back down.

"Do you need a moment Honey?" He asked holding on to me.

I wondered why he kept calling me 'honey.' I supposed that he couldn't remember my name. My father always calls me honey. I looked up at him and something passed between us but I had no idea what it was. I felt very vulnerable. I let him help me up and feeling the warmth in his arms I suddenly realized how cold I was.

Sali's and my job was to hold Monty's elbow on the affected arm and apply traction. I had asked him if he would like a shot of

Morphine also but he declined saying he had better not. I did not ask any further questions. Nash positioned himself behind Monty and gave him some directions which I couldn't hear. He then told me and Sali to hold steady and with one quick twist the deed was done. There had been a slight popping sound and I could see immediately the relief in Monty's face.

"Well done buddy. Now I'll take a swig of that pain killer if you don't mind."

I started to rattle off names of non-narcotic medications that he could choose from. Monty shook his head and asked if I was for real. I asked him what he meant. Nash answered for him.

"He didn't mean anything derogative, but in these parts of the woods they soothe their wounds with their own brand of medicine." He put his arm around Monty and led him off saying he'd see what he could find in his duffel bag before they got busy setting up camp.

"Just a minute Mr. Montgomery," I protested, "where do you think you are going?"

"Well to help set up camp of course; Nash can't do everything by himself."

"I have no idea what you mean by "camp", but if it involves physical labour I highly suggest you forego it. Your shoulder needs to be iced and put in a sling." I said assertively.

"No time for that unless you want to spend the night in this frigid tin can. I'll take you up on that sling later, but right now I got to cut down a few trees. Let's hit the trail Nash."

"A little help here Mr. Nash…" I pleaded.

"Perhaps she's right Monty; you could end up doing more damage to that shoulder."

"Screw the shoulder, let's go."

Nash shrugged. "I promise to keep him on a tight leash." He looked down at my feet. "Sali, you'll look after her I trust."

I asked Sali what he meant by that and why did he keep calling me honey.

She said she hadn't noticed. She told me to take a seat and picked up my left foot and removed my "sissy boots" as she called them. "These might be good enough for coastal weather but they'll freeze you solid the minute you step outside."

"I don't know what you are going to do about it Sali because it's already too late and I fear my feet are already frozen."

She reached for a pair of scissors from her oversized bag and cut the foot out of my nylon stocking. "Silly girl, you never wear nylon next to your skin in the winter; over a woollen stocking maybe, but never under."

"I didn't know I was going to be in a plane crash in the arctic or I would have dressed for the occasion." I stated in my own defense.

"Didn't your mother tell you that you should always be prepared for the worst?"

I couldn't argue with that. She massaged my ice cold foot back into circulation and then dressed it in some unknown fabric. I told her I hoped it wasn't wool because I was allergic to it. She laughed and said that I was in luck then because it was cashmere. I doubted it but didn't comment. She said she hoped I was a size 6 or 7 but had no idea how we sized our feet in Scotland. She slipped a beautiful beaded warm moccasin on my foot. It came about half way up my leg and my foot was in heaven. She quickly did the same for my right foot and I thanked her over and over again. She told me that the moccasins were called Mukluks and were hand-made and would keep my feet warm and cozy as long as the snow was dry. I asked her why she had an extra pair with her and she replied that her mother had always told her to be prepared for the unexpected. Evie giggled and stuck her foot out so that I could see that she had a pair of Mukluks on also. Sali told me to tend to Evie as she had to go and help the boys with the camp and get a fire going as soon as they returned with some wood. I wiped the wet window off and was totally surprised to see that a tent had sprung up about twelve meters from the plane.

"Where did that come from?" I asked in astonishment.

"What did you think when Nash said "set up camp"? Sali replied passing me a toque.

"I hadn't a clue…does he always pack a tent around with him? What's the hat for?"

"It's to keep your brains warm Dumpling. Nash is a wilderness outfitter and guide and he just returned from some sort of convention with all the latest gear. Lucky for us that he is scheduled to take a group out on an excursion after Christmas and is on this flight, wouldn't you say?"

"No, I didn't know that; how would I know that? He certainly doesn't look the part."

Sally laughed. "Well, he just got back from a couple of weeks in the city so he hasn't shifted back into Grizzly Adams mode yet. He does like to be clean and neat for all the ladies though."

"Are there a lot of ladies in his life?" I hoped I didn't sound too curious.

"Well, there is his sister and his mother…"

"That's not what I meant Sali."

"I know. He has not confided in me lately, so I do not know of any new conquests. He was engaged once though."

"Weren't we all? How do you know so much about him Sali?"

"I have known him for many years and his lodge is only a ten minute walk from where I live."

"You mean from Spring Valley?" I asked.

"No, I live in Akemantack."

"But I thought we were supposed to land in Spring Valley?"

"We were as it's the only town with a landing strip that can accommodate a cargo plane in the vicinity. Everything is either trucked or flown in there and we pick up our supplies from there. Five or six times a year me or my sister go outside to craft and trade fairs and so we usually always bring supplies back to our village. That way we save on transport fees. Our parents run a small trading post twenty miles from Spring Valley in Akemantack."

"I know you are anxious to get out and assist the men so please will you tell me more about your way of life later on? I have just one question for now though…what did you mean when you said you go "outside" to fairs?"

"Yes, we will definitely exchange stories later. Evie will fill you in on the "outside" thing."

With that she went to the rear of the plane where she began throwing duffle bags towards the door. I followed her and helped her throw them out onto the frozen snowfield stating that I would join her after I helped Evie and checked on Ace. She grinned at me and for the first time I noticed that three of her front teeth were missing.

Nash had left the medical cabinet in a state of disarray. I didn't blame him for the mess as I had urged him to be quick. I found myself wondering about the type of women he dated and his one-time fiancée. He was a little brazen for my tastes but certainly wasn't lacking anything in his physical attributes. I supposed one had to stay fit to live the life of a wilderness guide. He had dark brown hair with no visible signs of graying and so I estimated him to be in his late twenties or early thirties. He was about my father's height which is just shy of six feet. His face was weathered in a very good way. Something about him reminded me of my father. It certainly wasn't the eyes because his were dark brown and my dad's, as were mine, were deep blue. Oh God, my mother…how was this going to affect her pregnancy? Please, I prayed, let us be rescued before news breaks regarding the missing plane. I returned to the task on hand and that was to find a muscle relaxant for Evie. For the love of me I couldn't remember if I had packed any. I returned to the front of the plane and asked Evie how she was doing. She said it was only her neck that was sore. I decided to try a light massage. She said that it felt good so I upped the intensity a little. Fifteen minutes or so later I returned the pillow to the back of her head and gave her two aspirin.

She thanked me and then explained what Sali had meant by the word "outside." She said that the people of the north said that they were going "outside" whenever they were leaving the area they lived in. "Like," she said, "if I lived in Whitehorse and was going to Vancouver, I may say that I was going "outside"."

"Okay, but why don't they just say where they are going? By the way Evie, what is your destination?"

"That's where I am going in fact, to Whitehorse to spend the holiday with my sister and her family. I suppose I'll be late."

"Today is only the seventeenth so you will still be there in time for Christmas."

Evie said that she hoped so and would dearly like to lie down as she was tired of holding her head up. I told her I would see what I could do. I checked on Mr. Ace and he appeared to be sleeping so I squeezed out the partly closed cargo door and found Sali trying to make a table out of empty crates. I could swear it had only been minutes since I had last seen her and yet she had managed to get a fire started to the right of the tent. I thought it was a little too close to both the plane and the tent, but then, what did I know? I asked her where the wood had come from and she said Nash had brought her an armful…of course he had. I stood with my back to the crackling fire. It was much warmer outside then inside the plane. I told Sali that Evie wanted out. She said she could see no reason why Sali couldn't crawl into one of the sleeping bags in the tent and that Nash wanted to get Ace into the tent also.

It took both of us to get Evie into a standing position. She was very tense and reluctant to move if it meant she had to twist her neck or head. I reminded her that it was her idea to lie down. Step by step we coaxed her towards the door. I realized that there was no way we were going to be able to get Evie off the plane as the ramp had been destroyed along with the landing gear when the plane crashed. It was a big step down, and with her unwilling to move a muscle we were going to have to improvise. Sali suggested that we build a step out of snow and then perhaps we could ease her unto it. I said that maybe we should wait until the guys returned. As if on cue, Nash appeared pulling the travois that he had constructed to haul firewood.

"What are you girls up to?" He called as he entered the camp.

We told him about our predicament. He dropped the poles and offered his hand to Evie. She didn't budge. I told her that she was going to have to take the plunge sooner or later or she was going to seize up and so why not into Nash's big strong arms. He told me to show her how it was done. His grin told me that he was goading me.

"Right." I said boldly. "You should prepare yourself Mr. Nash for I am no lightweight!" I flung myself forward and landed squarely in his arms. Our eyes locked and I thought he held onto me a little too long. Evie said that she couldn't do it. "Of course you can, it's only a drop of one and a half meters."

Nash backed up to the door and sat down and told her to climb onto his back. She hesitated and so I climbed back up and Sali and I each took one of her arms and all but forced her onto Nash's shoulders. We followed him into the tent and helped him unload her. She had tears in her eyes.

It took us another few minutes to get her into the sleeping bag. Sali ran back to the plane and retrieved one of the small airline pillows for her. "I'm sorry if we hurt you Evie. If you are still in a lot of pain I can give you something for that."

"I'm sorry I was so much trouble." She sniffled squeezing my hand. "I think I will be all right. I feel much better lying down."

I asked her if she was warm enough noticing there was something that looked like it might be some sort of heater sitting in the middle of the tent. She said she was okay.

"Evie," I said, "why were you on this plane anyhow? Why didn't you take a commercial flight? I was under the impression that cargo planes don't take passengers."

"I'm afraid I fudged the truth a little. I left the booking too long and was put on stand-by for a flight to Whitehorse on the twenty second. I didn't want to wait that long and so I told the booking agent that my sister was going into pre-mature labour and I needed to get there as soon as possible. She told me to try Northland Transport and they agreed to take me. I guess this is my punishment for lying. Perhaps it's my fault we crashed as God is angry with me."

I told her that was just plain silly and to quit worrying as we'd be rescued tomorrow.

Nash was gone by the time I got back outside. Sali was still trying to construct a table but the boxes kept collapsing. I told her that I was certain we could find something sturdier inside the plane to hold Mr. Nash's implements. She said the table wasn't so much for Nash as it was for us to assemble meals. I'm afraid I laughed at her and asked her just where she thought we were going to find the ingredients to do that.

She looked at me oddly. "You do know that I have a store inside the plane don't you?"

"A store, what do you mean?"

"Did you miss the part where I told you that I was on a buying trip to replenish my parent's trading post and to purchase stuff for my village's Christmas dinner?"

"I heard you mention that you had been selling your wares and shopping for Christmas goodies. I thought you meant candy canes and chocolate and stuff to fill stockings. Are you saying that there is real food in the plane?"

She took my arm. "Come on Dumpling, it'll be lights out in no time."

I followed her into the plane. She said she had to check with Ace to see if there was enough battery power left to turn the cargo lights on. He assured her there was plenty and asked when we were getting him up. I told him as soon as Nash and Monty returned as we wouldn't be able to get him into the tent by ourselves. He laughed and said he guessed not as he had heard how much trouble we had getting little Miss what's her name off the plane. He instructed Sali what switches to turn on. She hit them all and the inside and the outside lit up like a Christmas tree. Ace said to leave them all on as Nash would get the hint and realize that it was time to quit for the night. It was only a little after three in the afternoon and so I didn't think darkness would descend upon us for another hour or so. Ace said that he had to pee. I said I would see what I could do.

"No time Doc; there's a jug in that cupboard for just such emergencies."

I found it and asked if I could help. He said he wasn't that indisposed yet. I wanted to help him undo his pants but he insisted he could do it. I left him alone with his make-shift urinal and joined Sali at the rear of the plane.

"See, now that most of Nash's paraphernalia is gone you can see the freezers and temperature controlled containers and the cases of staples. I pretty much remember everything I purchased but have no idea what is in the freight going to Whitehorse and Dawson City. It could be foodstuffs or something else entirely."

"There's more?"

"Yep, behind that closed grey tarp is a whole other load of goods."

I knew that it took a long time to starve to death and we would be rescued tomorrow so I hadn't been the least bit worried about food. On the other hand, just in case it took a day or so for us to be found it was nice that we wouldn't go hungry. Sali asked me what I fancied for supper and I asked her what she had in mind.

"I was thinking maybe some chicken noddle soup and fried Spam and eggs. What do you think?" She started rummaging through the boxes until she found what she wanted.

"Soup sounds good but I have no idea what this Spam is you mentioned. I hope that one of those cases has coffee as I could sure use a cup right now."

"What, I thought you Scots all like your tea? Spam is a tinned luncheon meat; you can eat it cold but my people like it fried, especially in the winter."

She handed me a pocket knife and pointed to a case with a coffee logo. I told her that I got my love of coffee from my mother and father and that the only time I drank tea was with the ladies. She asked me what ladies. I bit my tongue because I had been about to say that I drank tea when it was my time to host "high tea" at Avanloch Castle. No one needed to know that I was an heiress and second or third in line to become the next Mistress of Avanloch. No, no one needed to know that. I opened the case of Nabob Coffee and took one package out mumbling that I didn't know how we were going to perk it. What? What was I thinking? This was all a dream…I could manufacture a coffee pot couldn't I? I had invented this scenario; nothing was real and it was time for me to wake up. You can't crash land in the wilds of Canada in the winter and have everything on board that is essential to surviving. Where else but in a nightmare would this happen? I laughed a little remembering that I had played nurse pretending that I knew exactly what I was doing and had even contemplated stitching Ace's wound up with fishing line. What was going to wake me up? Did I really want to let go of these people I had created…especially Nash. There was something about him…

"Ava, what's wrong?"

I said "What, what did you say?" Okay, I wasn't awake yet…or was I?

"I think you went away there for a minute. I was saying that Nash would have something to cook the coffee in and you said of course he would and then you kind of went blank."

"I was just thinking that this is kind of like a dream."

"It's no dream Dumpling. Now let's get to work while we have the light. We don't want to use up all the battery power."

We decided to use the metal crate that the medical supplies were in for the base of our table. While we were unloading it I asked Sali what other provisions she had in her containers.

"In that cooler there is butter, eggs, milk, cheeses and an assortment of root vegetables. I am afraid the vegetables won't last and will probably freeze. The oranges and apples will freeze too so we'll have to eat them right away. There are turkeys in the freezer... eight if I remember correctly. There are cases of staples such as tin milk, sardines, tuna and soups, Christmas treats like cranberry sauce and tinned ham. Then there are things like ketchup, mayo, syrup, biscuit mixes and toilet paper and hygiene products and so on."

"So, in other words, you have a little bit of everything and we aren't going to starve and the cranberries will save us from getting scurvy,"

She laughed. "Yes, we will be just fine, at least for the time being."

We finished unloading the medical crate and got to work trying to move it towards the cargo door. After five minutes of useless tugging and pushing we collapsed on the cold floor laughing hilariously. There was no way possible that we could budge the heavy crate.

"Well, it's too soon for you two to be exhibiting signs of cabin fever so I have to assume that you found my stash of whiskey? By the way, thanks for turning the lights on for us." Nash had returned.

That's it, I thought... I've been drinking.

Monty peeked in and asked what all the commotion was about. Ace yelled that Sali and I had been into the juice. That only started us giggling again. I tried to explain through the laughter that had brought me to tears what we were trying to do. Nash told us to clear a path in front of the crate and asked Monty to bring him the tow rope from the travois. Nash ordered us off the plane while he secured one end of the rope to the crate. He climbed down and then all of us, including the dog, proceeded to play tug-of-war with the crate.

It made a loud thump when it landed but we had the structure close to where we wanted it. Evie emerged from the tent asking what was going on. I was very pleased to see that she was moving and asked how she was. She responded that her headache had subsided somewhat but her neck still hurt. Nash sat her on one of the rounds of wood by the fire. He said he was going to start the kerosene heater so that we could bring Ace into the warmth. I followed him into the tent.

"Is that what that is…a kerosene heater? How does it work?"

I could barely see him in the fading light. "Well," he explained, "you fill it with kerosene which I have already done, and then you light the wick. You might want to go back outside as it will smoke and smell a bit until it gets going."

"Why does it have a wick and isn't kerosene combustible? Wasn't there a danger that it would explode when we crash landed?" I asked concerned.

"You're just full of questions aren't you Ava Lane? Firstly, it has a wick which is made from cotton or fibreglass and it draws fuel from the tank much like a lantern does. Surely you know what a kerosene lantern is?"

He didn't wait for an answer but continued. "Cargo planes carry many different kinds of fuel. They are packed safely in non-combustible cushioning materials and sealed in a fuel compartment in the belly of the plane."

"Why wasn't it destroyed when we crashed? How much fuel are we talking about and weren't you worried that it would explode when we crash landed?"

"We were lucky I guess, and yes I was concerned that the bladder may have been damaged. I removed it from the compartment immediately after I checked on the passengers." He was kneeling in front of the stove and looked up at me smiling, "Anything else?"

There was a small glow coming from inside the heater and it was enough that I could make out his face. "I'm sorry for asking so many questions." I didn't know why I was apologizing.

"Honey, you can ask me as many questions as you like. I know this being here in these inhospitable conditions can't be easy for you so if I can ease your concerns in any way…"

"I'm not a city girl Nash. Where I was raised would be considered the boondocks to some." I left without explaining myself any further. He followed me out.

Sali and Monty were in the midst of laying ripped cardboard from the boxes on top of the metal crate and holding it down with cans of food and utensils from a box marked 'mess kit.' I was pleased to find a large blue coffee pot. It was a percolator; the same kind as the one Mary McDuff used in the kitchen at Avanloch. I offered to make the coffee.

"I guess you're going to need some water then." Monty said.

"How long do you think it will take to melt a pot of snow?" I asked.

"I think it will be quicker if we just use water." Nash proposed grabbing a pail from one of the opened boxes. I think he winked at me but it was hard to tell in the flickering lamp light.

"And, just where are we going to find water?" I asked sarcastically.

"I'm just guessing, but I think the creek will be willing to share its H20 with us."

Monty laughed and Sali told them to quit teasing me. She had just found out herself that there was a creek up the ravine. I decided to see this waterway for myself and said I'd go with him.

"If you're sure that you want to trudge through the snow then you may as well bring another receptacle." Nash picked up an axe and a flashlight and Sali handed me a large pot with a handle.

The path was already compacted because of the guys hauling the wood over it so I didn't have any trouble walking even though I could hardly see where I was going. Asta, Nash's dog ran ahead of us. Nash instructed me to step in his tracks as he veered off into unpacked snow. He said the creek was down a slope and perhaps I should wait at the top as it would be slippery.

"I don't even know why you think there is a creek down there; I can't hear any water running."

"Monty and I found the stream further up where we were cutting the trees. Don't worry, there is water and you can't hear it because it is frozen solid."

Now I knew what the axe was for. "Well, you are going to need someone to hold the flashlight while you chop and seeing I am the only one here…"

"All right," He relinquished, "but wait here until I check it out. Stay with her Asta."

I stood in the eerie silence of the evening convinced that I heard footsteps crunching in the snow behind me. I held on to Asta's collar. The two minutes it took Nash to get back to me seemed like an hour. He reached his hands up to me and I gladly took them. He asked me why I was shaking.

"I thought I heard something behind me but Asta didn't growl so it was probably just my imagination." I said not at all too convincingly.

"You are **never** to venture off by yourself Ava, never!"

I had no intention of doing so. "I'm sure I won't but why not? Are there wild animals about?"

"What do you think? I felt fairly safe leaving you women back at the plane in the daylight because Sali knows how to handle a rifle but one can never be too careful."

"Well, you aren't carrying a weapon and what makes you think I don't know how to use one?"

"And, what makes you think I'm not carrying one? You'd be surprised as to what this heavy coat is concealing and forgive me if I have mistakenly assumed things about you."

I did not comment any further. He passed me the flashlight and I held it up while he chopped vigorously at the frozen waterfall. I was about to suggest that he leave it until morning when a small crack appeared and a trickle of water ran down it and refroze almost immediately. Nash brought the axe down upon it once more and the crack widened, hesitantly at first and then it gave way to a deluge, spurting water everywhere and soaking Nash. He quickly filled our containers and we made our way back to camp. Thankfully all the outside lights of the plane had been turned on again which made our trip back a little easier. I sped up my pace wanting to get Nash back before his clothes froze on him as the temperature had plummeted. He assured me that wasn't going to happen but that he was looking forward to warming up by the fire. We were walking side by side with the camp only meters away.

"I think you're going to need a lot more warming up than that and you are going to need to get these wet clothes off and get into something dry. It's a good thing that you started the heater in the tent."

"You're right; I'm going to need a lot of warming up. Can you help me with that Miss Lane?"

"Whatever you are suggesting is not going to happen. You are becoming altogether too familiar with me."

He broke out laughing as we stumbled into camp.

Monty took the water bucket from me. "You two sure took your time; Ace is badgering us to get him out...what the hell happened to you Nash?"

I started for the plane and turned around and said. "I pushed him into the creek."

Sali looked shocked. "You didn't?"

"He needed cooling off. See that he gets into some dry clothes will you Monty? I need to check on our captain and then we best get him into the warmth."

Nash called after me still chuckling. "Last chance Ava."

I heard Monty ask what was going on between the two of us as I made my way to what was left of the cockpit. I knelt down beside Ace. He also asked me what was going on and were we going to leave him to freeze to death while the rest of us slept nice and cozy in a warm tent. I explained that we were waiting on Mr. Nash to change into dry clothes and relayed our little water episode to him. I questioned him as to what his pain level was and he said it was tolerable. I then asked him how long he had known Nash for.

His response was a little disturbing. "Six or seven years I guess. Why do you ask...don't tell me he's put the moves on you already?"

"What?" I said startled.

"Sorry, shouldn't have said that. Don't take anything he says seriously; he likes to kid around with the girls, that's all. He's not use to a prim and proper lady like you."

I stood up. "Is that your impression of me? Do you all think I am this strait-laced woman from the Isles who's offended by off color language or can't take a little ribbing? I only asked you how long you had known Mr. Nash for..."

I didn't get to finish my sentence as there he was; as if on cue again. "Did I hear you mention my name Miss Lane? Were you cursing me out again?"

"Again, when have I ever cursed you? I suppose you also think that I am this prissy Scottish maiden who has never encountered common scoundrels before..."

"Whoa there; where is all this coming from? Again, I am sorry if I have offended you..."

This time I didn't let **him** finish. "You have not offended me Mr. Nash so you need not apologise. Now what say we get Ace out of here?"

"I see you two are back with the Miss and Mr. thing again. What the hell has happened while I have been cooped up in here?" Ace questioned.

I laughed a little edgily. "Nothing and I assure you that I am still as captivated by Mr. Nash as I was the first time I laid eyes on him." I had no idea why I said that.

"Really...captivated, Miss Lane? I am flattered, but if I remember correctly, you thought I was the devil not more than a few hours ago, am I right?"

I didn't answer him but I am sure that my look said it all. I knew that something was going to develop between us...I just didn't know how far it was going to go or if it would have devastating consequences.

I suggested we enlist the aid of Monty and Sali and together we could all "drag" Ace and the sleeping bag to the open door and somehow lower him to the ground from there. Ace said he could probably walk with some help. We vetoed that immediately. We carried out the task without incident though Ace did groan a little when we lowered him from the plane to the ground. Evie came to take up one end of the bag while Nash supported Ace's body from underneath. We placed him into a dry sleeping bag and he insisted we place him in a sitting-up position. Nash looked at me for concurrence.

"Well," I said, "let's give it a try."

Monty brought a round of wood in and we placed it behind Ace cushioning it as best we could with a sleeping bag. The guys stayed with him while I went out to help the girls get the supper on. It was now six o'clock; five hours ago we had crashed landed in the middle of nowhere.

Sali and Evie had laid out an array of dishware on the make-shift table alongside of the two burner kerosene stove. Nash's mess kit contained two plates, two bowls, two mugs and two sets of silverware which included four spoons of various sizes plus utensils like a ladle and a spatula. Besides the coffee pot were two skillets and three different sized pots with lids. Monty had contributed to the service with two cups from his and Ace's thermoses, one rather rusty plate and an assortment of plastic picnic utensils. We decided we could use the pot lids as dishes and we would just have to make do with what we had. Monty said he'd hone down the soup cans and make them safe to drink from. I doubted that he could refine them enough but didn't say so.

Soup was warming on one of the burners and I placed the coffee pot on the other. As soon as it was perked Sali started into frying her "Spam." I took a cup of soup into Ace and told Nash to go and eat. He said he needed to string a clothesline up first so that he could try and dry his coat and the damp sleeping bag. Ace wasn't too keen on the soup but between it and the coffee I figure he got half a cup of liquid into him. I helped him to lie down and told him I would like to check on how his bandages were holding up. He asked for a pain killer. I asked if he could hold off for a couple more hours as I didn't want to overmedicate. He said he would try. I could definitely tell by the strained look on his face that he was hurting.

"I think it's time you took a little nourishment yourself Ava." Nash said when I emerged from the tent. He handed me a cup of soup. I thanked him and squished a handful of crackers into it. I ate it quickly and then rinsed my cup out and poured myself a much needed cup of coffee. Sali asked me if I wanted canned milk in my coffee. I told her I took it black. It was then that I learned that her provisions did not contain sugar or salt and pepper. Monty said he wasn't too fond of using honey in place of sugar. Sali told him to be thankful that there was coffee and honey and passed me a plate which contained a fried egg and a piece of the mystery meat. I thanked her and sat down next to Monty on an unoccupied round of log close to the fire. He nodded to me.

"Tomorrow I will carve out a few bench seats which hopefully will be a little more comfortable than these blocks of wood."

"Why are you going to do that Mr. Montgomery…are you of the same mind as Mr. Nash that we will not be found anytime soon?" I asked fearing that he thought as much.

"Anything is possible Miss Lane. I take it that we are back to addressing each other formally again? I am as hopeful as everyone else that we will be found but until then I may as well keep busy doing something useful."

"I'm sorry for the Mr. reference Monty; it just slips out. I do not mean to sound superior and I want you all to know that I am quite thankful that you all just happened to be on this ill-fated journey with me. I am somewhat comforted to have such resourceful people around." I turned around and smiled and hoped that I came off as being sincere.

"Yeah, I think you're right Miss…Ava; we are a resourceful bunch, you included." Monty agreed.

Evie laughed. "Speak for yourself Monty; I have no hidden talents to contribute to our survival. In fact, I may be a hindrance with this stiff neck."

Monty walked over to where Evie was standing. "Suck it up kid; we'll find a use for you yet."

Nash agreed and placed his hand on her shoulder. "I hate to say this, but we are lucky that we survived this horrendous crash at all with so little injury and only one casualty. I think it would be fitting if we have a little service for Grandfather Little Crow tomorrow; what do you think?"

We were all in agreement. Nash took the seat that Monty had just vacated. Asta came with him and sat down at my feet. I asked him if Asta could have my leftovers. He grinned and said that she could. He probably knew that I could not stomach the "Spam."

"She likes you Ava."

"That's good because I like her too. What breed is she?"

"She's what we call a bear dog. The original bear dogs originated in Russia. They are larger than Asta and have fur that is more like a husky. Asta has her winter coat right now but in summer she will shed and have a thin coat. I imagine her ancestors would be quite disappointed with her stature and her black and white coloring."

I bent over to pet her. "She's just beautiful the way she is. Why are they called bear dogs?"

"Originally, and probably still in Russia and other countries, they are used to hunt bear, moose and wild boar. They are not afraid of anything. Here in Canada, prospectors and trappers and hunters take them with them in case they encounter bears. An old trapper friend of mine retired to Prince George leaving a litter of pups in my care. Asta's sisters and brothers all went to good homes around Spring Valley. These dogs are rumoured to worry a bear to its death as they surround the bear barking and snapping. They are fast and small enough to avoid being swiped at. It's probably one of those backwoods tales but I don't doubt for one minute its validity."

Asta sat up and placed her head in my lap. I suddenly felt very sad as I stroked her. Nash asked me if I had dogs at home.

"We have four Labrador Retrievers, three are golden and one is dark brown and we have a German shepherd puppy. My Mother brought her home from Spain last..." I turned away as I could not finish my sentence.

"Ava, what is it?" Nash asked hesitantly.

I lied and told him that it was nothing. I brushed myself off and said I had better check on Ace. He offered to help but I declined and said that Sali had already offered. Monty was emerging from the tent as Sali and I approached. He said that he had shut off the heater as it was too hot inside. I asked him if he needed me to adjust his sling and he said it was fine. Ace was quite crabby. He said he had an itch that he couldn't scratch and that he was uncomfortable and couldn't sleep. I told him I had something that would relax him and help him get to sleep but I wanted to examine his wound area first. He grumbled but told me to go ahead. Blood had seeped out through the layers of bandages. I had a moment of panic fearing that I might have to stitch the wound up after all. I told Sali that I required Nash's help. She went to fetch him while I collected the dressings and sterile equipment and gloves. I needed Nash to hold Ace up so we could remove his coat and the binding that was holding the bandages in place. Monty and Evie sensed that something was wrong and came to offer their assistance. I asked Monty to hold the light steady above us and Evie said that she would assist Nash with the bandages.

Once the dressings were all off I let out a sigh of relief. "Thank God, there is very little new bleeding. I imagine that it was our dragging Ace that opened up the wound but it has clotted again. I'll just clean it and re-bandage. Nash, you know the procedure." He asked Evie to glove him and in no time we had the procedure completed once more.

"For a minute there I thought I was going to have to take you up on the offer of stitching Ace up with your fishing line Nash and one of Sali's fine needles. I hope we have averted that for now. Thanks for all your help everyone."

"Just to make a point here Ava; it's you who did all the work and I think I speak for everyone when I say it's you who deserves the applause. You told us going into this that you were not a nurse and were very unsure of what to do. I pretty much badgered you into taking on the role as medic… well young lady, inexperienced as you say you are I will gladly put my life in your hands any day!" Nash proclaimed.

I administered the Morphine to Ace amidst the applause. I said optimistically. "Let's hope it never comes to that Mr. Nash. Now that we are all here in this warm cozy tent I have a few questions for the pilots and I hope you will be honest." I looked at Monty and then Ace. "I think it's time that you two enlightened us as to what really brought the plane down. Was it the blinding snow storm, or were we struck by lightning? Isn't it unusual to have an electrical storm in the middle of winter? And did that flock of geese have anything to do with it?"

Ace told Monty to tell me as he didn't have the strength. "Bull tweedy!" I exclaimed. "You may be wounded but there is nothing wrong with your memory or your voice."

Nash snickered. "You tell him Honey."

I glared at him. "And you too, big boy! You know more than you are letting on, don't you?"

There was that gleam in his eyes again. "Yes, I have discussed it with the boys and they think it's a combination of all three…the unexpected whiteout, the lightning strikes and the geese. I will leave the experts to explain the phenomenon of the winter storm."

"Okay, I will give you a short blow by blow summary of what happened. We left Abbotsford air under clear skies as you all know at eleven ten;" Monty cleared his throat, "a few minutes late thanks to our late boarding passenger. We were…"

Nash cut him off. "Christ, am I the reason we crashed?" He asked mortified.

"You know what they say… life is measured in inches." Ace assured him that his tardiness had not caused the crash. "Ten minutes either way we may have still hit the storm and maybe worse as it was definitely coming from the north. There were no warnings coming over the airwaves. Now how about helping me to turn unto my side?"

"If you're trying to make me feel better you didn't, and my tardiness is something I will always wonder about." Nash said morosely.

I felt a knot in the pit of my stomach and smiled at Nash as I passed him a rolled up blanket and helped him turn Ace slightly onto his side. His breathing was laboured and I decided to give him an antibiotic. I knew I had included two different prescription orders in my packing and it was just a matter of finding them. I would do that after Monty finished his synopsis. I asked him to continue.

"Okay, where was I…oh yeah, so we were on schedule to touch down in Spring Valley at approximately twelve fifty. We ran smack dab into the storm at twelve thirty-two, only a few minutes before we should have started our approach. However, with zero visibility it was doubtful that we could have landed this boat anyhow. But the storm had more in store for us. It forced us to drop down in altitude where we encountered strong easterly winds propelling us drastically off course and then the lightning hit. My mind is a blur as to what hit us first, the lightening or the geese. I've heard of these electric blizzards happening now and then but have never encountered one before. What do you remember Ace?"

"I think they were both almost simultaneously. It was then that we issued a Mayday. Your guess is as good as ours as to whether it was even received. Our instrument panel was knocked out and we were flying by the seat of our pants. How we avoided taking out the forest is beyond me. I am not a religious man but someone was definitely looking after us."

"You have to take some of the credit for getting us down and into this trench though Ace."

He laughed. "You believe what you want Lass, but I don't mind telling you all that I was navigating completely blind and that we ended right side up on our belly was none of my doing."

"Yeah, well you won't convince any of us of that and as far as I am concerned it's just another feather in that legendary career of yours." Nash said.

"So", I asked, "if you were to guess, how far do you think we drifted off course and do you have even an inkling of how far we are from civilization?"

"Monty, you're the statistic man, give us your opinion." Ace threw the ball to Monty again.

"We were in the air for less than two hours as I said before so that means it was a good hour since we had passed over Prince George. If the wind had of been coming from the southwest we would have been propelled towards the Yukon border or even the B.C. / North West Territory border where we were headed for anyhow. However, it was a nor'easter and we were turned around and tossed as if we were a balloon and in my estimate we are somewhere north and maybe a little west of Dawson Creek; between the Fort Nelson/Toad River area and Spring Valley… just going entirely on the time factor as we crashed just before one. We could be as far west as Dease Lake, but I don't believe that we drifted as far as Atlin, but then anything is possible. What's your take on our location Nash? You've explored most of this northern area?"

"It's impossible to even make a good guess. Hopefully, the skies will clear tomorrow and I can get a fix on our location. I have not been able to find my compass and you say the one in the plane is smashed to smithereens so without one I have nothing to compare direction and latitude to on my maps. Let's just see what tomorrow brings; clear skies may prevail."

I was not ready to give up yet. "What about the "black box? Surely, it will relay our location?"

"Ah, that fabled black box…trouble with that is that there wasn't one on board." Monty said.

"But, I thought it was mandatory?" I really had no idea whether it was or not.

"Yeah, well ours was old and out-dated and we never got around to replacing it."

So much for that. Ace sighed and said that he would take the blame for that transgression and that it was time for us to get a little sleep-eye. Sali agreed and said she was going to crawl into her sleeping bag before the tent cooled off. Evie and Monty concurred. Nash helped me to settle Ace back down and advised Sali and Evie to change into dry clothes before they retired. He asked me if I would join him outside for a few minutes while he stoked up the fire. I told him I had to locate the antibiotics and dole out some sleeping tablets first and then I would see. I knew darn well that I was going to join him at the fire but he needn't know that. Ace didn't complain about the new medication and I gave him and Evie a light sleeping aide. Monty took a couple of aspirins and Sali didn't require anything.

I put my coat and mittens back on and said good night as I went out to brave the cold once more. Sali called to me not to let Nash keep me up all night. I closed the zipper on the tent as I exited and stood outside staring at the downed cargo plane. After a few minutes Nash asked me what was wrong.

"This whole thing is so surreal." I muttered.

"Not really, planes crash every day." He said matter-of-factly.

"Not with me on them they don't! But I don't just mean the plane crash…I mean the fact that you just happened to be on board with all your expertise and equipment and Sali with her store of foodstuffs…that's no ordinary everyday occurrence of passengers!"

"Come and sit down Ava Lane and I will make you a hot toddy and you can tell me what is really bothering you." Nash beckoned to me.

I sat on one of the blocks of wood nearest to the fire. Nash placed a wool blanket around me and proceeded to mix me a drink of hot water and honey and a sprinkle of what I assumed by the whiff

I got, was nutmeg. He started to add the rum and I told him to go lightly on it.

"You think that something besides the fact that our plane has crashed in the Canadian wilderness in the middle of winter is not enough to be upset about?"

"Nope, I fear there is something more."

"I need to get home Nash; my mother needs me. She is five months pregnant with twins and I am so fearful of what will happen to her when she finds out I am missing." I blurted out.

He passed me the tin cup and told me to be careful as it was very hot. "I don't mean to sound judgemental, but isn't your mother a little old to be pregnant? I don't blame you for being concerned, but surely there are other family members that are taking care of her, aren't there?"

"For your information, my mother isn't even forty yet."

"Well she must have been very young when you were born. Are there other children?"

"She was eighteen. Yes, I have sisters. Rosalyn is three years older than me and there is Tanny, an adoptee, and my baby sister Liliana, and Zoe who Mama brought home from Spain."

"There is that word "Spain" again. Why does it upset you so? What happened in Spain?"

"It's a very long story Nash." I took a long sip of the warm beverage; somehow it calmed me.

Nash moved his block of wood closer to me. "I'm not going anywhere Ava Lane."

"First, my name is not just Ava Lane. It is Ava Lane LaFontaine McAllister Quinn."

"That's quite the moniker for such a young lass to be carrying around. Tell me how you came upon all of those names."

"It wasn't always so. I was born Ava Lane LaFontaine. The Lane is from my maternal grandmother which she gave herself when she opened up her restaurant in Bridge Falls. She called it Lily Lanes. Do you know where Bridge Falls is?" Nash nodded that he did. "My mother and her mom and dad and two sisters moved there in nineteen fifty nine and in nineteen sixty she met my father and fell in love with him. She became pregnant with me the next year and my father went off to Italy and my mother went to Scotland to live with her aunt. When I was born she named me LaFontaine after my maternal grandfather. That's the first half of my name." I stared into the fire not sure that I could continue without revealing too much about Avanloch.

Nash placed his hand over mine. "You're not going to pull a Shahrazad on me are you?"

Startled I asked him what he meant by that.

"Well," he said, "my mother used to tell my sister and me bedtime tales when we were young but she never finished them. We had to wait until the next night to find out the endings. One day, I guess I was about six or seven when I complained to my dad about my mother's story telling. He said that she was just copying a woman whose name was Shahrazad. Of course I had no idea who that was and he explained her fabled tale to me. Surely you know what I'm talking about?"

"Yes, I do. It's strange because my father told me the same thing. However, I was much older; in fact it was only a few years ago that he made mention of my mother's ability to spin tales and leave one in suspense as to the endings…much like Shahrazad. Did your mother dance too? I don't remember her dancing much for Rosy and me, but my dad said she danced for him."

"That's quite the coincidence Ava. I don't think my mother danced for us either. Why do you think that your father never mentioned the similarities between the mythical Shahrazad and your mother's tales before?"

"I did not grow up with my father Nash. I did not even know that he was alive until three years ago. A chance meeting between him and my mother brought him into my life and back into hers." Again I stopped talking. I wanted to tell Nash my parents' story, and yet I was reluctant and worried that if I started I wouldn't be able to stop. I didn't think that I had my mother's ability to tell half-truths.

Nash offered to make me another hot drink and I passed him my cup. I watched him as I had before and something became hauntingly clear to me; this plane crash… me, him, meeting like this… it was preordained. He switched off the lantern and returned to his stump next to me and passed me my drink. He didn't ask me if I wanted to continue or if I would prefer not to. I could clearly see his face in the flickering firelight and the warmth I saw in his dark brown eyes made me want to tell him the story of Vienna and Rainey. I smiled and gazed into the fire again.

"My mother went to Scotland to live with her mother's sister, Aunt Jannie and her husband Uncle John. She was seventeen. She made her parents keep the truth from everyone; especially Rainey. They were to tell everyone that she had run away. She believed that this was the best strategy as my father did not love her and hadn't kept his promise to write to her every day. She knew that he would marry her but she didn't want him to feel trapped and she wouldn't interfere with his dream of becoming an architect. When my father came home and found her gone he nearly went crazy. My grandparents would not betray my mother though they wanted to. He learned from his best friend that my mother never received his letters just as he hadn't received hers. It seems as though the host family he was living with in Italy had a daughter who was interested in him...you get the picture... but no one knew this at the time. My father went back to Vancouver and university. He started drinking pretty heavily unable to except the fact that Mama had forsaken him. That summer he went to Wales to search for her."

"Why...why did he think she was in Wales?"

"My mother had told him that she had a gypsy aunt who lived there in a small castle and that she wanted to go and live with her. My father enlisted the aid of a friend from London, Stu and Stu's Welsh aunt to accompany him on his dubious quest. Of course he didn't find her but coincidences abounded. It is too much to go into right now; perhaps another time. My father came back here to Canada and my mother married L..." I had almost said "Lord" Jeremy McAllister. I corrected myself in time. "Excuse me; she married Jeremy McAllister who was Rosalyn's father. Mama and Jeremy were never man and wife. He was still pining for his dead wife Maveryn and my mother was still in love with my father. They married solely for the purpose of providing a home for me and Rosy. I was only a few months old at the time; Rosy was three. Jeremy owned a large estate and was hardly ever home as he had businesses in London. Although my mother was kept busy during the days with us girls and running the estate, the nights were a different thing and she suffered through many bouts of depression. She eventually sought help from a therapist but she never revealed the guilt she had about keeping me from my real father. She had nightmares and would cry out his name so I knew the name Rainey from an early age, but she would not talk about him. She told me she hardly knew him and that he had been killed in Italy. If he had meant so little to her she should have been able to rid herself of his memory, but she never could. I mean, how could she…here I was with my father's coloring and his deep blue eyes and me always asking questions. Jeremy took Mama to Vancouver with him on a business trip when I was ten. Something happened there because Mama was different when she came home. I know now that she went to see my father at his place of work. She saw him but she never let him see her. She let him go that day and I honestly think that she would never have told him about me if it hadn't been for that chance meeting in Hawthorne…but then there is the letter…" I quit talking then. Nash gave me a few minutes before he spoke.

"Is that also for another day Ava?"

I said it was and continued on. "My father never blamed mama for keeping me a secret. If anything he blamed himself. Anyhow, everything worked out. We went to Vancouver with him and I met my two brothers. He divorced his wife and he and my mother were married, once in Bridge Falls and then again in the chapel by our home in Scotland."

"So all is well and they are living happily in the highlands of Scotland?" Nash asked hesitantly.

"You would think so wouldn't you, but you know the old saying, 'the course of true love never runs smoothly.'"

"So what happened, I mean they are obviously together now aren't they? Just a minute; does this have something to do with Spain?"

"How very perceptive of you Mr. Nash; yes it does. My father found three antique Viennese silver bracelets in a run-down little shop in Italy in nineteen sixty and bought them for my mother. He wanted to give them to her for Christmas but of course he didn't because she was gone when he got home. He kept them all those years believing that one day he'd be able to give them to her. I guess he gave up because in 1964 he married a woman he wasn't in love with. Her father helped him get established as an architect and they had two sons, Morgan and Mason; my half-brothers. Mason is the reason I was in Vancouver. He had broken his leg playing hockey and I went to look after him because my father couldn't leave my mother. Anyhow, should I continue on with the story of the silver bracelets or have you heard enough?"

"Hardly; I feel you haven't even gotten to the heart of the matter yet…am I right?"

"I really don't know why I am telling you this Nash; I mean you are practically a stranger…"

"Because I asked you to tell me and I'm pretty sure you wouldn't be telling me if you didn't want to. We may have only met today but I don't consider us strangers. After all, strangers are just people whom we have never met before, aren't they?"

Nash placed his hand over mine and I felt the warmth even through my cashmere mitten.

"So, after twenty years my parents were finally together again and my father could, at long last, unlock the safe that had kept the bracelets secreted all that time. Strangely, Mama recognized them as ones she had read about some years ago. They had been presented to a woman by the name of Katarina from her husband Anton. They had been lost for over a hundred years. Legend had it that Katarina had been killed and that thieves had made off with the bracelets and her daughter. The bangles are very intricate and one has the inscription: **Mi muier Kat…Para siempre Anton…Infinidad.** It translates to: "My love Kat…Forever, Anton, For Infinity" and that is how they got the name Infinity Bracelets. Mother loved them but wanted to find their rightful heir. Of course, my dad could deny her nothing and with the help of her friend, Roberge Farradan, they were off to Barcelona Spain. Roberge's family are somehow connected to this Anton from another century. Significant information regarding the disappearance of the bracelets had just recently come into their hands. This data was entrusted to my parents as Roberge's family had not the means or funds to pursue it. The very next day, my parents set off to Nazeth, a small town in the heart of the Pyrenees in Andorra. That was the beginning of the end." I took a deep breath.

"My God Ava; I know this story! Rainey Quinn, he's your father? Ava, I have met him."

Nash was on his feet. "Ever since you mentioned your father's name things were clicking in my head. I have been thinking that Rainey was a very unusual name and was pretty sure that I had heard it before. I still hadn't made the connection when you said one of your names was Quinn, but as soon as you said Andorra, I knew it… I knew that I had met your father."

"This is a little spooky Nash. How can I be sitting here in the middle of nowhere with a man who knows my father? How Nash, how do you know my father?"

He sat back down. "I must correct myself; I don't actually know your father but I have met him. It must have been last winter. I was chatting with Lloyd Becker, the man who owns Outfitters Exclusive when your dad came in. Lloyd introduced me to him and said that he was the architect who had drawn up the plans for his expansion. We shook hands and I left. When I went to say goodbye to Stacie, one of the secretaries, I found her in tears. It was from her that I heard about your mother's unexplained disappearance in Andorra. She said that your father and family were heartbroken but no one had given up hope that she would be found. I left the next day for Akemantack and I guess I put it out of my mind. Now, here I am a year later sitting with that man's daughter and she is telling me her parents' history…what are the odds of that happening Ava? Tell me, what are the odds?"

"I don't think it is as unusual as you think Nash. A lot of people in the area of my father's firm knew that my mother went missing after the earthquake. You just happened to be there the day my father arrived with the blueprints. I was there too Nash. I stayed in the car because I wasn't up to answering any questions, especially from Stacie as she is a bit of a drama queen."

Nash laughed a little. "You got that right. Does that mean that I may have seen you and walked right by?"

"I don't think so because I would have remembered you if you had."

"How can you be sure?"

"Because Mr. Colton Nash, I never forget a face…especially one as fetching as yours."

"Why Miss Quinn, I think you just paid me a compliment. I'm pretty sure I wouldn't have forgotten your face either. May I now hear how your mother was found?"

"Apparently you already know that she disappeared during the earthquake …well, actually she was abducted. That's not even the right word because the two men that picked her up probably saved her life. She was cut and barely breathing. The one man, his name is Connie, took her to this little church where his boss was waiting. The other man died before he got to the church. Apparently seconds before the earthquake Mom had mentioned the name Katarina, and Connie assumed that it was her name. His boss's name is Antonio DeMarco who was obsessed with finding the Infinity Bracelets and the legend of Katarina and Anton. He was in Nazeth covertly to pick up some ancient scrolls. His pilot and friend Somner, flew them to the hospital in Verde El Mar which is also Anton's home. We cannot hate Anton for his quick actions, but we do hate him for keeping her from us because he knew exactly who she was. He claimed her as his wife at the hospital and never looked back. He fell in love with her and in his delusional mind believed they were the reincarnation of the fabled Kat and Anton."

I didn't want to go into any great detail as to what had transpired between Anton and my mother and yet I couldn't go to bed without answering Nash's question.

"I'm sure your mother had a lot to say about that didn't she?"

"No, she didn't. You see she was in a coma for two months and when she awoke she had no memory of who she was. She lived in that amnesiac state for almost two years thinking she was Katarina and that Anton was the father of her child. The night before the earthquake she had told my father that she was pregnant; he was ecstatic. Mama said she always knew that something was wrong with the picture that Anton had painted for her but could not disprove it. She tried through hypnosis to gain her memory, but all attempts failed. She was told she was one of those rare people who do not submit to hypnotic suggestion. It was all another lie perpetuated by Anton. Mama did come to care for him because he was kind and generous and loved her and Liliana. She married him for real and if Daddy's friend Stu hadn't ran into her in Verde El Mar she may very well still be there and under Anton's thumb and we would never know what became of her."

I was finished. I stood up and announced that I was going to bed.

Nash got up and put his arms around me. "Jesus Ava; that is the most heart breaking thing I have ever heard. I know there is a lot more to the story but I will not press you for anymore tonight."

"Thank-you." I said. "Good night Nash."

"Before you go I have something for you. Just give me a second to warm them up."

He pulled what looked like long underwear out from a box that had been sitting beside him. He held them up to the fire turning them every few seconds before passing them to me. "I want you to change out of your clothes and into this dry top and bottom and put these socks on also."

"If you think I am taking all my clothes off in that freezing tent then you are crazy! There is nothing wrong with what I am wearing and I am certainly not taking my mukluks off!"

"It's for your own good Ava. You will be more comfortable in clean dry garments and we need to dry your boots out. Now will you do as I ask? By the way, they are brand new and have never been worn before."

"I'm not wet and I'm allergic to wool."

"Lucky for you then because they are cashmere."

"What is it with you people and cashmere? I have to pee."

"Of course you do. Come on, I will help you into the plane. We may as well make use of the loo in there before it freezes up."

He passed me a flashlight. I hated this part of being in the wilderness.

Nash was still warming up my "night attire" when I returned. "You really expect me to climb out of my warm clothes and put those on?" I asked caustically.

"Yup, now be a good girl and get it over with. I'll give you some privacy before I come in."

"There are four other people in there you know."

"Yes, and they are probably all asleep so be quiet."

I grabbed the long-johns from him. "Yes Sir." I saluted him and scurried into the tent.

Nash and Monty had laid tree boughs along the inside perimeters of the tent to help keep the cold out so it smelled as though we had a Christmas tree in every corner. The tent was square and quite large. We had placed Ace perpendicularly at the top of the tent and closest to the kerosene heater. Monty was next to him against the inside of the tent. Sali and Evie's sleeping bags were horizontally below them. There was a walkway between the girls and Nash and myself. Our belongings and some food items were stored on the floor above our heads and my medical paraphernalia was below us. I could have fit in with the girls and was a little bothered that Nash had me sleeping next to him. I don't know when he had did it but he had strung up a rope from end to end and had draped a blanket over it so I had some privacy while changing. I started shivering as soon as I removed my coat. By the time the rest of my clothes were off I was quivering uncontrollably and my teeth were chattering relentlessly. I somehow got myself into my night attire which was now as cold as I was and climbed into the sleeping bag. I could not stop shivering. I didn't even hear Nash come in until Monty spoke to him.

"For God's sake man, do something with that girl before she freezes solid!"

Nash laughed a little. I heard him undoing the zipper on my sleeping bag. I tried to ask him what he was doing but I couldn't get the words out. The next thing I knew he was next to me and pulling me into his arms. I tried to struggle but he held me firmly against him. He rubbed my right arm and then my back and my lower body. I gradually warmed up limb by limb and started to relax a little.

"Good girl; now turn over." He ordered.

I hesitated as it would mean I would be lying beside him face to face.

"It's okay Honey; trust me, I am not going to molest you." He promised.

"I know." I managed to get out. "I hope you know that I am not accustomed to crawling into bed with a man after just one date."

He was massaging my left side now and my shivering finally subsided. He laughed again in a deep and sensual way. "If we were actually sleeping together my dear, you would know it; I can guarantee you that."

I relaxed a little more as he hugged me a little tighter.

"Thank-you." I whispered as I nervously put my arm around him.

"The pleasure is all mine, I assure you." He said kissing my forehead lightly.

"Good night Nash."

"Good night Ava Lane."

I guess I was stuck with that name now, but I didn't mind. I fell asleep feeling his warm breath against my face.

I was awakened the next morning by loud voices. I rolled over and adjusted my eyes to the flickering gas lamp. I sat up and was pleasantly surprised by how warm the tent was. The kerosene heater was doing its job. I asked what all the yelling was about.

Monty answered gruffly. "It's just Acerman being a total dumb ass; nothin to worry about."

"Convince these yokels that a little exercise won't kill me will you nurse Ava?" Ace retorted.

"Well that all depends on what you refer to as exercise. What do you want to do Ace?"

"I want to use **the john!**" was his astute answer.

I asked him why he couldn't use the bottle. He laughed and said not for the job he had in mind.

I said I understood and where was Nash and the girls. Evie poked her head out from under the covers and waved hello. Sali was making coffee and Nash was building a ramp out of snow so that Ace could get into the airplane and use the facilities. I asked what time it was and Monty said that it was 5:30. No wonder that it was still dark.

Nash came in breathing hard. "It's all done; let's make a stab at this Monty." He saw me and smiled. "Good morning Sunshine. Did you sleep well?"

I smiled back and said I did. I clamored out of the sleeping bag and joined in the task of getting Ace into a coat and boots. We got him standing and he winced in pain. I offered a pain pill and he said there was no time. The guys picked him up and. I opened the tent and followed after them prepared to help if they needed me. Sali and I heard him cursing all the way into the plane.

"Come on Dumpling; let's take this coffee inside as it's too cold to stand around out here."

I followed her and sat on one of the log rounds that had been wheeled in. "It is much colder than yesterday isn't it Sali? That means the skies will clear and the search party will be able to get a fix on us right? We could be rescued today right?"

She touched me on the shoulder as she handed me a cup of coffee. "Could be, could be."

"Is it just me, or does this tent now reek with the smell of onions instead of trees?" I asked sniffing the air. "I much prefer the later."

"Nash and I brought all the perishables in to keep them from freezing. Maybe we will have to throw the onions out as they are overpowering." Sali explained.

"Let's make soup." I suggested.

"Do you know how?" Evie asked pulling a sweater on over her head.

"How hard could it be? We peel and cut up potatoes and carrots and onions and throw them in a pot with a can of tomatoes and water and cook until the veggies are tender."

"We don't have any tomatoes." Sali said sombrely.

I said it didn't matter and we could use ketchup instead. Sali laughed saying we had plenty of that and that there was also some celery that was supposed to be for the stuffing for the turkeys but we may as well use it up. There were also some dried herbs. I said, "Good, then we are in business. Let's find some decent knives and get started. We'll need to get the boys to bring us a couple pails of water before they go off wooding."

Nash came in before I had finished my sentence. He asked why we needed knives and water. Evie told him that I was going to make soup. He grinned and said that sounded like a good idea.

I corrected Evie. "I'm not making soup, **we** are." I asked where Ace was as it was much too cold for him to be outside. Nash replied that he was finishing his cigarette.

"He smokes?" I asked a little surprised.

"We all do." Sali admitted.

"You do? Why haven't I seen any of you smoking? Do you think I would object? You all still think I am this prudish creature from Scotland don't you?"

"Ava, we don't think anything of the sort. We were just being respectful of you and Evie. Ace, Monty and I are the culprits…Nash doesn't smoke." Sali said apologetically.

"I've been known to pick up a butt now and then." Nash confessed.

"I have never smelled cigarette breath on any one of you before so how are you concealing it? I will tell you right now that I would welcome the aroma right now because the stench of these damn onions is starting to get to me. I wish we had some candles."

Sali jumped up. "We do. I have a dozen or so ceremonial candles that I bought for the tables for our communal Christmas supper. I can't believe I forgot about them." She looked at me grinning. "And the reason you don't smell smoke on us is because we already all smell like a bunch of Indians from standing around the fire." She hurried out of the tent laughing.

I asked Nash if "Indian" was not an offensive way to address her people. He asked me why I thought that. I said I wasn't sure.

"Her people refer to themselves as Indian although North American Native would be a more suitable name or Aboriginal. We should always be respectful of their rights as it was "us", the white man, who invaded their homeland. You will have to ask Sali what her people prefer to be known as."

"Thank-you, I would like to know about their way of life. My sister Rosalyn is in Brazil right now and I know that some of the tribes there are known as Indian also and I am sure they are in many other countries too. Now, you should get Ace in here and out of the cold. I want to make it known to all that I am perfectly fine with them smoking in the tent. As I said, I would welcome the smell over onions anytime! What about you Evie?"

She said it didn't bother her. Nash said he would bring Ace in unless he wanted to supervise his and Monty's opening of the crates. Nash explained that the cargo that was going to Whitehorse contained office supplies and they were much too large to just contain typewriters and paper supplies so Ace told them there was a possibility that one or two of the crates might hold desks and chairs. I hoped for his sake that they did. He took Nash's advice and came in out of the frigid weather.

I checked his dressing afraid that the trip to the lavatory may have caused his wound to open up but there was no evidence that it had. I told him that Evie and I didn't mind if he smoked. He thanked us in a round-about way and said he was good for a while as he had just inhaled enough nicotine to last for a few days. He asked if I, being a nurse and all, was going to lecture him on the hazards of smoking. I reminded him that I was not a nurse and I would let his wife do the scolding. He wanted to know who had been talking to me about his wife. Sali said it was her.

The over-sized scented candles definitely helped to mask the onion smell and they also produced a fair amount of heat so we turned the heater down low. I asked her how long she thought the kerosene would last. She said it was a question for Nash.

There were indeed chairs in one of the crates. Monty and Nash arrived with one that required a small amount of assembly. I suggested that they should omit putting the wheels on. Ace snickered but was overjoyed that he could now sit up in some comfort. The chair was made of leather and boasted a high back and cushioned arms. It looked totally out of place. Ace suggested that the boys bring in a few more for us girls. Monty said they had enough to do already. Nash winked at me and they exited laughing.

"What do you think they are up to?" Sali asked.

"Who knows? It is still dark out so they can't be going far. Let's get this soup finished just in case we are not rescued today."

Despite the cold, the clouds did not lift. Monty and Nash made a spit and fashioned a grill out of wood and airplane metal so that we could cook the soup. It turned out exceedingly well and we enjoyed it along with a half loaf of pumpernickel bread. There were five loaves of specialty breads among Sali's provisions. It was for their Christmas dinner; a little diversion from their usual white and whole wheat homemade breads. Her husband, Charlie George was the chief cook and baker at her house. Sali told us that she could fry eggs and make porridge and peanut butter and jam sandwiches; she left the rest up to her husband. They did work together preserving fruits and meats though. Evie said she did not cook either except for eggs and toast. She lived alone in a small apartment close to restaurants and fast food outlets so she either ate frozen entrees or ordered in. She and Sali were a couple of hours early for the flight yesterday so had gotten acquainted in the waiting area of Northland Transport. I had boarded ten minutes before our scheduled take-off and barely had time to introduce myself. I had wondered what we were waiting for and Sali said it wasn't a what, but a who. That's when I had my first glimpse of Nash. He had boarded and yelled at the pilot to "crank her up". I only saw his backside as he closed the cargo doors. I buckled up and prepared for the take-off hearing him take his seat and talk to Asta. I had immediately put my earphones on so did not hear him and Sali conversing.

The highlight of the cold day was when Nash and Monty interrupted our soup preparation to tell us to bundle up as they had a surprise for us. I said I hoped that they had found fur coats in one of the Yukon bound crates. Nash said they had something better. I couldn't imagine what. They led us to the corner of the downed plane. There on the frozen tundra three meters away and two meters apart stood two bright red toilets. My first reaction was one of disbelief and I was speechless, but then the insanity of our situation and the absurdity of there being two colourful porcelain commodes in the wilderness kicked in and I broke out in raucous laughter. Of course it was contagious and Sali and Evie joined in. Monty walked over to the farthest one away and said that it was the "gentleman's" and then he pointed to the other one saying it was the "ladies."

"You don't expect us to actually use them do you?" I asked still laughing.

"It beats anything else we've got. They came with plumbing and so we have done our best to make them useful. You'll have to bring a bucket of water with you though and perhaps the pipes may burst with the cold, but what the hell. We are going to enclose them on three sides with the cardboard from the boxes so you girls won't feel so exposed and it may very well blow away before we anchor it. What do you think?" Nash's voice sounded like he needed our endorsement.

I told them that they had outdone themselves and we were delighted. Evie and Sali agreed.

Evie ran back to the tent to get her camera and then we all had to pose in various positions around the toilets to have our pictures taken. No one had to remind us to smile because amusement was still written all over our faces. We made our way back to the fire where Evie continued to snap photos. She wanted one of me and Nash standing next to the tent and then the crash site. He had his arm around me and I couldn't believe I was so happy until the stark reality of our situation hit home.

"Your families were probably informed last night about our failure to arrive at our destination, but I don't know if word has reached mine yet. There is a time difference of eight hours or so…I am so worried about my mother…" I broke into tears.

Nash explained to the others that my mother was pregnant with twins and that I was extremely worried how the news that my plane was unaccounted for would affect her. Now everyone was concerned for me. I told them that I was fine because I had all of them. Nash suggested that we go for a walk. I asked him between sniffles where we could go.

He took my hand and said, "Down to the corner store."

He passed me a pail and he picked up another one and the axe. So, corner store meant the creek. Somehow he and Monty had found the time between assembling Ace's chair and the biffies to map out a new trail to the water supply. The pathway started right behind the tent and encountered the frozen pond a mere four minutes away. It was indeed much quicker and handier then the route Nash had taken me on yesterday. I sat down on a mound of snow while he chopped at the dribble of a small frozen waterfall. Eventually a steady stream of water emerged and he quickly filled our buckets. He plopped them down and sat down beside me.

"Do you believe that we are going to survive this Ava?"

"If you tell me we will then yes, I believe we will."

"I'm telling you we will. This is nothing compared to some of the situations I have been in. We have all the comforts of home here, shelter, heat, food and each other. We will face any challenge that comes our way, okay?"

I faked a little laugh. "So this is your idea of a comfortable home? Have you been in life and death situations before?"

"We are nowhere near that state Ava and yes, I have had a few harrowing experiences but none that I want to talk about right now. I want you to have faith that your family will know that you are alive and that you are going to come back home to them…can you do that for me?"

He was becoming more endearing to me by the minute. I asked him if he was a religious man.

"I don't think I would call myself religious. I believe that there is a deity that transcends beyond man's capacities to fully understand. I guess you would categorise me as a Christian. What about you Ava?"

"Oh, I definitely believe God exists, not only in heaven, but in our hearts. I hope I haven't used up all my time with Him as I probably overdid my allotted time when my mother was missing. I will keep on praying for her well-being though and for all of us too. There is a small chapel just down the hill from Avanloch in the village that I have been attending all my life. It is non-denominational which is what I think all houses of worship should be. Reverend Peters has always been the pastor and I know he will be of great solace for my family. Today is Sunday, do you think the rest will mind if we have a little prayer service?"

"No, they will not. I've known all of these people except for Evie, for some time now and I can say that they will welcome prayer just as they did last night for Grandfather Little Crow and it certainly doesn't just have to be only today, it can be every day. I think I would like very much to see this little chapel of yours." He pulled me up and suggested we get back before a search party came looking for us.

Did that mean that he wanted to come home to Scotland with me? I hoped it did.

Sali had the eggs all beaten up and ready to cook when we got back. I suggested an omelette and she said that would be delightful if I knew how to make one. Again I asked, "How hard could it be? Don't we just cook one side of the eggs and then add cheese and fold it over?"

We were each allotted one slice of bread which Nash toasted over the fire. Monty complained that the omelette needed salt and that last nights' eggs could have used some too.

Sali explained that we didn't have any salt or pepper and she thought he knew that. He asked what was wrong with the shakers in his tool box.

"As if we thought to look there and why didn't you mention it before?" Sali asked.

"You never asked."

Monty produced the oversized shakers and handed them over to me. I guess I was the keeper of the condiments. "I guess we had better salt the soup then!" I said cheekily.

Nash and Monty left for their woodlot with a thermos of hot coffee and we girls set about tidying up the dishes and the tent. I was glad to be "indoors" as my fingers had nearly froze while cooking breakfast. Nash had found his thermometer and it read 20 degrees Fahrenheit. I didn't need any damn thermometer to tell me it was cold. He expected that the temperature was going to continue to go down all day. I had asked how we would be able to keep the tent above zero once we ran out of fuel. He had just smiled and said not to worry. Well I wouldn't if the skies would clear up so that we could be found. It was only 10:30 a.m. It was going to be a long cold day. I felt guilty that we were inside while Nash and Monty were working outside in the freezing weather. We kept the kerosene heater as low as possible and climbed into our sleeping bags. Ace attempted to do a newspaper crossword puzzle and asked us for help every once in a while. Evie seemed to have the answers he required. She also had a dozen romance novels that she had brought for her sister. She gave them to Sali and I to choose from. I had never been a reader of fiction, but if it would help pass the time I decided to give it a go after I had written the events of the last twenty-four hours in my journal. I had mentioned earlier that I wished I had a notebook to keep track of our "so called adventure" in. Evie had come to the rescue producing reams of paper, pencils and pens. She presented me with a loose-leaf binder that I could keep my writings in. I objected at first as I knew that this was all stuff that she brought for her nieces but she insisted I take what I wanted because it could all be replaced, but memories couldn't. I thanked her and said that my mother always kept a diary and thank goodness Avaleena had or we would never have found out the truth about Avanloch. I realized what I had said the minute the words were out of my mouth and she asked who Avaleena was. I answered as my mother would have. "And that is a story for another time."

At three o'clock I decided to use up some of the apples before they froze. I couldn't duplicate my mother's recipe of mixing them with sugar and cinnamon because we didn't have either ingredient, but I could pour some maple syrup over them and cook them in butter. I'd give it a try. Sali saw I was up to something and asked if she could help. I jokingly said that she could run down to the corner store and get me some cinnamon and sugar.

"Okay," she had said, "be right back."

She bundled up and exited the tent. She was gone a good ten minutes and I thought I had better go and see where she had got to as we weren't supposed to be outside alone. I met her coming out of the plane. She had a handful of small packages in her hands.

She laughed. "Sorry, still no sugar, but we got spices!"

I hurried her back inside as the wind was howling and blowing billows of snow in our faces. I had stopped long enough to read the thermometer; it had dropped another five degrees. I hoped we weren't in for a blizzard. I was glad there was a lid on the soup. I had no sooner added the cinnamon and nutmeg to the apples and placed them on top of the kerosene heater when we heard Nash and Monty outside. I undid the zipper and told them to hurry in and bring the soup.

"What are you girls cooking that smells so good?" Nash asked.

"Ava made dessert." Sali said.

"The proof of whether it will pass as dessert will be in the tasting." I emphasized.

None of them knew what it was supposed to taste like so I guess it was a success as not a morsel was left. Nash winked at me and said how lucky we were to have a gourmet chef on board. I shook my head and said I was no such thing and not to get too excited over a simple apple concoction that any of them could have cooked up.

We played poker that evening. Monty had sawed up what would have been somebody's desk had the cargo made it to its destination. He had carved it just the right size for us to sit around on our log seats. Ace, of course sat on his throne. The table sat on two small stumps in the middle of the tent. Any more furniture and we would have been over-crowded.

Nash was surprised that I knew how to play half a dozen different poker games. I had explained that my brothers had taught me. I figure I had lost two hundred dollars to them in the last month. Nash said he thought my brothers might be con artists. I was pretty sure he was right. After only half an hour Nash asked if we would excuse him as he couldn't keep his eyes open one second longer. The poor man was exhausted and I think he was asleep the minute his head hit the pillow. We decided to call it quits for the night soon after. Monty escorted us gals to the biffy, stoked up the fire and let Asta have a good run.

The wind had died down and the air appeared warmer. I suggested that we should turn the heater off for the night to conserve fuel. Our sleeping bags were supposedly good to 45 degrees below zero. Hopefully we would not need to test that theory out. I slipped in beside Nash being careful not to disturb him. Asta plunked herself down between us. It was only 7 p.m.

I was awakened sometime in the night by Asta's' deep growls. I tried to get her to quieten by petting and talking soothingly to her. Off in the distance I heard coyotes howling. Nash stirred and asked what was wrong. I told him to go back to sleep as it was only coyotes.

"Yeah sure, coyotes." I heard Monty murmur.

Nash pushed Asta down to our feet and reached out for me. "Are you cold Ava?"

I answered that I wasn't. He said he was and put his arm around me. "That's better."

He fell asleep almost immediately again but startled me a few minutes later when I felt his body go rigid. He twitched rather violently. I patted his hand and nudged him slightly and he relaxed and hugged me tighter. I had no idea if he was aware of his actions or not.

Is this how it is I asked myself? Is this how love begins? Am I falling in love with this man next to me? I foolishly had thought I was in love once before when I was engaged to Randy for those few weeks, but it was nothing like this. If my mother and father hadn't found each other when they did I may have ended up marrying him. Seeing my mother and father together and the love that they shared I realized that I would never have that with Randy and so I had broken it off. Then there was that brief infatuation with Cam, and then my mother went missing so that was the end of that. There had been no one else. And now here I was in bed, so to speak, with a man I had just met. This was our second night lying next to each other and I didn't want to think of him not being here. Is it possible to fall in love with someone after only a day and a half? No, that wasn't right. I had felt something when our eyes met when we were attending to Ace and that had been within minutes of our meeting. My mother had fallen in love with my father almost immediately upon meeting him and that love had never ceased, so had it happened to me too? Suppose if Nash didn't feel the same way? My God, we haven't even kissed yet!

I felt his breath on my neck as he rested his head on my shoulder. I let out a deep sigh and whispered, "Good night Colton Nash."

We were all awakened by the tents' shaking early the next morning.
"Is that what I think it is?" Nash asked to no one in particular.
"Pretty sure it is Buddy." Monty answered.
"Yup, it's a Chinook." Sali affirmed.
"What's a Chinook?" I asked.

Nash got out of bed and lit one of the lanterns and looked down at me. "It's a warm wind and it can melt a foot of snow in a matter of minutes."

"Is that why it's so warm in here?"

"Yup. You stay in bed; Sali will fill you in. Monty and I need to batten down the hatches."

No way was I staying in bed! I wanted to see the effects of this Chinook for myself. I pulled the hanging blanket across the room so that we girls would have some privacy while we dressed. Ace asked for help saying he wanted outside also. He said he could walk if we each just took an arm. Evie maneuvered his chair through the door and Sali and I tried to ease him up. Getting him into a standing position was not easy. Sali and I did not have the upper body strength to pull him up as he was a big man and probably outweighed the two of us together.

"This isn't going to work Ace; we just aren't strong enough so you will just have to wait for Monty and Nash. It is one thing to lower you onto the floor, but quite another to get you up off of it. I'm afraid our tugging is going to reopen your wound."

"You're right Doc and I certainly don't want you gals injuring yourself on an old fart like me. That wind isn't going anywhere for a while anyhow."

"Is it dangerous?" I asked.

"I wouldn't say it poses any danger unless you are driving through it. It can be treacherous to an unfamiliar driver as blowing snow can cause huge snow drifts that seem to spring up right in front of one. The rapid snow melt can also be a hazard."

"I've never heard the wind called Chinook before; is it a Canadian weather phenomenon?"

Sali said it was a Native word that meant "snow eater". The Chinook people lived near the ocean. She said that the gusty winds pick up from the Pacific Ocean and travel as far away as the Rocky Mountains. The snow partly melts and partly evaporates in the dry wind and the temperature can rise 30 degrees in a few hours before it returns to normal. I asked if it would blow all the clouds away. She answered that it would not and that the skies would show off with a bank of clouds that would change throughout the day ranging in colours of light and dark blue and black and changing to orange and yellow hues by dusk. They will look like storm clouds and obscure the sun and mountains to the west. Well, we hadn't seen either yet so I guessed that nothing was going to change. She said that something may change but she didn't want to influence Evie or me and so would not elaborate. Evie and I looked at each other wondering what was in store for us.

Ace added that these winds were prevalent in the prairies and also occurred in the Okanagan and Fraser Canyon and Washington State and that he had heard of them reaching as far south as New Mexico and north to Alaska. Sali said she doubted very much that they could reach New Mexico. Apparently her little village experienced them once or twice a year and she knew that several years ago they had such a snow melt in a short time in Nash's home town of Quesnel that considerable damage had been done to homes.

Nash entered the tent just as Sali finished talking. I said to him that he had not told me that he lived in Quesnel. He said that he guessed it never came up in our conversations. I told him that my mother had lived there twice when she was young.

"Twice, how did that happen? Is it at all possible that I have met your mother also?"

"I doubt that you were even born when she left as you are much younger than she is."

"Are you sure about that?" Nash asked with a twinkle in his eye. "None the less, I think we have something else to talk about. You all need to come outside right now as it is so warm that you are going to be delighted. It looks as if you are chomping at the bit Ace? Hold on, I'll call Monty as I saw that your chair is already waiting for you by the fire."

I pulled the flap back on the tent and inhaled a deep breath in as the hospitable wind entered my lungs. There was no way that Nash could be forty was there I asked myself.

It was still pitch black as it was only six thirty. The only light we had was from the glow of the fire and the burner under the coffee pot. Monty poured us each a cup of his strong brew and produced a flask from his pocket and asked if any of us would like a little flavoring. I, uncharacteristically, held up my cup and asked for a dram or two not even knowing what he was offering. Everyone else followed suit except Sali.

Nash exclaimed that even though it was not yet dawn the weather had given us reason to celebrate, so what the hell. I asked him what the thermometer said.

"It says 43 degrees and that is up three degrees from fifteen minutes ago. I expect it will rise to at least 50 or so by days end."

He flipped my toque off saying that I should let my head breathe for a change. I flinched as I couldn't imagine what my hair looked like as I had been wearing the hat night and day. I ran my fingers through the tangled tresses realizing that I hadn't bother to comb it for two days. Evie had short light brown hair and hers was perfectly styled. Sali's hair was long and thick and her twisted braid that reached half way down her back was still intact. My shoulder length mane had not fared as well. Oh well, perhaps I would do something with it later.

By the time we had downed our first cup of coffee we had all removed one layer of clothes. Now if only the sun would come out from hiding it would be a perfect day. I knew that was not likely as according to Sali we would have cloud cover all day long. Monty remarked that if he didn't know better he would say that we were somewhere in the vicinity of Shadow Valley.

"Why do you say that Monty?" Nash asked.

"It appears as if we have definitely landed in some basin and I don't just mean this cavity that we are sitting in. Those mountain ridges we caught a glimpse of yesterday are not any that I am familiar with. You know the terrain better than me Nash…might they be the Coast Range? And look, it's the middle of December and the snow pack is unusually low for the north and this fog that has surrounded us is more like coast weather. That said, the plane could not have been blown that far off course or this far west so I'm just blowing smoke, right Ace?"

"Just a minute Monty…let's step back to those few minutes when we were fighting to keep control of the plane okay? Did we check the time? I think not as we were too busy trying to keep this old rust bucket in the air. Is it possible that we were so blinded by the lightning that we actually lost track of time? That storm was so powerful that it could have propelled us hundreds of miles off course. It's just a theory, but on the other hand, I have no recollection of landing this plane or being thrown out of my seat; do you? I'm wondering why we haven't discussed this before Monty…do we think something else was at work here?" Ace was dead serious.

"Yeah sure, divine intervention saved our bacon." Monty chuckled.

I asked where Shadow Valley was. Nash answered that it was an area between two ridges of the Coastal Range and was referred to as such because of the shadows the sun cast down to the floor of the mountains. I said that that didn't tell me much. He asked if I knew where Sitka Alaska was. I did not.

"I'll show you on the map later. What say we have a bite to eat and by that time it will be almost day-light. Monty and I have much wood to cut today and we had best get to it early as the snow may very well turn to slush and that will make hauling difficult. I would also like to be finished early today in preparation for tomorrow."

I asked Nash what was happening tomorrow and he replied that he would fill us all in later. I wasn't sure I liked the sound of that.

After our breakfast of Bisquick mix pancakes Monty and Nash took off saying they would be back before dark. I checked Ace's bandages out and then Evie and I went down to see if any ice had melted off the creek. A hole big enough to dip our small pail in had emerged so we would not have to wait for the guys help. We filled our pails and hung them on the tripod over the fire and waited for the water to heat. We took full advantage of the 49 degree weather and took turns washing each other's hair. Sali declined saying hers would never dry. We told Ace to keep his eyes closed while we stripped down and bathed ourselves. We giggled all the while keeping a watch out for Nash and Monty. Ace complained, but he agreed to a sponge bath. We also did some laundry. I wondered what Nash would say when he saw our unmentionables draped over his rope clothesline.

It felt like picnic weather so we cooked up the last of the potatoes and boiled a dozen eggs and added mayonnaise and a little onion and some cut up pickles and called it potato salad. We buried the bowl in a snow bank to keep cool. This mock refrigerator also served to keep the milk and other dairy products from freezing. I was learning much from Sali and Nash about life in the north. Sali said it was like a holiday and we should open one of the five tinned hams to serve with the salad. The hams were also meant for Christmas day dinner in Akemantack.

I learned that Akemantack was home to twenty-six people. It was so named because of the abundance of tamarack trees in the area. There were nine separate family residences, the Long House, which served as their church and community center, Sali's parent's trading post, a smoke house where they dried all their game and fish and did their canning and some out buildings which housed their outdoor equipment like snowmobiles and canoes. There was also a workshop. Two small barns sheltered their chickens and milk cow. I asked why she had purchased the twenty dozen eggs and twelve gallons of milk if they had chickens and a cow. The two dozen chickens were molting and only laid a couple of eggs a day and the cow would not freshen until sometime in March. I should have known that but I hadn't taken much interest in the farm animals at Avanloch for a long time.

Sali was explaining about how her village came to be when the guys returned with a small load of wood. It was only noon so it was a little early for them to be calling it a day. Apparently the saw chain was dull and needed sharpening and they chose to come back to camp to work on it. Nash asked what we had been up to and I told him that we had bathed, washed our hair, prepared supper and made four trips to the creek for water. I added that there was lots of warm water for him and Monty to wash up in. Evie asked what she could offer them to drink. Nash said that a beer would be nice but would settle for a whiskey with a nice chunk of ice. I offered to go to the creek and chop out a block of frozen water. He said he would tag along because he wanted to witness my expertise with an axe. He wasn't so smug when I accomplished the task in a few strong hacks.

He grinned and said he had no qualms about my ability to survive in the backwoods or while he was gone.

"What do you mean by *gone* Nash?"

He placed the chunk of ice in the pail and asked me to sit down. I said I would rather stand.

"Let's go back to camp and have a look at those maps first and then I will explain what my plans are. You may not like it Ava but I have to do it. Promise me you will keep an open mind."

"I think you had better tell me right now Nash. If this is something I am going to disagree with I need to hear it so I have time to react. I don't want to make a scene in front of everyone."

"Ava, there is nothing I want more than to see you reunited with your family, but hanging around here waiting to be found may not happen for some time. I need to do something to get us out of this mess. The only way I can see that happening is if I go on a little walk around and see what's beyond our camp. Do you understand what I'm saying?"

"Yes and no. Is it the same as what the Scots called a stravaig?"

"Seeing I don't know what that word means I can't answer that."

"I think it means to wander about; is that the same thing? How long will you be gone?"

"Yes, sounds like it is. I'm thinking that I will hike for three days and if I find no signs of life I will return, so six days in all. I'm going to follow the creek and trek downstream. It may prove fruitless as I may be going in the wrong direction, but I have to try. What do you say; are you okay with it?"

"I am not your keeper Nash and my opinion does not matter. It is your decision and who am I to disagree with it?"

"You are this amazing girl who has adjusted to this unfathomable situation that we find ourselves in. You are not only our nurse and cook, but you are funny and have kept our spirits up and are a friend to all of us... especially me. I thought there was something going on between us... am I wrong to assume that there is?"

"I am not this amazing person you have painted; I am scared to death all the time. I have done nothing that anyone of you couldn't do." I picked up the bucket. "Let's get back and I will help you pack.

There is nothing going on between us Nash; I cannot and will not let myself feel something for someone I may never see again after tomorrow." I turned away from him but he grabbed me so forcefully that the pail went flying and I slipped and fell into a snow bank taking him with me.

He laughed saying he was sorry but that he really wasn't as he had me where he wanted me. I tried to push him off but he was too strong for me.

"I think you have pretty much confirmed what I wanted to hear my dear so deny it no more. There is no way I am not coming back. Have you forgotten what I do for a living? This may be uncharted territory for me but I know what I am doing. I may not know "where" I am going but there is no way I am going to get lost. Can you have a little faith in my abilities? By the way, I like your hair; where did the curls come from?"

"Wouldn't you like to know? The curls are just one of my many secrets."

"So you have secrets? Now I am more intrigued than ever. Come on; let's get you up before you freeze your butt off."

"Well, who put me here in the first place?" I took his hand and he pulled me up. "I am not worried that you will get lost so much as I am about you falling and breaking a leg or being attacked by wolves or freezing to death."

"None of that will happen Ava, I promise you. Especially not now that I have a real incentive to get back…"

"Don't come back just because of me for there may very well be nothing to come back to!"

He retrieved the pail and followed me. He was talking all the time but I covered my ears so I couldn't hear him. He laughed and said that he liked this side of me. I had no idea what he meant by that. I marched back into camp and announced that Nash was going to leave us for six days.

CHAPTER 2

Avanloch Castle

December 18th

I put my pen down. I couldn't concentrate on the Christmas menus. They would have to wait until later; perhaps when Amma returned home from her shopping trip with the girls. For some reason my mind was wandering back to last summer.

Everyone at Avanloch thought that Rainey and I had slipped magically back into the life we had shared before I had disappeared and we had, for several weeks at least… and then it all started to fall apart. We had been inseparable; neither of us had wanted to lose sight of the other. Then one early August morning I broke the bubble. I had snuck into Liliana's room and silently snatched her out of her crib.

"Come on Cara Mia; let's go wake your Papa." I whispered to her.

He heard us coming and turned over. Lili put her arms out and he pulled her down beside him as she cooed "Daddy, Daddy."

"Honey, it's your P…" I had started to say Papa but stopped myself as I realized that the man in my bed was Rainey, and not Anton. I backed away.

"Vienna, what's wrong Sweetie…you're white as a ghost."

I made up an excuse about having a blinding headache and escaped to the bathroom. I washed my face with cold water and peered at the woman staring back at me. Where had I just gone? Had I thought I was back in Spain and that I was Katarina?

"Oh no, no," I cried.

There was a knock on the door. "Honey, are you all right? Lili needs changing."

I opened the door and let them in. Rainey told me to go back to bed and he would tend to Lili. I didn't want to go back to bed because I didn't want to close my eyes…I was afraid of who I would see. I smiled and said that the headache had eased somewhat.

It was later that very same day that I received the letter. It was late in the afternoon when the post arrived. Caron, one of our new employees had delivered it to me. I was bustling about trying to keep myself occupied. I thought that if I was physically busy I could keep my mind shut off. I asked her to leave it in my parlour and I would tend to it later. She commented that she had never seen such a beautiful postage stamp in all her life. I asked her where it was from.

"Oh," she said a little flustered, "it has a Spanish postmark."

I relieved her of it saying I had changed my mind. My name was spelled out in very bold letters:

LADY VIENNA QUINN,
AVANLOCH CASTLE,
AVANLOCH SCOTLAND

In the return address spot was the name:

Somner Stamos
Pilliar Pier,
Verde El Mar, Spain

With trembling hands I unsealed the envelope; I did not withdraw the letter. I was still holding onto it when Rainey found me. He came over and planted a kiss on my forehead.

"Sorry I'm so late but we had one hell of a time unloading that new mare. All's well though. I'm going across the hall and fix a drink, what would you like Hon?"

I handed him the letter. He asked who it was from and I told him.
"So, did he explain everything?"

"I don't know, I haven't read it." He asked me why "I'm afraid of what it might say."

"Honey, nothing he says can hurt us. Isn't this what we have been waiting for? Do you want us to read it together?"

"I suppose; you read it, let's get it over with."

August 8ᵗʰ

My Dear, Dear Vienna,

I do not even know where to begin. Saying I am sorry for all the heartache that I was part of I suppose is a fitting place. I am just as culpable as Anton in deceiving and keeping the truth from you. I made the decision to stand by his wishes and I will have to live with the choices I made for the rest of my life.

WE did not know who you were at first. Constantine told us that you said your name was Katarina just before you were clobbered by the falling bricks. I suppose I am right in assuming that you asked him if he had ever heard the name Katarina before. He and the priest's aide Sandez put you in the truck after they themselves were assaulted by the flying bricks. Sandez died as they collided with a tree. Connie was draped over your body when we found the two of you. If we weren't in such a hurry to get the helicopter off the ground before another earthquake or aftershock we may have had time to question him but he passed out and Anton insisted that I fly you both to Verde El Mar. I like to think that we saved your life that day. Anton made the decision immediately to list you as his wife. He said that you were so broken and helpless that he just had to do whatever it took to heal you. I know that it is of no consolation to you that he did that very thing. I did not expect that he would fall in love with you or believe that you were the fabled Katarina reincarnated and that his plans were to never tell you your true identity or return you to your family. It was an added blessing to him that you were pregnant. A childhood illness had rendered him incapable of fathering a child, and so he convinced himself that Liliana was his. He is a very delusional man and knowingly I went along with his sick plan. When you accepted him as your husband I absolved myself of any wrong-doing...or so I thought.

Anyhow, I want you to know that I am no longer in Anton's employ. I left the day after your family rescued you. I moved here to Pilliar and here I will stay until Lelani is released from prison. After that I know not where we will go, perhaps somewhere in Greece. I have much to make up for...not only to you but to her.

It's true... it's all true what you accused Anton of. He did want Delaney to take the name Katarina and he did pay the analysts to lie about you not being able to be hypnotised. He had everyone in his pocket except Dr. Zaccaris. No, he is the real thing.

What else do you need me to tell you Vienna? Do you want me to say that I went to Nazeth and *found out who you really were? It's true, I did. In my own defense I will tell you that I told Anton that we had to contact your family but he would not hear of it. I am so full of regret for my actions. He was holding nothing over me…I hid the truth and there is no going back from that.*

Lelani has convinced me that I must beg for your forgiveness for it is only you that can save my soul. I loved you like a sister Vienna and mourn the loss of my best friend every day.

I pray you have found peace again in your life. I remain your servant for eternity.

Somner

I thanked Rainey for reading the letter to me. He said that was pretty much what I had thought all along wasn't it except for the part as to how I was rescued by Connie. He asked me if I felt any closure and could I forgive Somner. I told him I didn't know how I felt yet and that I was going to have to think about it. I folded the letter back up and put it in my dress pocket and told Rainey I was going to go for a little walk. He offered to come with me. I told him that I needed a little alone time. He kissed my forehead and said he understood.

I walked briskly at first, passing through the rose gardens without even slowing down enough to take in their sweet smell. When I was well out of sight of the castle I collapsed on one of the benches and wept. When there were no more tears to shed I pulled Somner's letter from my pocket and reread it. I then walked back through the garden and stopped at the potting shed. Inside I went directly to the one orchid I had been trying to grow. It was in its first stages of bloom, a beautiful delicate lavender color. I wondered for a brief second what had become of Somner's prize orchids now that he was no longer at Casscadia Casa. I picked up the potted flower and along with the letter deposited it in the compost bin. "Thank-you for robbing me of almost two years of my life Somner; good-bye." With that action

I hoped I had banished my life as Katarina and could resume my life as Vienna, Mistress of Avanloch, mother to my children and wife to the only man I would ever love. Ah, but it was not to be. I tried to lay the past to rest but that Vienna who once worshipped that man had disappeared and was replaced by an unloving and cynical woman and I seemed to be powerless to stop her from ruining a perfect marriage. She was out to destroy it and I watched it all unfold from within.

It was September 2nd, one day before the party. I returned to our bedroom from spending the night in Miss Mary's room and found Rainey having his morning coffee on the balcony. He was standing at the balustrade looking out over the valley. I made a quick stop at the bathroom and went out to join him.

"It amazes me how you can be out here in the cold in just your shirt sleeves." I shivered.

He came over and handed me a cup of coffee that he poured from the carafe and placed an afghan around my shoulders. I placed the cup on the table in front of me. He asked if he had heard me being sick. I told him that he hadn't. He went back to where he had been standing. He was probably surprised that I was talking to him.

"I've been contemplating going away for a while and giving you a break. After this weekend is over and done with I think I will visit with Stu and Daisy for a day or two and then cross the pond to spend some time with the boys. How would that sit with you?"

"Your idea of giving me a break is to leave me alone in this colossal house to deal not only with it, but all the estate duties and the children as well… how very noble of you." I stood up and headed for the door.

"Vienna, this has been your domain for twenty years before I came along and you managed very well without my help and you certainly won't be alone… so what is different now?"

"Suit yourself." I said testily. "I had my little holiday for two years so I suppose you are entitled to some time off away from me and the girls. Thank-you for including me in your decision; I was not given the opportunity of selecting my own vacation."

"Why are you bringing that up? No one has ever referred to your time away as a holiday and I'm not going to get away from you. I have been breathing down your neck for almost two months now and I thought you might like sometime to yourself. We've hardly spoken two words to each other for weeks so I thought you'd be glad to be rid of me."

"Is that your excuse for taking a little holiday? Well, don't let me hold you back. I never for one minute believed that you didn't find solace in the arms of other women while I was gone anyway. Perhaps it started with Mrs. Macleod and God only knows with whom afterward. Don't lie to me Rainey…just go and get it over with!" I stormed out and headed down to the kitchen in my night clothes. I heard him calling after me.

"Vienna, what the hell…."

I made sure I was not alone with Rainey for the remainder of the day. He tried to talk to me, but I rejected his every attempt and finally he just shrugged his shoulders and gave up. I was too busy to be bothered by him anyway. I spent the night in Miss Mary's room again.

The party was in full swing; the band was playing, liquor was flowing, people were dancing. Rainey came over to me and said that I was the most beautiful woman in the room and would I care to dance. I thanked him for the compliment and said no, I would not like to dance.

"Very well then, maybe later." He said.

Ava said she was glad he was enjoying himself as she had been afraid that he wouldn't. I followed her gaze and saw her father twirling the Duchess of Calendria. He was laughing. I excused myself saying I needed some air and marched upstairs and into the useless little foyer and passed through the bookcase as I had done so many times before.

Rainey

I had first become aware of Vienna's edginess right after she received Somner's letter. I should have discussed it with her but I chose to let her have her space. Perhaps I could have prevented her aloofness, but I kept quiet and watched silently as her emotional state built up to the point where she accused me of being unfaithful. I have no excuse as to why I did not confront her except that I was afraid to. I was terrified that she was going to tell me that she didn't love me anymore and that she wanted to go back to Verde El Mar and Anton. Unspoken words and jealousy had led us to an impasse. I was dreading the party, but I was determined that one way or the other Vienna would be back in my arms before midnight.

It had been some time since I had last seen her. She should have been easy enough to spot in her shiny silver gown as it sparkled when she walked as though it was made of a thousand glistening stars. I felt a woman's arms encircle me.

"Lord Rainey, please say you will be my partner in a rousing game of bridge?"

I removed the arms of Lauren, the Duchess of Calendria, from around my neck and asked her if I looked like the kind of man who sat around playing cards.

She laughed and whispered in my ear. "And, do you think that is really what I meant?"

I didn't even want to know what she had in that scheming mind of hers. She was the wife of Vienna's and my good friend, Roberge Farradan. According to him, no one was good enough for her and him being the Duke of Hennessey and from a foreign country would make people sit up and take notice. Truth of the matter was that his title meant nothing and he was penniless and she knew this from the beginning, but he was charming and looked good on her arm. He played the good soldier and went along with her masquerade. He often pointed out that she wasn't hard on the eyes, paid him fairly well and he got to hob-nob with the idle rich.

"Sorry Duchess but I must decline your invitation. I am sure anyone of these esteemed gentlemen would be only too glad to join you in the games room."

I had been sitting with half a dozen other men listening to them discuss the sad state of the economy of Great Britain, the senseless acts of war and the general poor health of the planet. I had been invited to join them on the small terrace outside of the upper tier of the ballroom as smoking was permitted there. I thought it was part of my duties as host and so I accompanied these total strangers keeping one eye on the dance floor at all times. Lucky for me Lord Rokenberry said he would be delighted to be the Duchess's partner and she sulked off with him.

Sam Worthington, a London legislator said. "You dodged a bullet there son."

"I'm sure the Lady Lauren is quite harmless." I replied.

"Sir, I can assure you that the title "lady" does not apply to that woman! But speaking of Ladies, where is that lovely wife of yours? I don't believe that I have seen her for some time."

"I was thinking precisely the same thing Sam. If you gentlemen will excuse me, I believe that I will track her down."

I met Ava in the large reception hall where she and Rosy were supervising the laying of the buffet tables for the midnight supper. It was the only room big enough to serve the seventy guests. From there they would be welcomed to take their meal into the dining room, the small drawing room or back into the ballroom.

"Daddy, where is Mama? I haven't seen her since she went outside for a breath of air and that was hours ago. I want to make sure this is to her liking."

"I'm sure it is Ava. I'm sure your mother is in the kitchen or upstairs with Lili."

After half an hour we still hadn't tracked Vienna down so we decided to enlist the help of Evan, Johnny and Amma. At ten minutes before the bewitching hour we were ready to give up searching as the possibilities of her whereabouts had been exhausted. Vienna was not at Willowisp, nor was she at the stables, Brackenshire manor, the mausoleum, the pavilion or the unoccupied residence above the garage, or anywhere in the house. She was nowhere.

"Thank the good Lord that Aunt Jannie and Uncle John had to cancel out on this weekend because of poor health. I don't think she could go through this again." Ava bemoaned.

I put my arm around her. "Honey, we'll find her. As usual, I am the culprit here. Vienna has been upset with me for several weeks now and I have yet to discover the reason for her coldness. Thinking that she was tired of me breathing down her neck I suggested that I should go away for a while and give her some space. Her reaction to that was to accuse me of having mistresses."

Rosy laughed nervously. "Well, that is just absurd? Where would she get such a silly idea?"

"She said that since she had been unfaithful to me while she was on her "two year holiday" that it only stood to reason that I was also unfaithful because she knew damn well that I couldn't live without a woman in my bed, and then she told me to go and get it over with."

"Oh God," Ava cried, "has she really gone back there **again**?"

"I'm afraid so Honey. I just can't see her abandoning the party to get back at me though. Johnny, do you think we should alert the authorities in case something more sinister has happened?" Secretly I was worried that Anton was on the property.

"You mean like her abduction in Nazeth? Myself, I do not believe that Anton is behind this. She has probably fallen asleep in some obscure place where we failed to look. I think that we should wait until morning and hope that she shows up just as she did all the other times. What do you say girls?"

"That was so long ago Johnny, and Mama was despondent then and…"

I interrupted Rosy. "What's happening here? Are you all saying that Vienna has disappeared before? Why am I just hearing about it now?"

Rosy bowed her head. "Yes, but it was a long time ago…before you Rainey."

"There was never any "before me." You all know that everything she did stemmed back to the day I left her alone to pursue my idiotic career! I've read her letters; I know better than any of you how she was feeling for those twenty years. She wouldn't have done anything to worry you as she loved Avanloch and all of you, but you are saying that she did…just where do you think she went and how long are we talking about?"

Amma spoke in a very low and soothing voice. "She would only be gone overnight Rainey. The first time was when Ava and Rosy were quite young. They called us when they couldn't find her. We searched the whole castle and grounds just like tonight. We were very concerned and spent a sleepless night worrying. We were about to call the authorities when she showed up bright and cheery early the next morning. We asked her where she had been and she said that she hadn't been anywhere but asleep and why would we ask her such a silly question."

"How many times are we talking about?" I asked.

"Five or six times." Amma answered.

"You mean five or six that any of you know about? Tell me, to your recollection, did anything out of the ordinary precede her disappearances… like say, had she received a letter or disappointing news? Did she ever mention a visit from the Grey Lady?"

"I don't think that we took any of that into consideration Dad and we told you before that we had never even heard of this "grey lady" until you mentioned her last year. Do you think she has something to do with Mama's vanishing?"

"Your mother has not vanished Ava. Everything about her persona seemed to change after she received the letter from Somner. She made me read it and did not want to discuss it afterwards. She said that she would like to be alone and went for a walk. This is not something I am proud of but I kept an eye on her from a discreet distance. On her way back she went into the potting shed and came out rubbing her hands. After she was back inside the house I checked the potting shed. She had disposed of the orchid she had been nursing and underneath it was Somner's letter. I retrieved the letter as I was sure she would want his address some day. She never mentioned it and I have never brought the subject up. I would find her staring into space and once when I asked her what she was thinking so seriously about she said she had been wondering what the Grey Lady would do. I asked her what she meant by that and she said, "You know, what would she have done if she had been kidnapped? Do you think she would have known that she was Avaleena?" It made no sense to me then and it makes no sense today, but I have this uncanny feeling that if we could only unravel this damned Grey Lady enigma we will have our answer."

"Suppose if Mama had of went back to retrieve the letter daddy…wouldn't she have wondered what happened to it?"

"I thought of that and so I emptied the bin. Lucky for me she never inquired about it. Perhaps all of this has nothing to do with the way she has been acting but I think it is all connected… Verde El Mar, Anton, Somner's letter and somehow the Grey Lady, though I have no idea how.

"I think someone just walked on my grave Daddy." Ava was shivering.

Rosy's answer was to go to the mausoleum and talk to her dead mother Maveryn.

Yeah, I thought to myself, that's going to help because as far as I knew Maveryn never answered. It was nearing the midnight supper hour so we had no choice but to abandon our search for the time being.

As usual, Mary McDuff and her kitchen staff put on one whale of a feast. There was roast beef, racks of lamb, ham, oyster patties, scallops and shrimp. Chicken, potato and green salads accompanied the meat dishes along with breads, cheeses and fruits. Small cakes, tarts and meringues and ices awaited the sweet tooth. Champagne was set out in crystal glasses on silver platters. Vienna had asked my advice on one of the rare occasions when she was talking to me before the party, what after dinner liqueurs to serve. I had suggested brandy, sherry and port having absolutely no idea if this was what the Scots and Brits preferred. I did know however though that Drambuie was a Scotch based whisky and was probably a favorite. I consulted with Mrs. D and she said that it should definitely be included. She said the recipe originated in Scotland and was originally made from aged Scotch whisky and a secret combination of heather honey, herbs and spices. She said she couldn't speak for it now as the brewery was no longer in Scotland but I should include it anyhow. She had told me that in days gone by the dinner fare would have been much different. There would have been wild game birds like pheasant, quail and duck and golden plovers…whatever the hell they were. Venison, rabbit and even squirrel had been a staple. Now venison is only hunted when the deer population explodes. I was very glad that hunting was no longer a sport at Avanloch and tomorrow the guests would have to settle for croquet on the lawns or skeet shooting at the rifle range. That would happen only if Vienna returned from wherever she was.

Rosy and Evan announced that supper was served in the main reception hall. I stood back and watched as the revellers filled their plates. If anyone asked about Vienna our story was that Liliana was not feeling well and Vienna was tending to her. We were using a little girl to explain away a mysterious disappearance. For some strange reason I joined in at the end of the buffet line and heaped generous amounts of food onto two plates. Lauren came up behind me and asked if one plate was for her. I dismissed her rather rudely and retreated upstairs to wait for Vienna. I was awakened the next morning by Liliana tugging on my shirt sleeve.

"Sorry Rainey, she was up and running before I was even aware that she was awake."

I swung my feet over the bed and picked Lili up. "No need to apologise Zoe, I should be up anyhow. What time is it and have you seen Vienna?"

"It's only seven. No, I haven't seen her. Why does it look as though her side of the bed has not been slept in?"

"I'll fill you in later. Right now I need you to take Lili." I kissed my daughter. "Sorry Sweetie, but I need to go and find your mother."

I trudged down the back stairs. Mary must have heard me coming as she greeted me at the kitchen door with a cup of coffee.

"Run along then Mr. Rainey; the rest be a waitin you in the den."

"Thanks Mary. Do you know what is going on?"

"Not much gets by these ole eyes or ears Sir."

I gave her a quick hug and meandered down the hallway stopping at the open door of the den.

"Who's in the ballroom?" I asked to no one in particular.

"No one, "Amma answered, "I was in there five or ten minutes ago. The cleaning crew will be arriving in the next hour or so."

"So you turned the stereo on for them?"

"No, why?"

"Because there is music coming from there."

They all followed me to the ballroom. We stood in the doorway watching Vienna deposit dirty drink glasses into the waste basket that she was holding. She was swaying to the music. I halted everyone and walked over to her.

"I believe you owe me a dance Mrs. Quinn." I relieved her of the basket and took her into my arms. The slightest trace of a smile crossed her face and she slid into my arms for about thirty seconds until she seen the rest of the search party standing in the doorway.

"Oh," she said, "you're all dressed already." She looked down at what she was wearing which of course was her silver evening gown. She giggled. "I suppose I had better get changed. Rainey, why do you look as though you slept in your clothes, or have we not been to bed at all?"

Ava stepped forward. "Mama, you kind of disappeared on us last night…where did you go?

"What do you mean by "kind of"? To my knowledge I didn't go anywhere. Now I best get out of these duds and go and see if Lili is awake."

I nodded to Ava and Rosy and they offered to go with her. I stayed behind to question Amma and Johnny. They said her reaction was pretty much the same as it had been all the other times.

By the time I got upstairs Ava and Rosy had already undressed their mother and she was lying down. I tiptoed over to the bed; she did not open her eyes or acknowledge me in any way.

We needed to leave for the rifle range by ten as the skeet shoot was scheduled to begin at eleven. Vienna would have been incensed with me if I let her sleep through it and so I went to awaken her. I was quite surprised to find that she was already dressed in her riding garb, boots and all. She was sitting at her dressing table with Lili who was attempting to brush her hair. As usual, as soon as Lili spotted me she yelped, "Daddy, Daddy." and put her arms out to me.

"Why don't you finish your mother's hair darling?" I said.

"I'm done." was her answer and so I picked her up.

Vienna's eyes met mine in the mirror. "I want to ride with the girls and Duffy in the carriage over to the range. I would like to ride Atlantia home though so would it be too much trouble for you to have Zoe ride her and tag along with you? I know Atlantia can be quite spirited at times and I am not comfortable with Zoe riding her unsupervised."

"Of course; she can ride along side of Johnny and me. We'll take it slow."

"Yes, she would like that; thank-you Rainey."

"There is no need to thank me. Her safety is important to me too."

Abruptly she changed the subject. "Did you have a good time at the party Rainey?"

"I suppose it was all right…that is until my wife went missing."

She ignored the reference to her disappearance. "From what I saw you were definitely having a good time… especially with the Duchess."

"Then perhaps it's time you got yourself a pair of spectacles." I was tired of her insinuations but what she said next floored me.

"Do you want to bed her Rainey?"

"What…what did you say?"

"You heard me, you're not deaf. Do you want to take the Duchess Lauren to bed?"

"I will not dignify that with an answer." I turned and walked out of the room with Liliana.

The next time I saw Vienna was at the rifle range. She had Lili on her hip and was strolling behind the shooters talking to each in turn. I met her in the middle and as luck would have it right behind the Duchess of Calendria.

"Darling," she cooed, "poor Lauren just can't seem to get her stance right. Do you think you can help her before she injures her shoulder?"

"I'm hardly the person to be giving instructions to anyone in the art of skeet." I stated firmly.

"Oh Darling, you are too modest. I know you have taken your lessons seriously. I have watched you and I have been impressed with what you have learned in such a short time. Do you trust that he can help you Lauren?"

The Duchess smiled brazenly at me. "Oh yes, I know he can help me. I will be a perfect student, I promise you Rainey." She lowered her rifle and beckoned me to her.

I stepped forward and put one arm around her shoulders and the other around her waist. Apparently that was what my wife fancied. I wanted to strangle both of them.

I lost sight of Vienna after that. I did wonder if she watched my futile attempt to keep Lauren focused on the task at hand. I was perfectly aware of the fact that the Duchess liked my arms around her and was only pretending to not understand my instructions. After an exasperating ten minutes I stepped back and told her to give it a try. She failed miserably by missing the clay pigeon by a country mile. She turned back and laughed saying she needed more instructions. I said I would see who I could find to aid her.

"But Rainey, it is only you I want." Her voice was all too seductive.

"You are barking up the wrong tree Lauren. I am much too old for games and I have no desire to be anyone's partner but my wife's. Good day to you."

Half an hour later I spotted Vienna sprawled out on a mossy mound with Roberge. I sauntered over. "Am I intruding?" I asked.

"Not at all my good man. It appears as if we might be off together on a new adventure. I was intrigued last night when the sisters approached me and offered an insight into my somewhat cloudy ancestry. And now, your lovey wife has informed me that she has all the answers. I admit I am more than a little mystified as to what information they have found that has been unobtainable for me. Are you privy to this information Rainey and when are we leaving on our next excursion?"

"I don't want to get your hopes up nor do I want to leave you in the dark, but I'm afraid the girls may have jumped the gun Roberge. We have come upon a diary[1] and there is some mention of the name Ferrani. We are not through translating as the diary is not only in Spanish and French but some unknown dialect. Vienna remembered that your surname translates roughly into Ferrani and so she thought there might be some connection. Is that what you told him Honey?"

"Sort of; I'll leave you two as I want to get home before Duffy does with Lili and Tanny." Vienna was on her feet and reaching for the reins of Atlantia that one of the newly hired grooms had brought her.

"I'll ride home with you." I offered.

"I'll be long gone before you even collect your horse." She mounted and was gone.

---

[1]   Diary of Avaleena, Mistress of Avanloch, circa 1850, found by Rainey last year

"Well, that was very brusque of her!" Roberge explained.

"Think nothing of it; she's been off her oats lately."

Roberge laughed. "No doubt, it's been a long time since a soirée of this magnitude has been held here. Go, go chase after your wife and I trust you will keep me informed regarding this mysterious diary? If you require my expertise in translating I will be most happy to oblige."

I thanked him and said we'd talk more at another time. I found my steed and set off after Vienna. I took the high path as I was certain that would be the trail she would take. I caught sight of her from the bottom of Widow's Hummock. I think she was waiting for me. Her horse reared when it saw us. I held my breath but Vienna held firmly and the two of them disappeared over the knoll. I did not catch up to her. She had avoided being alone with me for some time now and had even gone so far as to sleep in another room so I guessed she didn't want me riding along side of her either. She still had been saying goodnight to me but then she would go down the hall and lock the door behind her. Several times I stood outside of Miss Mary's room tempted to break the door down and demand an explanation from her but I couldn't bring myself to do so. She was somewhat polite to me when in the company of others but I am sure they all felt the tension between us. I had decided to let it pass until yet another disastrous Labor Day weekend was over. My solution had been to leave Avanloch for a few weeks and give her the space she seemed to want but that had gone over like a lead balloon so I was at a loss as to what to do. Something was definitely up with her but I was clueless as to what it could be. I didn't want to face the obvious and that was that she had abruptly stopped loving me; for what reason I could not fathom. What had I done; what had I said? Did she really want to go back to the man who had kept her away from me… did she love Anton more than she did me?

The first sitting of the afternoon luncheon was to be held at three P.M. for those who had to make train connections at Waverly. The last train left at six P.M. Vienna's sister-in-law, Ash and all her friends were spending another night at the castle and so they would take their meal later. I joined up with Zoe and the young girls in the upstairs hallway.

"Where is Mama?" Tanny asked.

I picked Lili up and said that I hoped she was waiting for us downstairs. The door to Miss Mary's room was half open. Tanny pushed it the rest of the way.

"Maybe Mama is in here…oh my, what a mess!" She exclaimed.

She was right; Vienna's riding gear along with six or seven other outfits were strung out across the room. Drawers were left opened and jewellery and lingerie dangled out of them.

"Who is going to clean this up Rainey?"

"Your mother made the mess Tanny so I think it's her job to clean it up don't you think?"

"Yes, but we'll help her won't we Zoe?"

We took the lift downstairs and stopped at the kitchen doorway. Lili yelped. "Mama, Mama!" and practically jumped out of my arms. Yup, she knew her mother even from behind. Vienna turned around, knelt and hugged her daughters.

"Look at you my darlings! How beautiful you are! Zoe, thank-you; they look every bit the little princesses that they are."

Vienna raised her head and smiled at me and I fell in love with my wife all over again. She was just as beautiful as she had been on that New Year's Eve so very long ago. No matter how insolent her behaviour had been I still adored her and I couldn't imagine life without her. I knew at that moment that I would do whatever to right what was wrong between us.

She was wearing what I would call a "flapper dress." It was dark brown in colour and was decorated with golden tassels. She had on a long single strand of pearls; I was pretty sure that she was wearing the pearl earrings that I had given her. Somehow she had managed to cut her hair since I had last seen her. It was very short and little curls escaped from under the gold headband that encircled her head. She was wearing mascara and eyeliner which was very unusual for her. Her lips were painted a gingery color as were her cheeks.

"No Mama, you are the beautiful one, isn't she Rainey?" Tanny boasted looking up at me.

"Yes, she certainly is." I wanted to take her in my arms and kiss her all over; to hell with dinner and the guests!

"Get you all to the dining room!" Mary ordered. "We be bringing the soup right away, you dinna want to keep your guests waitin. Now off with ye all!"

Vienna took my hand and we walked to the dining room. I was pretty sure that I had the love of my life back but not in a million years could I have predicted what was to come. The dinner crowd was already seated and they all rose when we entered the room. Vienna beckoned them to sit down. We deposited the girls with Johnny's and Emma's daughters at a small table directly behind us. I was not overly pleased that Lauren had claimed the chair to the right of me. She placed her hand on top of mine.

"Thank you so much for lending me your charming husband this afternoon Lady Vienna."

Vienna was quick to respond. "Rainey is not mine to lend Duchess; he is his own person. However, if he were mine to lend, I can assure you that you would be the last person on earth that I would even consider loaning my husband to!"

I don't know who laughed harder…Lauren or Roberge. A few of the other guests joined in the laughter but most of them just sat with quizzical smiles on their faces. I felt like I was some bargaining chip in an age old feud between two beautiful women with only one possible outcome…Vienna would win, hands down. Ava's and Rosy's probing eyes met mine.

Vienna passed on the soup and salad and loaded her plate with everything carbohydrate. I raised my eyebrows at her choices as she dug in ravenously. I remarked that I had never seen her eat like that before.

She shrugged her shoulders. "I need to keep my strength up and besides I'm eating for two."

Alarmed I said "What?"

"I just meant that I haven't eaten for a while so I am consuming two meals in one and it's going to be a long, long night." She squeezed my leg and winked at me.

I wondered if she had consumed too much wine but her glass was still untouched. It took a full hour to get through all the courses before desserts and coffees were even brought out. No one was in any great hurry. Frankly, I had had enough of idle chit-chat to last me a lifetime.

Vienna asked Rosy to collect the kitchen staff so that we could toast them. She turned to me.

"Darling, I seem to have dropped my serviette; would you mind retrieving it for me?"

I pushed my chair back slightly and leaned down. I felt her hand on my knee and then she took it and ran it up the inside of her leg. I wondered briefly if she was amusing herself at my expense. It became abundantly clear that she was serious when her hand directed me further up her inner thigh and I shockingly discovered that my wife, the Mistress of Avanloch, had come to the formal dinner table sans underwear. She let go of my hand when Rosy returned with Mary McDuff and the kitchen staff. Vienna magically produced her napkin as she thanked me and asked if I would make the toast. Her eyes were highly suggesting that she had more in store for me. I told her that it was indeed my pleasure. It was my turn to wink at her. I cleared my voice and wondered if anyone had noticed our under the table antics. I didn't give a damn if they had.

Everyone stood and clapped and cheered when the ladies entered the room. They raised their glasses as I saluted them for keeping us all well fed. I promised that there would be a little something extra in their Christmas stockings. As they made their exit I asked that everyone be seated as I was not finished with the toasts yet.

"First, I would like to thank our daughters, Ava and Rosalyn for suggesting that we host this bash and to all of you for attending our Canadian holiday Labour Day party." Rosalyn was teary-eyed…I surmised because I had called her my daughter. "It's no secret that Vienna was lost to us all for almost two years. It was the Labour Day weekend that she went missing and so the girls thought that it was about time that we did something positive to celebrate our holiday. I don't mind saying that it has not been a particular favourite time of the year for me for one reason or the other. I'm pleased to say that this year is shaping up to be the best of my life." I looked at Vienna and her smile promised me that it would be. "So, raise your glasses with me as I thank our daughters for all their hard work in making this weekend happen." The wine carafes were nearly empty and I asked Johnny if he would refill them. While he was doing so I continued on with my thank-yous. "Nothing at Avanloch succeeds without Johnny O'Shea and his lovely wife Amma; they are indispensable and I am so thankful that they were here all those years with Vienna when I wasn't. They, along with Rosy's fiancé, Evan Govern, worked night and day so please raise your glasses because without them this soirée would never have happened." I turned around to address the young people. "And to the O'Shea girls for all their invaluable time keeping Tanny and Liliana amused, and to our own Zoe who is always ready to take up the slack. Oh, and to Ash and Gray, who are still outside doing God knows what, for helping with the guest list and other contributions. Thank-you; we love you all."

Vienna took my hand and whispered. "And I love you."

I suddenly felt very vulnerable and was pretty sure that I would choke up with my next toast.

"Lastly, but certainly not least, I want to thank my remarkable wife Vienna, not just for everything she contributed to the weekend, but for being my Lady. Quite frankly, I don't think I could live another day if she wasn't in my life. These past two years without her was a nightmare. I will be eternally grateful to the people who looked after her and yet, they were also the ones who kept her from us…" Vienna squeezed my hand and gave me the grit to go on. "Excuse me; it's all still too recent. I think you all get the gist of this and that is that Vienna had barely been home a month when she agreed to the girls' request because she thought it would do us all a world of good. I have no doubt that she could have pulled this affair off single handily. I know that she wouldn't agree with me, but believe me, she was the force behind all of this so please everyone; give a whoop and a holler to the Mistress of Avanloch."

Vienna brought the clapping and whistling to a halt when she stood up and began drumming on her glass. She held up her hands. "Thank-you, but if you will allow me, I have a few words I would like to say also." She picked up her goblet. "Please join me in another toast to my daughters, every one of them, and Amma and Johnny and Evan and all of you for coming." She turned to me. "Rainey is too modest. He actually has an intense distaste for huge gatherings and yet he jumped in with great enthusiasm and took full charge of the skeet shoot. I believe he did a superb job for someone who had no knowledge of the sport in the beginning."

Interrupting the cheers I admitted that at no time did I really know what I was doing. Lauren spoke up and said brazenly. "I strongly disagree; Rainey, you are an excellent teacher."

"I must agree with you Mrs. Farradan, my husband is a gifted teacher, especially in matters of the heart."

I had to chuckle as Vienna had just put the Duchess of Calendria in her place. She absolutely hated being referred to as Mrs. Farradan. Vienna extended her hands out to me and I stood up and put my arm around her waist.

"Something always kept me going those many months while I was living another life. I always felt that somewhere someone was waiting for me and I spent many a sleepless night trying to piece it all together. I was reborn the moment I was reunited with Rainey and my heart sang as it does now." She faced me. "I love you Rainey and I shall until the day I die…no matter what."

There was much clanging on the glasses…not that I needed any coaxing to kiss my wife. In between kisses she whispered. "Get me out of here Rain."

I did wonder about her phrase, "No matter what." though.

I addressed the guests asking to be excused as we needed a bit of a break before the next sitting of dinner and that Johnny would make sure that none of them would miss their connections back to London or wherever. Vienna waved a final goodbye saying that we might just do it all over again next year. Lord, I hoped not. We stopped at the girl's table and hugged them all and told Lili and Tanny that it would soon be their bedtime and we would see them tomorrow. Zoe said she had everything under control and not to worry about a thing.

I watched my wife sashay up the spiral staircase. I was thankful her chemise wasn't any shorter for I knew all too well what wasn't under it. Ava and Rosy had corralled me and had a dozen questions for me. How was their mother? Had she confided in me as to where she had disappeared to the night before? I put my hand up to halt them.

"No more questions tonight girls; I have a date with your mother and I don't want to keep her waiting." I kissed them both lightly on the cheek and started up the stairs after Vienna.

"What do we do now Daddy?" Ava asked.

"Anything you want Honey; it's your party."

"You are coming back for the next seating aren't you?"

"What do you think Ava?" I said winking at her.

Rosy laughed and said. "Come on Sis, let's go entertain the minions."

Vienna was entering the bedroom door by the time I got to the top landing. I closed and locked the door behind me and turned to see her sitting on the edge of the bed. She held one leg up and said, "Hi Rainey."

I bent down and placed her leg on my knee. "Hi yourself." I started to unroll her thigh high stockings slowly and sensually.

She leaned back on her elbows expressing delight with her eyes. "I see someone has shown you the proper technique to removing a lady's hose. Would it be that socialite bitch Priscilla or that wafer-thin Italian model…Zeta, was that her name?" She paused. "I am pretty sure it wasn't that cold wife of yours Louise, or maybe it was someone else entirely, but my money is on your little exotic dancer friend."

I pulled the rest of her stocking off and dropped her leg. She had just taken the fun out of the seduction.

"What?" She cooed. "I didn't say her name. I promised you I wouldn't and I never will."

"You know perfectly well it was you Vienna and I can guarantee you that I have never removed another woman's stockings."

"I doubt that very much." She said giggling.

She held up her other leg and I took it rather roughly and quickly removed the stocking. "Stand up and turn around." I ordered. She did. I unzipped her chemise and let it fall to the floor. "I see panties is not the only under garment you forgot to wear tonight."

"I didn't forget Rainey."

"Sometimes you act like a little school girl."

"Did you like me when I was a naïve, love-struck teenager?"

"Yeah, I liked you, but there was never anything naïve about you."

"Do you like me now Rainey?"

"Not always." I drew the quilt and sheet back from the bed and told her to get in. I pulled them back over her and stepped away. She sat up.

"Aren't you coming to bed with me Rainey?"

"I haven't decided yet."

"Why, are you angry with me for what I said? I didn't mean anything; I was only teasing. Please come to bed Rainey; I've been waiting for you all day." She pleaded.

I bent over her. "Where does it say in our marriage vows that you get to ignore me for days on end and turn your back on me in bed, but when you want me I am to come running? Where does it say that you can randomly accuse me of wanting to cheat on you and then throw me to another woman and then when you decide that you need a little lovin think you can seduce me under the dining room table and invite me to your boudoir and all will be forgiven?"

She started to say something but I hushed her by placing my fingers on her lips. "I'm not finished yet. If you have a problem with my past and the women in it then we had better have a talk. For some ungodly reason you want to throw them in my face and it seems as if you have forgotten that you were the reason there even **were** other women. You left me high and dry in 1961, and I am sorry that I didn't stay true to you like you did to me, but as far as I knew you were never coming back to me. I tried to replace you but you know how that turned out. I've told you a hundred times that I never even so much as looked at another woman while you were "away" these past two years, but if it makes you feel less guilty because of your life with Anton then go ahead, believe what you want about me." I stood up and started to back away. "That's all I have to say. The ball is in your court. You can tell me what's troubling you or not...I'm done."

She grabbed onto my arm. I didn't want to look at her but I did. Little tears were forming in the corners of her eyes. I wish I could cry as easily as she could.

"Please don't go Rainey. I know I have been neglecting you and that I have been sullen and I promise you I will tell you everything tomorrow…tomorrow, not tonight. I need you Rainey. I need you to hold me…please. I've never cared about the women in your life, you know that. I don't know what made me bring them up. I know I spoiled a perfectly wonderful moment and if you will just let me make it up to you…"

"I'm not feeling very amorous at the moment Vienna so you will have to excuse me. You know when I first saw you in the kitchen earlier this evening dressed in that sexy dress and sporting a wild haircut, I felt a renewed love for you. I wanted to take you in my arms and cart you upstairs, but it wasn't up to me to make the first move…and then you took my hand and again I knew that I would follow you wherever you would take me. I guess I'm a fool that way."

Big tears were rolling down her face. "Will you just lay with me Rainey? We don't have to make love, I just want to hold you and I need you to hold me."

"Tell you what…you scoot over to your side of the bed and I will lie on top of the bed and we can hold hands and I'll stay until you fall asleep, how's that?"

"You're sitting on my side of the bed." She said sniffling.

I walked around the bed and undressed down to my skivvies and crawled under one of the coverings. She reached for my hand and asked if she could give me a good-night kiss.

"No, no kissing, no kissing!'

"Okay, I promise." She kept inching closer and closer and then she just placed her body on top of mine and kissed me like there would be no more tomorrow."

Breathlessly, I said. "You promised."

"I lied." She whispered and then she kissed me again.

I rolled her over and tossed the covers aside and muttered. "What the hell."

I woke early the next morning. Vienna was sound asleep curled up facing me with her hands in the prayer position on her pillow. She looked peaceful and content. I hoped I was the reason. I wanted to kiss her but decided to let her sleep. I scribbled a few words on a slip of paper and placed it on my pillow where she would be sure to see it. I grabbed my clothes and hurriedly dressed in the parlour and made straight for the kitchen where the sweet aroma of coffee was wafting up the stairs. Amma and Johnny were already seated at the big wooden table.

"Why aren't you two sleeping in this morning?" I asked pouring myself a cup of the robust brew. I took a sip. "Must be the Saimaza blend that Vienna bought when we were in Saragossa; am I right Mary?"

"That you are Sir. She not been drinking me coffee lately so I sent Duffy downstairs to bring up a package of the Spanish concoction. Is she right behind you?"

"No, I left her sleeping. I didn't hear a peep from Tanny's and Lili's room so I suspect they are tuckered out too."

"Actually, they are not even here Rainey. Our girls took them and Zoe to our house for a sleepover. They were all still awake except for Lili when Johnny and I got home at two." Amma said. "I expect they will be asleep for a while yet. Now tell us what did our fair lady have to say for herself about her disappearing trick the other night?"

"I'm sorry but the subject never came up Amma." I replied winking at her. "What am I saying…I am not sorry at all but she did say that we would talk today so we will just have to wait and see if she confesses or not."

I asked them how things went after Vienna and I had left. Amazingly well they said. Ava and Rosy took charge and Ash played hostess until the last guest was out the door. They figured there were a half dozen or so of Ash's friends still holed up in the towers. She had informed them that breakfast was from eight until ten and then the kitchen was closed after that for a week or so.

I laughed. "And it should be. Mary, you and Lois need to take a few days off; go visit your sister or go shopping, whatever. Ava and I can handle meals and I seem to remember that my wife is a fairly decent cook herself."

"I already sent Lois off for a week as she was the main cook here this last week so you just never mind as this will be like a holiday for me with everyone else gone." Mary insisted.

There was no arguing with the woman; she would do just as she pleased and we wouldn't want her any other way. Johnny and I were discussing dismantling the skeet arena when the house phone bleeped. Amma said that it was Vienna's room. I told her to answer. After a brief one sided conversation Amma hung up and said that I had been summoned.

"See you all later." I said cheerily as I pushed myself away from the table.

"You bring her down here and there had better be a light back in those big brown eyes of hers you hear Mr. Rainey! We bout had enough of her brooding and only you can bring her out of her doldrums." Mary instructed.

"Oh, so it isn't just me who has noticed things haven't been sitting right with her?"

"You'd have to be blind as a bat and dumber than a doorstop not to see that she be troubled."

"I'm hoping I'm already half way there Mary. Now I best not keep the Lady waiting." I freshened up my coffee and poured a cup for Vienna and took the lift to the second floor.

The bedroom door was still shut so I entered through the parlour.

"You rang my Ladyship…what's going on here?" I asked puzzled by the heap of clothes scattered on the floor. She was standing in the middle of them.

"Any fool can see that I am cleaning out my closet." She replied sarcastically.

I swore under my breath. "At seven thirty in the morning you decide to tidy up your closets…"

She interrupted me. "I'm not tidying. I might keep the clothes in this pile, but not those."

She pointed to the mess in front of me. I asked her what was wrong with them or was she just tired of them. She dropped the dress she was holding and rubbed her stomach and said that she was too fat for them. Well, she had put on a little weight but she had needed to as she had come home thin as a rail from Spain, but I certainly wasn't going to tell her that. I told her that we would box up the ones she didn't want and I would take her to Edinburgh or London and buy her a whole new wardrobe.

"Is that before you go away or after you come back Rainey… that is, if you even come back?"

She turned her back to me. I suddenly realized that I was holding two cups of hot coffee and set them down on the chest of drawers. I crossed the room to her and turned her around and put my arms on her shoulders.

"I'm not going anywhere Vienna and you know that." I said emphatically. "Now, I think it is high past time that you tell me what the hell is going on with you. When did you become so unsure of my commitment to you?"

"Is that what I am to you…an obligation?"

"That's not what I meant and you know it. I promised to love you forever and nothing has changed there. I'm devoted to you and no one can ever take your place. Where are these crazy notions of my infidelity coming from? I thought we were solid. What did I do or say to make you turn your back on me?"

"I was gone a long time Rainey and I know from experience that you need someone to share your bed with. If it was just casual sex then I am all right with that… but, if it was with someone you fell in love with while I was gone…

"Stop it Vienna! You know perfectly well that I have never been in love with anyone but you and I sure as hell never even contemplated having sex with anyone while you were away. It's all a figment of your overworked imagination. Now sit down and start talking before I completely lose all my patience with you."

"Isn't it true Rainey that all women are alike from the neck down? If you put a paper bag over their head you can pretend that you are with the woman you love and still get fulfilment and not even feel guilty? Men are like that, right?"

I shook my head. If she wasn't so serious it would be funny. "Where the hell did you get such a cockamainy idea from?"

"I don't know. It's true though isn't it?" She asked in her little girl voice. "Men have their needs."

"And so do women, at least the woman I love does. I think you have skirted around the issue long enough; it's time you started talking." I gave it a shot hoping I had hit the mark. "Let's start with Somner's letter…that's the day things all went sour with you isn't it?"

She scooted up on the bed and put her head against the headboard. She tried to cover up her legs by stretching her short nightgown over them. I passed her a pillow and she smiled at me. She reached out and touched my face.

"I thought I buried Verde El Mar that day when I buried Somner's letter but obviously I didn't. I went back there Rainey and I hated myself all over again for being unfaithful to you. I thought if I could make you out to be adulterous also everything would be all right and so I planted the seed…or should I say, Katarina did."

"We've been over this several times already Vienna. You were never untrue to me and I thought that you had come to terms with yourself that you were not responsible for what happened when you had amnesia and were led to believe that you were someone else?"

"I see her in the mirror Rainey. She looks back at me and tells me to take Liliana to her Papa. I know she means Anton because Lili never calls you papa. She always calls you daddy."

"That's because I am her daddy." I got up and picked up a hand mirror and told her to look in it. "Who do you see in there?" I asked.

"Right now I see me, Vienna… but sometimes I see Katarina."

"Katarina can't hurt us; she was not a malicious person. How could she be, she was a re-creation of you. I can handle her; you just have to tell me when she makes an appearance, okay? Now are you done with all this nonsense of me being unfaithful?"

"I wish I could be. I wish we could go back to that day in 1981 when you came looking for me in Bridge Falls and we renewed our love at the Palace. I didn't care how many women you had wooed. You assured me they meant nothing to you and I believed you because I was so happy to have you back in my life. I couldn't imagine being any happier and when I got pregnant my happiness increased twofold. But then Nazeth happened. I was faithful for twenty years to a man I never thought I would see again and then in the blink of an eye I undid the magic."

I sat down on the bed beside her. "I assure you that the magic is still here Vienna. It's here when I look into your fabulous brown eyes, when you smile at me and when you touch me. Nothing has changed for me and I thought you felt the same way but I guess I am wrong. You've made this all about me. You want to paint me as a conniving, adulterous womanizer because you somehow believe that it exonerates you, is that right Vienna? Well, you have nothing to be forgiven for and I have told you that over and over but you just can't seem to let it go. It's time you forgave yourself and until then I can't see us moving forward. We haven't made any progress here at all. All you talk about is me wanting to be with other women and that Katarina has been making an appearance. Is that it Vienna, do you want to be Kat again…do you want to go back to Anton? Is he better at everything than I am? Do you love him more than you do me?"

"No, no Rainey!"

"Are you sure about that? I won't stop you from going back to him but you will not take our daughter with you. Do you hear; you will not take Lili with you? I will march out of here with her this very minute and you will be powerless to stop me. I will not be so cruel as to keep you from seeing her like you kept me from Ava though."

She was blubbering and grabbed onto my shirt.I brushed her aside and headed for the door. I had got down and dirty and I wasn't very proud of myself but I was tired of her beating around the bush and never getting to the crux of the problem.

She jumped off the bed and ran to me throwing herself at my feet. I told her to get up.

"No, no, not until you hear what I have to say. I never want to see Kat again when I look in the mirror…why do you think I cut my hair? I had to get rid of the last trace of her. I don't want to hear her voice in my head anymore and as for Anton…I hate him. I loathe him with a passion and you know that. He kept us from each other for almost two years; I have nothing but remorse for the time I spent with him. None of this is your fault Rainey. I have been in my own personal hell and I didn't want to bring you into it and it was up to me to find my way back. I have been in the darkness many times before but it was never so dark as these last weeks have been without you. I quit punishing myself last night and prayed that you would forgive me for my insanity."

She fell back onto the floor. "You haven't forgiven me though have you Rainey? And, if you can't believe me about this then you will never believe me about the baby either."

Now she had completely lost me. "What baby? What are you talking about?"

She rubbed her stomach. "This baby... this baby Rainey. We made another baby Rain, but you won't believe that it's yours will you?"

I pulled her up off the floor and sat her down on the settee. She was shivering. I grabbed a blanket off the bed and wrapped it around her. She was a mess; her eyes were red and swollen from crying and yesterday's make-up ran down her face. I pulled a handkerchief from my shirt jacket and dabbed away making more of a mess by uniting the tears with the mascara.

"I'm an ugly duckling aren't I Rainey?" She said through more tears.

"You're **my** duckling, my beautiful duckling." I said trying to appease her.

"Do you still want me Rainey? A minute ago you said you were going to take Lili and leave?"

"And, I still might if I don't get the answers I want. Are you really pregnant or is it a ruse?"

"I would never lie to you about such a thing Rainey."

"So why do you think I won't believe that the baby is mine? Have you been fooling around with somebody else?" I asked idiotically.

"Of course I haven't! It's just that the timing may be suspect to you?" She was still sniffling.

"Why is that Vienna?"

"Because I think I conceived the night you rescued me and brought me home. It was your birthday; do you remember?"

"Well it's not a night I will soon forget but that means that you are almost two months along. Why am I just hearing about this now?"

"Because I was afraid to tell you; I was afraid you would think the baby was Anton's."

"So you were going to hide the fact from me and everyone else that you were pregnant? How long do you think you could do that for? Why in hell would I think it was Anton's baby? Didn't you tell me that Kat hadn't been with him for months before we found you? And, what about the fact that Somner told you in his letter that Anton was sterile?"

"I hadn't decided what I was going to do. I was too confused…"

"Just a minute, just a damn minute; are you saying that you thought about aborting the baby?"

"Oh God, no Rainey, I could never do that! I meant that I hadn't decided how to tell you. I was so scared and then I got those stupid notions in my head that you had a girlfriend and you wouldn't want to have another child with me. I let it fester in me and the jealousy and mistrust just grew and grew."

"First of all, I am thrilled that we are going to have another daughter, so get rid of that idea immediately. But, I still don't have an answer…what did I do that started you on this merry-go-round of distrust? How could you ever doubt my love for you?"

"I wish I knew. You were right, we were gloriously happy… too happy I guess. I started to imagine what could go wrong because nothing had ever gone right for us before. Who was I to think that we could live in perfect harmony and bliss forever? And then I got the letter…"

"Well, it's time you did something about that letter. It's time you forgave Somner for that is the only way you are going to be able to forgive and vindicate yourself. He was your friend Vienna and I think you need to take another look at the words he wrote."

"I can't Rainey because I buried it and it's gone."

"I have the letter Vienna." I then told her how I had followed her and retrieved the letter from the compost bin. She wasn't angry with me and rewarded me with a kiss and asked me over and over again if I could ever forgive her.

"Let's talk about the baby; have you seen a doctor?" She shook her head. "Then that is number one on our list to do. You do know that this means I am never going to let you out of my sight for the next nine months…well, I should say seven months. This is going to be our last chance Vienna and nothing is going to come between us again; do you understand?"

"Yes, nothing will. You do love me though don't you Rainey? You didn't mean it when you said you would leave with Liliana did you? I thought you had forgiven me for keeping Ava from you for all those years. All I can say is that I'm sorry again. I made a huge mistake and when I see the two of you together I hate myself all over again."

I squeezed her hands. "I shouldn't have said that Vienna and I am sorry that I did. I was so exasperated with you that I just lashed out. It's not like me to be so insensitive but that's what you do to me. I have been so worried about you and your indifference and then once in a while you would almost smile at me across the kitchen table and so I had hope, but then you pulled that disappearance trick on us Saturday…if you hadn't shown up the next morning it would have been Nazeth all over again."

"Oh Rainey, I am so sorry."

"Don't you start crying again. I won't be at all placated until you remember where you were."

"I know Rainey, I know where I was."

She caught me off guard. "You do? When were you going to tell me?"

"I'm going to better than that, I'm going to take you there."

I was too stunned to say anything.

She kissed me and grabbed a slip from her closet and stopped at her dresser and gathered some underclothes. At the bathroom door she asked me if I would pick out something for her to wear.

"Sure," I said to myself, "if I could only remember which pile of clothes was taboo and which were acceptable." I chose one from the wardrobe instead and waited for her wondering where she could possibly be taking me. We had searched methodically for her on Saturday night and I couldn't fathom any place that we would have missed, but then, it **was** her castle. She did not protest when I slipped the yellow daisy print dress over her head.

"You always liked this dress didn't you Rainey? I best grab a sweater as it is cold down there."

I had laid a pair of flats out for her and she slipped her feet into them and told me to grab a flashlight. She took my hand and led me out into the hallway where she stopped and peered over the banister. I asked her what she was looking for. She said that she didn't want anyone to see us. I followed her into the little foyer where she walked to the corner of the bookcase. She looked back at me and smiled and told me to stay close behind her and to turn the light on. I watched in astonishment as she stood on her tiptoes and reached up and pressed on some books. The walls separated and she passed through pulling me in with her.

We stood on the narrow landing above a stairwell. She asked me to direct the light to the wall in front of her. She reached over and flipped a switch that activated power to a dim dangling light bulb six feet above the stairs. I grabbed on to her fearing she might lose her balance and fall. She thanked me but said she had done it many times before and had never fallen once. She smiled at me and asked me if I was okay.

"Define 'okay'. I have just entered into a stairway that was hidden behind a bookcase and I have the uncanny memory of being here before, but not only that, my wife has told me that she has no idea how to gain entrance to this hidden area and yet… here we are."

"I don't always remember that I know things Rainey. I know that makes no sense but it will, I promise. I will tell you the whole story just as soon as we get into 'the room', okay?"

"By 'room', you mean Avaleena's don't you?"

"Actually, it was not Avaleena's room at all. Come on."

She started down the stairs but I stopped her and asked her to let me go ahead as I didn't want her falling. She said she wouldn't and said again that she had been down them hundreds of times before. I asked her if she had been pregnant then and she said "no" and let me take the lead. I guess she realized that I was counting the steps because she told me there was twenty two, just like in my dream.[2]

[2-3]   In "The Curse of the Infinity Bracelets" Rainey is led through the bookcase and down 22 steps and into the room in the cellar by the Grey Lady in what he believed was a dream. The next morning he awakens to find an oversized book titled "AVANLOCH" in his room.

I could see myself walking down these very stairs following the lady in grey[3]. I shook my head hoping that I was dreaming again for it couldn't be so…I couldn't be in another secreted part of the castle because if I was then it meant my darling wife had been lying to me about her knowledge of the area. I didn't for one minute think that she suddenly remembered its whereabouts. The backside of the Grandfather clock greeted us at the bottom. I sighed and asked Vienna if we could get back out the same way we came in. She said that she had never been able to. I asked her what was beyond the door down the corridor to our left.

"It doesn't open; it is just a false door but I think it once opened into the grand reception hall."

"Why do you think that?"

"I think you will think so too after you hear me out. You still like my story-telling don't you?"

"Yeah, and I have the feeling that this is going to be a story to end all stories."

She giggled and led me down the right corridor and stopped at a door which I believed was the one I had visited in my hallucination. I asked her why there were no locks on the door and where was the table that held all the candles.

"I have no control over what you saw Rainey in what you think was a dream. Are you ready?"

She put her hand on the doorknob and we walked into a room from another time, a room that I uncannily remembered.

CHAPTER 3

The Diaries

I watched Rainey as he walked around the room running his hand along the top of the mantle and the table, checking for dust I guessed. He picked up the small portraits of Robert McAllister and asked me if I knew who he was. I answered that I did.

"So, you frequented these rooms for what…twenty years? Why, why would you come to such a dismal prison-like place?" He said without emotion.

"Maybe seventeen or eighteen years ago and I didn't regard it as a prison, but a haven." I answered truthfully.

He shrugged his shoulders. "Same thing; so are you going to tell me why?"

"I told you I would but you are not going to like it."

"It doesn't matter much what I like does it? I wasn't here, so whatever your reasons, they have absolutely nothing to do with me."

"That's where you are wrong Rainey; they have everything to do with you. I was invited here by the Grey Lady just as you were. At first I thought it was all a dream and maybe the first time was, but after three or four recurring experiences I realized that I was in control. I had found a sanctuary where I could come and cry my eyes out and no one could see or hear me. I believe Avaleena showed me the way for a reason. She had weathered the storm and when I found the diary, I realized that I could too."

"So, you believe that Avaleena is the Grey Lady; listen to me talking as if I believe in ghosts. And just what storm were you weathering?"

"You Rainey, you; it was September 1964 and I had just found out that you had married."

He took a deep breath before speaking; there was no compassion in his eyes.

"So, the reason you came down to this dungeon is my fault…. well, I think I have taken the blame long enough. It was you who didn't trust me enough to wait for me. There never was any other plan for me but to come home from Italy and be with the girl I wanted to spend the rest of my life with. You say you fell in love with me the first time you saw me…well, what about me? Love was nowhere in my plans, but there you were, this sweet sprite of a girl who stole my heart away and then promptly broke it into a thousand pieces when she up and ran away and took my unborn child with her. I suppose it is a blessing that I never knew that you were pregnant. I never got a say, you never gave me a chance. I will take the blame for not telling you I loved you and I have regretted it for twenty some years, but my God Vienna, you had to know that I loved you… you had to know. You made a life for yourself and our daughter, but what, I was not allowed to try and do the same? Is that what you are telling me Vienna? Did you want me to wait forever for you and never try to make a life without you? I thought we had put our past behind us but clearly that is not the case. I wanted desperately to fall in love with someone else and feel the way I once did with you but it didn't happen and I guess I will never be able to convince you of that. So, the question is, where do we go from here?"

He was sitting on the divan bent over with his head in his hands. It reminded me of the night he had told me about Jorja. She was the closest he had ever come to loving someone else. That had all come crashing down the day he found her with another man. She had sworn she loved him but behind his back she was sleeping with other men for money. It had crippled him to think that he had once thought that he could replace me with her. Mindlessly, I had insinuated her into my jealous rant last night about the women in his past. I was ashamed and I needed to tell him so.

I went over and sat on the floor and took his hands in mine… just as I had done that night two years ago when I had told him that whatever happened while we were apart had no bearing on the here and now and asked him to marry me. I needed to tell him that again.

"Look at me my darling. You asked me where we go from here and my answer is that we are already there. We are together and we will always be, no matter what befalls us. Do you remember what you made me promise you the night you brought me home from Spain? You made me promise never to cavort with any other men and never to leave you if I ever became pregnant again…do you remember? Well, I never will and we are going to be together through this pregnancy, come hell or high water, I swear before God!"

Rainey looked up at me through moist eyes. "I seem to remember that there was one other condition…"

I laughed as I dried our eyes with the sleeve of my sweater. "Do you mean the 'witch thing'? Well I haven't met any lately that I know of so I can sort of promise that I won't be hanging around with any."

"All-righty then, there is just one other thing that we have to clear up and that is this ridiculous idea you have that I have a girl-friend. You don't really believe that do you?"

"Sometimes it gets into my head that you do or did. Two years is a long time to be alone. But no, when I am sane I know you love only me."

"Good because I don't want to have to get you a new head. I have grown very fond of this one." He ruffled my untidy locks. "And, I was never alone. I had Ava and Morgan and Mason and the bottle."

"What? Did I drive you to drink again?" I asked distraughtly.

He pulled me up off the floor and into his arms. "No, it wasn't like when you went away the first time. Just a couple drinks at night to try and take the edge off. My behaviour was monitored pretty heavily by the kids so I couldn't even if I had wanted to. I'm afraid that I put them through hell at times. I love you so very, very much Vienna. Please don't ever desert me again. Do you know how many times I wanted to break down Miss Mary's door and cart you off screaming and yelling?"

"I wish you had of. I needed a scolding, maybe even a spanking. But you need to promise me that you won't keep things from me too. Why is this the first time that I am hearing how much you resented my keeping Ava from you? Why did you never tell me before?"

"I didn't want to burst the bubble. I had you back and I had a gorgeous younger replica of you in Ava; I was happy; we were all happy. Then you went away again through no fault of your own. Ava pulled me through those agonizing days and nights. Yes, I regretted not raising her but I was not blameless and so I kept it locked up. Thankfully, you came home again and you brought me another beautiful blue eyed living doll and now we are going to have another little girl and I am going to be with you every step of the way; every single step."

"You know that our baby will be a girl then, don't you?"

"Well I have been told that the LaFontaine women have no use for boy children, so yeah, I am okay with her being a girl on one condition."

"Dare I ask what that condition might be?"

"You may; I get to name her."

"You have seven months to come up with something spectacular so start thinking!"

"It's already done and no, you may not know. Now, isn't it about time that we get to the real reason for being in Avaleena's room?"

"I told you that it was not her room, not at first." I took his hand and pulled him along with me into the bedroom. "Come, and I will tell you a most dastardly tale of love and lust."

"If this is just a ploy to get me into the bedroom then let me assure you that I need no coaxing."

I laughed. I had my Rainey back and life was wonderful. He lay down on the bed and beckoned for me to join him. I glanced over at the bureau that had kept Avaleena's diary buried for one hundred and thirty years and another hour one way or the other wasn't going to change anything. In fact, as far as I knew, I was the only one who knew how to access the chest and extract the **real** diary.

I turned the lamp off and stepped out of my dress and cozied up beside Rainey. "What the heck," I said, "but there had better be a whole lot of kissing."

"I wish the woodpile wasn't depleted as this room could certainly use some warming up." I said as I chose a long sleeved silk kimono from the closet. I put it on over my dress.

"I thought we warmed it up considerably." Rainey quipped. "How in the world did you manage to bring firewood down here without being seen?"

"Oh, I didn't. It was all here piled up against the back wall next to the grandfather clock."

"And, it lasted you all these years?"

"No, I ran out years ago. There are no plug-ins so I couldn't bring an electric heater. I thought of buying a kerosene heater but I didn't. If the cold was too unbearable I would take my writings upstairs to my parlour."

"Your writings; is this where you wrote all the letters to me? No wonder some of them are filled with despondency. It breaks my heart picturing you down here in these cold and gloomy rooms and all because of me."

"You were not to blame my darling. I did it all myself and I could have tried to right the situation but instead I chose to play the role of the forsaken damsel." I walked over to the bureau and pulled open the second drawer and then immediately shut it and was attempting to open it again when Rainey offered his help.

"Here let me help, it must be stuck. What's in it anyway?"

"It's not stuck; see there is a hidden drawer and it is only activated by the opening of the drawer twice. I discovered it strictly by accident. I was snooping and originally this drawer wouldn't open so figuring that something was stuck in it also, I slammed it shut and reopened it and Voila! Here within is **the** book."

"I see that." Rainey removed it and held it awkwardly in his hands. "When and why did you bring it back here Vienna? Was it Saturday night when you disappeared on us?"

"It's not the same book Rainey."

"What do you mean? I can see perfectly well that it is the book of Avanloch."

"There are two books; this is the real one."

"You've lost me Hon; what do you mean by 'the real one?'"

"This is the one that Avaleena penned. The one upstairs locked up in room one is the one that I wrote." I let that sink in for a few seconds but I could see that I had only managed to confuse Rainey even more.

He gestured to me to sit down on the divan and placed the book between us. "What the hell Vienna? Why would you make another copy of Avanloch? Were you afraid that the original would be lost, or stolen, or what?"

"They are not exactly the same Rainey. Mine is fiction and this one isn't."

He skimmed through a few pages. "Looks exactly the same to me."

"Yes, and some of it is. I copied it verbatim in many places, but when it took a decisive turn into how Robert Bruce McAllister was conceived I took exception and decided that Avaleena should be the one who had the love affair and not Stewart."

"I have so many questions Vienna but I am going to try and sit quietly while you explain yourself, but first I need to ask you one thing, okay? All along you have been able to read Spanish...when we were in Spain and Abella showed you Anton Christovals diary that contained information about the Infinity Bracelets, you could have translated it, but pretended you didn't know how, and when I showed you Avaleena's diary, you pretended again that you didn't know Spanish...why?"

"It wasn't deliberate Rainey. I told you that I don't always remember things and that is one of them. I was not being deceitful. On the plane home from Verde Del Mar you suggested that I had a selective memory and only chose to recall what was important to me like conjuring up images of Avanloch. Perhaps I do for I cannot explain why I could see it but not you or the girls for you are all more important to me than this old castle. There was this one thing though that I couldn't explain at the time. It was New Year's Eve. I couldn't dance much because of the pain in my hip but Anton wanted me to try a slow waltz. I said that I would try. The band started up and some memory tried to make contact with me and I became disoriented and I fainted. I didn't recognize the song then but I do now. It was "The First Time I Ever Saw Your Face." It was our wedding song and I guess that is why I was so disturbed by it."

"That must have been traumatizing for you Sweetheart. I can't imagine what it was like for you and I am so sorry that I accused you of having a selective memory."

He put his arms around me. "It's all right Rainey. Don't ever think that you weren't in my head because you were…I just couldn't hold on to the visions long enough to make contact with them. I'm positive now that it was you trying to communicate with me but for some reason we just couldn't connect. That was then and this is now and I'm never going to lose sight of you again." I felt tears forming in my eyes and quickly wiped them away.

"Sorry Babe, I didn't mean to accuse you of lying." Rainey apologised. "And speaking of your troublesome hip… I guess that your surgery is not going to happen next week?"

"It's okay, I know you didn't and yes, there will be no surgery if I am pregnant and I'm pretty sure I am. I'm still a little miffed myself as to why I had no inkling of understanding Spanish when it is very clear that I can sometimes. When I first opened the book and realized that it was not in English I was quite disappointed. I leafed through the pages and then suddenly the writing turned into a language I recognized…French. Though I was not fluent in tongue or the written word I could make out some phrases and my curiosity was aroused as to why the sudden change in dialect. I decided right there and then to decipher the whole diary. I knew it was going to be a formidable task, but perhaps it was just what I needed to take my mind off my situation. I had Henry, our chauffeur back then, drive me into Waverly to pick up some books on how to translate Spanish into English and my two years of high school French would not be sufficient so I would also need a French dictionary. I wasn't happy with the selection I found in Waverly and so I asked Ash to see if Stu had what I wanted. I think she thought I was crazy to want to burden myself with such a task of self-teaching myself new languages, but she came through for me. Stu had exactly what I wanted and two weeks later I started my arduous task. It took me four years to translate Avaleena's diary and another two years to rewrite it."

"May I ask you a question Hon?" Rainey asked warily.

"Of course; you can ask me anything." I answered affectionately touching his hand.

"Do you know this book off by heart or can you read/translate it right now?"

"I think so…let me see. Well of course I have memorized the first few lines so I will skip ahead to after Corinthia has made an appearance. This is what Avaleena says."

"I have had my first meeting with the woman who is going to give me the child that I so desperately want — So much so that I have gone along with Stewart's demented plan. He does not know that I have found his secret entrance into the underground room that he had built to house his whore mistress."

I quit reading. Rainey's eyes were questioning. I asked him if he wanted me to explain and he said, "Yes, definitely. While you were away Ava and Zoe managed to translate the diary upstairs and nowhere does it ever mention that Stewart had a mistress; only that Avaleena had a lover."

"Avaleena didn't have a lover and neither did I. Stewart moved another woman into the house in hopes of impregnating her and you had gotten yourself married so at that point in my life I had no use for men. Stewart was having way too much fun with Corinthia and I pictured you doing the same with Louise so I turned the tables and gave Avaleena a lover as she was much too sad. I could not do the same for myself as I could not betray my love for you. I imagined I was Avaleena and on paper I gave her a lover and I guess that meant that I gave myself one too. Do you hate me yet Rainey?"

"Do you think I would hate you for wanting to find someone to love? Of course I don't, but if you gave Avaleena a relative of Roberge's to cavort with does that mean that you secretly wanted Roberge to be your lover?"

"Heavens NO, why would you say that?"

"Because in the book upstairs, the one that **you** supposedly wrote, Avaleena's lover is Jacques Ferrani and you so acutely pointed out that Ferrani is an alternate spelling of Farradan and I only know of one Farradan and that is Roberge, so…"

"I did not make up the Ferrani name Rainey. There really was a man named Jacques Ferrani and you will see in a little while how he fits into the picture. But as for me wanting Roberge for a lover you are way off base."

"All righty then, it won't be the first time I have insinuated that he was more to you than just a friend is it? Sorry, I apologize."

"Just a minute, you may not be too far off base here. I mean I didn't know very many men except Jeremy's friends and most of them were old and unattractive. I met Roberge in nineteen sixty four, I think. It was here at a party we hosted. I have to admit that he did flirt with me then and every other time we were in each other's company, but I did not reciprocate. Perhaps subconsciously I thought of him, I don't know. The name Ferrani did not ring a bell with me when we were in Spain with Roberge and he mentioned that it was an alternate or Basque spelling of his name."

"Yes, I remember and we will question him about it at some time down the road." He chuckled. "Roberge hey…I always figured he had a crush on you?"

"Quit teasing Rainey; it may just turn out that we are related!"

"Say what?"

"Do you want to hear the story or not?"

"The floor is all yours My Lady."

I picked up the diary and started with how Robert McAllister came to be.

After four years of Marriage I had yet to conceive. Stewart had me to doctors in Edinburgh and London. It was finally determined that I would never be able to get pregnant because my ovaries were basically non-existent. I had suffered great abdominal pain when I was a girl of thirteen and an exploratory surgery found that cysts had developed on my ovaries. They had ruptured and I was left with a great amount of scar tissue and labeled "infertile". I was not told this at the time. It was my fault that we would not have children. This was not acceptable to Stewart as he needed an heir to carry on the family name as he was the last of the McAllister's. I was desperate to have a child of my own but would not go along with his hair brained scheme and that was that the only way to accomplish this was for him to have another woman carry his child. When it was born we would pass him off as mine. He would move this surrogate into the house and no one would know who and why she was here except the servants. He was a very powerful and somewhat ruthless man so for fear of their lives they would not cross him. I locked myself in my room for days protesting. It did not work and Stewart sent two of his faithful soldiers off to find a woman with my stature and coloring. Meanwhile he started the construction of these rooms. He proposed to keep her in isolation away from me and the rest of the household. Seeing that he would be visiting her often he wanted to be comfortable also so did not scrimp on anything. Corinthia arrived two months later.

"Excuse me for a second Vienna…just like that, this woman agrees to be his concubine and bear him a child? She must have demanded something in return and where did his men find her? We know there was a child but suppose if she hadn't bore a son, but a daughter, what then?"

"You are the impatient one aren't you? Of course she was going to be rewarded; Stewart was a very wealthy man for the times. She was of Spanish descent and it is not clear exactly where she was found. If she had of given birth to a girl…I am getting ahead of myself. Shall I go on?"

"Of course Darling; sorry."

"It is a matter of record that Stewart's son was born in 1852 and from Avaleena's diary we learn the exact date and the circumstances. I will do my best at translating but it has been a long time and I am sure I am a little rusty." Rainey said he wouldn't know the difference anyway. I opened her journal to the page that I had earmarked and read from it.

October 03

I have suspected for some time now that "SHE" had arrived as Stewart was coming later and later to bed. Sometimes he didn't bother at all. For months I had heard loud noises coming from beneath the castle's floors but that had all ceased in early September. I surmised that the construction of Stewart's mistress's room was completed. What mockery of that word! I was Mistress of Avanloch and yet the title also referred to my replacement as she lay with my husband.

For months Stewart had tried to convince me of the necessity of this so called surrogate to be under our roof. No amount of my ranting and crying had changed his mind. He wanted her under lock and key at all times. His argument was that if she was a woman of suspect character then what was stopping her from cavorting with other men? No, there was to be no chance of that; she had to be "pure" from the moment she came to him. I had laughed in his face. He promised me that the moment she was "with child", he would be through with her. He made it sound obscene. I hated him and told him that I wanted to go home; I wanted to go back to Spain. He forbid me to do so and said he would put a guard on me night and day if necessary. So like the woman downstairs I was also to be his prisoner. I decided to find a way to visit her. It was not easy but I succumbed to his demands, yet secretly I was plotting my escape. I let him to believe that I wanted a child so badly that I had come to realise that he was right and that I would not interfere anymore. He told me that he loved me and that the very idea of him being unfaithful made him ill. Did I believe that... not for one minute. I was not as naïve as I led him to believe that I was. My husband is a very powerful man and he is often called upon to settle disputes within the territories. He is gone from the castle for long periods of time fighting for one cause or the other, commandeering titles of lands from rival clans and distributing them to those in his favor. I did not think for one minute that he had not found comfort in the arms of some maiden when his travels kept him away for long periods of time. However, this was an entirely different situation...this affair was going to be under my roof!

After two months I gave into my curiosity about the woman in the cellar and decided to visit her. Our cook, Dacha, was rather a simple woman and I decided to make her my friend by pretending to be interested in cooking. I knew that it was she who was preparing and delivering meals to the woman downstairs so my ulterior motive was to get her to trust me so that I could find the entrance to the forbidden room. I did follow her clandestinely and learned that the entry was in the Grand Reception Hall. Why it was called that I had no idea as we certainly didn't receive any guests; at least I didn't. But my efforts were thwarted as I soon discovered that the door was locked and required a key to gain entrance. How many keys existed I did not know, but the one that I was interested in hung from a cord around Dacha's neck. I thought of drugging the woman with laudanum but I was not sure how many drops it would take to put her to sleep. Stewart had his doctor prescribe the drug for me citing that I suffered from rheumatic pain and a never ending cough probably all brought on from the dank conditions of the castle. The past summer had been advantageous to my health and I had not partaken of the solution for five months. I had successfully weaned myself off my dependency of the narcotic. Then Corinthia arrived. Stewart said he would not, could not tolerate my outbursts of anger and highly suggested that I needed to calm down and that laudanum would see to that. I had resisted at first as I had no intention of "calming down."

However, I had talked myself into a drop of the tincture every evening with my nightly tea as I was unable to sleep knowing full well what was going on in the room under my bedroom floor. I would pace back and forth and get myself into such a state that I felt like pulling my hair out so what could a little drop hurt? And, I was still planning on escaping my prison so I needed to stay healthy. One drop and sometimes a little bit more and I was asleep in twenty minutes, but how much would it take to down Dacha? I did not know and I did not want to kill her. I put that idea away for a while and tried a different approach.

I persuaded her to tell me about her life away from the castle. She lived in Doome which was the hamlet down the hill from Avanloch. Her husband had run out on her and she was left alone with three hungry mouths to feed. She had little time to spend with her children as she didn't leave the castle until nine every evening and had to be back at four the next morning. I had never thought about the hardships of the help before and found myself sympathizing with her and promised to do what I could to alleviate her situation. I was the Mistress of Avanloch wasn't I? Yes, and I was going to assume the role and initiate my authority and Stewart had better go along with me or I might just add five drops of laudanum to his whiskey!

Within three days I had the key to the secret room. I awaited Stewart's departure for Edinburgh and with Dacha keeping the other servants busy I unlocked the door to my husband's lair.

"Ah, I see. The wild look in Avaleena's eyes can now be explained. She wasn't demented, she was a heroin addict." Rainey declared.

"I'm not too sure about that Rain." I said defending her. "Should I continue?"

"Of course; I can hardly wait to meet Corinthia."

I smirked. "Perhaps you may have already met a distant relative of hers."

"Are we talking about Roberge again?" Rainey asked.

"Maybe I am and maybe I'm not." I teased.

He looked at me questionably. "Good things come to those who sit and wait quietly." I said. I turned the page and took up reading again what Avaleena had written in her diary one hundred and thirty two years ago.

December 9ᵗʰ

I turned the key in the lock. The door swung open and I was met by a blast of icy air. I wrapped my shawl around me a little tighter and proceeded down the steps. Dacha had provided me with a lighted candelabra but I was pleased to see that walls held lamps so I lit some of them from the candles. The dirt floor was very uneven and I stumbled several times so decided to douse the candelabra before I burnt myself. I laid it on a little table next to half a dozen or so other candles. The door to the right was locked with a deadbolt.

"Aha again; I told you there were lots of candles on that table didn't I?" Rainey contended.

"And, I thought you were going to sit quietly and listen?" I left the question dangling in the air.

He smiled and gestured to me to go on.

I pulled back the bolt and tried to open the door but it did not budge.

"Is that you Dacha? Wait, I will let you in." A voice called out.

I heard another lock open and there she stood... the woman who would carry Stewart's child and make me a mother. I was not shocked to see such a beautiful young girl as I was sure it had been a quality that Stewart had insisted upon. She was younger and taller than me and had bright blue eyes. She was fair skinned with light long auburn hair, just as I. My eyes were a much duller blue/grey than hers, but we were identical in figure. It had been two months and if she was with child she did not show.

She stepped back when she saw me and clasped her hand to her mouth. It was obvious that she knew who I was. I lost all revulsion for the girl immediately. I made sure she knew that I meant her no harm. We sat on a shabby settee and she offered me tea if the pot was still hot. The fire in the hearth was nearly out and the room was none to warm. She told me that she could not replenish the woodpile as her door was barred. Together we went for an armful of wood from where it sat outside the door. I cursed Stewart for not seeing to her needs. She was very shy and apologetic...as if any of this was of her doing. She set me straight on that right away saying that she had accepted the "offer" straightway as it was a way out of her current situation. Stewart's lackeys had found her begging on the streets of Barcelona. She had *feared that she would soon have to take up the profession of prostitution so that she could provide for her little brother and herself. Their parents had both died from the plaque. She and her brother, Alain were on the verge of becoming homeless. She accepted the offer on the condition that her brother would be cared for. She believed that Stewart's men offered the church a good deal of money to harbour him. So, she said she had chosen to prostitute herself for a good cause. I asked her if she had contact with her brother and she said no. I asked her if Stewart was kind and gentle with her and she said yes, but that she was very lonely. I told her that I would remedy that but it was going to have to be our little secret as Stewart was not to know that I had befriended her. She cried and hugged me. I surveyed the room and her meager belongings and vowed to make her more comfortable. Corinthia was only seventeen.*

"This is not at all how I thought Avaleena would react." Rainey uttered.

"I think Avaleena surprised herself that she was so accepting of Corinthia, but then the woman was supposedly going to give her a child so… I am not going to go into great detail about what transpired between the two women over the next months as it is only more of the same. You can read it all another time. Suffice it to say that they became friends. I believe that Avaleena thought of Corinthia as the sister she never had. She hated Stewart for what he had done to their marriage and still planned on escaping once the baby was born. She knew she would need a lot of help so she befriended the holy sisters of the little convent in Doome. She visited the abbey once a week with donations of food and monies. Stewart was not against her doing so but always sent guards to accompany her. Even though she was essentiality under house arrest she was allowed to go wherever she chose as long as he sanctioned it and he was not stingy at all with his sixpence so Avaleena had the funds that she needed for bribes. She had learnt to be just as cunning as her husband. She was gifted at doctoring the books and whatever he doled out to her for household expenses she put a portion away for the day that she would take flight with her new born child.

In early March Corinthia announced to Avaleena that she was pregnant. Avaleena thanked God as it meant that Stewart would no longer have a reason for spending anymore nights away from her. She had decided to forgive him as she truly did love him. However, Stewart liked the idea of having two women to share his bed and did not adhere to Avaleena's request. One day she told Stewart that she wanted to meet the mother of his child so that she could monitor her pregnancy and see that she stayed healthy. He forbade it of course. She argued that she had as much at stake as he did and that if he became ill or died there would be no one to see to the birth of his child. He still did not surrender and so Avaleena poisoned him."

"What?" Rainey gasped.

"Don't be such a dunce! I'd probably do the same thing." I stated.

"You'd poison me?"

"Honey, I wouldn't have put you through such agony; I would have just shot you and been done with it and besides, I have no idea where I'd get hemlock or any other poison."

Rainey smirked and kissed me. "Oh, my beautiful Vienna LaFontaine, I think I have underestimated you. I think though that your gypsy friend, Meggie Magan, could supply you with anything legal or illegal your little heart desired. Does Avaleena say where she got the hemlock from or how she knew how much to give him because it can be fatal you know?"

"I do know. Isn't hemlock the poison that Plato used to kill Socrates?"

"Plato probably had nothing to do with his death. I believe that Socrates was sentenced to death for not recognizing the gods of the state and it is said that he chose his own death by drinking a cup of hemlock."

"Well, I don't always get things right. I don't have ten years of university like some people and I seem to have this memory problem so excuse me with mixing up the facts."

"Are you being sarcastic or flippant? College degree or not, you have more knowledge in that perplexing beautiful head of yours than anyone else I have ever known."

"I don't know if that is a compliment or not but I am going to take it as one."

"Good because that is how it was intended."

"Anyhow, I am planning on visiting Meggie tomorrow so…" I returned his kiss and asked him if I could continue because I wanted to get the saga over with as I was starving.

"We can take a break as I am sure lunch will be on the table in a matter of minutes."

"No, I'll persevere. Of course Stewart didn't die as his dear wife had given him just enough hemlock to make him very sick. Here are her words."

March 19th

Stewart is recovering from his "bout with the flu." I nursed him through the vomiting and nausea and diarrhea. He had mild convulsions and his heart was racing. I feared that I had perhaps given him too much. Seventy two hours after the dose he began to rally. He was very grateful for my care as I had barely left his side. He was worried that I or Corinthia would contract the same illness and admitted that I was right regarding Corinthia and he surrendered the key to me. He begged me not to judge her as she was really a very nice woman. Ha, she was but a child! Without his knowing, {while he was ailing} I had stairs built that led into the cellar. There was this empty space across from our bedroom and I deemed that was a good place to erect them. Stewart asked me over and over about the banging that was going on. I told him I was having a bookcase installed across the hall. That was not a fib. I made sure that the two men who created the concealed door that led to the underground room was Stewart's idea and that they would be penalized by death if it was ever revealed. I had learned a lot about threatening from my husband. He would not know of the secret passageway... only Corinthia, my handmaiden Gracie Darling, and I would.

Stewart recovered completely. Sometimes I would catch him looking at me strangely and I wondered if he suspected me of having a hand in his illness. Oddly enough, I still loved him and I believed that he loved me also. Soon he was off on one of his quests again and I was left alone with Corinthia. I took to bringing her out of the dungeon and would even smuggle her outside for some fresh air with help from Dacha and Gracie Darling. Corinthia had an uncomplicated pregnancy. She was great company for me and I knew I would miss her when she was gone.

Stewart returned at the end of April and was very pleased that I had accepted the mother of his child. Oh, if he only knew of our conspiracy! He never touched Corinthia again. Her due date was sometime in September. Stewart was gone off and on again. His last trip was to Aberdeen in August to acquire a new herd of cows at an auction. He planned on being home in time for the birth of his baby but things did not go according to plan.

"This is where things get a little dicey." I said to Rainey.

"What do you mean Honey, what happened?"

"The baby came early or maybe they just miscalculated. It was early evening on August 12th when Corinthia went into labor. Dacha went off to collect the midwife in Doome but she was not anywhere to be found and so she went to the convent and enlisted the help of Sister Agnes." I turned to a page I had earmarked and read.

August 13, '52

Corinthia had begged off a game of cards after supper citing sheer exhaustion. She did not want to rest in the room I had allotted for her a few doors down from my bedroom. She complained that it was too hot and preferred to return to her room downstairs. I insisted that she take the back stairs as they were not as narrow as the bookcase ones. I accompanied her to the reception hall and unlocked the door for her. We still kept it secure because of nosy servants; enough already knew of our subterfuge. We had barely entered the corridor when she doubled over in pain. I managed to get her into her room and onto the bed before she screamed and writhed in agony. Fearing that she was going into early labor I left her crying and went for help. Dacha was on her way out. I instructed her to fetch the mid-wife and ran back to Corinthia.

It seemed like an hour had passed before Dacha returned. The mid-wife was off attending to another birth. Word was left for her to attend Avanloch castle the moment she returned. Thank the good Lord that Dacha had the sense to stop at Our Lady of Angels and beseech Sister Agnes to assist us. She was the nun I trusted completely and she did not let me or Corinthia down.

I left momentarily to summon my faithful man-servant Quinn. I instructed him to collect Gracie Darling from her quarters and to bring the articles that we had assembled for birthing and boil lots of water. Quinn was to guard the entrance. I suggested that he treat the guards that had remained to protect the castle to a drum of mead and to send for half a dozen wenches from the tavern to keep them occupied. I especially wanted the two guards at the drawbridge to be relieved of their duties. I don't know why, it was just something I felt.

"It did not go unnoticed by me Rainey that you gave me a very curious glance when I mentioned the name Quinn. Can you imagine how I felt when first I saw the name? I did look the name up and apparently it is Scottish for the fifth born into a family. He was very loyal to Avaleena and I think that it is fitting that he was there to watch over her."

"Oh, you do, do you? Here I always thought I was Irish. I don't suppose Vienna makes an appearance in this journal does she?"

"You are just going to have to wait and see."

Rainey raised his eyebrows and gave me a quizzical look. I continued.

The difficult labor continued well into the night. I may as well have been the one giving birth as I felt every contraction that Corinthia underwent as I held her hands and cradled her body next to mine. Finally, just a few minutes before the clock struck twelve Robert Bruce made his appearance into the world. He was red and kicking and howling. Sister Agnes cut the umbilical cord and passed him to Gracie to swaddle. Corinthia's discomfort did not diminish. She let out a yelp and there emerged another little head. Sister Agnes quickly attended to the unexpected arrival of another baby. It was a girl. She was silent and blue; the cord was wrapped around her neck. I left Corinthia's side and assisted Sister Agnes in removing the obstruction that was suffocating the baby. The sister breathed life back into the lifeless infant and we all exhaled in relief.

Corinthia asked for her daughter. She looked at me with pleading eyes. "Can I keep her Avaleena? Please, can I keep her? No one needs to know as Stewart only wants a son. I need her, please let me go and take Vienne with me. You need never see us again...please Avaleena, please."

It was almost as though she knew that she had been carrying twins and that one was a girl. I asked her if this was so but she denied it and said that the name Vienne had just come to her.

The baby was not out of danger and Sister Agnes suggested that mother and child come with her to the convent to receive proper care. She said that the child needed its mother. We could decide what to do about its future at a later date. I agreed and called Quinn to assist us with our furtive scheme. An hour later we had Corinthia bundled up with her daughter. Quinn picked them both up and left with Sister Agnes for the convent. I knew then why I had wanted the guards off the drawbridge; I had had a premonition. I kissed Corinthia and the wee babe she held next to her bosom. I whispered to her that I loved her and told her to cherish little Vienne. I said that the name was beautiful and that I would remember her in my prayers at night as little Vie. She liked that. I feared that I would never see the two of them again.

Rainey had not interrupted me at the name of Vienne. I had lost count of the times that he had suggested that my father had named me Vienne but that mother was the one who had added the "a". He could no longer hold back.

"You have got to be f... ing kidding; you expect me to believe that she named the baby Vienne? I think you have put me on long enough my teenage V…Quinn and Vienne…really?"

"Are you saying that I made this whole thing up Rainey?" I was hurt that he may think so.

"Well Darling, you are the mistress of storytelling…" He saw the look on my face as I started to move away from him. He grabbed me. "Sorry Babe, I'm out of line. I think it's the hunger talking, but even you have to admit the sheer magnitude that the two of you share the same name is an enormous coincidence."

Tears were stinging my eyes. "It was very traumatic for me when I came upon those two names Rainey as I was already in a fragile state of mind. I put the book away after that but curiosity got the best of me and I took up my quest once more. Every word is true, I swear it!"

He held me and apologised again. "Of course it is. Don't cry my sweet; I need to be slapped for upsetting my pregnant wife."

"Yes, you do; just don't do it again. We have months to go in "our" pregnancy and I expect to be treated like a queen."

"You will be, I promise. Now, can we get out of this dungeon?"

"Yes we can, but I am not through yet. There is one interesting fact that I have not mentioned yet and maybe then you will under-stand that Corinthia's daughter's and my name are not such a coincidence after all. Corinthia's last name was Novia. What do you think about that?"

"Just because your great, great whatever grandmother's name was Novia does not mean that you are automatically related to Corinthia you know? We did find out that Novia is a very common surname, but I guess anything is possible. I best digest all of this on a full stomach so can we talk on the way to the kitchen?"

"Yes." I answered. "I won't know for sure if we are related until I open up my father's package. I think the time is now." I extracted another little booklet from the bureau and handed it to Rainey.

He didn't ask what it was and picked up Avaleena's diary and we walked to the grandfather clock. "I hope you remember how to get out."

I did. "Now that you know about this secret room I think we can work on finding another way in and out like through the reception hall."

"Does that mean you are planning on spending more time down here?" He asked concernedly.

"No, not really; I just want to see if there is a door hidden there."

Rainey helped me through the clock and asked if I knew whose idea the grandfather clock's exit was. I did not. The clock was never mentioned in Avaleena's journal. "Are we going to tell everyone everything?" I asked.

"Of course we are and don't worry, I won't let anyone accuse you of lying."

"But you believe that I lied to you so what is the difference if they think so too?"

"Just because a fox is found inside the hen house with all the dead chickens doesn't mean that he is guilty of killing them. Maybe he has a reason for being there."

"Thank-you Darling; that makes no sense at all but thanks for comparing me to a fox. I think the female is called a vixen, and she is very crafty isn't she?"

"That she is and I am proud to say that you're my foxy lady." He winked at me. "I will join you in the kitchen in a few minutes. I want to run upstairs and grab the "other" diary and your father's envelope. Keep me a seat next to you."

I left Rainey at the bottom of the main staircase and sauntered down the hall and into the kitchen. Everyone was there except Ash. This involved my sister-in-law so I hoped she hadn't left yet.

"Hi," I said casually. "Rainey and I are famished so I hope there are lots of leftovers."

They all looked over my shoulder. "He's coming. Is Ash still here?" I assured them.

Ava said she was outside. "Would you mind asking her to come in Honey? Rainey and I have something to tell you and we don't want to have to repeat it twice."

Ava got up but looked alarmed. I supposed that she thought we had decided to separate.

I sat in my usual spot and started filling my plate with a variety of last night's scrumptious supper. Ava returned with Ash just as Rainey snuck up behind me and kissed me on the cheek. He sat down and greeted everyone. He asked what we were eating and answered himself by saying "everything" as he stole a glance at my heaping plate of food.

I heard Ava take in a deep breath and Ash asked what was up. Rosy said she was curious as to where we had been all morning and what did we want to tell everyone.

"All in good time Red." Rainey winked at her and she beamed as she always did when he called her "Red".

Mrs. D placed cups of coffee in front of me and Rainey stating that it was the coffee I had bought in Saragossa. "Now yous all just let these two eat in peace. Whatever they been up to and I suspect it was old fashioned hanky-panky by the way they are devouring their food can wait."

Johnny laughed. "Well it's about damn time!" He patted Rainey on the shoulder. "I told you she would come around didn't I ole man?"

"Have you been talking about me Johnny?" I asked coyly.

"Yup and it was all no good."

Everyone laughed at that because they all knew he would never talk ill of me.

I bowed to him. "I will take this time to apologise to you all. I know I have been acting in a most unbecoming way and I really have no excuse except to say that I am a dunce and my own worst enemy. Rainey has set me straight once again and I promise to behave myself."

"Don't get too sanctimonious on us now Honey. We kind of like the spunky V." Rainey stated.

"Why did you call her "V" Daddy; you never do?" Ava asked inquisitively. Rainey said it was a slip of the tongue.

I asked him if he would mind getting me a glass of milk. I never drank the stuff so was met with a lot of curious glances. I took a few sips and asked Mary if there was any of the children's chocolate NesQuick left. Ava offered to get it and as she squirted some into my milk said she didn't know why I was drinking milk if I hated it so. I smiled but did not offer an explanation.

Rainey squeezed my hand. "I have had the most interesting morning. It started with Vienna being in one of her moods "again". After a few unwarranted threats on my part and tears and tantrums on hers we came to an understanding."

I giggled a little. Ava said that we were going to drive her to drink.

"Speaking of that, I could use a good stiff drink." Rainey got up but Mary silenced him with her hand and said she had just what he needed. She asked Johnny to get her stash out from under the sink. Amma collected the glasses and Johnny poured everyone three fingers. I thought I may as well get on with the story while they were all enjoying a little nip. Ava made a face every time the amber liquid touched her lips; she was definitely my daughter.

"This is a fairly long tale so you may want to sip slowly."

"Amen to that." Rainey tipped his glass to me. "You have the floor my love."

"Jump in whenever you feel the need to." I directed. "Okay, here goes. I know you have all been wondering where I disappeared to the other night…well, I won't keep you in suspense any longer. I know exactly where I was and I have been retreating there for a great many years. It is a place beyond the bookcase in the upstairs foyer. I have been there hundreds of time and now I would like to take you there and in doing so we are going back one hundred and thirty years."

Ava interrupted. "I don't understand Mama. Are you telling us that there is indeed a secret room in the foyer behind the bookcase that we have searched dozens of times and that you have always known how to open it?"

"Yes, but in my own defense, I did not always remember that I knew." I answered sheepishly.

Rosy had to add her two bits worth. "That makes absolutely no sense at all. You either know something or you don't; are you saying you forgot? That doesn't sound…"

Rainey interjected. "I believe your mother has what is known as a selective memory disorder. I thought as much when we brought her home from Verde El Mar last summer and so I did a little research with help from my secretary back in Vancouver. I'm afraid I have not been very supportive of her as there have definitely been times when I thought she was lying; case in point, the mysterious bookcase. This ability to supress certain things make it convenient for her and she doesn't believe that she is keeping secrets. In fact, it can make her happy as all the down sides of life can be forgotten. Vienna admitted to me that when she first started making regular trips to the room down under was when she found out that I had married, so I am to blame again."

"That's when the dreams started; when Lara told me that Rainey had married. At least I thought they were dreams at first. Then one day or night, I don't remember which it was, I found myself opening up the bookcase and the Grey Lady was nowhere to be seen so I realized that I wasn't dreaming." I admitted.

Rosy swore. "What is it with you two and that damn grey woman? No one else has ever seen her so why does she only make herself visible to only you two?"

I started to answer but Rainey interceded. "No, let me handle this Honey." He glanced around the table. "Who here has seen Rosalyn's deceased mother, Lady Maveryn? Who has actually witnessed her presence?"

I held up my hand as did Rosy and Ava. Rainey reluctantly held his up too. "What about the rest of you, why hasn't she presented herself to you?"

"I cannot answer that Mr. Rainey, but I think we have all felt that she is watching over us. Sometimes for no reason I start thinking about her and a tear will cloud me eyes, but then a ray of light will shine through the window on what was a very bleak day. I feel as though I have been hugged by a warm wind and I know it tis Lady Maveryn."

Rosy got up and hugged Mary. "That's the most beautiful thing I have ever heard. Thank you so much for sharing." Mary returned the hug with one of those tears escaping down her cheek.

Ash spoke for the first time. "I do not speak of such encounters, you know that Vela."

"Oh, no one has called me that for a long time Ash." I gushed.

She laughed. "Yeah, well…anyhow you and Rainey are probably the only ones here that know that Jeremy and I had encounters with the covert militia when we were children. We only met them in the court on the rooftop. They were our own very band of soldiers. We never told anyone else about them and we believed that they only appeared to us, but now I understand that they have also presented themselves to Morgan and Mason?"

It was a question directed at Rainey. "So they say. I think you have made my point Ash and that is that spirits only present themselves to whomever they damn well feel like engaging at that particular moment in time. Some are playful and some are downright scary and those like Lady Maveryn are here to give comfort and guidance."

"Why Rainey Quinn," I declared, "you never cease to amaze me! What about the Grey Lady, why do you think she came to you and me?"

"You know why Vienna; she came out because she knew you would be the one to tell her story. I am not too sure why she came to me."

"Maybe it was so that you could find the diary Daddy." Ava suggested.

"But that was before we found your mother so what bearing would it have on anything?"

"I had not been in "the room" downstairs since Rainey came back into my life. I had put it "away" without even knowing that I had. When he showed me Avaleena's diary it must have triggered something in this addled head of mine and when I was distressed as I was the night of the party, it all came tumbling back. And now, I am ready to tell the rest of you Avaleena's story. There is no doubt in my mind that she is the Grey Lady."

The room was silent. All eyes were on me and Rainey. I asked him to get the journals.

"You mean there is more than one Mother?" Rosy asked.

"Yes Dear, one is the real diary and the one you all know about is the one I wrote."

There were a lot of "what's?" Johnny said that the plot was thickening by the minute.

"I think dessert can wait; let's clear the table girls. I think I need to get the Duff for this." Mary scuffled off to get her hubby.

Rainey plopped the two tomes on the table and opened them to the first page and stepped back as one by one they all came to inspect them.

"I don't understand Mama, they are both identical. Why would you want to make another copy of Avaleena's journal?" Ava looked mystified as she scanned the two diaries. "And they are both in the exact same handwriting." It was more a question than a statement.

"Your mother is a very good forger or copier; however you want to spin it." Rainey flipped ahead to the pages we had tagged when Corinthia had arrived. He asked Ava if she could translate and to compare one with the other. She said they were not the same. "And so the true story unfolds. Vienna, do you care to enlighten everyone?"

I started to reiterate at the point where it was deemed that Avaleena could not conceive and Stewart had come up with a plan as to how they could become parents and why and how Corinthia had come to the castle.

"That dirty rotten bastard!" Ash exclaimed.

Johnny commented that she probably wouldn't be here today if that union hadn't happened. He looked at me. "It certainly sounds like that is how Robert Bruce came to be born, am I right?"

"I see you know the McAllister history Johnny. Many a royal monarch fathered children with women that were not their legal spouses. They did what was necessary to carry on the blood line. I guess I was appalled at the idea also so that is why I gave Avaleena a lover of her own. I never expected that my account would ever be read…sorry Ash that it led to you and Rosalyn believing that you were not the entitled heirs to Avanloch. I hope with this true account you will be able to forgive me."

Rosy came around and hugged me. "There is nothing to forgive Mama but you sure do make life interesting around here. I must say though that I am a little relieved that Roberge Farradan has no bearing on the lineage."

I smiled and asked her to sit beside me because I was going to prove that belief to be wrong. I continued on with the story right up to the part where Quinn had carried Corinthia and Vienne off to the convent. There were a few eyebrows raised at the mention of the name Quinn and little Vienne or Vie as Avaleena had called her.

"Oh, I see now why you called Mama "V" Dad. It is all so very strange don't you think?"

"I should be used to all the shenanigans that go on around here and to your mother's colorful story telling but what you are going to hear next will astound every one of you, just as it did me."

"Before we hear your next revelation Vienna, can you answer a few questions for me? You know I have never taken much interest in the family tree. I much prefer to live in the present and do my part in running the shipping business, but all of this is arousing my curiosity in the past. How large a town was Doome back then? I mean, it housed a convent and what sounds like to me, a house of ill repute and who knows what all?" Ash queried.

"I cannot answer that Ash because nowhere did I come across that information. Perhaps it is mentioned somewhere and I missed it. You all have to remember that I translated Avaleena's journal many years ago. It took me a very long time to learn how to transcribe Spanish and French into English and then to compose my own version of the tale. I have not retold all the days that Avaleena wrote about as they are far too lengthily." I opened up the envelope that held my booklet of the diary that I had transcribed into English. "This might help those of you who do not wish to translate the actual dairy."

"One more question Mama; what is that third language that you wrote in? None of us could figure it out." Ava asked.

I looked at Rainey and managed a half smile. "Those pages have nothing to do with Avaleena and I do not know why I included them. They were real words at one time but I cannot even remember for sure why or when I wrote them. I think they were a conglomeration of my emotions and I just mixed up the letters because that's how I envisioned life. I was living a fairy-tale life in this castle; I had two magnificent daughters and all of you my friends and I should have wanted for nothing but there was always someone missing." I half smiled at Rainey.

He put his arm around me and squeezed me as a little tear escaped from my eye.

Mary sniffled. "Now we will have none of that dearie; that all has come to pass."

"Yes it has Mary. Put your tears aside for now girls because there is to be no more sadness in this house! Now Vienna, are you going to reveal the piece de resistance or am I?" Rainey asked.

I put my hand on my father's envelope. "What's in here may or may not confirm what I believe is true or not. There are a few details that I have not told you yet. I have not told you of Corinthia's and Vienne's fate nor have I told you what Corinthia's maiden name was."

Rosy covered her ears. "I don't think I want to hear this Mama; this is where you are going to tell us how Roberge fits into the picture aren't you?"

"Why don't you quit conjecturing Red and let your mother finish the story?" Rainey suggested.

She clasped my hand. "Sorry Mama."

I carried on as if I hadn't been interrupted. "Corinthia's last name is one that I am familiar with. It figures into my father's ancestry. You have all heard me mention that my great great grandmother's name was Novia…well, that was Corinthia's too."

There were a few gasps and more "WHATS?"

"Does that mean that we are related to her and Vienne…oh my, what does it mean Mama? If Corinthia is Robert Bruce's mother and your grandmother down the line…does it mean that you are a rightful heir to Avanloch?" Ava was dumbfounded.

"Let's not get ahead of ourselves here. Novia is a very common French name and just because Corinthia's last name was Novia does not mean that she is in any way related to me as your father pointed out to me. I know you are all anxious to hear what became of Corinthia and Vienne and I will not keep you in suspense any longer. I asked Rainey to pass me Avaleena's diary and I read from it.

August 14th

Yesterday was the longest day of my life. There was much to be done to protect Corinthia and her child. Stewart was never to know that he had fathered a second child. As much as I would have liked to keep Vienne for my own I could not. Corinthia deserved more than just a stipend for what she had endured. My conscience was clear. Gracie Darling was sent to a little hamlet outside of Doome to fetch the wet nurse whom we would need. Stewart had engaged her as such. His reasons were that I was not keen on nursing. My pregnancy had been masqueraded by the use of bustles adjusted around my midsection.

They were all gone, Quinn, Sister Agnes and Gracie Darling. Dacha was busy with the clean-up. I took to my bed with Robert and awaited the arrival of Bibi, the wet nurse. It seemed to take forever for Gracie to return with her and Robert was most agitated. After a thorough sermon from Bibi telling me that I had to be patient as my milk would come in and that I just had to keep trying. Gracie asked her what she was being paid for and told her that she could soon be replaced if she con-

tinued to bully me and the Laird would not be pleased with her disrespect. She soon had Bibi and Robert settled in the nursery.

Stewart had strongboxes hidden throughout the castle. The few I knew about only contained paltry amounts of coin. I feared the main treasuries were secreted in the underground rooms. The guards were in their quarters beneath the kitchen galley so I could not access the cellars from there. Quinn had returned from the convent but had gone to reinstate the guards at the drawbridge. They were not in very good shape. He had highly suggested that they pull themselves together before Lord McAllister returned. It would have been amusing had the situation not been dire. I had no doubt that Stewart would seek Corinthia out and learn about Vienne. I needed to send them as far away as possible but that would require a great deal of currency. Stewart had never discussed with me what he was planning on paying Corinthia after she delivered his child. If I could only find one of his main treasuries I was sure there would be enough in it to send her wherever she chose to go.

There existed a concealed stairway just beyond the master bedroom. I had never been down it as it was not safe and I had no desire to venture into the obscure. Now was not the time to be skittish. Quinn brought two lamps and we descended into the abyss. He put his hand into every nook and cranny. Twice he extracted rats that had been hiding inside. Thank his lucky stars that he was wearing steel gloves. The castle was mostly free of *varmints because of the large population of cats that roamed freely about but I surely didn't want Quinn to be bitten.*

"I'm going to quit reading now as I am getting rather hoarse so I will just make it quick and say that Avaleena and Quinn did find a bonanza. Rainey is going to verify this later but I do believe that it was found in the rooms that he uncovered last year under the back stairs. Corinthia and her daughter were long gone before Stewart returned home. He was very upset that his wife had paid her off and helped her to flee the country. He banished Quinn and Gracie Darling from the castle and made Avaleena a prisoner of it again. For years she believed that Stewart had executed Quinn but one day when Robert was five years old he and Grace Darling returned via the secret stairway to rescue her. However, she chose to stay as she was devoted to Robert and would not risk their being hunted down by her estranged husband. As I said earlier, you can read all the details yourselves, but now it is time to open my father's letter." I turned to Rainey.

All eyes were on him as he carefully unsealed the package. He handed me some photos which I put aside. He scanned page after page until he came to one that seemed to interest him. He asked me if I was ready to learn my roots. I was. He cleared his throat.

"Joe writes that he hopes this will answer your questions regarding the Novia name. The record he has only goes back to sometime in the 1850's. He says you already know that his parents, Joseph and Juliette both died before he was two and that he was raised by his maternal grandparents, Genevieve and Francois Hebert. Here goes."

Mother: Juliette Marie Bessette Lavoix....1883-1903
Married: 1889 to Joseph LaFontaine...........1873-1903
Grandmother: Genevieve Margo Bessette...1868-1938
Married: at 18 to Francois Lavoix {12 children}
Great Grandmother: Vienne Corzine Novia...1852-1902
Married: Jacques Ferrani in 1871
Children: Genevieve and Franklin {no info.}

Great Great Grandmother: Corinthia Novia No dates or marriage info.
Great Great Uncle: Alain Novia: married Angeliqua
Children: Evangelina D 1890-1911
      Ester Louise 1892-1975
      Married: Daniel LaFontaine 1911-1939

"Your dad says that Daniel was his uncle and that he died from a boating accident. His dad drowned while swimming in a pond near their home; tragic coincidence that water was the culprit in both of their deaths. He said that there are several cousins but that they have never kept in touch. He left the family farm when he was fifteen and never went home again."

"So that's that." Rainey said. "It appears you were right Vienna; you are a descendant not only of Corinthia, but of Stewart McAllister also, and I guess a fourth or so cousin to Roberge Farradan if it can be proven that he is indeed a Ferrani as Vienne married Jacques Ferrani. Did you know that Bessette was also a family name? Is it possible there is a link there also to Anton's Uncle, Father Bessette?"

I did not want to think about that.

"Wait a minute, wait a minute…we can't jump to conclusions just like that. Oh, I don't mean about you Mama, I mean about Roberge. He may not be from that branch of the Ferrani's at all." Rosy exclaimed.

"It's all right Dear, I know what you mean. It doesn't matter one iota to me that I may be an heir to Avanloch and no one else even has to know about this. It's up to you and Ava what you do about it." I stood up. "Now, you will all have to excuse me as I am dead on my feet and I haven't even seen the little girls yet. You can discuss this amongst yourselves."

"Yes, go rest Mama. Ava and I will go over everything thoroughly before we make any decisions, won't we Ava?'

"You're the one who told Roberge that we might require his help in deciphering the diary so I am sure you have already piqued his curiosity and it's only a matter of time before he'll be calling…"

"Dang," Rosy cursed, "I forgot about that."

Rainey took my arm and escorted me to the door. He grinned boyishly. "Have fun girls… oh, by the way, Liliana is going to have a baby sister in about seven months."

There were a few gasps. Mary McDuff banged her hand on the table. "Mary, Queen of Scots, I knew it! I told you didn't I Duff that there was something off with that girl? She be not drinking her favorite coffee and either hungry as a horse or refusing to eat at all!" She pulled herself to her feet and beckoned me to her and enfolded me in her arms. "My Darlin, you is blessing this house with another wee one, just what we need. You get over here Mr. Rainey as I pretty sure that you had a hand in this as well!"

Everyone came over to congratulate us and there was much crying and laughter. Ava asked why we hadn't told anyone sooner.

"I just found out myself." Rainey confessed. "Your mother was afraid to tell me."

"Why?" Amma asked. "Why would you be afraid to tell him Vienna?"

Rainey hugged me. "Because she had the foolish notion that I would think the baby was Anton's and that I would think that she had been deceitful regarding their recent relationship. She was too distraught to remember that Somner had mentioned in his letter that Anton was unable to father a child. So she went through weeks of agony for nothing. I hope you all know that I would have accepted the baby regardless of who fathered it."

"We do Daddy. Oh Mama, no wonder you were so withdrawn; if only I had known."

I kissed my daughter. "No one is to blame but me Ava. I am so ashamed that I didn't trust Rainey's love for me, but as usual, he has forgiven me."

"Yeah, that is just our past coming back into play again. Anyhow, I am going to need all your help to keep this woman safe and under surveillance for the next seven months because she is too much for me to manage on my own, what do you say?" Rainey asked grinning mischievously.

Johnny laughed and shook Rainey's hand. "You got it man." He kissed me and shook his head. "It ain't gonna be easy though."

I thumped him and asked Rainey if we could go now.

"Mama," Rosy implored, "can you please show us how to open the bookcase? I don't know about everyone else but I would very much like to see that room down there."

I sighed. I had hoped that I was done with all that business for the day but apparently I was not.

"Very well; give us fifteen minutes with the girls and then we will meet you all in the foyer."

We found the three girls watching a Disney movie in the upstairs den. Tanny was ecstatic that she was going to get another sister and Zoe promised that she would look after me just as she had when I was expecting Liliana. Rainey and I had discussed her enrolling in school some time ago but she said she was not ready yet and could she please just do home studies. We wanted her to meet new people but she said she had all our family and Alexa, Brie and Shannon O'Shea and Jeanette and Caron, and that was more friends and family then she had ever had before so that was enough for her. We had relinquished and now I was glad that she would be with me through another pregnancy. Lili fell asleep in Rainey's arms and he carried her to her bedroom. Zoe and Tanny chose to stay and watch television.

Ava and the McDuffs were the only ones not waiting for us in the upstairs foyer. I pointed to the bookcase. "There it is."

"We know that Mother, but how do we open it?" Rosy said impatiently.

"It's really quite simple and I don't know why you girls never figured it out before. Have I not always said that all roads lead to Rome?" I didn't want to make things too easy.

"What does that have to do with anything Mother?"

My daughters only called me "mother" when they were annoyed with me. Rosy looked at Rainey expecting him to know the code for opening the bookcase.

"Don't look at me; I have no clue as to how to get in!"

Johnny seemed to have figured something out. "So that quote is the clue, right Vienna?"

"Yes. I will get you started. There are five books on the top shelf and the first word is "All". Do you get the drift?"

Amma and Rosy stood looking up at the books. Rosy grinned and turned to me. "Really Mother, couldn't you have just shown us?"

"I had to figure it out by myself so why shouldn't you?"

"But you had help from the Grey Lady."

"OH, do you mean the apparition that only exists in Rainey's and my head?"

Rainey smiled at Rosy. "Have you figured it out Red?"

She used her finger as a pointer. "The **FIRST** word is "All" as mama said. It is taken from this book "All Saints Parish, London England". The **SECOND** word is here, I believe though spelled differently. "Cecil Rhodes: Quotes and Biography: Rhodes is the second word. The **THIRD** word is in this book that refers to metals: "Tin, Copper, Lead etc." Lead is the third word. **FOURTH** word is "to". Here it is in "English Dictionary A to Z." "To" is the fourth word. And last but not least is "Rome" so "Religious Cults of Ancient **ROME**" is the last clue in the quote. Very clever Mama; I particularly like the spelling of 'roads'; now what?"

"This is not of my doing my dear. The person or persons who devised all these secret entrances and rooms and codes inhabited this castle way before me or your father or grandparents even existed." I took her hand and one by one, I had her push firmly on the key words starting at "all" and ending with "Rome." "Don't take too long to pass through or you'll have to do the sequence all over again. As long as someone is in the "portal" so to speak, it will remain open."

Everyone scurried through and I yelled to them just as the entryway closed. "You'll have to go out through the grandfather clock though. We'll come and find you if you are not back in an hour." I shrugged my shoulders and cackled slightly.

Rainey shook his head. "Did you have fun with that my Ladyship?"

I poked him. "Yes, and don't call me that! You know I hate it."

"Yes, sure you do. Now let's get you off to bed for your rest."

"Are you going to join me?" I asked playfully.

"Not at the moment my love, but ask me again later."

I said that he could count on that. He helped me get comfortable in bed and snuggled the quilt around me. He said he'd check on Liliana and then he'd be next door in the parlour working on his plans. I was in the middle of talking myself into staying in bed for the rest of the day when I felt a presence beside me. I opened my eyes to find Ava peering down at me.

"Are you sleeping Mama?"

It should have been obvious that I wasn't. "What can I do for you Ava, and why aren't you exploring with everyone else?"

"I'm not that interested and I wanted to talk to you?"

"Okay, I am listening."

Her voice had risen substantially. "Mama, I need you to promise me something."

"I will if I can; what is it you want me to promise you?"

"It's not just for me; it's for all of us and especially Daddy. You have to promise that you will never do that to him ever again!"

Out of the corner of my eye I saw a movement. It was Rainey standing in the archway between the parlour and the bedroom. His "working" glasses were perched on his nose. He reminded me of "Owl" from Winnie the Pooh. I held back my giggles.

"Ava?" He said rather coarsely.

She stiffened. "I didn't know you were here Daddy."

"Obviously, or you wouldn't have spoken to your mother in such a tone. Now just what is it you think she has done to me?"

"She's barely spoken or looked at you in weeks. She forgot how much you love her and she accused you of having a mistress. No one knows better than me how ridiculous that is!"

"And don't you think that is between your mother and me to sort out? Were you not listening to us downstairs when we explained everything?"

"I know her hormones are acting overtime, but her actions affect us all. I just got you Daddy and we were all so happy and then Mama went away for almost two years…I just couldn't bear it if I lost one of you again." Ava sobbed, big tears streaming down her face.

I reached out for her. "Come here sweetie pie." She lay down beside me and I encircled her in my arms. "I am so sorry that I was such a bitch to your dad and I do know how much he loves me and you know perfectly well how I love him. Now what is this bit about losing one of us?"

Rainey came over and rubbed her back looking over her at me with his eyes raised to the heavens. She turned to face him and blubbered. "It's your fault too you know Daddy. You should have demanded that she tell you what was wrong and then to make matters worse you go and dance with that horrible Countess Lauren on Saturday night! I've lost count of the times you told me that you don't dance with anyone but Mama and then you go and do it right in front of her with a woman she can't stand! No wonder she ran away!"

"Don't blame your father Ava; it was all me. I suppose it was all meant to happen or else I may have never remembered about Avaleena and the room downstairs, don't you think?"

"NO, and you can't keep explaining everything on fate! I don't care a flying fig about our ancestry or that room down there. I just need you two to get along."

"Honey," Rainey tried to calm her down. "I don't know what has brought all this on…you know that your mother and I are crazy in love with each other. I think you need to get out of this fortress for a while and get on with your nursing career…"

Ava cut him off. "Do you really think I am leaving mama now and going off to school?"

"You won't be leaving me Ava and you'll be home on weekends. It'll be good for you to get on with your life and you shouldn't put nursing school off while everything you learned last year is still fresh in your mind." I tried to sound encouraging.

"But it's all right if Zoe skips going to school for another year?"

"It's not the same situation Ava and you know it. Zoe has never attended a regular school and she isn't ready yet. Besides, she wants to help your mother through her pregnancy just as she did when she was pregnant with Liliana." Rainey was becoming a tad agitated.

"Zoe, Zoe, Zoe…why does she get to look after Mama and I don't? Is she more qualified than I am? Haven't I been caring for her all my life?"

"That isn't fair Ava. No one is saying you are not qualified but…"

Now it was time for me to interject. "Why does everyone think I need looking after? My God, I am under house arrest as it so I don't need constant supervision. I am pregnant, I am not ill."

"That's right Mama, you are pregnant and that means that you will be leaving daddy again."

Rainey pulled Ava up and into his arms. "Is that what this is all about? You think she's going to somehow get away from me again? I can guarantee you that will not happen this time."

"You can't guarantee that Daddy."

"Yes I can, and I do." He held her away from him and looked into her eyes. "Do you hear me Ava? No one is going to force you to go to school. If you want to stay here and help me keep tabs on your mother then I welcome the help as I know she is a force to tend with." Rainey winked at me.

She bent down and kissed me. "I love you Mama." She turned to her father. "And you too Daddy. Please don't fight anymore. Now I am going to go and see if Zoe needs my help."

"We don't fight Ava but couples do have disagreements and misunderstandings. You will find that out for yourself one day. Your father and I will have a lot more I am sure but I won't let it go so far next time." I may as well have been talking to the wall as I am sure my words fell on deaf ears as shrugged her shoulders and walked away.

Rainey shook his head. "What do you make of her behaviour?"

"I think she is lonely. We are all coupled up around here and she has no one of her own. I hope we can talk her into enrolling in the nursing program so she can meet new people."

"I think you are right Hon. All the time she was with me and the boys at the coast she never went on a date. She had a few friends at work and the clinic but she never went out for drinks or dinner with them. She was like a dutiful wife and mother coming home to cater to me and the boys. Let's see how things go before we approach the subject again."

I agreed just as Amma and Johnny appeared at the door. The rest of the explorers had exited via the grandfather clock but Johnny was able to find the mechanism which opened the bookcase from the other side. He said it was an obscure little switch recessed into the wall at the top; much like the one in my parlour that led to another stairwell. Rosy arrived breathless.

"Come on you guys, Evan thinks he has figured out where the door to the cellar once was."

I told them all to go ahead while I rearranged myself. Rainey decided he had better close up his drafting table just in case inquisitive little hands decided to write all over his plans. Liliana had done so a few weeks back. The next to arrive at my door was Tanny.

"Hey, where is everyone off to?" She asked.

I explained to her about the hidden door and invited her to join us. I asked her to pass me my dress that Rainey had draped over the chair by the closet.

"Oh my God," she exclaimed, "who made this mess? Vienna, why are you so messy?"

I didn't know whether to laugh or scold her for her language and her brazenness. Rainey handled it for me.

"What did you just say to your mother young lady?"

"Well it's true Rainey. Look at all these clothes on the floor and remember what she did to Miss Mary's room?"

"That's still no way to speak to your mother. And for your information, though it is none of your business, Vienna is donating those clothes to charity as they no longer fit her. I believe you owe her an apology."

"Okay, but we should get her a maid don't you think Rainey?"

"What's with the Rainey and Vienna thing? Now tell your mother you're sorry and vamoose before you get yourself into any more trouble with your mouth."

She hugged me. "Sorry Mom and don't worry, Zoe and me already cleaned up Miss Mary's room." She turned to Rainey. "I just like saying Rainey and Vienna, that's all Dad."

As she skipped out of the room I thanked her for cleaning up my mess.

Rainey slipped my dress over my head. "First Ava and now Tanny…are you wondering if you will be getting a scolding from Rosalyn also?"

"And don't forget you Darling; you scolded me too." I took one look at myself in the mirror and yelped. What had I been thinking when I had chopped off my hair? I tried combing it but it didn't help so I decided to stick my head under the faucet. Rainey was talking to me but I couldn't hear him over the running water. I towel dried my hair and asked him what he had said.

"I think Tanny is right…we should get you a hand-maiden."

"Oh yes, and let's dress to the nines for dinner and reinstate the butler, and reopen the servant's quarters downstairs and have everyone call us My Lord and My Lady!"

"I'm not saying we go that far but someone to help you might be a good idea."

"You think I should have someone like Grace Darling? I already do; in fact I have several. Lili combs my hair and helps me pick out jewelry and Tanny and Zoe clean up after me and you help me dress, so why do I need anyone else?"

"Okay, but just so you know I am not opposed to the idea."

"We would never have any privacy then you know."

"There's always the room downstairs; speaking of which, we had better get a move on. Go put your head under the faucet and let's go."

"I already did…are you insinuating that my hair looks ugly?"

He passed me a hand mirror. "Not at all my Lady."

I soaked my head again but it didn't help much. "What was I thinking?" I asked myself again.

The whole family of Avanloch including Ash and her permanent fiancé, Grayson, our house Maidens, Jeanette and Caron, along with the McDuffs were all assembled in the Grand Reception room. Johnny and Evan had an array of saws and other implements set out on a canvas drop sheet below the wall where Rosalyn's and Ava's portraits once hung. I asked what they were waiting for. They said for my permission. I told them to hack away.

"What do you think Rain, power saw or axe?" Johnny asked.

"Hey, I erect things not dismantle them, so your choice."

Bits and pieces of white chalk-like material fell to the floor the second the saw blade hit the wall. I asked what it was and Johnny replied that it was pre-historic plaster. In a matter of minutes the damage was done and together the men lowered the panel to the floor exposing a dark cavity in between the wooden supports.

"My Lady…" Rainey beckoned to me.

"I stepped forward and peered into the void. Johnny shone a flashlight down the black hole for me. "I guess that answers that." I said and backed up so that everyone else could take a peek into the corridor that would most assuredly lead to the room that was built for Corinthia.

"Mary Queen of Scots," Mary McDuff exclaimed. "in all my thirty some odd years here did I ever think this secret room existed!"

"What about the rooms under the kitchen stairs Mary?" Amma asked.

"You be right Miss Amma. What more secrets do these old castle walls conceal? I dare not even to think." Mary said as she scuttled off down the hall. "Supper be in one hour."

"Didn't we just eat?" I said to no one in particular.

Ash hugged me. "So sorry Darling, but Gray and I must take our leave. I fear Winston will have to drive like the wind so we don't miss the train or else we will be here for another night. I can hardly wait to see what awaits us on our next visit. Will you uncover yet another lost room? This has been a most extraordinary weekend and I do so hope that we can do it all over again."

"Not bloody likely! Vienna is now a Lady of leisure so there will be no new escapades." Rainey stated.

Ash laughed. "Love you too Rainey and good luck with keeping our girl out of mischief. See you all in December." Ash waved to us from the front door.

Johnny asked what we wanted to do with the hole in the wall.

"Let's just move the credenza in front of it for the night and tomorrow we can rustle up a fitting door for it. I don't want my little wife on those awful stairs anymore and knowing her she will probably be visiting the room again so I think refitting this entrance will be the answer. What do you think Honey?" Rainey asked.

"Yes, please. I don't have reason to go back there anymore but some of you may want to check it out more thoroughly. I am wondering if there is a hidden exit that leads to the crypt though."

"Mother!" Ava had decided to join us and voiced her disapproval.

"Not to worry girls, I've got this covered." Rainey said trying to reassure them. "Do we think that there may be rodents down there?"

Amma said that she would fetch the cats from the back door. "They are getting fat and lazy so some new territory should arouse their curiosity."

Tomorrow would be the first day of school for Tanny. She should have been in attendance today but seeing it was still part of our Canadian holiday, we kept her home. Rainey would walk her down the hill and get her settled in. We finally managed to get her tucked into bed at eight thirty. The weekend was finally over…or so I thought.

I was relaxing in bed reading Rainey's journal that he had kept since my going AWOL, as he so aptly called it. I spoke to him through the open bathroom door. "I like it when you found me in the kitchen yesterday and say that you fell in love with me all over again."

He came out with toothbrush in his hand. "It's not just a one-time occurrence Babe; it happens quite often. Oh, by the way, there is a note from your father marked: "For your eyes only," on the night table."

"What does it say?"

"Did you miss the part where I said it was for you only?"

"We both know you read it so just tell me what it said Rain."

He asked if I knew that my father had been married before. I said, "What?"

He emerged from the bathroom again. "I gather you didn't. Joe says that he was going to tell you when you were twenty-five but you were over here and things seemed to be okay with you so he decided not to spill the beans. Your mother and he decided they would go to their graves not revealing that part of his life. Recent events, mainly your abduction made him rethink his decision. He fathered two sons with his first wife…you have brothers Vienna."

"WHAT?"

We discussed it at great length over the next few days. My astonishment was met with a small amount of detachment. Rainey finally convinced me to call my father. I did and I sort of understood why he had kept the secret for so long. His first wife Anne had taken the boys who were three and two at the time, and returned to France where she had grown up. He tried tracking her down but she was not at the family home in Bayonne; in fact it appeared as though the whole family had vacated the area. He met my mother soon afterwards. She convinced him to keep looking but their finances were very limited and they gave up after a fruitless few years. They married though I believe illegally as it does not appear as though my father and Anne had divorced. I suppose that made me and my sisters illegitimate.

Rainey asked me if I wanted to make an attempt to locate my brothers as we had the funds to do so. I thanked him and suggested that we put it off until after the baby was born. He agreed.

I was indeed pregnant. Dr. Macintosh confirmed it and referred me to Dr. Beatty, who was a gynecologist. Mac said he did not deliver babies anymore as he was too old. I suspect he was also worried that **I** also, was too old to be having a baby. I discussed that with my new doctor. She assured me that was not the case at all and that women much older than me were giving birth every day. She wanted me to have a Sonogram. It was then that we found out we were having twins. My due date was April the nineteenth.

The whole household was overjoyed that we were having twins. Never in a thousand years had I entertained the thought that I would be carrying two babies. Rainey was Rainey and he was excited but would worry double about me for the duration of the pregnancy. I asked him if he would still love me when I weighed two hundred pounds. His answer was that there would be more of me to love.

Rainey and I spent many hours outside. Soon the weather would be changing and I wanted to soak up as much of the sun and gentle breezes as I could because no doubt I would be housebound by December. We would take long walks through the meadows and down to the ponds and return via the path to Miller Floss Bridge. Sometimes we would wander down to Brackenshire Manor and have a cool drink with Amma and Johnny if they were at home. If we didn't have Liliana with us we would climb the rock steps that led back to the rose gardens. Everyone had been helping us put the gardens to bed for the winter. Many fall flowers refused to accept the cooler weather and were still blooming, and that included the roses. Early snows were already glistening on the faraway mountains. One day as Rainey and I rested on one of the benches that overlooked the valley I told him that I was going to miss my rose gardens most of all. He said that he would see that we had flowers delivered every week from the florist in Waverly. I had told him that wasn't what I meant and I explained.

"I mean when we go home Rain."

"Home, we are home Babe."

"I mean when we move back to Canada."

He was stunned. "Are you saying you want to move back to Bridge Falls? Honey, you only lived there for two years and you have been here for over twenty years. I can't believe you still think of it as home…what's going on here?"

"It's where we met Rainey and we have a house there. I love that house. I miss Lara and Jimmy and our parents aren't getting any younger. I think we need to be closer to them and to Morgan and Mason too. They must miss you something terrible."

"All of that makes perfect sense Vienna, but what about your life here? What about Amma and Johnny and Mrs. D? Rosy and Ava would be devastated, and do you think this estate and village could function without you?"

"Well first of all, I don't run this estate, Amma and Johnny do; anything financial Gray and his brother Chandler look after. Ava will no doubt follow us and it's time that Rosalyn took her rightful place as the Mistress of Avanloch. She and Evan will be married soon and they will be starting a family and there is no better place to raise children than here. Evan loves this life. Rosy will be just fine. Of course I will miss everyone just as I miss those back in Canada, but it's time Rain, it's time. Your mom and dad will be selling the ranch soon and I am not sure I want them to do that and my parents are only a short plane ride away from Bridge Falls. It makes sense. I want to raise our children in Canada where you and I were born.."

"You've certainly given me something to consider. I can honestly say that I never thought you would ever think of retuning permanently to Bridge. What did you mean about not wanting my parents to sell the ranch?"

"We could have our own Avanloch there Rainey. Do you remember when you said that you wanted to build me a house someday? That someday has been over twenty years in coming and I think I would like to give you that opportunity. I'm done here; I'm ready to move on."

"I think I like your idea but it's going to take some planning. I'm not sure the Palace is large enough for our brood and I can't expect you to be chief cook and bottle washer to five children and still have time for me."

"Oh, "tis yourself you be worryin about 'tis it now?"

He pulled me up off the bench and kissed me and said it was time to go home. I said that is what I just said.

He laughed and said that we had lots of time to discuss it but that we should keep our tentative plans to ourselves until after the babies had arrived. I agreed.

He helped me compose a letter to Somner. I told him that I accepted his apology and that I would like to stay in touch. I wished him and Lelani many happy years together.

Towards the end of October I received a distressing phone call from the Duchess of Calendria. She practically begged for me and Rainey to come to London. Apparently she was ill and needed to find her husband. I had no idea how we could help her as we had not talked to Roberge since the September party. It was then that I found out that my eldest daughter had taken Avaleena's diary to London to get Roberge's take on the Ferrani name. Roberge was most intrigued and decided to track his father down. The only person his father stayed in touch with was Roberge's sister, Pilar. Rainey and I had met her along with the rest of the family when we were in Saragossa gathering information on the Infinity Bracelets. Pilar had informed her brother that their father was on an expedition in South America searching for some lost gold mine. How he expected to find their father was puzzling. The last time she had heard from him was when he was leaving a remote village in Brazil a few weeks ago.

Rainey agreed to take me to London though he was not happy about the idea. He truly thought that Lauren had an entirely different agenda in her warped little mind. He was wrong. We were met at the Calendria Palace by Lauren's faithful companion Mrs. Spencer. She was also in charge of everything related to the palace. Her gratitude that we had come was so sincere that I believed Lauren's health was definitely in jeopardy. It was confirmed a few minutes later when I was escorted to her bedside.

This was not the vibrant, glamorous woman from September whom I had accused my husband of wanting to have an affair with. Her once shiny golden locks lay plastered like dead leaves on her colourless face. Her eyes were shut. I put my hand to her forehead. Her lifeless blue eyes stared back at me. She murmured my name.

"Yes Lauren, it is me; Rainey is here too. Shush Dear, we are going to take care of you." I glared at the nurse sitting ten feet away. She seemed unconcerned. "Why isn't this woman in the hospital?"

"She refused to go."

"Can you not see that she is severely dehydrated and by her wheezing I would say she has pneumonia? Did you get your nursing degree in a box of cracker jacks?"

"I don't think I like your tone! Who are you to talk to me like that?"

"I am her friend. You have no idea who Lauren is do you?"

"Just because she has some fancy title doesn't make her any more important than anyone else."

"Exactly", I said, "and that is that she is a human being. You have been neglectful of your duties and you can be assured that I will be reporting your dereliction to your supervisors."

That poor excuse for a caregiver told me that I had no business undermining her authority. She informed me that anyone could refuse treatment and Mrs. Farradan had done just that.

"Oh, and she has a "do not resuscitate" clause as one of her wishes?"

"I wouldn't know about that. She has been like this for days and I see no reason to go against her wishes as she isn't getting any worse; she's still breathing isn't she?"

I saw red. "Get out of this room!" I yelled at her. "Get out of this house…now!"

She sneered at me. "And by whose authority do you think you can order me to leave lady?"

"That would be my wife, Lady Vienna with a capitol "L" and cousin to the Countess. You are relieved of your duties immediately and I highly suggest you go voluntarily." Rainey had heard me shouting and had come to my rescue. He pointed to the door.

She stormed past us muttering that we had not seen the last of her. Rainey put his hand on my shoulder and asked if I was okay. I said that I was but that we had to get Lauren to the hospital.

He came closer to the bed. "She doesn't look very good does she?"

I summoned Mrs. Spencer and she entered the room all flustered and wringing her hands. "I should not have listened to that nurse should I have? It will be my fault if she dies."

"I hope that it won't come to that. Now bring me some warm water and cloths. We need to make her presentable; she would not like anyone seeing her like this." I asked Rainey to call an ambulance and he suggested we take her ourselves as it would be faster. He had Mrs. Spencer order Lauren's driver to warm up the limousine and meet us at the front door. I bathed Lauren as quickly as I could and changed her sodden nightdress. I brushed her hair away from her face and applied lotion to her hands. She clutched them with hers.

"Did you find him Vienna…did you find my Roberge? I need to tell him how much I love him; he doesn't know. Oh, there you are Roberge, come closer, come closer." Lauren was looking at Rainey. "Oh Roberge, I didn't think you would make it back."

I squeezed her hands. All she could do was whisper Roberge's name over and over.

"She's feverish Rainey; let's get going."

He picked her up and I wrapped the coverlet around her and ran ahead of them downstairs. Mrs. Spencer was crying and said she would meet us at the hospital as she had to collect the Countess's information. She had already phoned ahead to St. Francis Hospital to prepare them of our impending arrival. A gurney and two attendants were waiting for us at the emergency doors. We sat and waited for word on her condition. After fifteen minutes I decided to go and phone Rosalyn. Rainey offered to do so but I said it was my job.

A nurse steered me in the direction of a public phone. I rang my daughter's private line. There was no answer and so I had to dial the main reception office of McAllister Enterprises. I was told that Rosalyn was in a board meeting. I directed Irena, the receptionist, to inform Miss McAllister that her mother requested to talk to her immediately. Of course Rosy assumed that something was wrong with me.

"No Rosy," I assured her, "I am just fine, but the Duchess of Calendria is not. Rainey and I found her near death at the Palace and we have brought her to the hospital. She is delirious and thinks that she sees Roberge. We know that is not possible don't we Rosalyn because you sent him on a wild goose trail to Brazil to track his father down? I thought we had decided to leave the matter aside for a while…what possessed you to spill the beans child?"

She knew by the tone of my voice that I was most displeased. "Oh Mama, please don't be angry with me. Ava wasn't interested and you had the pregnancy to think about. I just wanted to discover the truth about the Ferrani name and there was only one way to do that and that was to confront Roberge. Is Lady Lauren going to be all right Mama?"

"We have no news at the moment. We will stay here until we have word on her condition which I am sure is forthcoming shortly. We have much to discuss and I expect that you will be waiting for us at the apartment?"

"Yes Mama; may I bring Evan?"

"I'm thinking that he is your cohort, so yes, by all means." I hung up the phone and returned to find two doctors talking with my husband, a Dr. Caruthers and Dr. Taylor.

Lauren had been moved to the Intensive Care Unit. Her condition was most dire. Left for much longer the excessive fluid on her lungs would have caused them to collapse. It was most fortunate that we had arrived to intervene when we had. Rainey had filled them in on the circumstances as to why we had come and to the condition we had found her in. One of the doctors had spoken briefly to Mrs. Spencer before she was shuttled away to fill out forms.

Dr. Caruthers spoke openly. "We were told that Ms. Farradan had a bout with influenza in September and did not seem to fully recover from it. She had not consulted with her doctor about the lingering effects as he was off on vacation and she did not wish to visit his replacement. She may have had a viral infection and the consequences of it not being treated have undoubtedly led to her current condition. A portable x-ray machine has shown inflammation in both alveoli, the microscopic air sacs in the lungs. Bacteria have entered her lungs probably while she was trying to fight off the flu bug. When the alveoli don't work efficiently the lungs cannot extract oxygen from the air and breathing becomes both labored and painful. There are different types and causes of pneumonia. We believe that Ms. Farradan has what is referred to as "walking pneumonia" as it seems to have presented itself weeks after her initial illness."

Rainey interrupted Dr. Caruthers. "Sorry Doctor, but I do not like the term bacteria…is this type of pneumonia contagious? My wife is pregnant and if there is any danger…"

Dr. Caruthers held up his hand. "Let's not jump the gun here Mr. Quinn. You are entitled to be worried about your wife's condition," he nodded to me, "but as of yet we have not determined what type of bacteria is causing the infection. The lab is busy analysing her cultures and blood work as we speak. Most types of pneumonia are not contagious, but if results show otherwise you can be certain we will contact you immediately. Once we have settled Ms. Farradan you may visit her. You will be asked to wear a gown and mask; it is as much for her protection as well as yours. Once we have determined if Ms. Farradan has enough red blood cells to carry oxygen and if her immune system can fight off the infection or if the bacteria is in the blood stream we will have more answers. Now if you will kindly excuse us, we need to check on our patient. A nurse will direct you to the I.C.U. ward. I caution you not to worry excessively Mrs. Quinn."

We both thanked them and awaited the nurse. I told Rainey that he could go and sit by Lauren's bedside if it was allowed and I would continue on to the apartment to meet with Rosy.

He laughed. "In what realm is that likely to happen? Are you suggesting that you go out into the streets of London and hail a taxi?

You do remember Jack the Ripper and Sweeny Todd and the Water Rats don't you? It will be a sunny day in Hades before I let you out on these streets alone my dear."

"Would you enlighten me as to whom the water rats are and wasn't Sweeny Todd a fictional character and Jack the Ripper…really Rain?" I was slightly amused by his list of characters. I assured him I would be quite safe on the modern streets of daytime London.

"Said you as you crossed the cobblestone road in the tiny village of Nazeth…"

I smiled satirically. "You win Darling…just as you always do."

"Thank-you and I take my wins when they are warranted."

We made our way to the I.C.U. ward. We stood at the window and watched as two nurses fiddled with the equipment that was providing hydration and medication to Lauren. She was enclosed inside an oxygen tent. One nurse noticed us and came to tell us that Lady Lauren was resting comfortably and that her breathing was less worrisome as the oxygen was doing its job. She asked if we would like to "gown-up" and we replied that we would not disturb Lauren at this time but we would return in several hours.

She said that was a good plan. "Your cousin is in very good hands here Lady Quinn. You can be assured that we will provide the utmost care for the Countess. We will look forward to seeing you later then." She backed up a little and I swear she curtsied. She nodded to Rainey and said, "Sir, I mean Lord Quinn, your decision to bring the Countess to us surely saved her life."

Rainey replied that it was a no brainer. She smiled. I'm not too sure she understood his lingo.

I grabbed his hand and pulled him towards the elevator. "My cousin, Lord, Lady, did you tell them who we are?"

"That would be Mrs. Spencer. She made it perfectly clear that the Countess of Calendria owed her life to Lady and Lord Quinn of Avanloch."

Thank heavens there was a little bench to sit on while we awaited the arrival of the elevator. Rainey sighed and asked if our lives would ever be normal again.

"It will be when we move back to Canada and we can be just Mr. and Mrs. Quinn; just plain ole Rainey and Vienna."

He laughed. "Yes Mrs. Quinn, I am looking forward to that. Now I suppose we must confront the next Mistress of Avanloch. You won't be too hard on her will you?"

I did not answer.

Rosy had prepared an afternoon tea for us of fancy sandwiches and pastries. After a few initial pleasantries Rainy broke the ice by asking if there was anything besides watercress in between the thin layers of bread. Rosy apologized. Evan passed Rainey a beer which he graciously accepted. I sat in one of the comfortable wing chairs expecting Rainey to sit in the chair next to me but instead he chose to sit beside Rosy on the sofa. He took her hand.

"Well Red, let's hear your story."

She smiled, but tears were stinging her eyes. "There is no story Rainey. I am sorry Mama; I never knew Lady Lauren was that ill. She had a slight cold but she was all for Roberge tracking down his father. She willingly financed the trip. She was most intrigued that you and he may somehow be related and that he may have a stake in Avanloch."

"Yes, I am sure that is what interested her the most. But when and why did you decide to confide in Roberge?"

"I thought Ava and I would approach Roberge together but she flatly refused. I couldn't bother you as you were newly pregnant and you and Rainey had quit fighting so I asked Evan what I should do because I truly wanted to lay the matter of lineage to rest one way or the other."

I was about to speak but Rainey corrected Rosy before I could. "First of all Rosalyn, your mother and I were not fighting, we were just 'not talking'. It was all a big misunderstanding wasn't it Darling?" He reached across and took my hand and winked at me flirtatiously. "I would think you would have known that you could have come to us with your plans no matter what?"

"I wanted to have it all settled so Mama wouldn't have to wonder if we had to share our properties with a stranger." Rosy looked at me for approval.

"Roberge is hardly a stranger. I have great respect for him even though he was not in my good books when first we met. I am very fond of him and if it turns out that he and I are distantly related, in fact to you also, we will welcome him into our fold… will we not?" I had not seen my oldest daughter so flustered since the day she discovered that I knew that she was no longer living in this apartment but was co-habiting with Evan.

"Yes Mama, we will. And you should know that Evan advised me against my plan."

I loved Evan. He was the son I would never have which was odd because we were very close in age. He knew I did not care for tea except the lavender and heather brewed concoction that Mrs. D. made for me and so he had bought some blackberry juice for me. He set a glass down on the table in front of me and sat down next to me. I thanked him and smiled.

"Yes, I am sure he felt like he was between the woman he loved and the deep blue sea. We are not angry with either one of you. However, I fail to see how you expect that Roberge will be able to track his father down in the Brazilian jungle. You do know that they are not the best of friends don't you?"

"I had no idea that his father was not in France or wherever he was living when I first visited Roberge. He was much intrigued as was the Countess when I told him what we had discovered in Avaleena's journal. Ironically his father had asked him to join him on his expedition to Brazil. Roberge had declined because he did not want to trek about some mosquito and alligator infested swamp. However, as soon as he heard the name Ferrani, he was as I said, most intrigued and he changed his mind about the hazards."

"Do we have any way of contacting him?" I asked.

"No, but I know his itinerary so he should not be too hard to track down."

"And, just how do you expect to do that if there is no way to contact him?"

"We will fly into Minas Gerais just as he did and contact Father Baptiste who will direct us to a guide who will take us to the lost gold mine that his father is searching for. I will make this right Mama." She looked at Evan. "Will you come with me?"

"Well, I'm certainly not letting you go alone." He answered sharply.

"Just a minute, just a damn minute; neither one of you are jetting off to some treacherous jungle in South America! Has it not occurred to you that lost might actually mean **lost**? If there are guides that know about this mysterious gold mine why aren't they amassing the treasure themselves?" Rainey questioned sombrely.

"I don't know Rainey; maybe none of them believe in the legend."

"Come on Rosy, surely you can see that none of this makes any sense at all?"

"Mr. Farradan would not have embarked on this expedition unless he was sure that it existed."

I leaned forward and stared into my daughter's unflinching green eyes and stated that I was not aware that she had met Roberge's father and was an expert on his character.

"I never met him Mama but Roberge says that he is very astute and always checks out the validity of his ventures before he commits to them. I trust that was true in this instance."

"I understand your concern and believe me I am not too keen on the idea of trekking through the unexplored jungles myself, but if Rosy has made up her mind… I think you both know what I am saying." Evan said candidly looking directly at me and then Rainey.

I sighed. "Yes, I know what you are saying Evan, but we have yet to hear any prove that this mine actually exists. How was Monsieur Farradan informed about its possible existence and who financed the expedition? From what I understand he is not a man of means? Have you considered the possibility that he and his cohorts are being bamboozled?"

"Why Mother, why would someone finance such a project unless it was highly credible? Roberge told us that it was bankrolled by business acquaintances with whom he had worked for before. Apparently, this is not the first treasure expedition his father has been on and besides that, he has a map."

"A map… well that makes everything plausible then doesn't it?" Rainey said mockingly.

"Are you in possession of a copy of 'said map'?" I asked.

"No, we don't have one but Roberge has a copy and Evan and I have both seen it. I'm sorry I never thought to photocopy it."

"Why would you Rosy; you had no plans to follow Roberge did you?"

"No, we didn't, but the thought did cross my mind that he might get lost and we may have had to send out a search party for him. I was neglectful in not only that but not noticing how sick the Countess was."

"She probably was not showing any signs of distress at the time so you are in no way at fault there. When did all of this take place?" I asked.

Rosy recited the dates. "Evan and I came to Calendria Palace on the eighth of October just one week after Roberge's father had left on his expedition. Roberge left for Brazil on the fifteenth of October, exactly two weeks ago. We are not that far behind."

Rainey got up and walked to the window like he always does when deep in thought or fretting. We respected that he was contemplating all that had been said. After a few minutes he came over to me and placed his hands on my shoulders. "We cannot and will not forbid you to go; not that you would listen to us anyway, but just so you know, we are not encouraging you to go either. We will support you in any way we can, but we are not one bit happy about your decision to go traipsing off into the unknown."

"Do you feel the same way Mama? Do we have your permission to go?"

"My sentiments are exactly the same as Rainey's. We are not endorsing your hair-schemed plan and we will not prevent you from going by barricading you in the cellars of Avanloch."

That brought a few chuckles to a very tense situation. Rosy positioned herself at my feet and put her head in my lap. "I just want to try and find Roberge for Lauren. I realize that it is a shot in the dark that we can find a guide that can follow his exact route and that we might fail. Or on the other hand, maybe it will be easy. Thank-you for respecting my wishes and I promise I won't let anything happen to Evan."

"I think it is me who is supposed to be protecting you my dear." Evan countered.

"I trust you will have each other's back. Now get up here little girl so that I can hug you and tell you that I love you just as I love all my children. I shall worry about you night and day until you are back where you belong." Rainey brought both Rosy and I to tears. He had to clear his throat several times so I knew he was on the verge of tears himself.

"Sometimes I am envious of the relationship you and Ava have. I see you together and I am sad that I never had that closeness with Jeremy. I was so prepared to hate you when first we met and more so after that stunt you pulled pretending to be mother's chauffeur, but Ava was right, I would soon come to love you and I do. I want to call you Daddy…." Rosy was crying so hard that she couldn't speak.

Rainey had tears in his eyes as he pulled her a little away from him and smiled into her eyes. "Well Darlin, why don't you then?"

"Maybe Ava wouldn't like it." She said sobbing.

I couldn't say anything as this was a moment between father and daughter. Evan and I stood together holding hands.

"Well, I hardly doubt that. You know that your mother and I are adopting Tanny and Zoe and you are already Vienna's daughter, so what say I add you to my list or would it be disrespectful to Jeremy?"

Well now he had really done it! Rosy was crying so hard that she was having trouble breathing. She finally managed to ask me if I would be okay with that. I could only tell her the truth. "When Rainey and I talk about our children you are always included. Jeremy and Maveryn will always be your biological parents, but they left you a long time ago. I have been your mother for twenty three years and I will be honoured if you let the man I love become your father."

Rainey said that it was settled then and that Rosy would officially become one of his girls. "I trust that since you are the eldest of the brood you will keep your siblings in line?"

She answered that she would try but that it wasn't going to be easy, especially with that spirited Tanny. We put the tears away for another day. Rosy wanted to change clothes before visiting Lauren so she and Evan left promising to meet us at the hospital in an hour.

As soon as the door shut behind them I thanked Rainey. "You have made her very happy. I think she has been envious of yours and Ava's closeness for quite some time. Whether you legally adopt her or not, just the idea of it makes her feel like she is truly one of ours. Am I included on your list of Rainey's girls?"

He laughed. "You know perfectly well that you are on top of the list and you always will be."

We stayed in London for three more days. We would have stayed longer but we needed to get home to our little girls. I sat with Lauren for several hours that first night after we were given the green light that it was safe to do so. There was a small flap in the oxygen tent that I could fit my hand through and hold her hand. Rainey and Rosy would relieve me from time to time. We talked to her continuously so that she wouldn't feel alone. She squeezed my hand several times so I knew that she was hearing us. A few times a tear escaped and rolled down her face. The doctors were optimistic that she would make a full recovery and that it was highly possible that within ten days she could conclude her convalescing at home. The day we left she was able to sit up for short periods of time. She was quite alert and knew of Rosy's and Evan's plans to bring her husband home to her. She besought us to prevent them from making the arduous and virtually impossible journey. We left her saying that we would try as we did not want to argue with her. She asked me if I had forgiven her for flirting with Rainey. I told her "no", but that we would discuss it when she was feeling better. She tried to laugh but couldn't quite manage it. She asked if we could be friends and I told her that we already were. I blew her a kiss and Rainey hurried me out before the damn broke again.

Evan and Rosy couldn't leave for Brazil until November fourteenth as their vaccines were not up to date and it was highly suggested to them that they wait out the two weeks for certain ones to take effect. We talked to them the night before they were to leave. After all the cautionary words were echoed again, we wished them a safe trip although our hearts were not in it. They were to call us as often as was possible. I told Rosy to keep a detailed journal.

Rainey's youngest son Mason broke his leg the next day at a hockey practice. Morgan called us from the hospital saying he didn't know how he would be able to look after his brother and continue with his studies. Neither one of them wanted their mother to know as she would be more of a hindrance than help. She was on a Mediterranean cruise anyhow. He asked permission to hire a nurse. Rainey was sick that he could not be there for his son because he would not leave me. I tried to talk him into going but was met with such hostile resistance that I dropped the matter immediately. Of course Ava had the solution; she would go and care for her brother. She left the next day.

It was now December the eighteenth. We had not heard from Rosy and Evan for weeks. Father Batiste, the Jesuit Priest who was their contact person had managed to get through to us from some remote village and inform us of their progress. Apparently, all was going well. He had accompanied them to a fishing village but was called back to Minas Gerais for an urgent matter. He told us that Rosalyn and Evan had been received favorably at the Indian villages. The gifts of colorful beads, bangles and colorful materials were indeed appreciated. He had left them in good hands with a tribe known as Pirantas who were very intrigued with Rosalyn's fiery red hair. Their guides had left to secure safe passage across a very treacherous river. It was the last barrier before they would reach the enchanted land of the Green Seas and the supposedly rich caves.

The clock chimed eleven bells. I had been reminiscing for almost two hours. Rainey stuck his head in the parlour door and asked how I was doing with the holiday menus. I laughed and told him I hadn't made any progress at all. It was the last time I would laugh for a very long time. He said he would be right back as the phone was ringing and there was no one was answering it and it might be Rosy. He returned five minutes later and I immediately knew that something was wrong. I assumed it was dire news about Rosy and Evan. It wasn't; it was regarding our other daughter. Just two days before she was to fly home she had been approached by her former boss Malcolm Deans and asked if she would accompany a medical shipment to some destination in northern British Columbia. Of course she said yes.

Rainey was trembling as he told me that the cargo plane had not reached its destination yesterday. The last contact with it had been sometime before one yesterday, Canadian time. Search planes had been dispatched immediately from Prince George and Edmonton Alberta but were recalled almost immediately due to unsettling storms. They would be attempting to resume the search today at first light…weather permitting. It was three a.m. Vancouver time. He would keep us updated a he received reports. I think I stopped breathing for a few seconds.

Rainey sat on the round-about in front of me and took hold of my hands and lamented. "Both our girls are missing Vienna."

"They will be all right Darling; you'll see." I rubbed his shoulders trying to comfort him. I couldn't afford to panic and I tried to speak in a calm voice though I was scared to death. "We have to have faith and believe that they will be."

He looked up at me and placed his hands on my stomach. "We have to keep these little girls save Vienna; we can't let anything happen to them. Yet, if it wasn't for them I would have been the one to go to Vancouver to look after Mason and Ava would be home here safe and sound, and I should never have consented to let Rosy go to that dark and perilous continent. What's wrong with me Vienna… why do all my girls desert me?"

"This is not the time for you to be having a pity party or second guessing anything. For God's sake man, snap out of it! No one could ever take the place of Ava and Rosy but don't you dare go blaming these precious little souls that you and I made out of our love for each other…do you hear me? Now let's go and find Amma and Johnny and Mrs. D as we are going to need all their love and support in the next few days." I didn't want to be the brave one but perhaps I was going to have to be if my husband was going to fall apart.

Malcolm phoned several more times during the day; there was no news. The weather was still unsettled and the search planes could not rise above the clouds that were still threatening the skies along the route that Ava's flight would have taken. We were told that the pilot was a decorated war veteran who had flown many missions during the Vietnam conflicts and that if anyone could land a plane safely during a blizzard it would be him. That was little consolation but it was something along with knowing that there was a young man, aboard who was a wilderness guide and had all the skills to survive in the backwoods. Malcolm had yet to receive the manifest from Northland Transport but thought the only other person on board besides him and Ava was the co-pilot.

Rainey had pulled himself somewhat together when we had the unpleasant task of informing the rest of the household of the missing plane. Amma wanted to call Mac immediately and Rainey agreed that I should be checked over. I wanted Mac to prescribe something for Rainey so I said that it was probably a good idea. As soon as Mac had assured everyone that all seemed well with me and the babies I asked to see him alone where I conveyed my worry over Rainey's unusual manic behaviour. He said that he had noticed the feverish pitch of Rainey's voice and actions also and left a mild tranquilizer for me to administer to my husband. I knew that he would refuse it, but when he said he was going to stay and monitor the phone downstairs all night I insisted he take one reminding him that we had a phone in our bedroom and this was not the time for us to be alone. He apologized and we slept fretfully in each other's arms until Lili came bouncing into our room. Rainey caught her just before she jumped on me. Zoe rushed in after her apologizing for letting her get away. Lili was what we needed and she managed to distract us from our worries briefly until the telephone rang. Rainey bounded out of bed and grabbed it on the second ring. I watched his facial expressions warily as he answered. He inhaled and then let out a breath of relief.

"That is very good news Red; your mother and I have been sick with worry wondering why we haven't heard from you and Evan."

It was Rosy. I shook my head feverishly instructing him not to tell her that Ava's plane was missing. Rainey told Rosy he loved her and passed the phone to me. The connection was very poor and she said that we could lose contact at any time so she talked fast telling me that they were well and back in Minas Gerais. They would be home in two days. I think she said that they had found Roberge but before I could confirm or tell her that I loved her, the line went dead. Rainey tried to reconnect but all he got was a busy signal.

"Sorry Honey, I'll try again later. I know only too well how hard it is to get an overseas operator who speaks English or will listen to your plight…"

He seemed to lose focus. "Rainey, where did you just go?" I asked hesitantly.

"Back to nineteen sixty one." He said pensively. "You'd think there would be better long distance phone management nowadays wouldn't you?"

I felt tears stinging my eyes because I realized he was remembering how he had tried in vain to connect with me from Italy that fateful winter so very long ago. "Come here my darling, Lili wants you and I need you."

He climbed back into bed snuggling up to me and rescuing a lively toddler from me.

"At least one of our daughters is safe Vienna. Now we can focus all our efforts on finding Ava. After you fell asleep last night I made a few calls to a few old buddies at the coast who own a helicopter service. I told them I didn't care who they had to bribe or what it would cost to get search planes in the air. I expect to hear from one of them any time now. I'm praying I have better luck with these guys then I did with the private investigators I hired to find you."

Was Ava's disappearance so soon after mine going to be more than Rainey could handle? Suppose if she was already dead…I wanted to scream and cry. Lord, give me strength.

CHAPTER 4

Camp at 57 Degrees North

Nash and Monty brought our makeshift table out into the light and spread two maps out. Of course Monty already knew of Nash's decision to leave our camp and look for help. Ace had not been aware of Nash's plans but was not surprised and neither was Sali. Evie felt as I did; apprehensive, but sort of confident that he knew what he was doing.

Monty charted out the flight plan using one of Evie's red markers. "So as you can see our route follows Hiway 97 to Mackenzie and then over the Rockies and Ft. Nelson and straight on into Spring Valley. However, I am doubtful that we made it to Ft. Nelson. I vaguely remember flying over a body of water. Normally that would be the Prophet River and then the Ft. Nelson River, but somewhere in between the storm struck. At first it was light gale winds that rocked the plane a little, but within minutes it had turned into a full force tempest. That's when Ace instructed you to prepare for turbulence. The Contessa was pummelled by lightning and hail and by the way our instrument panel was lighting up I'm pretty sure we changed direction several times. We had tried to rise above the storm but couldn't; flying any lower would have put us on a collision course with the Rockies or whatever mountains were in our path, so we just had to ride it out... and we were until that bolt of lightning struck the tail and all hell broke loose." He stopped talking and took a swig of whiskey.

I took that time to ask if Contessa was the name of the plane as I hadn't heard it mentioned before and I hadn't seen any name on the plane. Monty said if I looked carefully I could see a few letters still visible under the wing. It was in dire need of repainting. He explained that Contessa was what Ace called his wife. I said it was lovely and nice that the company allowed him to name the plane. It was then that I learned that Ace and Monty were the sole owners of Northland Transport.

"So, where do you think we are and where is this Sitka Alaska you referred to?"

Nash took my hand and ran it over a very large area. "Here, somewhere. The boys are pretty confident that the plane was turned around and was propelled in a westerly direction which puts us here… somewhere in the vicinity of Spatsizi Plateau Wilderness or maybe closer, say in one of these other wilderness parks. Hopefully, this creek will lead down to a river and give me some idea of where we are."

"I don't see how that is going to tell you anything. Look at all of these rivers; there is the Muskwai, the Finlay, the Toad, the Skeena and half a dozen more. Are you saying that you know which river is which just by seeing it?"

Nash grinned. "Well no, it is not as simple as that but I'm hoping the skies will clear and I will recognize the landscape."

"Well, the skies could clear here too! I still don't see any Sitka Alaska."

Monty showed me where it was located. "Why that is way over on the coast, surely you are wrong?" I turned to get Ace's take being careful as I raised my head because I had this terrible ache in the back of my neck and it was travelling rapidly up to my face.

"I told you all that we were in Alaska." Ace said matter of factually.

I grabbed the back of my head and said I was going to lie down as I had a dreadful headache.

Sali followed me into the tent saying it was the "Chinook Effect".

"What?" I said crankily.

"Do you remember me mentioning to you and Evie that the wind can have consequences; well I meant health wise. I've heard of people having severe headaches and feeling irritable and some even speak of a sudden depression. I think you are one of these special people. Are you prone to headaches Ava? I certainly know that you are not grouchy so I'm going with the Chinook as causing your discomfort, but it will pass soon enough so how about a couple of headache pills?" Sali said positioning the pillows behind me.

Nash came in and asked how I was. I told him that according to Sali I was suffering from some ancient hocus pocus that this lovely warm wind was the cause of my headache and irritability.

"It happens Ava; my mother suffers from Chinook Fever as she calls it. I'll make you an ice pack and you can rest. As soon as the temperature starts levelling out your headache will disappear, I promise. Are you warm enough? Don't you want to get inside the sleeping bag?"

"It's just a headache, so all of you quit fussing please."

"All your life you have been taking care of someone; first your mother and then your father and you came all the way over here from Scotland to care for your brother when he broke his leg. When you should have been on a plane going home for the holidays you chose to help the people in the remote north by delivering medical supplies…don't you think it's time someone looked after you?" Nash asked rather curtly.

I held back a sniffle and managed to say thank-you. I took the aspirins and hoped that I would be able to sleep.

I was awakened by a little wet nose nuzzling my cheek. I spoke to her in a very calming voice and followed her outside. Evie saw me first and asked how I was feeling. I replied that I felt refreshed and that my headache was almost gone. Sali said they had been waiting for me to have supper. I volunteered to get the salad. The second I bent down to retrieve it from our snow refrigerator, the pain shot up the back of my head again. I righted myself slowly and it subsided somewhat. I didn't want anyone to witness my discomfort so I put a little food in my bowl and turned slightly away from everyone. Asta had not left me since she had woken me up. She sat down along side of me and placed her head in my lap. Two spoons of salad and I knew I was going to be sick. I threw the bowl down and covered my mouth and ran as far as I could down the wood trail before I had to bend down and upchuck. I felt a hand on my shoulder and another one holding my hair back. I crawled up the path a ways and collapsed into the snow. I felt much better with my head immersed in the cold slush. I lay there for a few minutes trying to compose myself. I was well aware that Nash was with me.

"Are you all right now Ava? Here, take my hand, let me help you up…careful, take it easy, you may have hurt yourself when you planted yourself in that snow bank." He sounded worried.

"I'm okay Nash." I smiled into his eyes and then the world went dark.

"I'm worried Nash; I think this is more than just a case of the Chinook Fever."

It was Sali and she and all of my new cohabitees, even Ace, were hovering over me. I asked why they were all staring at me.

"What's the last thing you remember Ava?" Nash questioned.

"Well, I remember being sick if that is what you are wondering and then…how did I get back here? I can't recall coming back into the tent; did something else happen?"

"I'm not sure. I helped you out of the snow bank and asked if you were all right. You said you were and smiled at me and then you blacked out. I picked you up and brought you back here."

"That sounds like one of my mother's performances, not mine. I have never fainted before in my life…wait a second…it's you Nash, you're the boy from the ski hill! Oh my, I must have had a déjà vu experience."

"Ski hill, déjà vu, what in the world are you talking about?" Nash implored.

I sat up and suggested that someone get Ace's chair as he shouldn't be standing. Monty said that he was on it. I asked Nash if he had ever had a déjà vu experience. He said he hadn't. Apparently, no one else had either. I asked Nash if he remembered the year he was in Bern.

"Do you mean Bern Switzerland, and how could you possibly know I was there?"

"So you admit being there?"

"Yes, but I fail to see what that has to do with anything."

"I was there too Nash. Do you remember helping a little girl who had careened out of control on the ski hill and landed in a snow bank?"

The look on his face said it all. He said he had to sit down. Monty rolled a stump of wood over for him. "Are you saying that young girl was you? I had forgotten all about that incident…it was so long ago. Hell, it was my senior year and a bunch of us had gone to Switzerland for the winter break… how do you remember that… you were probably only five or six?"

"I believe I was seven and that it was nineteen sixty nine; does that sound right to you?"

"I would have been seventeen so I guess so. It still doesn't explain…I'm lost."

I took his hand. "When you helped me up just a few minutes ago you asked me if I was okay and was I hurt and that is almost exactly what you said to me all those years ago. Something triggered my memory banks and when I looked into your eyes I knew I had been in this same situation before with you. That is when the moment of recognition took hold of me. Did I reach out to you?"

"I believe you tried but you just went limp and I caught you before you fell. This is all too uncanny for me to comprehend Ava."

"I told you that the two of you had met before didn't I, well I was right wasn't I? Sali chuckled.

"Yes, you did suggest that Sali, but what Nash and I shared fourteen years ago was barely a meeting. It was my first time on a skiing vacation and I was not very skilled in the sport. I threw a ski and went tumbling down the hill landing in a snow drift. Nash was the first one to get to me. My mother arrived on the scene a few seconds later. Nash had offered to carry me to the first aid station but there was no need. Mama thanked him and that was it; no names were exchanged, nothing. It may be unnerving for you Nash but if you lived in my world you would know that there is nothing unnatural at all about experiencing sensations such as déjà vu."

"What do you mean by "in your world" Ava?" Nash asked inquisitively.

"And that is a story for another day." I replied.

"I've heard you say that before Ava and I am beginning to think that you are a story all in yourself waiting to be told." Evie stated.

I laughed. "Who knows? By the time we get out of this place I am sure you will have all heard about the adventures of a Scottish girl just because we will have run out of things to talk about. I can assure you though that my life is no more adventurous than any of yours. Now let's say we get out of here and enjoy what is left of the day?"

"Amen to that! Enough black magic for one day people, let's go back into the light." Ace exclaimed.

"Oh, if you think what I just experienced was witchery then you ain't heard nothing yet!"

I was itching to tell my new friends about the spirits that haunt my Scottish home but the time wasn't right yet, and on the other hand, maybe I never would tell them. Nash said that nothing would surprise him about me at all…well, we'd just see about that.

There wasn't much preparation to be done for Nash's venture. He had purchased a week's supply of freeze dried meals at the outdoor convention he had attended. They were light-weight and besides a thermos of the homemade soup and two tinned ham sandwiches that was all the food he would be taking. Coffee and one of the small pots, a sleeping bag, two pairs of woolen socks and an extra shirt would fill up his backpack. Asta had a small pack that held her rations strapped to her back.

I still had a faint headache and excused myself early. I decided to separate Nash's and my sleeping bags and settled down with a project I was working on. I used the novel I was reading to hide it from view. I pretended to be reading when Nash came in.

"What the hell Ava?" He said rather crossly.

"I'm very restless Nash and I don't want to keep you awake so I thought it best to unzip us and besides I am still warm. You need to get a good night's sleep so don't be angry." I looked up at him. "I shouldn't be sleeping next to you anyhow. I can't be a substitute for the one you left behind." I turned over and said good night not knowing why I had said that.

He called Asta and moved his sleeping bag a little further away. "Is that why you think I want your company…never mind, I'll be sure not to bother you again."

I slept restlessly and wanted Nash back next to me but told myself I had done the right thing.

Monty's voice woke me the next morning. He was asking Ace if he thought they would work. I rolled out of my cocoon and asked him what he was talking about. He held up what looked like a tennis racquet entwined with rope and said he hoped it would help Nash stay on top the snow. I slipped my Mukluks on and walked out without saying a word and right passed Sali who was frying eggs. Nash was cleaning his rifle. He asked me where I was going in such a hurry.

"To the imaginary red toilets because even though all of this is a hallucination or else I am just plum crazy and this is my asylum, I still have to pee." I snapped.

He picked up his gun and followed me.

"You don't have to watch over me Nash as this is my own personal nightmare and I will have to deal with it myself. Oh, and what I said yesterday about Bern and us meeting before… well, that was a memory of someone else from another lifetime, it was not you!"

He took hold of my arm. "I remember it too so don't give me that crap! And, we are all in the same nightmare so quit thinking you are living this alone! What has got you so riled up so early in the morning?"

I pulled away from him. "Who brings a tennis racquet to a plane crash anyway, can you answer me that?"

He did not answer me and we did not talk again before he left. He shook hands with Monty and Ace and they wished him good luck. Sali and Evie hugged him and said they were going to miss him. I did not look up from the log I was sitting on. He said, "See you all soon." I heard him whisper to Sali to look after me. Evie sat down beside me.

"They are not tennis racquets Ava; they are cheap badminton racquets that I brought for my nieces. I doubt that they will hold up under Nash's weight, but you know Monty had to try. Why are you treating Nash like the enemy Ava? I truly thought you cared for him;

what has happened?" She asked tucking my wayward hair back under my toque.

I fiddled with the little object in my coat pocket. "I do Evie…I made him something to keep him safe, but I didn't even give it to him." I felt a tear roll down my cheek.

"It's not too late." She squeezed my hand and I was up and running calling out his name.

He turned. Asta came to greet me running circles around me barking as if she hadn't seen me in days. I stopped when I was face to face with Nash. "I'm sorry; I have no excuse for my childish behaviour. It could be because I don't want you to leave us but I know you feel it is your duty so I won't ask you to stay." I took the tartan scarf off from around my neck. "My Aunt Jannie once told me that the Scottish women always sent their men off to war with a memento of themselves like a handkerchief or a scarf so that her man would remember her. Will you wear mine Nash?"

"I'm not going off to war Honey, but I would be honored to wear your scarf and you are going to be on my mind day and night so there is no worry there."

I helped him loop my scarf around his neck and then I reached in my pocket and placed the little flag in his hand. He opened it and asked what it was and where did it come from. I told him that I had made it for him last night out of a piece of a cloth bandage and colored it green with one of Evie's markers and affixed it to a piece of Monty's wood cast-offs.

"Did you draw this magical little fairy sitting on a lily pad and do these red berries signify anything? I am very impressed with your talent Ava and that you made it for me. Is there is some sort of message here?"

"Graphic Art was my major and this is no great talent, believe me. I borrowed from a legend that comes from Dunvegan Castle. It goes like this. The fairy wife of a Scottish Lord presented her husband with a flag before his departure into fields of the unknown. He was to wave it three times if he came face to face with danger and the danger would be averted. It is known as a Fairy Flag. The three red berries mean that he can use its power three times over… but then the magic will be gone. A flag as such still flies at the castle today." I smiled at him wondering if he thought I was indeed bonkers.

Instead he tilted my face up so that he could look into my eyes and said the words that would carry me through until he returned. "I have never been more touched by anything or anyone in my life before Ava. You just made this journey a lot easier for me. I wish I had something to give to you to keep you safe. I have to trust that you won't do anything reckless and that you will be here waiting for me; do I have your word?"

"Yes, I will be right here waiting for you. Even if a rescue party comes I will not leave without you, I promise."

"Right here; you will be right here?"

"Well, I may be down at the corner store, but all you have to do is call my name and I will come running. Now off with you, get going before I cry!"

"One kiss and then I will go."

Our lips touched ever so slightly. I stepped back. "Remember, three times, wave the flag three times and don't use up the magic carelessly."

He started to turn away saying that he wouldn't. He stopped and said, "Ava, just to set you straight on that comment you made last night regarding me leaving someone behind… I didn't. I didn't leave anyone behind. There hasn't been anyone in my life for three years now, not until I stepped on that plane and met you."

"Oh go Nash, just go." The tears were in my voice. "May God travel with you."

He blew me a kiss. I stood and watched until he disappeared out of sight.

The snow was crusty from yesterday's thaw and the overnight freeze. I hoped it would stay that way for Nash as I was pretty sure those makeshift snowshoes would not carry his weight for very far. I held my head up as I trudged back to camp wondering if anyone would say anything. I didn't have to wait very long.

"I say it's about time girl! For a minute there we all thought you were going to let the boy leave with a heavy heart. Kudos to you for coming to your senses." Ace commended me.

"I assure you there is nothing wrong with my senses." I stated smugly.

"And Bob's your uncle, right?"

"That's a British adage, not Scottish." I corrected him smiling. He asked what it meant.

"I think it means, "You're all set." or something like, "you've got it made.""

"Thanks for clearing that up. I always thought it was a strange saying."

Monty had to get his two-bits worth in also. "I hope we don't have to put up with you sulking around here until he returns and pretending that nothing is going on between the two of you."

It was more a question than a statement and I answered as such. "I don't sulk and I am sure I have no idea what you are talking about. I just wanted Nash to know that I was sorry for the way I had been acting…you know; the Chinook fever and all."

Monty laughed. "Chinook fever, my ass! More like lightning bolts following the two of you around. Have you just discovered what the rest of us have known since day one?"

Again I told him I had no idea what he was presuming but I smiled coyly when I said it. Sali told him to quit teasing me.

"It's all in good fun Sal and I think she likes it. Come on Evie, the wood isn't going to cut itself you know."

"So Evie is your designated helper now is she and what does she have to say about it? Perhaps she doesn't wish to and maybe Sali or I want a bit of exercise… do we have a say?"

Monty loaded up the travois with the saw and axe and slung the rifle over his shoulder. "Nope, Evie already volunteered and besides, I am going to teach her how to shoot. Three blasts on that whistle and I am here Sal. Don't let that pistol out of your sight. See you in a couple."

They left with big smiles on their faces and I felt as though I had been left out of some important decision making. "So this was all decided in the few minutes I was gone? I doubt that Evie has even seen an axe before."

"Come on Dumpling," Sali said taking my arm, "we have some sorting out to do in the plane. Are you comfortable out here by yourself Ace?" She put the gun in his lap.

"Yeah, yeah, but I'd rather have one of those flares. This pea shooter won't be much good if mama grizzly decides to visit."

"Sure and you fall asleep and drop the flare in the fire…good plan Ace. There ain't gonna be any bears dropping by. They would have been here already if they were around."

"Yeah, well we don't have the bear dog anymore."

Sali shook her head and told me to pay him no mind. I said that I thought bears hibernated for the winter. Ace laughed and said that I should go on thinking that. I hadn't been all that scared of wild animals invading our camp when Nash and Asta had been here. Now, I wasn't so sure.

We spent a couple of hours sorting out all the remaining tinned and boxed food items placing them on the airplane seats in an orderly fashion. We checked on Ace every few minutes. The whirring of the saw off in the distance comforted me somewhat.

Yesterday had been a delightful day despite my battle with the Chinook headache. We had basked in the warmth as if it was the first day of spring. The continuous changing of the colors and formations of the clouds entertained us all day. At dusk the sky was a hue of oranges and yellows that seemed to form an arch like a rainbow. Within the next hour the temperature had plummeted back to the seasonal normal and an icy thick fog had crept in. I had lived in a country all my life where a common saying regarding the weather was, "Now sun, now rain." This Canadian North Country had that all beat to heck.

The day and night passed without incident. The night grew cold. Monty lit the heater and a few candles after supper. We played a few hands of poker and then decided to shut the heater off to conserve fuel and crawled into our sleeping bags. Sali and Evie had moved theirs next to mine so I wouldn't feel so alone. I appreciated the gesture but slept fitfully all night worrying about Nash.

The next morning heralded our fifth day in the remoteness of the Canadian wilderness. It was Wednesday, December 21st. We were all awake early as usual. Monty asked us girls how we slept and we replied fairly well. He had already made coffee and passed us a cup. We sat on our makeshift beds and drank it. Monty read us an excerpt from Evie's' Farmer's Almanac.

"It says here that this December is to be one of considerable storms and unsettled weather in the northwest…nothing we don't already know hey? Anyway, apparently there was a full moon on the nineteenth, the day of the Chinook. Anyone see it because I sure didn't"

"Well that explains my mood that day then… I always go a little crazy when the moon is full!" I said laughing.

"Could be Ava. My people believe that the moon influences all earthly things; mainly human and animal behaviour and plant growth. We have been gardening by the cycles of the moon for centuries." Sali stated.

I added that I thought the crops at home were also planted by the moon's cycles. "As far back as I can remember Duffy, Mary D's husband, did all the planting. Now he only supervises as age had caught up to him." I asked Sali to tell us more about gardening in her village.

"Our season is very short so there are many things we cannot grow; for instance, tomatoes, watermelons and celery. Cool weather crops like lettuce and spinach and cabbage we plant during the new moon. Just before the full moon things like beans, peas and squash are seeded. After the full moon wanes is the time to plant beets, carrots, onions and potatoes. Corn and cucumbers do not always mature. Sometimes we get pumpkins and sometimes we don't. Ours is a community garden and we all work at keeping it up. We have been saving up to build a greenhouse. Because of our short season we go a little crazy with planting hardy flowers that can live up to the weather like sweet peas, Alaskan nasturtium, and pansies and perennials like daisies and lupines which also grow wild along with bluebells, tiger lilies, wild roses and Indian paintbrushes. What flowers grow in Scotland Ava?"

I wanted to buy her people their greenhouse, but how could I do so without revealing how I could afford to do so. "Our meadows come alive in the spring with the rainbow colors of tulips and daffodils that have been scattered over time. Heather and lilies and iris and of course the Thistle follow close behind. My mother tends the rose garden. I would not even fathom to guess how many bushes or varieties exist. I only know that it is a whole days work just deadheading.

Evie sighed. "I have several houseplants and one window box of petunias and geraniums on my little patio in the summer. I would love to have a house that sat in a field full of beautiful flowers and with a creek running nearby."

"Maybe you will someday Evie." I said optimistically. "At home we have Miller's Creek. It supplies the whole village with water and runs through the property of our resident mystic. Her name is Meggie Magan and she is a gypsy by birth. She came to live in the house after her grandmother Mollie passed away. Mollie was a dear friend of my mother's. When my sister and I were young we made many trips to Gypsy Hollow's bubbling brook which branches off from the creek to watch the fairies dancing and frolicking. Of course they were really fireflies but you couldn't make a young girl believe that. I remember one magical evening sitting on the mossy bank being mesmerized by the little creatures flitting about when the moon announced its arrival by bolding lighting up the sky. We all applauded and Mollie gave us a little lesson on moon lore. She said that the moon is this wondrous elliptical sphere that comes out to enchant child, woman and man and that the tides rise and fall with it and it tells man when it's time to plant and when to harvest and that it's a time to fall in love. She also said that there is a dark side to the moon and that many chilling fables were composed when the moon was full. It is a time for magic and that vampires and werewolves and witches come out to play."

I added that Mollie had cackled a little at the end and that Rosy and I were somewhat fearful. We loved Mollie but we believed that she was akin to sorceresses. Evie laughed and asked if we knew that the little crescent shaped moon at the base of our fingernails was called the Lunula; it was named after the pale quarter moon. We all looked at our fingers; it was much more dominate at the base of our thumbs. I now had a name for something I didn't even know had a name.

Ace added that it was all very interesting but could we drag ourselves away from moon talk and story-telling long enough to bring him some food.

After breakfast Monty and Evie were off to gather more wood. Ace had done too much sitting up and walking the day before so decided to stretch out on his bedroll for a few hours. Sali and I were the only ones left so it was the perfect time to find out more about her village and their way of life. It was obvious that the sun was not going to make an appearance again. The temperature was tolerable and we sat with our backs to the fire most of the time. The first thing I asked her was how her village got its name. She said it was an Algonquian name for the tamarack trees that were abundant in the area; it also meant "wood for snowshoes." Hackmatack, the name of Nash's lodge and Wilderness outfit was another name for tamarack.

"We are made up of many different tribes. We come from Canim Lake, Blueberry River, Athabaska and the Yukon. My husband is from the Pelly Crossing region and his tribe are the Kaska and Slavey people. My family live around Beaver Creek and are known as Tanana. I met my husband George Standing Bear one summer at White River. It was an unusually good run of salmon that year and hundreds of small and large family groups camped along the banks reeling in the rewards. Wild mushrooms, raspberries and low growing blueberries were also abundant. We exchanged information and ideas with each other. George and his family along with two other families came east to Spring Valley. It got its name because it is in this valley where the snows leave early. They had heard that a white man with the name Lander Champion had purchased three hundred acres from the government. His wife had died giving birth to his daughter so he wanted to get as far away from civilization as possible. He left his daughter Charlotte in the care of his sister in Prince George. He built a small cabin on the land and panned for gold in the river and nearby creeks, trapped, and had plans to log the area. Word had circled that he was hiring and men were welcomed to camp on a certain parcel of his land. George was seventeen at the time. He became Lander's right hand man. I met up with George twice more in the next two years and in the autumn of nineteen forty nine George came to my village and we were married. Ten years ago Mr. Champion suffered a debilitating stroke and had to leave the land and people he loved. He moved to Quesnel where his daughter Charlotte lived."

"That's where Nash was raised isn't it? Was it through them that Nash bought his property?"

"And that is what I am going to tell you Dumpling. Lander Champion was Nash's grandfather; Charlotte or Char as she likes to be called is his mother. Every summer Nash and his mother and father and sister would spend several weeks with Lander. Nash tried going to college when he graduated, but the call of the wild was in his blood. When he was twenty two he moved to his grandfather's property, built a larger cabin and eventually the lodge. He started his wilderness guide business about four years ago. Ladner had deeded two hundred acres to Nash and the other hundred to my village. And that my dear is why I have known Nash for such a long time. He and my three boys have always been friends. Their escapades of the area are legendary. He is exactly the man I would have chosen to be my daughter's husband, but of course I was not blessed with a daughter. He has his eye on this little gal that I am very fond of so I think Char's and my wish for him to find love and happiness is right around the corner."

All I could say was, "Oh." but I am pretty sure that my heart stopped beating.

Sali roared with laughter. "Oh Dumpling, if you could only see your face! I didn't mean to scare you, but you got to know that gal I am speaking of is you, don't you?"

I was very near to tears. "I've only known him for a few days Sali so I really don't know if he is just taking advantage of the situation we find ourselves in to flirt with me. I want to think that he has genuine feelings for me, but I really don't know."

"In your heart I think you know or you would not have run after him like you did yesterday. What made you do it and what did you say to him Ava?"

"I had acted badly Sali and I needed to apologize and tell him that I would be waiting for him."

"Is that all? Didn't you tell him that you loved him?"

"Oh no, I don't even know what love is. I am really a novice in that department. I know that he sets my heart to fluttering and I miss him something dreadfully. Is that a sign of love?"

"I met that little bleached blonde that he was engaged to and never once did I hear him call her honey or sunshine or look at her the way he looks at you. No, his feelings for you are genuine and I pray yours are for him too."

"Look at me Sali; I am just this plain Scottish girl with stringy hair and a dirty face…what could he possibly see in me? I have to admit that I am a little afraid of my feelings for him."

"First of all, there is nothing plain about you inside or out! Why someone hasn't grabbed you up already is beyond me and yes, I can say the same for Nash. There are plenty of available ladies in Spring Valley and I have seen my share of them come parading through the village in pursuit of him, but not a one has captured his heart. I think he put his love life on hold after Avery, but then you appeared out of the blue and well, things just fell into place. You heard what Monty said about us all seeing the chemistry between the two of you…"

I laughed a little. "I think that maybe I came in with the storm and that it is responsible for the so called electricity between us. I only hope my heart won't get broken in the melee. Funny that our names are so much alike… don't you think?"

"What?"

"Avery, Ava…"

"That's just plain silly so quit looking for trouble. Ah, here comes Monty and Evie and they don't have a load of wood. Wonder why and what has brought them back so soon."

Monty informed us that he and Evie had stockpiled the rest of the cut wood and would gather it when need be seeing we still had a three day supply at camp. He was running dangerously low on fuel for the power saw so would have to revert to chopping saplings with the ax if Nash didn't return with help. I asked him if the fuel from the airplane could be used in the saw. He said that it certainly wasn't recommended because it burns too hot but with the right amount of oil added it just might work. He laughed and said he hoped it never came down to that.

We spent a quiet afternoon sitting around the fire. I was asked a lot of questions about my family and I told them a shorter version of what I had disclosed to Nash. We had a simple supper of soup and cheese and crackers. Evie brewed a pot of tea. I usually refused it but decided to be polite and have a cup. Ace made a comment about the Brits and Scots being tea grannies so he wondered why I preferred coffee. I told him that I got my love of coffee from my mother and that she used to dread having tea with the ladies on Fridays. Drats, I had said too much and of course was asked, "What ladies?" I covered by saying that it was an Avanloch family tradition to invite the ladies from the village up for four o'clock tea and tidbits once a week late spring and into autumn. It was adjourned for the winter months. My mother found it tedious but carried on the ritual anyhow. The teas had been suspended indefinitely upon my mother's disappearance and she had chosen not to carry on with them when she returned.

"Sounds like your mother is regarded as some royal queen-like persona by the villagers. Good for her that she has chosen not to carry on the age-old customs. Evie Honey, would you mind getting me a refill? I've been meaning to ask you Ava why you don't have much of an accent. Is it because both of your parents are Canadian?"

I was about to answer Ace when I heard something behind me and I turned around to see Evie standing motionless not far from the front of the plane with Ace's cup dangling from her hand. Not three meters away from her was a magnificent silver wolf staring at her. Without thinking I grabbed the long stick I had been stirring the fire with and slowly stood up. "Don't move anyone; Monty, wolf." I knew his rifle was leaning up against the tent.

I had an adrenaline moment and rushed to stand between Evie and the beast thrusting my burning twig at him. He backed up a meter or so, but now his focus was on me. I was slightly mesmerized by his penetrating yellow eyes. Behind him, twenty meters away, three more wolves stood watching. Monty arrived and shot a warning round into the air. The silver lupine raised his head and let out one eerie howl, turned, and ran into the woods. The rest of the pack followed after him.

"What the hell were you thinking Ava?" Monty demanded.

"Leave her alone Monty; she saved my life. I couldn't move I was so petrified, I couldn't even move or yell." Evie hugged me and said, "Thank-you Ava; you are so brave."

"Nash would have my hide if anything happened to you so don't do anything so reckless again…do you hear me Ava? On the other hand, I'm glad you're on my team." Monty took each of us by an arm and led us back to the fire shaking his head. "Keep an eye on these two will you Sal while I go check to see if those critters actually high-tailed it out of here."

"No, don't go Monty!" Evie sobbed but he ignored her.

"You girls stay put; I'm going with Monty." Sali passed the pistol to Ace and followed Monty.

Ace and I tried to calm Evie down but she continued crying and shivering until they returned assuring us that there was no sign of the wolves. Monty cautioned us that we would have to be more vigilant now that we had been found out. He was pretty confident that they meant us no harm as wolf attacks on man were very rare. He had a few more choice words for me. I think we all slept with one eye open all night. I prayed that Nash was safe and that the sun would come out of hiding tomorrow and chase the clouds away. It didn't.

It was the twenty second of December. Nash had been gone for over two days. We spent the day pretty much the same as we had every other one; cooking, eating, chopping ice from the creek for water, stirring the fire, trying to nap and reading or playing cards and trying to keep warm. We were much more aware of our surroundings however. We had expected to hear the howling of the wolves in the night, but we had not. Darkness was closing in fast and Monty said he may as well light the kerosene heater as it was going to be another cold evening and we may as well be comfortable. Just as he was getting up I heard something off in the distance.

"Did anyone else hear that?" I asked.

Evie shivered and stood up. "Oh no, are they back?"

"No," I said, "listen; it sounds like a vehicle or something."

We all stood up and looked in the direction the droning was coming from. It was getting closer and closer. Suddenly this black and white form appeared at the top of the hill and ran towards us barking up a storm. Right behind her followed a contraption which I took to be a snowmobile. Asta ran straight at me with such a force she almost knocked me over.

"Well, I'll be go to hell, it's Nash!" Monty yelled.

I thought my heart was going to jump out of my chest. He parked the machine a good distance from the fire and waved. "Hello, the camp!"

Monty asked him where the rest of the troops were.

Nash came directly to me and took me in his arms. "I have missed you Ava Lane."

I told him I missed him too. He kissed me quickly and then took my hand and walked me over to stand beside him in front of the fire. He did not let go of my hand.

"Sorry to disappoint you guys, but I am the lone cavalry. The good news is that you'll all be out of this camp by the end of the day. The bad news is that there is still no way to contact the outside world." He consulted his watch. "Just a few hours or so by snowmobile and you'll all be in a Four Star Lodge. It's all ours as it has been closed up for the season but all the amenities of life are there and should sustain us until…well, whenever."

Evie handed him a cup of coffee and asked him if he was hungry. He said he could eat as long as it was fast as he had to get going if we were all going to make it out tonight. He had spent the first night on the trail under a fir tree and had come upon the Lodge early the next morning. He had spent the rest of that day and all of today working on getting the sleds running. His plan was to take Monty back with him, hook up the toboggans so that we could load them with our provisions and return for us two at a time. Monty vetoed that idea immediately.

"Sali can run one of those things better than I can so take her back with you. I'll stay here and wait for the last bus; yeah, that's best if we do it that way."

Monty had looked directly at me when he spoke. Nash was suspicious and asked if something had happened while he was gone. Evie couldn't help herself; she had to tell Nash.

"Ava saved me from getting eaten by a wolf yesterday."

"He wasn't going to eat you Evie." I said calmly.

"Hold on…what's this? What happened here?" Nash demanded.

I tried to speak but he said that perhaps I wasn't the right person to be telling the story as he was pretty sure I would downplay it so he wanted to hear Monty's version. He listened and then asked me if that was the way it happened. I said, "Pretty much."

He asked me if I was scared. He was still holding my hand. His grip tightened a little when I said that I wasn't. He asked me why.

"It all happened so fast that I didn't have time to be scared. It was all over in a minute."

He loosened his grip on me. "Okay; I think you and Ace will be the first two out of here. Are you ready to go Sal? Hopefully, if all goes well with the sleds we'll be back in a little under two hours." He looked at me. "Be ready to go when I get back."

I didn't answer him. Monty asked if he had gotten a sense of where we were in this God forsaken country. Nash said he knew the lodge was on a lake but it was so socked in that he wasn't able to see ten feet in front of him.

"In fact, I may very well have missed it completely if it wasn't for Asta. She had gone ahead of me and was barking up a storm so I followed her thinking she was in danger or had treed something. She was probably an eighth of a mile ahead of me and ignored my calls. I was literally taken by surprise when the fog suddenly lifted and I came upon her sitting on a mound of snow in front of a large building. I swear that dog smiled at me and if she could talk she would have said, "Nash, you dumb ass. Good thing I went left when you were set on going right."

We had a good laugh. I bent down to pet her and tell her what a good girl she was.

"Anyhow, the sign over the front entrance says Blue Heron Lodge. I can honestly say I have never heard the name before. What about you guys?"

Sali, Ace, and Monty shook their heads saying it didn't ring any bells.

Nash continued. "Okay then; I'm sure we will find information on where it is tomorrow. I didn't spend much time inside except to light the wood stove in the kitchen so I could make coffee and heat up some soup. There are two fireplaces, one in the den and one in the lounge. I lit the one in the den in the evening so I would have some place warm to sleep. I didn't snoop through any drawers or anything but I did find that part of the radio phone was missing. I suppose it had been removed for repairs. That's it for now. We better get a move on Sal."

Nash put the leash on Asta and passed it to me saying I had better tie her up for a while.

"Be back as quick as we can. Stay out of mischief will you Ava?"

"What?" I protested throwing my hands up. "I haven't done anything!"

He grinned. "And see that you don't."

I shook my head and told him to get going.

Soon as he and Sali were out of sight we went to work pulling two of the lighter crates off the plane that would fit on the toboggans and then we collected an array of goods to be loaded onto them. It was after seven when Nash and Sali returned. Apparently one of the machines had been acting up and Nash had to make a few adjustments. They circled the plane and pulled up to where we had the crates ready to fit onto the toboggans. We loaded them and the guys tied them down with rope. Nash asked me if I was ready. I told him Evie was going and that I was staying with Monty.

"Why? I want you out of here too Evie but I think that Ava is better qualified to care for Ace. The trip will probably be very hard on him." He scrutinised our faces suspecting that something had happened since he had been gone. "Okay, what is it?"

"It's me Nash." Evie blubbered. "We heard them and I panicked."

"The wolves are back, is that it? How close are they, did anyone see them?" Nash questioned.

"They aren't close Nash but for her state of mind we think Evie should be the one to go. Ava is calm, cool and collected and no offense to Evie, but it's Ava I prefer to have waiting with me."

"Yeah, that's what I am afraid of. Tell you what Monty, I'll stay behind and you take Ace and Evie can ride with Sali, okay? There, that settles that." Nash was pretty sure he had the solution.

Monty disagreed. "Not so fast there Buddy. I know next to nothing about those contraptions and if one acts up again I haven't a clue as how to fix them. Ava and I are perfectly fine here so get on your horse and ride, time's a wasting."

"Why do I get the feeling that you two had this all planned out right from the start?"

"I am not unfamiliar with wildlife Nash. There have been no wolves in Scotland for centuries and the only bear are in captivity, but we do have wild cats, red fox and coyotes. I know wolves are a different breed and you can be assured that I will keep my distance if any come calling."

"Oh, like you did before?"

"Let's get Ace on board okay? You can rest easy Nash, Monty has everything under control and Evie is perfectly capable of tending to Ace, so no worries."

"I didn't get much of a say in this Nash. I volunteered to stay behind and let the two girls go but I am afraid they all conspired against me. Never thought Monty would choose a girl over me but he and Ava are two of a kind…stubborn." Ace grumbled.

Sali started her machine and took off. Ace suggested to Monty to see if there was any life left in the plane's batteries and to turn them on if there was because we wouldn't be needing them anymore. Nash told me to mind Monty.

"Yes sir!" I saluted him. "You know Nash, the wolves don't want me…I am not Little Red Riding Hood." I said cheekily.

He shook his head and said. "Very funny Ava, very funny!"

I backed up and waved them off.

Monty and I quickly gathered what was left of the food stuff and our personal belongings for the last trip. I perked a pot of coffee hoping it would help us stay alert. A bitter wind had rolled in and we decided to wait in the tent because no one had thought to shut the heater off so it was nice and toasty inside. Monty said he would shut it off a half hour before we expected Nash back so that it could cool enough to store in the plane. I took Asta in and she curled up on my sleeping bag and was snoring in no time. I hadn't spent any time alone with Monty and he had never let anything slip about his personal life so I decided that I had the perfect opportunity to do so since we were alone. I had sensed something going on between him and Evie and I didn't want her to get hurt if he had someone waiting for him. He laughed when I asked him.

"Afraid not Ava; I gave women up a long time ago."

"I don't believe that for one minute, I see the way you look at Evie. You can't deny that you have eyes for her?"

"I think she's a delicate flower, but alas, not one that belongs in my bouquet."

He looked away and I thought that was a very odd thing for a man to say. I was about to say something when he surprised me and sat down beside me and continued talking.

"Two failed marriages and one son that doesn't even acknowledge that I am alive, so believe me when I say I am not worthy of someone like Evie. I am not in the market for romance and I trust that I can count on you to set her straight on my wicked ways. I enjoy her company but that's as far as it goes, understand?"

"Your wicked ways? You are going to have to convince me that any exists."

"Oh, they exist all right. I got my wings flying commercially and graduated to overseas passenger flights. Worked for three different airlines and was fired from them all due to my drinking and gambling and romancing of female employees. I knew Ace from flight school; he was one of the instructors so we go way back. Hadn't seen or heard from him for years and then out of the blue he shows up at my run-down apartment door and has a proposition for me. Apparently he had heard from my first wife who was a friend of his wife's that I was on the skids. I was too proud to accept help but he continued to harass me until I caved and here I am, seven years later, no better and no worse for wear. So what do you think Ava Lane… am I worthy of such a refined lady like Evie?"

"She sees exactly what I see and that is a hard-working, intelligent and caring man. We all have our little crosses to bear and I think you have worn yours long enough. It's time to move on. Yesterday is dead and buried and tomorrow is uncertain. Today is for the living and you are definitely in that category. You don't have to make any promises you know, but why not see where things go. Just be honest with yourself and with her."

"Well aren't you the advocate of romantic advice? Just because you and Nash have hit it off doesn't mean the future bodes well for me and Evie."

"Oh Monty, I fear I am expecting too much. I am a novice at affairs of my own heart. I have watched my own mother who has an undying love for my father make horrible mistakes. Her choices have cost her dearly and for twenty years she had too much pride to make amends. They say pride goes before a fall and I have seen her fall time and time again, but she picks herself up and carries on. Now she has my father to lean on but I fear there will always be some force trying to pull them apart and I am terrified that love will not be able to save them one day. Oh, sorry Monty; I didn't mean to get so melancholic."

Monty reached over and patted my hand. "You certainly worked yourself into a state Ava. I imagine it's because you think they believe you are dead…is that it?"

I shivered. "I don't know Monty; something just came over me. Forgive me for going all maudlin. I started off wanting to tell you that I have no expectations for me and Nash…"

"Like hell you don't! You can't kid a kidder. I was there at the get-go remember? The two of you are smitten and I, for one, am going to enjoy the fireworks."

"How did this end up being about me? I thought we were talking about you?"

"We were Ava darlin but we're through talking about me. You just admit to ole Monty that you're in over your head with Nash man and then I am going to whoop you at a game of crib."

"Well you can try but I doubt that you will succeed and yes, I will admit that Nash sets my heart aflutter. I've only known him for a few days but he is exactly the kind of man I want to spend the rest of my life with and if you tell him that then I am going to have to blab to Evie. He's a little bossy though don't you think?"

"Nash, bossy, whatever gave you that idea? I don't have to tell him how you feel because it's written all over your face. Now, shuffle up and cut the cards."

We didn't hear the snowmobiles until they were right outside the tent. Monty jumped up swearing because he had forgotten to turn the kerosene heater off. He grabbed his coat and went out apologising to Nash who said it didn't matter and where was I. Monty said that I was getting dressed. I was bent over pulling my mukluks on when Nash burst in.

"Monty said you were getting dressed…why were you undressed Ava?"

His words caught me completely by surprise. "What?"

"You heard me, why were you undressed?" His tone was accusatory.

"What the hell are you insinuating?" I demanded. "Never mind, it doesn't matter." I brushed past him grabbing my coat and mittens.

He grabbed my arm. "I'm sorry Ava, I was out of line. I didn't mean anything…"

"Like hell you didn't! Let go of me please."

He did and I walked out and stood next to Sali. Monty had the sleds already loaded and Nash helped him tie the load down. Sali asked if Monty could drive because her arms were tired.

"I'll ride with you Monty because I don't want to ride with Nash." I said hotly.

"She doesn't mean that guys. Take off; we'll be right behind you." Nash promised.

"Quit telling me what I can do and what I can't! I don't want to be around you right now!"

"Whatever you two are quarreling about, we don't want any part of it. Come on Sal, let's go." Monty started the machine and they took off.

"I guess I'm stuck with you." I climbed on the back of the snowmobile and crossed my arms and said, "Let's go."

"You don't really mind being stuck with me do you?" Nash asked teasingly.

"Yes, as a matter of fact I do. You are bossy and boorish. You make up your mind about things without even considering that you may not be right. I think you have been living up in the sticks too long. You do not own me Colton Nash and on the back of this machine is the closest to me you will ever get!"

He sat down in front of me and told me that I was going to have to hold on to him. I said I did not. He got up and sat down facing me. "Well Honey, it's for your own safety."

There was still enough light from the dying fire that I could see his face. I wanted to wipe that grin right off of it. "Don't call me honey and I will take my chances that I won't fall off."

"You know you like me calling you honey, but if you prefer that I call you darlin then I will."

"You're a male chauvinist…" I did not get to finish because he pulled me into his arms and kissed me until I couldn't breathe. I gasped. "What was that for?"

"I have wanted to do that since the day we met so I just thought this was the perfect opportunity…do you object?"

"Yes, as a matter of fact I do."

"You didn't like it then?"

"I didn't say that, but you should ask a girl's permission first."

"Oh, is that how they do it in Scotland? Sorry, I'm not up on my foreign kissing policies. May I kiss you, pretty please Miss Lane?" He was playing with me and I may as well play along.

"Well, you have already taken me into your bed on our first date and I can most definitely assure you that that is against our laws so I guess you may as well kiss me again."

He did and I obliged him. He laughed and said that he had finally met his match and that if I thought that he had already taken me to bed then I was in for one big surprise. He said that we were in for one hell of a ride. I didn't think he meant just the ride down the hill.

CHAPTER 5

Sanctuary

It was a very long and cold trip. It took all of my strength to unfold myself from the hard seat. Nash took hold of me and led me into the lodge. Monty met us at the door and steered me towards a chair. Nash asked the girls to look after me while he unloaded the cargo. Evie handed me a cup of hot chocolate and Sali took my boots off and rubbed my feet. She had made the trip back and forth three times and barely had time to warm up herself and yet she was seeing to me. I asked how she did it. She smiled up at me and said it was nothing but she was certainly glad that Nash and I had settled our lover's quarrel.

Evie took a kettle of water off the stove and suggested that I follow her into the den. I was so fatigued that I didn't even take notice of any of my surroundings. I found Ace half asleep reclined in what looked like a very comfortable chair. I asked him how he had made out and if he was in any pain. He said the trip had jarred him up pretty bad but Evie had given him a "happy" pill and he had been in "La La Land" for a while now. I didn't like the sound of that thinking that he may have become dependent on the meds but I was too tired to give it too much thought.

Evie gave me a warm pair of pyjamas, a present that had been meant for her sister no doubt, and a pair of knitted slippers. She directed me into the bathroom and poured the warm water into the sink so I could wash up. There was a pail of water on the floor for the toilet which was actually melted snow because the faucet in the kitchen only yielded a drip now and then. I had to walk over two mattresses and quilts on the den's floor as I had entered…more of Evie's work I presumed. She said she had been here for hours and wanted everything to be ready for the rest of us because she had done so little so far. I hugged her and told her that wasn't so. I threw my wet, dirty clothes into the hamper she had supplied and washed quickly. The pyjamas were deliciously comforting. I sat down on the chesterfield planning on staying awake until Nash was finished and I could join him wherever. My body betrayed me and soon I was fully reclined with my head resting on a tiny soft pillow. I felt someone tucking a quilt around me. I sighed as I recognised the hands touching me. I looked up into Nash's dark brown eyes and reached out to him uttering his name.

"Tomorrow my darling, tomorrow; sleep peacefully now." He kissed me on the forehead and I drifted off into dream land.

I awoke the next morning to giggling. I pulled myself up and peered over the back of the chesterfield to find Sali and Evie at the bottom of the stairs attempting to pull one of the mattresses up the stairs. I slipped into the housecoat that Evie had provided me with last night and went out to help them. An extra pair of hands was not much help but we managed to get it up and unto the bed that was in the bedroom at the top of the stairs. Apparently it was Nash's room. I was informed that there were seven bedrooms and that three of them were to the right of Nash's room. I had been assigned room number three which was right next to his. Evie showed me that there was an adjoining door between his and my room…just in case we wanted to visit each other. She tried not to chuckle.

"Come and look Ava." She said as she walked over to a window. "You have a perfect view of the lake from both your windows as do Sali and I. We figured that we girls would appreciate the vista more than the guys. There is a huge linen closet between your room and Sali's and mine. I hope you don't mind that we took the liberty of assigning rooms but we wanted to get everyone's possessions in place.

Are you okay with the arrangements because you can change rooms if you are not happy?"

"It suits me just fine. You gals must have been up for hours if you have already found and sorted out our belongings. I wish that I had more than one change of clothes but who knew I would need more. Thank-you again for sharing your wardrobe with me Evie. I know these pyjamas were a gift for your sister so I am in debt to you once again."

"Think nothing of it. I am only too happy to share and do something for you after all you have done for me…especially the wolf thing."

I told her we were a team and helping each other was what it was all about. I asked where the guys were. Sali said that they had left Ace in the kitchen drinking coffee and that Monty and Nash were in the basement figuring out the hot water system. I left them putting the sheets and blankets back on Nash's bed saying that I would join Ace. I hoped it would be warmer in the kitchen than it was upstairs. I was on my second cup of coffee when Nash emerged from the basement. His smile sent my heart aflutter as usual.

"Good morning Sunshine! How are you this fine morning?" He asked.

"I am afraid I have overslept as everyone else is already hard at work."

"Speak for yourself young lady." Ace complained. "I am still good for nothing except causing more work for everyone else."

"Cheer up Acerman; you'll be good as new in a few days, won't he Ava? Believe me, I wish it was you and not me who had to climb that icy hill and dig out the water line. Well, I best quit bellyaching about it and get on with it." Nash said unenthusiastically.

I offered to make him and Monty breakfast but he declined saying they would eat when they got back. He gave me a peck on the cheek and told Ace not to be too hard on us girls. I waited a second and then followed him. He turned when he heard me behind him.

"Is that all I get…just a peck on the cheek?"

He grabbed my hand and shone the flashlight on the steps in front of me. "Please be careful; I don't want you falling."

He took me in his arms at the bottom of the stairs and told me that he had a lot more in store for me and that he would rather be spending the day with me than with his boss. The only light was from two lanterns hanging from the ceiling rafters as there was none getting through the windows as the snow was covering them. Monty emerged from behind the furnace brandishing a very large wrench.

"YOUR boss, that'll be the day! I think Ava and I are in agreement that you are the boss Nashman, aren't we Ava?"

I laughed a little. "Well, at least we will let him think he is. Now through which of these many doors are the pantries? Ace is hungry and I would like to see if they contain anything that can be used for breakfast. We will check them out more thoroughly later and sort out the supplies we brought down from the camp."

Nash said he only glanced in them so I best see for myself. He opened the door to the first one for me and it contained an array of cereals and canned articles. I chose a box of corn flakes and a large tin of peaches. Nash took them from me and escorted me back up the stairs amidst my protests that I was perfectly capable of carrying them myself. Monty laughed and said that I had better just let Nash have his way. I intended to. He set the goods on the kitchen table and said he would be back as soon as possible. His kiss was full of promises as was mine.

After breakfast Sali took Ace out to the front porch for a cigarette while Evie and I cleaned up. I suggested to her that we make bread. She asked me if I knew how.

"How hard could it be? Let's look through those books." I answered pointing to a shelf that housed a dozen or so more cookbooks.

We found what seemed to be an easy recipe and set off to collect the ingredients from the basement pantry taking pen and paper with us as we would need to document everything that we borrowed. Hopefully there would be enough provisions along with Sali's cache to sustain us until we were found and then we would replace all the "goods" that had kept us alive. We decided to wait for Sali to do a complete inventory.

We mixed up the dough and took turns kneading it until it was pliant and shiny like the recipe said. We placed it back in the big glass bowl and were about to set it in the warming oven above the stove to rise when Sali came into the kitchen. She looked at it and said it looked just like her husband's bread and congratulated us for our efforts.

I laughed. "Don't be too quick to judge Sal; it's not actually bread yet. If it does turn out, I am sorry to say that there is only enough yeast for two more batches."

"We can always make sourdough you know Dumpling." She suggested.

I asked her how we did that and she said she hadn't a clue but there must be a recipe for it in one of the books. There was. After reading several recipes over and over we decided on one and concluded that it was going to be a long drawn out procedure and we had best get to starting it right away. Evie made up a schedule for the "feeding" of the sourdough.

We retreated to the basement pantries once more and took stock of all the food stuffs. We concluded that we could survive quite nicely combining Sali's and the lodge's supplies for a month or two. Hopefully, we would be out of here long before that! Of course there was no meat, but we had turkeys and lots of tuna, four tinned hams and several cans of salmon, which we would keep and use as a treat. I didn't know much about the preservation of food, but I was sure the cheese would keep for quite some time. We would have to freeze the butter and maybe even the milk. I had no idea what to do about the eggs. Evie wondered if we could crack them and freeze also. Nash had said that he would get the generator going so that the deep freeze could be started. The frozen turkeys were already sitting in the freezer and keeping the butter and milk cold. Christmas was only two days away so we took one of the turkeys upstairs to thaw out. I gathered the last loaf of pumpernickel bread, a block of cheese and a large tin of chicken noddle soup to make for lunch. Supper would be spaghetti and tomato sauce and hopefully, fresh bread. We would dine like kings.

I was alone in the kitchen stirring the soup and flipping the grilled cheese sandwiches when I felt a presence behind me. I had just yelled to Sali to collect Ace and Evie as lunch was almost ready so I expected it was one of them but the warm breath on the back of my neck told me it was not. I turned knowing full well that it was Nash.

"How did you get in here without me hearing you?" I asked pretending to be startled.

"I think you were preoccupied thinking about me weren't you?" Nash asked teasingly.

I let him kiss me. "Do you think I have had nothing better to do all morning?"

"By the smell of this kitchen I would say you have been very busy."

"She has." Evie said entering through the swinging door that led to the dining room. "I hope I am not intruding but we were summoned."

"You are not intruding Evie. Suppose you fill me in on what this one has been up to?" Nash suggested.

"To start with, she made bread."

"Let me correct Evie…**we** made bread, she and me, and I had no more of an idea of what we were doing than she did, but here it is." I took the tea towel off the raised loaves and showed him. "What do you think? Half an hour more and it will be ready for baking."

"I think you city girls are amazing." Nash answered taking a whiff of the unbaked bread.

"Where is Monty? You two must be famished?" Evie asked.

"He's adjusting the water flow downstairs." Nash reached under the sink and turned the water shut-off valve on and then he slowly opened the tap. A brown sputtering trickle erupted. He let it run until it ran clear. "There you go girls, no more melting snow. If you will excuse me, I will see to the rest of the house."

"What about lunch?" I inquired.

"First things first…I trust you'll keep mine warm."

He was gone before I could respond. I shook my head. "Men!"

"What's that you say Missy? Is he giving you trouble already?" Ace said as he settled into a chair at the table.

"Nothing I can't handle." I assured him.

He smirked and said that he sure as hell hoped I could.

I really didn't see Nash again for more than a few minutes until supper. He had wolfed down his lunch, thanked me with a smile and left to track Monty down. It seemed as everything around the lodge was in disrepair and the power plant was no exception. They had aspirations of getting it running before days end. I sighed as he walked out the door. Ace had gone to have a rest and Sali and Evie were in the basement still sorting things out. I put the five loafs of bread in the oven and then washed my hair with hot water from the reservoir. I collected my journal from my meager belongings that Evie had moved upstairs and recorded the events of the last few days. I ended with: *I am anticipating that Nash and I will be together tonight. I am not nervous. I only hope that I am woman enough for him.*

The bread was delicious. We went through one whole loaf eating it with the spaghetti and with strawberry jam for dessert. We sat around the table and talked for an hour or so. Ace had spent a better part of the day in the lodge's office rummaging through drawers trying to find answers as to where we were. He spread out a large map on the table that outlined the Spatsizi Plateau Wilderness and pointed to a red dot in the middle of the plain.

"Apparently, this is where we are. This lodge is situated somewhere in the vicinity of Bob Quinn Lake Any relation to you Ava?"

I said I doubted it but really had no clue and he continued "There are several other lakes around so that this lodge could be on any one of them but considering it is called Uncle Bob's Cabin, I'm assuming it is Bob Quinn Lake."

Evie said she thought Nash had told us it was called Blue Heron Lodge.

"Apparently, it has two names. The title is registered in the names of Cicily and Al Jones of New Westminster B.C. Besides ten years of record books of guests I have not uncovered any other useful information. Mind you, I have not tackled the file cabinets yet. The last entry into a daybook reads: November 11, 1983, 10:A.M. Time to get out of here. First snow last night. Radioed for Denver to pick us up this a.m. We were hoping we were good until end of month but weather forcing us out. Everything locked up and secured, winterized. Date of return unknown at this time. Al taking radio phone as it is in need of an overhaul. Cicily Jones.

"So it appears as if you were right Monty; we are definitely somewhere in the vicinity of the park and Skeena Valley. Sorry people but I very much doubt if this area has even been considered as a search route. If we are indeed here and this map suggests that we are, then it may very well be months before help arrives. Anything is possible though and perhaps when the weather clears we will discover that we are in a flight path of sorts."

"Thanks for that Ace. At least we have a clue as to our whereabouts now, not that it makes much difference. I do not know this area but have thought of exploring it several times and now it seems as though we are in the heart of it." Nash looked at me. "We may have to make our supplies last longer than expected. You and the girls would know more about that."

"Yes, a more thorough inventory is needed and we'll get on that after Christmas. I am not in the least bit worried though and we all may be a few pounds lighter when we get out of here. I'm pretty sure that none of us are going to starve to death."

"We are not. There is game in the hills and fish in the lake and like you said Ava, after Christmas is soon enough to take stock. Shall we see if we can get anything on the radio or television?" Monty suggested.

The guys had managed to get the generator started so we were enjoying the glow from the dining room chandelier while the freezer was doing its job downstairs. The batteries in the radio were all dead and we had not found any more but now we could plug it in and get some news. The only station we could get was the Canadian Broadcast Company, and it was from Vancouver. There was no weather information for the area that the men thought we were in. There was a satellite dish that brought signal in to the television but it seemed to be on the frizz, so no help there. The guys said they would see to it tomorrow. It didn't really matter anyhow as all we had to do was look outside and we could predict our own weather.

Nash and I walked Ace to his recliner in the den. I hadn't checked on his bandages yet and so did so while Nash went upstairs to clean up. I was most pleased that Ace's dressings were still all in place and that he required no pain medication. He was still experiencing some discomfort but insisted that he could deal with it. I walked with him back to the dining room table where Monty was waiting for the girls to finish the clean-up so they could play cards. I said I was going to check on Nash. Monty asked me as I was heading up the stairs if we were coming back down to join them. I turned and smiled ever so slightly. Ace laughed and told Monty to quit teasing me. I knocked lightly on Nash's open door. He peered at me from around the corner of the bathroom door. Half his face was shaven and the other half was covered in shaving cream.

"Hi, may I come in?" I asked coyly.

"Please do, and perhaps you can help me with these tough whiskers?"

"Oh no," I said, "straight razors scare me." I sat on the edge of the bed. "Do you mind if I watch you though?"

"Certainly not; did you like to watch your father shave?"

"No, I never grew up with him."

Nash had stripped down to his waist and the suspenders he had been wearing were hanging off his waist. He was quite muscular and somewhat tanned. I knew I was staring but I couldn't take my eyes off his half naked body. He walked over towards me.

"I'm sorry Ava; forgive me for bringing up which is probably a painful time for you."

"No need to apologise Nash, I am good with it all now."

"Are you sure you don't want to take a swipe at me with the razor?" He asked suggestively.

I shook my head and stood up saying that I should get going. He asked me where I was going and I replied, "Just next door."

"Good. There's a little warm water left in the kettle if you would like it."

I thanked him. He said he had turned a lamp on for me in my room. I smiled and thanked him again. He said he had found some old but clean clothes in one of the drawers that had been left behind or perhaps belonged to the owner of the lodge. They were a little on the large size but would do for tonight. I told him that I had also discovered articles of ladies clothing in the closet next door too but unfortunately, except for several oversized sweaters they were for somebody a lot smaller than me. He told me he would see me shortly as soon as he finished washing. I told him not to wash too much of the "woodsy" smell off.

"Ah, so you like me a little primeval? No Old Spice for you then Darlin?"

I shook my head. Suddenly, I was very anxious and scurried off through the connecting door.

I tossed my clothes onto the bathroom floor and quickly washed my body from top to bottom. I shivered as I donned my three quarter length cotton nightgown. I looked at myself in the vanity mirror. "Are you sure you want to do this Ava Lane? You know it could quite possibly be more than you can handle and though you think you are in love with him, he may not be in love with you. Then what will you do stranded out here in the wilderness with a man who may rebuff you? How will you…" I closed the door on the disapproving lovelorn in the mirror and sat down at the vanity and ran the brush through my hair thankful that I had chosen to wash it earlier.

Nash came up behind me and took the brush from my hand. "It's been a long time since I have brushed a ladies hair Ava. Will you do me the honor?"

I wondered how many ladies tresses he had brushed. He answered without me having to speculate. "I guess I was about six or seven and I was jealous that my sister always got to brush my mother's hair so I asked her if I could and she said that she didn't see why not. I grew out of wanting to do so shortly and so did my sister and I have never even thought about it again until just now."

I placed my hand over his. "Rosy and I use to brush our mother's hair also but she was usually the one brushing our hair. Are you close to your sister Nash?"

"I only see her and the family two or three times a year. We keep in touch through the mail. Her name is Ruby. She's almost three years older so she has always considered herself the boss of me. She married when she was eighteen to her school sweetheart. They have two children and live in Quesnel. I trust they will be up to visit this summer."

"That's nice Nash. We haven't compared notes about Quesnel yet have we?"

"No we haven't Sweetie and we are not going to tonight. You are shivering and I think we best get you into bed."

He helped me up and I slid under the covers grumbling that the sheets were colder than the sleeping bag ever was up the mountain. Nash turned the lamp down low and slid in beside me.

"And that is what I am for my dearest…to keep you warm."

I slid willingly into his arms and knew that there was no other place I would rather be in the whole wide world. He rubbed my arms and my back just as he had done that first night which now seemed so long ago.

"I don't mind telling you that this has been the longest day of my life Ava."

"You needn't have worked so hard Nash. We did without running water and central heat for a week so just having a roof over our heads was enough for a few days." I murmured softly.

"That's not what I meant Honey. I am accustomed to hard work and long days because that is my life and I don't have much to look forward to at days end, but I did today. Every time I saw you I anticipated being alone with you and holding you in my arms and kissing you and laying with you like this and hoping that you felt the same way. Do you Ava; do you feel the same way…do you want to be with me?"

"I do Nash and I think it's time you kissed me like you did the other night."

"I'm warning you Ava…if I start kissing you I don't think I'm going to be able to stop."

"And that is what I am counting on." I said surrendering my lips and my body to him.

We lay together for a very long time just holding hands and breathing. Finally Nash broke the silence and asked me if I was all right. I told him that I had never been more all right ever in my life before.

"I swear I heard music Ava or maybe it was just my heart singing."

I laughed. "Do you know how corny that sounds Nash?"

He laughed too. "Did those words actually come out of my mouth? Look what you have done to me Ava Lane! It's at a time like this when a guy could really use a cigarette, but I promised you I wouldn't smoke anymore and I won't."

"I don't mind if you smoke Nash and you never promised me that you wouldn't. You must have me mixed up with one of your other women."

"Believe me Sweetie; I would never have made that promise to anyone else." He said candidly.

"Not even to Avery?" I asked.

"I see someone has been talking to you; was it Sali and what did she have to say?"

"Not much. I don't think she liked her very much."

Nash snickered. "That is an understatement if I ever heard one."

"Tell me about her Nash and all your other lady friends."

"What…now? You want me to tell you about my disastrous relationships and my so-called engagement…why, why now?"

"Why not; we are not doing anything else right now and I think we are both too wound up to sleep. You don't have anything to hide do you?"

"We could be doing something else." He answered squeezing my hand. "But no, I do not have anything to hide. I'm afraid you will find my non-existent love life very boring, but I'll confess all on one condition."

"What's that Nash?"

"That you do me the same courtesy."

"Well that will take all of two minutes." I had already mentioned my short engagement to Randy before so there wasn't much more to tell. I told him about me meeting Cam at my parent's wedding and thought that something might develop there. He worked in northern Canada and I lived in Scotland so it was only a relationship on paper. We had plans to meet up that autumn, but my mother went missing and that was the end of that. "I'm pretty much a relationship virgin Nash so if this thing between us turns into something more than what it already is, I'm probably going to make a lot of mistakes along the way."

"No more than me Honey, but we will find our way together. I told you we were in for one hell of a ride didn't I? That was all wishful thinking, but now I know it's a reality and I hope you are willing to see how far we can take it. What do you say?"

"Maybe I should wait to answer that after I have heard about all the women in your life. Maybe you are too much of a playboy for the likes of this innocent Scottish lass…"

He laughed. "I'm going to prove how wrong you are about that, and maybe you **were** innocent, but I think we can remove that adjective from your resume now."

I smacked him playfully and told him to get on with his story.

"If I must…my very first girlfriend was my first grade teacher. Stop laughing Ava; it's true."

I apologised and told him to continue.

"Sadly, she did not return my affections and preferred those of a much older man, the principal, who just happened to be her husband. I walked to school and had play dates with the little girl next door; I think her name was Betty. She moved away so nothing ever developed between us. Then in fourth grade…"

"Nash," I interrupted, "could we skip the school years?"

"I thought you wanted to hear everything."

"I will be asleep by the time you reach puberty; just get to the juicy stuff." I pleaded.

"Oh, so you just want to hear about my sexual conquests?"

"No, I am not into voyeurism. I just want to know about the women you loved."

"Oh well then, that narrows the field. I guess I mistook sex for love when I was sixteen… you know how that is…all of a sudden you're not interested in sports or hanging out with the guys anymore because you have suddenly developed this mysterious feeling in your loins when you are around the opposite sex?"

"No, I don't know about that Nash."

"Lucky for you because it was a pretty embarrassing time. So I had a few girlfriends but nothing serious ever developed and I left home for college the summer after I graduated. Some of those gals still live in Quesnel so I have run into them a time or two. They are either divorced or have some agenda so I pretty much avoid that scene. That's about it."

"I don't think so; there must have been others after your teenage years and before Avery, someone else who you promised to stop smoking for?"

Nash was playing with my fingers. "Believe me, there was no one I cared that much about. Avery had a pack and a half a day habit so it surely wasn't her. No, it was you Ava and if I didn't tell you, I meant to."

"Okay, I believe you...now what happened with you and Avery?"

"Why is it so important to you?"

"I want to know what I am up against."

"I thought I told you there had been no one in my life for over three years so you are not up against anyone or anything. My God Ava, not one woman I have ever known could hold a candle to you!"

"Avery must have had some attributes...enough for you to ask her to be your wife. Surely you wouldn't marry someone you didn't love?"

"Well I didn't marry her did I and since you are dying to know I will tell you why I didn't. I will make this short. I met her through friends that I stay with when I am in Vancouver. We saw each other off and on during the winters over a period of three years. I usually come "out" from December to the end of March spending a month with my family, one or two at the coast and a few weeks in some tropical country."

"Is that why you are so tanned Nash? Have you just returned from a holiday in paradise?"

"Let me make this clear Ava; the north country, this north country is my paradise. I could not survive for very long in the tropics. But to answer your question, yes I was on a little vacation with a couple of buddies in Belize. It was not my idea to get married. Avery thought it was a good idea because neither one of us was getting any younger, and if we wanted to have a family then we should tie the knot so we became engaged. I am not sure if at any time love even entered the picture. I'm not even sure if I know what the word means. Anyhow,

I took her home to meet my family and that was a huge mistake. My mother and sister could barely tolerate her. She considered Quesnel a hick town and said I was lucky to have escaped it. I asked her where she saw us living when we got married and she said, "The city, of course." Apparently she wanted me to get a white collar job, buy a house and become domesticated. Reluctantly she agreed to come to Akemantack and see where I lived and worked. She grumbled from the minute we left the airport until we landed. Then there was the twenty mile ride from Spring Valley to my house. It was early April so the road was rough and muddy and not only that, she had to ride in a jeep! We stopped at Sali's parents store where everyone was gathered awaiting our arrival. They had planned a big pot-luck welcoming supper but she pretended to be sick and made me take her to my "cabin" as she called it. I took her into the house and showed her the spare bedroom, dropped her luggage at her feet and told her not to bother unpacking because I'd be taking her back to Spring Valley the next morning and she could await there for the next flight out. I went back to the party with "my heathen friends" as she called them. It took all I had not to slap her silly. And that is it Ava…I dropped her at the airport knowing full well that she was going to have to spend the night because there wasn't a flight out until the next day. I gave her the taxi's phone number, asked for my ring back and told her to have a nice life. That was the last I ever saw of her. What in the hell had I ever seen in her? Don't ask me if I still ask myself that question because I never think of her at all. No one can insult my friends, my dog, my family or my home, do you understand that Ava?"

I rolled away from him because I was laughing so hard that I thought my bladder was going to burst. I grabbed my nightgown off the floor and stumbled half blind into the bathroom.

"Ava," Nash yelled at me, "Get back here!"

"Do you mind if I pee?" I yelled back at him. "Turn the lamp on please." I emerged from the bathroom still giggling and crawled back into bed.

"You thought that was funny did you? Get over here you wench." He pulled me into his arms.

"Yes, Kemosabe."

"You're a little too sassy for your own britches you know that?"

"What do you want to do about it?" I asked running my hands through the hair on his chest.

"If you take off this stupid nightdress, I will show you."

I was cold. I rolled over to put my arms around Nash but he wasn't there. "Oh no," I moaned, "oh no!" I pulled the covers over my head.

"What's wrong Ava? Did you have a bad dream?" Nash appeared out of nowhere pulling back the blankets.

"No, I woke up and you were gone."

"Just where did you think I had gone?" He inquired snuggling in beside me.

"I don't know…in your room next door, downstairs, I don't know."

"Nature calls you know and I am right where I want to be. I should be up but it's fairly warm in here so I guess Monty had already stoked up the furnace. I want to talk to you anyhow; are you up to a little early morning chat?"

"How early is it?"

"Five thirty four to be exact," he said checking his watch, "too early for you?"

"That depends on what the subject is and if it can wait until I am a little more conscious." I answered wanting so much to close my eyes and go back to sleep.

"Okay," he kissed me on the cheek and rolled away from me, "go back to sleep. It isn't important anyway. I just wanted to tell you that I love you."

His feet were already on the floor. "Where do you think you are going Colton Nash?" I said grabbing at him. "You can't just tell a girl that you love her and then leave?"

He turned the lamp on and turned to look at me. "Why not?"

"Because you didn't give me a chance at rebuttal?"

"You want to argue the fact that I love you? I will inform you young lady that I have been falling in love with you from the first moment I saw you. I told you last night that I didn't know what love was; well, you have proven me wrong. I've been watching you sleep for the longest time and I wanted so badly to wake you up and kiss you and tell you that I loved you, but I talked myself out of it, or at least I thought I had. Have I miss-spoken Ava? Is it too soon?"

My eyes were very moist and my lower lip was quivering. "Rebuttal was the wrong word. What I want to say is that we should discuss it…I mean… I don't know what I mean. You have got me all flustered." I couldn't stop the tears.

"Hey, hey Baby; I'm sorry, I just couldn't help myself. It's too soon I know…"

"You big boob," I said crawling out of bed and unto his lap.

"Woman, have you no shame? Suppose someone were to walk in and see this naked lady attacking me…" Nash laughed holding on to be so I wouldn't fall unto the floor.

"I don't care!" I said kissing him. "You love me Nash, you really love me?"

"Yeah, I am pretty sure I do."

"I love you too Nash. I have loved you from the first time our eyes locked and our hands touched and you spoke my name. I knew I was head over heels in love with you but I knew I wasn't in your league…"

"Hold on a minute there Lassie, there is no league and if there was, you would be leading the pack! No girl, it's just you and me and this crazy thing called love. I want to take it as far as we can. I'm asking you again, are you up for the ride?"

"I am Nash, I am!"

We kissed until neither of us could breathe and then we fell backwards unto the bed. Nash said to hell with the fires, we would make our own.

Twelve hours later my new life was about to come crashing down on me.

The day started out quite wonderful. It was the day before Christmas. Nash and I were the last ones up and we had to endure a few rounds of lively teasing before we were even offered coffee.

I was somewhat embarrassed but managed to smile through it all. After a quick breakfast of cereal and horrible powdered orange juice, Monty and Nash set out to find out what the problem was with the satellite dish. Sali took Ace out to the front porch for a cigarette which left Evie and I alone. She asked if we could make shortbread. I asked her if she knew how. She laughed.

"How hard could it be?"

I guess that was going to be our catch phrase. Shortbread required butter and Evie felt guilty about using a whole pound of butter. We still had lots and it was Christmas, so why not? The first batch almost burnt because we had made the cut-outs too thin and the oven was too hot. We rolled the dough thicker and waited for the oven to cool down before baking the rest. I should say I waited as Evie had left me to join Sali in making Christmas decorations. Nash had popped his head in the door an hour earlier and said that he and Monty were going tree shopping. I joined the girls after I had collected supper ingredients from the basement and the last batch of shortbread was done.

Evie asked if the guys were back and I told her I hadn't seen them if they were.

"The forest is full of trees, so what's taking them so long?"

"They will be here when they get here Evie. I'm sure they didn't want to cut anything down that was close to the lodge and some-times a small tree is hard to find." I sat down at one end of the large dining room table which was covered in craft supplies that Evie had brought for her nieces. There was sparkly kids' jewellery making kits, construction paper, crayons, stickers and everything else under the sun that would keep a youngster busy let alone grown women. She was attaching colorful paper chains together.

Sali was stringing some of her moccasin beads onto thin threads. She said she guessed this was the reason that she had stocked up on beading materials. My job was to create a top for the tree. I chose to construct a star out of some cardboard I had found in the basement. I colored it bright yellow and told the girls that I was going to go and pop some popcorn so that I could make holiday balls with it and get the casserole ready for supper. I was just about to "feed" the sourdough when I heard someone rapping on the back door and a "Ho, ho, ho!"

I wiped my hands on my apron and opened the door. "Sorry, but we are not in the market for any wares that you are peddling Sir."

"Can I not interest you in an exquisite little orphaned tree my lady? It has no home and would like to spend the holiday in a nice warm house with some very nice people." Nash said in a little boy's voice. "It promises not to shed."

I was momentarily stunned when he called me "my lady" but recovered quickly. "Well then, that is a different story and I think it will look quite lovely in the lounge."

Nash bent down and kissed me. "God, you taste good but not half as good as you smell."

I laughed. "I think that is Evie's shortbread you smell, or on the other hand, it could be fermenting sourdough. Where is Monty? Evie would not like it one bit if you lost him."

"Really, is something going on there that I am not aware of?"

"A lot happened while you were on your journey that brought you to this haven."

"You are going to have to catch me up. Monty is in the workshop constructing a stand for the tree. You can let Asta out now and I had better get this little guy to the basement to dry out."

"Asta is curled up by the fireplace in the den. Ace has been in there most of the day going over maps again. By the way, what took you so long to find one little old tree?"

"Are you checking up on me already? Okay, I'll come clean; we were tracking deer."

"Just what kind of deer would that be?" I teased.

"The four legged kind, **my dear.**"

"You didn't shoot one did you?"

"No, but when we get tired of turkey we know where they hang out. You're not opposed to that are you? And also, I wanted to stay away long enough for you to miss me."

"Mission accomplished." I kissed him and sent him on his way.

It was finally my turn to have a shower. Nash had suggested that we leave an hour between showers so that we would be assured of hot water as he wasn't sure that the boiler was working to full capacity. I volunteered to go last because I was still unthawing the turkey and I wanted to be finished with it for the night. It was five-thirty Christmas Eve. The tree was all trimmed and the rest of the gang had settled down to watch the news on the television. They were tuned into a station in Edmonton Alberta. I told Evie she could put the casserole in the oven at six.

I laid my newly laundered underwear, grey slacks and olive green blouse and nylon stockings out on the bed. I was tired of the same old clothes, but what could I do? I had packed only one change of clothes because my trip was only supposed to have been an overnighter. I hadn't seen my carry-on bag since we left camp but Evie had found it and delivered it to my room. I opened it and dug into the bottom where my mother's travel case was. I had forgotten to pack essential toiletries for my trip to Vancouver and had been on the way out the door at Avanloch when I suddenly remembered. I wasn't worried as I could get whatever I needed in any pharmacy but my mother insisted I take her overnight case as it was already packed. She had sent my father upstairs to fetch it and we had a few extra minutes alone before Johnny would be driving me to the train in Waverly. Daddy found us hugging and both in tears when he returned.

"Hey you two, it's only for a few weeks you know." He had hugged me. "I'm gonna miss you too Pumpkin."

That was almost two months ago.

A tear fell down my face and I whispered to an empty room. "I'm all right Daddy, I'm all right Mama; I'm alive, I'm alive." I grabbed my mother's sweet lavender shampoo and conditioner and escaped to the bathroom and let the hot water wash away my tears. Fifteen minutes later I was dressed and had towel dried my hair. I sat on the edge of the bed and picked up my mother's travel bag. "I think this is just the right occasion for jewellery so let's see what kind of jewels you have in this thing Mama."

I put my hand inside the velvet lining and it touched something peculiarly familiar. "No, it can't be." I whispered out loud. A little voice told me to stop being so skittish. I reached inside the pouch again. At exactly the same time that I extracted them the connecting door between Nash's and my room slammed shut. I threw them on the floor and screamed.

I heard footsteps on the stairs and Nash calling my name. He didn't bother to knock but crashed into my room breathlessly. "Ava, what the hell was that?"

I was still sitting motionless on the bed. "I didn't know I had them Nash…honest, I didn't know. I'm the reason the plane crashed, I killed Grandfather Little Crow…it's all my fault. How am I ever going to tell them Nash, I could have killed them, I could have killed you!" I cried.

He came over and knelt on the floor beside me and took my hands in his. "I don't know what you are talking about but you are not the reason the plane crashed Ava. Where did you get such a bizarre idea?"

I pointed to the floor. He reached over and picked up the bracelets. "Don't touch them Nash; they're cursed!"

"Honey, relax. Look, they can't harm me." He held them out in front of me. "They are just inanimate pieces of silver and they don't have any power; not over you or me and they certainly didn't bring the plane down. I thought we had agreed that it was Mother Nature's doing?"

"But you don't understand…they are the Infinity Bracelets and they are just as my father said… they are cursed!"

"Yes, I am well aware of what they are. They are exactly as you described, delicate and beautiful and I can see why your father picked them out for your mother and why she loves them. Now, come on, you're smarter than that. They don't have any super natural powers so you can't give into the myth. I realize that it was probably a shock when you discovered them …how come you didn't know they were in your jewellery bag?"

"It's not mine, it's my mother's and I never opened it in Vancouver because I didn't have any reason to dress up but I wanted to look nice for you so…"

"Oh Honey, you are beautiful without any bangles and you always look good. What else do you think your mother has in here? Could there be a ring?"

"A ring, no; my mother only wore the rings my father gave her."

Nash dumped the contents of the case out on the bed. He picked something up and asked me what it was.

"Oh," I said a little surprized, "it's the little ruby ring Rosy and I bought for my mother's twenty fifth birthday. I thought she had lost it."

"Do you think she would mind if I borrowed it?" Nash asked me coyly.

"Whatever for, what could you possibly want with a ring?" I asked through tears.

He took my hand. "It's customary I believe that a man have a ring when he asks a woman to marry him." He started to put it on my finger.

I pulled my hand away and moved to the end of the bed horrified. "You don't know what you are saying; you don't want to marry me!"

"I beg to differ with you because I do want to marry you."

I got up and walked over to the south window and peered out. It was pitch black outside. I stared into the darkness. "You don't know me Nash… you know nothing about me."

He came and stood next to me." I know enough about you to know that you're the woman I want to spend the rest of my life with."

"I can't marry you Nash." I said solemnly.

"You can't, or you won't, or you just don't want to?" He asked brusquely.

"I can't." I answered.

He put his hands in his pockets and shrugged and started to walk towards the door. "I thought you loved me, but I guess you were only saying the words, you didn't mean them."

"I do love you Nash. I just can't marry you and believe me when I say if you knew why, you wouldn't want to anyhow."

"Are you already married?"

"Don't be absurd."

"Are you betrothed then?"

"Oh Nash, that is such a sixteenth century word." He'd almost made me laugh.

"Well, are you?"

"No, it is nothing like that. I wouldn't lie to you about such a thing!"

"Then you better have a damn good reason why you can't marry me so start talking!"

"What was wrong with things the way they were Nash? I was perfectly happy…why did you have to go and spoil things by asking me to marry you?"

He took my hands and led me over to the bed and sat me down. "Because I didn't want you getting away on me, that's why. We could be rescued tomorrow and you would go back to your Scotland and I would go back to Akemantack and never would we meet again."

"That's crazy."

"Is it? I've never felt this way about anyone ever before. You make me feel alive in a way I didn't even know existed. I love you and I respect you and I don't just want you in my bed. I want the whole ball of wax. I don't want us to make the same mistakes your parents did. And I don't want them thinking that I took advantage of you and our situation to get you into bed,"

"Oh, and your answer is to marry me so you can have a clear conscience and keep sleeping with me? If I remember correctly I was a very willing participant, so you needn't marry me to save my reputation and we are not my parents… our situation is entirely different."

"That's not why I want to marry you. I do not feel guilty about our love making, and I hope you don't either. If you feel you can't, or don't want to get married, then so be it." He smiled Sadly and said he'd better get downstairs and assure everyone that I was okay.

"You're going to make me tell you aren't you Nash?"

"Nope, you don't have to tell me anything. You should know though that no matter what your little secret is it will not change the way I feel about you."

"I can't marry you Nash because I have been lying to you…I've been lying to everyone. I'm not who you think I am and I don't live where I said I did." I blubbered.

He sat down beside me. "I'm listening. If you are not Ava Lane etc. etc.; then who are you, and why would you say you lived in Scotland if you don't"

"I am Ava Lane, and all those names are mine and I do live in Scotland and I do live at Avanloch, but Avanloch isn't just a house, it's a…" I couldn't get the word castle out.

"It's "a what?" Come on Ava, spit it out."

"It's a castle!" I blurted out.

Nash started laughing. "A castle…a castle? My God Ava, I swear I thought you were going to say a house of ill repute!"

I smiled a little. "Thanks for that and my mother and sister thank you also."

He raised his eyebrows and grinned. "Sorry, but why wouldn't you want us to know that you live in a castle? They are not uncommon in Scotland are they?"

"Because you all saw me as a simple little Scottish lass who lived a rather solitary boring life and I liked it like that, but if you knew I had a title and lived in a castle you would all think differently towards me."

"First of all, there is absolutely nothing simple about you and none of us ever thought so. You have been the glue that has kept us all together in one way or the other. Now about this title…are you some sort of princess or something? Oh, I get it, you are some sort of royalty and you can't marry me because I am just a commoner. Is that it Ava?"

"I am not royalty Nash. When my mother married Rosy's father, Lord Jeremy McAllister, she became Mistress of Avanloch and took on the label as Lady McAllister or Lady Vela as she was known then. Rosy was Jeremy's true daughter and so she was automatically a Lady and because he adopted me, so too was I. It means nothing. Just because some king from another century dubbed a McAllister with the title of Lord has no significance today, but customs are customs. My father became a Lord or Laird when he married mama, but don't you dare call him that or he will probably throw you out of the house."

"Does that mean that you still want me to go to Scotland with you?"

"Yes, of course I do!"

"So while we are walking up your driveway, you were going to say: "Oh, by the way, I live in a castle and here I am known as Lady Ava.""

"I don't know Nash; I guess I hadn't thought that far ahead. I didn't think that it would come to this. I always felt like something was going to happen between us, but I wouldn't let myself believe that it would turn into love. Yet here I am, head over heels in love with you, and you tell me that you love me too and that you want to marry me, but you don't anymore do you? I lied to you and that is not acceptable. I'm so sorry Nash." Tears filled my eyes.

He took me in his arms. "Do you think what you told me changes the way I feel about you? What the hell is a castle anyway? It's just a really big old house right and I can get used to calling you Lady Ava. I wouldn't say you lied to me Honey; you just omitted a few things about your life."

"That's not all Nash. I'm heiress to a really large fortune." I stopped crying and looked up at him to see his reaction.

"Yeah, that changes everything. I'm not sure I can live with a woman who has more money than I can ever make."

I pulled away from him but he pulled me back. "Just kidding Honey."

Monty was at the door. "Everything all right in here kids?"

"Yup, we'll be down in a few. We just have one more thing to settle."

"Okay, take it easy you two." Monty held two fingers up and left.

"So?" Nash asked taking my hand.

"So, what?" I asked.

"Are you going to marry me or not?"

"I want to be with you always Nash, so yes, yes I will marry you. For now we can be engaged to be engaged." I held out my hand.

He pulled the ruby ring out of his pocket and placed in on my finger. "I love you Lady Ava and this is going to be the shortest engagement in history."

"That depends on how long we are marooned here doesn't it?"

"No, I want to marry you tonight. It's Christmas Eve and the perfect night for a wedding."

"Colton Nash, now I know you are crazy! You must have hit your head one too many times on those low hanging pipes in the basement! Are you forgetting where we are? It's not like we can dial up a minister you know." I shook my head smiling.

He winked at me. "I know a man."

"Yes, I am sure you do, but let me reiterate…" I never got to finish my argument.

"Acerman, it's Ace, he's my man, he's *our* man." Nash stated confidently.

"Does he have the power to do so? I know the captain of a ship has the authority to perform a wedding ceremony but I didn't know the captain of a plane could also. Are you sure Nash?"

"I don't know about the captain thing but Ace wanted to officiate at his daughter's wedding and so he took some course which enabled him to do so and he can do the same for us." He smiled. It all made sense to him.

"I've never heard of such a thing! Why would he want to do that?"

"Maybe it wasn't his daughter's, maybe it was a niece or something. You will have to ask him that yourself. Apparently you can get a licence to do anything these days. Are you with me Ava? Can we go downstairs and ask Ace to marry us?"

"This is crazy Nash, just plain crazy. What's your hurry? I told you I am not going anywhere."

"I already gave you all the reasons. I can't imagine living my life without you in it. Are you afraid to take a chance on me?"

"No, I am not because if you turn out to be a Mr. Hyde or Dr. Jekyll I can always get a divorce. You better kiss me again just to make sure there's still a spark."

He did. It was a very long and passionate kiss and I replied that we better get going so we could make it legal. He gave me a smack on my bottom as I went off to wash my face and comb my hair. "Ha, Ha." I heckled the doubting Thomasina in the mirror, "I win. He loves me, he loves me and he wants to marry me, so there! Next time you see me I will be Mrs. Colton Nash!"

I pinched my cheeks and applied a dab of coral lipstick and opened the bathroom door to find Nash leaning up against the wall. His arms were crossed and he was sporting a very amused grin.

"Pray tell my Lady, to whom were you talking?"

"Oh, just this woman in the mirror who told me last night that I should not count on you falling in love with me. I think I knocked the wind out from under her when I told her we were getting married. Now, Mr. Nash, I would like you to refrain from calling me "Lady" as you know very well that I am no lady."

He laughed. "I won't tell if you won't."

He offered me his arm and we went traipsing downstairs and stood before the man that Nash said could marry us. All our friends were sitting around the large dining room table. Ace was doing a crossword puzzle as usual, Monty was whittling and Sali was knitting. Evie put her book down and said she would have supper on the table in two minutes. Nash asked if she could hold off for a little bit as he and I had some business to conduct with Ace.

"Yes," Ace said laying his book and spectacles on the table, "what can I do for you?"

Nash didn't beat around the bush. "We want you to marry us."

Evie sat down and covered her mouth but we all heard her say, "Oh, my!"

Sali exploded. "I told you all! I told you something was up with those two didn't I?"

"You mean besides hanky-panky Sal?" Monty said winking at me.

"So you want to get married do you? Don't you think this is a little hasty?" Ace looked directly at me. "Has he somehow coerced you into marrying him Lass?"

"Yes, he has. He has told me that he loves me and doesn't want to live if I won't marry him. I have no choice Ace…I have to marry him to save his life." I squeezed Nash's hand.

"Aha, I see. Well then I guess I have no choice either, I'll have to marry you two lovebirds. Give me a few minutes will you to bone up on the nuptial vows."

Evie jumped up. "Come on Sali; let's get Ava ready for her wedding."

"But I am ready Evie; there is nothing more to be done." I protested as they each took an arm and led me up the stairs. I looked back at Nash wondering what they could possibly do for me. He told them not to make me anymore beautiful.

"I am not Cinderella and you two are not my fairy Godmothers, so what's this all about?"

"Give me some credit Ava. Did I not transform a plain little fir tree into a work of wonder? I have a lot more to work with here. Get her out of those drab clothes Sali and get working on her hair, I'll be right back." Evie chirped as she dashed down the hall towards her room.

"What's she up to and what's wrong with my hair?"

Sali said she hadn't the slightest idea and asked me what all the stuff was spread out on the bed. I discreetly covered up the bracelets and replied that it was my mother' stuff. She rummaged through it and picked out three pearl hair combs remarking that my mother had very good taste. Evie entered the room twirling a pale blue three quarter length dress and her camera.

"What do you think Ava…do you like it?"

"It's lovely Evie." I said feeling the cool velveteen fabric between my hands. "Is this another present for your sister? I hope you aren't thinking that I should wear it."

"Of course you are going to wear it! You can't get married in slacks! And for your information, it isn't for my sister. I bought it for myself hoping that I might get invited to the New Years' Eve dance; ha ha, fat chance of that happening, but I don't care anymore anyhow. Come on, try it on."

"Thank-you Evie, but it can't possibly fit."

She threw my blouse on the floor and slid a silky slip over my head and then the dress. To my amazement it fit perfectly. I smiled as my two best friends clapped. Sali ordered me to sit down and in a few minutes she had assembled my hair in rolls and secured them in place with my mother's combs. She left little tendrils of curls spilling down my cheeks. I asked her where she learned how to arrange hair in such a fashion. She laughed and said that she was the resident hair dresser of her village and did I like it.

I stared into the mirror. "I like it very much. I look like Angeliqua."

Evie asked who that was and what was I going to wear for shoes. I said it was a long story and for another time and that I didn't require shoes at all. My mother had been married in bare feet and I would be too. Sali said that I had something new, that being Evie's dress and my mother's combs were something borrowed and now I needed something blue. She took the turquoise beads off from around her neck and placed them around mine. I was ready and I took the arms of my new friends who were also to be my bridesmaids, and together we walked slowly down the stairs. Monty met us at the bottom and handed me a bouquet of plastic flowers. I tried to say "thank-you" but my voice broke and it came out garbled. A tear slid down my cheek.

Nash was waiting for me in the lounge. He was wearing jeans and a white shirt and a suede sport-like jacket. I would ask him where he got them from later. I realized that I was trembling as the girls surrendered me to his hands. He smiled lovingly and said I was beautiful but why were my hands so cold and why was I crying. He asked me if I was having second thoughts.

"Second, third and even fourth thoughts, but if you are sure you want me than I am ready to make the biggest commitment of my life."

"I am more than sure. Ace, you heard the lady, let's get this show on the road!"

"All righty then. Dearly beloved, we are gathered here in the most unusual of places and set of circumstances. It appears as though these two young people before me, Ava Lane Quinn and Colton Nash have fallen in love and wish to be married in the eyes of God. It is my pleasure to unite them on this day of the Lord, December twenty fourth, nineteen eighty three. Nash, I believe you have a few words that you would like to say to your bride to be."

Nash cleared his throat. "You all know me as a straight shooter and so when I say that this woman here has captured my heart, you know I speak the truth. That fateful day when we were all aboard the plane that was on a collision course with hell changed my life forever. You're my angel Ava and I'm pretty sure that you descended from heaven."

I whispered that he was being "corny" again.

"Maybe I am but from the first moment I looked into your deep blue eyes I felt a stirring in my heart that I had never felt before. I tried to pass it off but it only got stronger every day. Perhaps subconsciously I remembered those eyes from another time…the day I looked into them as I pulled you out of the snow bank in Switzerland. My love for you is growing by leaps and bounds every day. I promise to look after you and protect you and love you forever. We are in for one roller coaster of a ride and I am honored that you want to take the journey with me. I do so love you Ava Lane."

"I do so love you too Nash. Ditto to everything you said and even though I thought you were the devil at first, I came to quickly realize that there was nothing but kindness in those dark chocolate eyes of yours and they stole my heart away and they are doing so right now." I was overcome by emotion and there was no stopping the tears that had been trying to escape. Sali and Evie were both crying. Nash was holding my hands tightly and his eyes were moist as he said that he loved me again. I looked at Ace. "For God's sake Ace, would you please marry us?"

"I can do that Lass. Seeing this is not your typical wedding we will skip a few steps such as "Who gives this bride away…""

"You will not!" Sali interrupted as Evie and she stepped forward. "Evie and I are standing in for Ava's parents and it is our pleasure to give her hand in marriage to Nash as we know they would be honored to do so."

I thanked them for their thoughtfulness. Here I had thought that they were just my maids of honor but they had taken it upon themselves to stand in for my parents also. I was very moved.

Ace said he knew there was no one to object to our marriage and so he would carry on and asked Monty for the rings. Monty stepped forward and produced two shiny round objects.

"Sorry kids," he apologized, "I couldn't come up with anything better on such short notice."

I recognized them as the oval rings from the pencil cases Evie had brought for her nieces. I reached out and hugged Monty. Nash was grinning from ear to ear. First the posy of artificial daisies and now creative rings… who was this bearded man anyway? My make-shift ring went on easily but I could only get Nash's barely past his first knuckle. He grimaced and I stopped saying that would have to do. Ace agreed and said it was the thought that counted.

And so I became Mrs. Colton Nash. I was now Ava Lane LaFontaine McAllister Quinn Nash. God willing, Nash was the last name I would ever add to my name.

Ace did not have to tell Nash to kiss me because he took me in his arms and did so the second Ace had pronounced us man and wife. Then he told Monty "to hit it" and whisked me unto the hard-wood floor for the wedding dance. The tune was hauntingly familiar. I asked Nash if he had picked it out. He said he did. I told him that it was the same song my father picked out for my mother's and his wedding song. He said that it was fitting then that he had chosen it too. We didn't dance so much as just held each other and swayed to the beautiful voice of Roberta Flack singing "The First Time Ever I Saw Your Face."

"Are you happy Ava?"

"I am very happy Nash. I could stay in your arms like this for-ever. I feel so safe and comfortable when you are holding me and it is the only time I am completely warm. If this is all a dream then I never want to wake up."

"Me neither Honey."

Bob Seeger's voice was the next to come blasting over the record player. Monty grabbed Evie and the two of them put on a show for us jitterbugging. It was like they had been dancing together for years. Nash asked me if I would like to join them. I declined saying I would much rather watch them. The music abruptly came to a halt a few minutes later and the lights went out. The generator had run out of gas.

"Guess we'll be eating by candlelight." Ace remarked. "And speaking of such, it better be soon as I can feel myself fading away."

Nash lit the candles, Evie put the food on the table and Monty opened a bottle of sparkling wine. He poured us all just enough for a few toasts informing us that there was only four bottles left in the liquor cabinet and so we had to ration it. Sali did not drink alcohol but held up her glass to make the first toast. Everyone else followed in turn wishing us happiness and good luck. Nash stood up and thanked everyone for spontaneously going along with our crazy plan to be married. He turned to me as he held up his glass.

"To you my darling…thank-you for making me the happiest man in the world."

"One thing is for sure Nash," Monty declared, "and that's that you are never going to go hungry! If this tuna casserole is any indication of what your bride can throw together, you are going to be one well fed man!"

"It is delicious Ava, but why are you not having any?" Ace asked.

I finished swallowing a mouthful of last night's spaghetti and answered. "I do not eat tuna; in fact, I hate it, but my brothers love this dish so I thought you all might too. We have lots of mushroom soup, something else I don't eat, and noodles and tins of tuna so this may just become a weekly thing."

"No problem there." Monty said.

Sali brought out coffee and Evie's shortbread. Ace remarked that we were dining exceptionally well for castaways. We all agreed. I excused myself saying I needed to get something from upstairs and dashed away not too sure if I was really going to expose myself to these people who had become my family. I tried not to think of what they would say about what I had been hiding. I returned to the dining room and stood behind Nash. I placed the bracelets on the table in front of him. He reached up and patted my hands.

"This is the reason the plane crashed. I am responsible for it all."

Monty picked the bracelets up and with a mischievous glint in his eye winked at me. "So, these are what brought the plane down? Never did take any stock that it was bad weather that did it. Yeah, cursed bracelets; that makes far more sense, don't you agree Acerman?"

"Yup."

"You told them?" I squealed beating on Nash.

"I just wanted to soften the blow a little Honey, that's all."

Monty passed the bracelets to Evie who admired them. "So these are your mother's Infinity Bracelets? They are beautiful. I doubt very much that they have any malevolent power. From the story you told us, I believe love is the only power they possess and I think you should wear them tonight on this your wedding night."

"There is no way I am wearing them! I don't care what any of you say… I am not at all comfortable knowing that they were hidden away in my mother's jewelry bag. I will not jinx anything else! What else did you tell them Nash? Did you tell them that I am an heiress and that I live in a castle? Did you tell them that I live in a fairy-tale world and that my sole mission to Canada was to find a man who would fall so deeply in love with me that he would obey my every command and wish?"

Nash pulled me down on his lap before I could escape. "Nope, I didn't, but I think you just did. Do you want to explain yourself, or do you want to leave everyone wondering what the hell you are ranting about or do you want me to?"

I hid my face in his chest. "You start."

"All right, but I want you to turn around…thank-you. That scream you all heard earlier was Ava's reaction to discovering that she had the bracelets with her. I calmed her down and that is when I asked her to marry me. She refused. She said she couldn't marry me because she had been lying to me about who she was and where she lived. I told her that just because she had left a few things out about her life didn't mean she was lying. I will let her tell you the how and why she kept her real identity a secret from us."

I apologized for being a buffoon and repeated what I had told Nash earlier leaving out the intimate parts.

"So that's it; na, I don't think so. There has to be more…like ghosts and hauntings and things that go bump in the night isn't there Ava Lane?" Monty joked.

"Oh yes," I said smiling, "there be ghosts."

"Just a minute," Nash said grinning from ear to ear, "nobody said anything about ghosts. Ace, I think I might need a refund on those marriage vows."

I don't think so my dear; you may have a man, but I have a woman…a gypsy woman."

Through howls of laughter Ace managed to speak. "I told you that you had met your match didn't I Nash old man?"

There was much talk about moats and drawbridges and turrets and towers. I left the telling of wandering spirits for another night.

Nash insisted upon carrying me over the threshold. He kicked the bedroom door shut with his foot and deposited me on the bed and started kissing me. I pushed him away.

"Stop, this is Evie's dress and I need to get out of it before any monkey business!"

"That was next on my agenda my dear."

"Yes I am sure it was." I stood up and he unzipped me. I hung it up in the closet.

"I think we should buy the dress from Evie because you looked like a vision in it I want you to wear it again on our anniversary. What do you say?"

"Ha!" I said retreating into the bathroom. I took my mother's negligee off the hook and held it up to my body. "Really, you were seriously thinking about wearing this?" I glanced at myself in the mirror and laughed and replaced it with my cotton nightie and went out to greet my husband.

"Is that woman in the mirror giving you trouble again?" Nash asked.

"Nope, I was going to wear my mother's sexy red negligee but I talked myself out of it. I mean, what was I thinking wearing what I'm sure my father bought for my mother? Anyhow, don't expect me to be able to fit into that dress a year from now because I won't be able to."

Nash crawled into bed and reached to turn the lamp off. "Why do you say that?"

"Leave the lamp on for a little while please. You do know that there is every bit the possibility that every time we make love we could be making a baby, don't you?" I wanted to see his face for his reaction.

"I guess it has entered my mind a time or two but there isn't much we can do about it is there? Believe me, finding the love of my life on this trip was the last thing on my mind. How would you feel about having a baby Ava, my baby?"

"Yes, I want to have babies, your babies. When you meet my baby sister Liliana, you will want to have half a dozen little girls just like her and that is all we can ever have is girls Nash. How do you feel about that?"

Now he looked confused. "What do you mean?"

"The LaFontaine women don't have male children; they can only have girls;" I replied matter of factually, "something about not having the patience to deal with boys and their tantrums."

"You know that makes no sense whatsoever, and I do believe that the male determines the sex of the child. Sounds like the ladies in your family believe in some fairy-tale curse passed down through the ages by some gypsy woman or sorceress." Nash was teasing but he was going to have to learn a few things.

"My sister is a half-blooded gypsy." I said as if that explained everything.

"Rosalyn?"

"Yes, her mother's family came from Romania and settled in Wales many years ago. I had the pleasure of meeting Rosy's grandfather a few times. He was still mourning the passing of his wife when his beloved Maveryn died. There are two more sisters but Rosy rarely sees them. Maveryn's portrait hangs in the main reception hall and you will see how Rosy resembles her. I don't think you will be meeting her in person though."

"Well if she's dead I guess not."

"Oh," I said, "slip of the tongue."

"No, I don't think it was. What are you not telling me Ava?"

I looked him straight in the eyes. "She is our resident spirit."

"Do you mean ghost? Does Rosy's mother haunt the castle?"

"She doesn't haunt Nash, she just visits. She looks over us and when she sees that we are all right she goes back to Jeremy in the mausoleum. She's beautiful, she floats on air and we all feel a peace and calm after one of her visits."

Nash scratched his head. "And you believe that you have actually seen her? I was hoping that you were joking when you said that you lived with ghosts, but apparently I was wrong. How long have you been having these visions?"

"I don't know…since I was five or so. She won't hurt you Nash. I didn't really want to get into this with you on our wedding night."

"Well, it is out now. My wife fantasizes that she sees dead people floating around…."

"Nash," I interrupted, "it is not a fantasy and she is the only one I have seen."

"There's more?"

"You'll have to talk to my parents about that."

"Just a minute…your dad is buying into this?"

"Like I said, you can take it up with him. Oh, he may deny it but if The Grey Lady hadn't of come for him we may very well have never uncovered Avaleena's diary and the real truth about our ancestry. It is because of "her" that mama remembered things that she had locked away in her mind. Now I am done talking for the night so let's put it away for another day."

Nash turned out the lamp. "So, you are pulling a Shahrazad on me are you?"

I ignored that reference. Instead I thanked him from rescuing me from living a long and lonely life as a spinster in the north tower with my fourteen cats.

"Ah, so twenty two is regarded as spinsterhood in the Isles is it?" He mocked.

"Yes Dear, it is, and I am not getting any younger so I suggest we get on with the honeymoon."

I was awakened the next morning with a passionate kiss.

"Good morning sunshine! Look", Nash pointed to the window, "it's snowing!"

"Goody," I complained, "more snow, just what we need."

"Okay Miss Grumpy, go back to sleep. I'm going to grab a quick shower." He covered me up and retreated to the bathroom.

I closed my eyes but they popped back open. What was wrong with me? I shuffled my way to the bathroom, opened the door and pulled back the shower curtain. "Is there room for two?" I smiled at my very receptive husband.

"And Merry Christmas to you too Mrs. Nash!"

CHAPTER 6

Christmas at Avanloch

My bladder had been sending me signals for the past hour and I could no longer ignore it. I tried not to disturb Rainey as I attempted to roll out of bed but he heard me and asked me where I was going. "I'm sorry Darling, I didn't want to wake you but I simply must get to the bathroom."

"Do you need my help?"

I said I didn't. He asked me if I was coming back to bed. I told him that my back ached and I needed to walk and stretch.

"Please Honey, just for a little while; I need to hold you."

I smiled and said I would. Last night was the first decent night's sleep we had both gotten since we had learned that Ava's plane was missing. I contributed it to the fact that our older daughter was home.

Rosy and Evan had arrived early yesterday morning. Their flight from Brazil had been delayed so it was late in the evening when it had landed and they had to spend the night in London. Evan's landlord had let the information regarding Ava slip. It had been impracticable for me to believe that I could keep such news from her. We received the phone call from her at eleven p.m.

Of course I was already in bed and asleep but was awakened by the shrill ringing of the telephone. I heard Rainey's voice coming from the parlour. Before I could rouse myself he was at my bedside speaking in a very calm tone to Rosy.

"Don't upset your mother any more than she already is Red. Love you and we will see you in the morning then. Promise me you won't push Evan to fly that helicopter faster than it is capable of going okay?"

He handed me the phone and sat down next to me. For ten minutes I listened to her cry and carry on. She kept saying that we should have told her when we talked to her in Minas Gerais. I did my best to soothe her but she wasn't letting me get a word in edgeways so I asked her to put Evan on the phone. I passed the receiver to Rainey. He held it up so that I could hear.

"Why Mama; don't you want to talk to me anymore?" Rosy was still on the line.

"I asked you not to upset your mother didn't I Rosy? Do you think that this has been a cakewalk for us? For weeks we hadn't heard from you and then Ava's plane goes missing…we are hanging on by a shoestring. We need you home here with us so please try and get all your negativity and morose thoughts out before you come home. This isn't about us; it's about Ava. Now put Evan on the phone like my good little girl, okay?"

Evan assured us he would be able to calm her down and that they would be at Avanloch first thing in the morning. He said that Rosy had tried to tell us that they had found Roberge when she called from Brazil but the phone line had gone dead. They had found Roberge, and he had come home with them. His father's work wasn't done so he would be remaining at the site of the lost gold mine. They had found out that there was indeed a lost gold mine, but because of volcano eruptions over the past hundred or so years it had slipped into the sea.

Yesterday had been very difficult. I had waited at the kitchen table with Amma and the McDuffs for Rosy's and Evan's arrival. Rainey and Johnny went out as soon as we heard the helicopter touch down. After ten minutes or so of tearful hugs and outbursts of rage Rosy finally sat down asking us to forgive her for her ranting. She said that she and Evan had the solution all figured out. They were going to take a commercial flight to Vancouver or thereabouts. From there they would rent a bush plane or helicopter or whatever it was that was used as search planes in Canada and they would search for Ava themselves.

I sighed. Rainey bobbed his head up and down several times as if in agreement "Why didn't I think of that?"

Rosy was sitting between me and Rainey. Evan was across the table and looked distraught.

Rainey took hold of Rosy's hand. "In theory it is a very good plan, but there are a few holes in it. For one, it is winter in northern Canada and I don't just mean a foot or so of snow… I mean six or eight feet of the white stuff. The weather is unpredictable; blizzards and freezing temperatures are everyday occurrences. Canada is a vast country and Evan does not know the terrain, or am I wrong in assuming that?"

"No Sir, I am not at all familiar with Canada." Evan admitted.

Rainey smiled I assumed because Evan had called him "Sir."

"All righty then. Now little girl, what makes you think that you and Evan can accomplish what no other aircraft has been able to do so far? Search planes have only been able to be air bound for half an hour or so before they are forced to return to base because of fog and storms. When the skies clear they will be at it full force and they won't give up until a thorough scouring of the flight area is completed. No, my dear, you will not be attempting something so foolhardy. Have I made myself clear?"

"But Rainey, we have a personal stake in this and they don't and what's to say searches may be suspended because of the cost?"

"You know perfectly well that we will personally cover any over costs. You should know that these search and rescue teams do everything in their power to find missing planes and people. They spend hundreds of their own personal time and their own money just doing so. You might think that Ava is just a name to them but believe me they know everything about her and her companions and they take a personal interest in them all. Their mission is to reunite the missing or lost with their families."

"I'm sure that's all true, but…"

I interjected. "Rainey has already hired a private helicopter firm out of Vancouver. Everything possible is being done. No one has the power to control the weather so we just sit and wait hoping that the next phone call will be good news. We are pretty much drained. Don't forget we not only had Ava to worry about, but we also hadn't heard from you and Evan for weeks so our anxieties were two-fold. Thinking that you could do what no professionals can is just plain ludicrous. I can't handle your pessimism and tears right now so if you can't offer support then I suggest you head back to London." I got up from the table saying I had to tend to Lili.

Of course she was crying again and holding on to me saying she was sorry and she hadn't meant to insinuate that we weren't doing enough to find Ava. "I can't even begin to imagine what you have been going through and I am so sorry that Evan and I contributed to your worries. I haven't had time to process anything yet Mama. All I can think of is that my sister is missing just as my mother was and you want me to leave…"

Rainey took us both in his arms while the rest of the family tried to keep control of their own emotions. Mary and Amma were not doing a very good job.

"Look at me Rosalyn," Rainey said in a soothing voice, "your mother doesn't want you to leave. We need you here and here you are going to stay. Ash and Jannie and the rest will be here later today so we are going to need you to run interference with them…are you up to it?"

Rosy said she was and she was also going to take over caring for Lili if we would let her. Rainey nodded to me over Rosy's head. I had no choice but to say thank-you and I would welcome the help. It wasn't true as I had no intention of relinquishing my baby's care over to any-one, not even my daughter. Lili's stories and her funny little ways were the only things that kept me from going to pieces, but I would share her as I knew Rosy loved her. She still preferred Rainey over me but that was okay because I preferred him over anyone else also.

"You should know Rosy that your mother has been the brave one here and she has been my saving grace. Her faith has never fal-tered. She trusts that God is keeping Ava alive and she has made believers out of us all. Oh yeah that, and hers and Meggie's sixth sense." Rainey beamed at me. "Isn't that right Sweetheart?"

Rosy asked if Meggie had seen Ava. I told her that she had. She had seen Ava just as she had seen me…she was alive but she could not see where she was. She had a vision of a downed plane and survivors, but that was all. Rosy seem appeased. Rainey said he was going to escort me upstairs and then he would be back to give Rosy and Evan the full details of the search so far.

"Why don't you and Evan get dressed and we'll go for a walk. I'm sure you are going to want to visit Maveryn just as Vienna did yesterday." He winked at me. "Yes Dear I know you snuck out. You can't pull anything over on me anymore."

"Really Rainey, how did she get out without any of us noticing?" Amma asked.

"It was on my watch, but not to worry, I had her in my sights all the time."

I made it to the bedroom door before I broke down. I couldn't stop the sobs that were wracking my body. Rainey managed to get me inside and shut the door and sit me down.

"What is it Sweetie?" He tried wiping my tears away with his shirt sleeve.

"I was so stern with Rosy." I lamented between tears. "This is the second time I have scolded her in the past few months. This is not like me Rainey. I should have comforted her but all I could think of was how asinine her idea was and that she was adding more stress to the situation. I need to go downstairs and apologise; not just to her but to everyone for my outburst."

"You need to do no such thing. You were justified in both instances and Rosy knows that. Here, let's get you into bed; there, that's my girl."

He kissed me and said he'd make his apologies downstairs because I needed him. I told him that I would be all right and that he should escort Evan and Rosy over to the mausoleum as he had promised. He tucked the coverlet around me and smiled.

"For weeks you have been my rock; you have provided me with hope and comfort…now it is time for me to look after you. I think maybe you have reached your breaking point so there is no damn way I am leaving you alone. You are my priority, not just now but always, you know that don't you?"

"Yes, but…"

"But nothing; give me two minutes okay?"

I threw my arms around him. "I love you Rainey."

"And I you; you are the most precious jewel in my world and don't you ever forget it. Oh, and by the way, I think we have a little matter completely unrelated to discuss don't you?"

"Do you mean my visit to the crypt?"

There was a knock on the open door. "May I come in Mama?"

I sat up. "Of course you can; come in and sit by me."

"I will, but just for a moment. I know I upset you both and I won't let it happen again. I just couldn't bear it if you were angry with me Mama."

"I am not angry with you Sweetie and I am the one who needs to apologise. You were just expressing your grief and I should have recognized that you needed to vent. From now on we'll do our crying together and tomorrow we are going to sit down and you and Evan are going to fill us in on your adventures in South America okay?"

"Yes, and I'm going to try and be brave for you. I am sure there will be many more tears. Now I am going to leave you to rest. Mama needs you right now Rainey so you look after her. Evan is pretty zonked out, thanks to my ranting, so he needs some down time too. We'll do the walk thing later okay?"

"That was what I was coming to tell you Rosy. We have plenty of time to catch up. If you have any questions that you want answered right away Johnny knows just as much as I do."

We all hugged and said our "love yous." Rainey walked Rosy to the door and crawled under the blanket with me and took me in his arms. He rubbed my back and asked where we had left off. "Oh yeah, we were at the crypt…"

"I don't see how you heard me go out. I was as quiet as a mouse and I was very careful. I was going to tell you eventually you know?" I said defensively.

"Something in your voice alerted me, can't say what it was for sure. I emerged from the office and saw the entrance door closing. I went to the window and watched you step gingerly through the slush holding onto the umbrella as a crutch. I was pretty sure where you were going so I followed you."

"What do you mean, you followed me? I kept peering over my shoulder and I never saw you."

"I watched until you were on solid ground and then I ran down the path in the cellar and I arrived at the mausoleum before you. It was easy to keep an eye on you from my vantage point."

"You are not making any sense…how could you have gotten there before me? What path?"

Rainey sighed. "I wasn't going to tell you this for a while but I guess I may as well now. Remember the day that Amma took you and Lili down for lunch at her mother's? That was the same day that Johnny and I barricaded the entrance to Avaleena's/ Corinthia's room behind the bookcase. I mentioned to Johnny that I had found it strange that Avaleena had mentioned a secret entrance from the outside when Gracie Darling and Quinn came to rescue her and the child. He said it was the perfect opportunity for us to search for one and so we did. One by one we started to remove bricks from the outside wall at the end of the passageway and sure enough there it was…a door. You won't believe what was etched into the wood…well maybe you will."

"All roads lead to Rome?"

"Yup; I'm amazed as to how often that motto keeps popping up. Needless to say we broke the door down which had been barred and bricked, I assume by Stewart. We entered through it and followed a dirt trail it and it took us inside the crypt into a small antechamber behind the actual resting places. There is a small opaque window-like opening between two of the burial compartments. I could see you through it but I could barely hear you. I am sure you whispered as you believe that it is respectful to do so in the house of the resting souls. It is just as you always thought Vienna. From inside that little room is another door that leads outside that undoubtedly leads into the forest. I assume that is the escape route that was created many, many years ago as a way of exodus from marauding enemies. It is not visible from the outside at all. Remember how Morgan and Mason scoured every inch of the crypt looking for an entrance…there was no way anyone was ever going to find it from the outside, but it was visibly apparent from the inside. I didn't have time to explore as I had to keep my eyes on you. When you left I exited and watched you until you were safely home. Are you angry with me for not telling you about our discovery?"

"No, I know you had my best interests at heart. I will see it one day when I am not so cumbersome. Thank you for watching after me. Have you disguised the door in the cellar?"

"No, I have thought about it but other things came up. I thought locking the entrance to Avaleena's den was enough and you have never asked for the key, so all is well."

"You have unlocked most of the mysteries of this castle Rainey and I should be grateful to you for that, but you know what, I really don't care anymore. I only want our Ava to come home." I buried my head on Rainey's chest and he let me cry all over him.

"Me too Darling, me too."

One extra guest arrived on Christmas Eve with Aunt Jannie, Uncle John, Ash and Gray. It was Chandler, Uncle John's other son. Winston had picked them all up from the train station in Waverly. Rainey and I met them at the door. Ash complained about the long tedious ride and said she hoped we didn't mind but Chandler was downcast because he would be spending Christmas all alone and so she had invited him. I knew he had alienated himself from his ex-wives and all three of his children. His response when I welcomed him was to take me in his arms and kiss me.

"Ah, here she is, the Lady who stole my heart so many years ago. How different my life would have been if I had insisted you marry me then! And look, with child again and not one of them mine. I am crushed as always."

"Oh for the love of God Chandler," Ash moaned, "the girl was only twelve! We've heard it all before; give it a rest will you?"

I actually wiped his kiss off my lips. "I don't believe you have met my husband."

"Ah yes, the auspicious Rainey Quinn. I salute you Sir; to the victor goes the spoil, but in your case what you won was the cream of the crop. I am sure we will get along splendidly as we have one thing in common and that is this beauty here." Chandler winked at me.

Rainey shook his hand for a little too long I thought. "My wife is not anyone's prize Sir and please do not make the mistake of assuming that we will be friends."

He took my arm saying that Caron and Jeanette would show them to their rooms and that supper would be served in the dining room at six-thirty and cocktails would be served in the drawing room at six. I heard Gray chastising his brother behind us as Rainey suggested that we stop at my parlour. Johnny picked up Aunt Jannie's suitcase as he passed by us and whispered that he hoped I wasn't in trouble again. I shot him a dirty look.

Rainey closed the door behind us. "Is there something I should know about you and Chandler, Vienna? Is every man you ever met in love with you?"

"Is this another of your ridiculous inquisitions?" I asked cheekily.

"I just want to know what I am up against."

"You are up against nothing. Chandler is a boorish, pretentious little man. Even as a young girl I could see right through him. He has none of Gray's or his father's charm or good manners. Please don't read anything into any of his innuendoes; they are merely castles in the sky."

"You know all about the women in my life… how come I keep hearing about new ones in yours? Are there anymore who are going to come out of the woodwork?"

"The difference between the men in my life and the women in yours is simple…I never slept with any of them." I had hit below the belt but I was tired of his unwarranted jealousy.

He hit right back at me. "Did you want to Vienna; did you want to sleep with any of them?"

Should I lie and tell him no? "They were all married Rainey and I was never that kind of woman as you very well know. I was lonely though and so yes, I did entertain the thought of taking a lover, but that is as far as anything went and you know that." I was hurt by his questions but I would not bow down.

"It was Jack wasn't it?"

"You want me to tell you that it was don't you even if it wasn't? Okay, then I will; yes it was Jack. Are you happy now?"

"Now how hard was that to admit the truth? I knew it all along you know? I hope your feelings for him won't cause any dissention between the two of you when we go home…he is with your sister after all."

"Damn you Rainey Quinn! It might have been easy for you to crawl into bed with someone you had no feelings for just to satisfy some hunger in your loins, but not so for me!"

"I believe we have had this conversation about my ex's before and I don't want to rehash it."

"Well, you started it so I think you can take what you give. You know a lot of things happened over the course of twenty years and I am sure that we are going to discover a lot more about each other's lives as the years go on. I'm sure one day I'm going to find one of your little lovers at my front door and then we will see how you explain yourself."

"That is never going to happen. You know very well that you were, and are, my only love."

"That is just your word. We have never addressed your early college years have we?"

"No, and we aren't going too because there is nothing to discuss and I have told you that a hundred times!"

"And if I have told you once I have told you a hundred times that I love Jack just as I do Jimmy and Johnny. It is the same way you love Lara and Amma. The love I have for you is something entirely different. I tire of this tete-a-tete so get out of my parlour and leave me alone to compose myself before I have to face the masses!"

"I am not leaving you alone. I did that once already this year and I won't make the same mistake twice. Now come to Daddy and tell me you love me despite my stupidity. Have I crossed over the line once again and are you angry with me yet again?"

"I find your behaviour quite amusing and if you hang around I am going to beat on you. However, I don't have the time and this is all so petty…your obsessive jealousy is irrational. Have you forgotten our daughter is missing and may be dead?"

He pulled me into his arms. "Don't say that Vienna, please don't say that."

"I'm sorry; I didn't mean to, it just came out." I kissed him. "Now let me go now as I barely have time to check on the table and dress myself and the girls."

"Are we dressing for dinner?"

"Suit yourself; you are the Laird of the Manor and you can do as you so choose." I smacked him on his backside as I skirted around him. He was sporting his usual whitish colourless shirt but had changed his khakis for blue jeans. I did not disapprove as he fit them to a "T". I left him cringing at the word "laird."

I crossed over the great hall to the dining room. The girls had done a great job. I counted making sure there was an extra place setting now that we had an unexpected guest. Tonight was our Christmas feast because it was easier to obtain extra help as all our regular staff would be sitting down with us and tomorrow Mrs. D and Lois could rest. Caron and Jeanette would be leaving for Ireland to spend the holidays with their family immediately after dinner. I wandered down to the kitchen and found Tanny and Liliana having dessert with the extra staff that was finishing up with their dinner. Lili reached out to me with her blueberry tainted hands.

"I think not young lady!"

Zoe rushed to wash her hands. "Sorry Mum, I'll take her up for a bath."

"No, I can see that you are busy and you have already done enough for the day. Remember you have to change too." I picked up Lili who somehow managed to plop her hand into what was left of her pie. She licked her fingers. I put her down. "Really Lili, did you have to do that?"

I took her dirty hand and headed for the elevator. Rainey was half way up the hall whistling "When Irish Eyes are smiling." Lili broke free of me and ran to meet her father. He bent down to pick her up and she smeared her purple hands all over his white shirt and face. He looked at me over her little curly head with a not-so amused grin on his face.

Tanny pulled me towards the lift. "You're in big trouble Vienna. Come on, hurry up!"

"Don't you dare press that button Tanny!" Rainey called as he ran up the hallway.

She did. We laughed all the way up to the second floor where she kept tugging at me to hurry. "Where should we hide? I know, in my closet. Now be quiet as a mouse Mama so Rainey won't find us." She put her hand over my mouth.

We heard Rainey running the water in the bathtub and talking nonsense to Lili.

"You can come out of the closet girls because we know you are in there, don't we Lili?"

"I guess the jinx is up Tanny so let's go face the music." We emerged from the closet still giggling. Rainey had taken off his shirt but his face was still lined with little streaks of blue. I remarked that the color looked good on him.

He said that if this was my ploy to get him to change clothes then I had won.

"Come along Tanny; let's go find something for me and you to wear."

Without looking at me Rainey suggested I should wear the green paisley. I told him that I didn't have a green paisley. He said I should look in the closet and there might just be something for Tanny in there too.

Tanny ran ahead of me and pulled the closet doors open. "There is a present here with my name on it. What do you think is in it? Look, there is one for Lili too!"

"I am sure I do not know what that man has been up to. Why don't you open yours and see."

She tore at the paper and opened a box and pulled out a red taffeta dress. "Oh my," she exclaimed, "it's beautiful!" She held it up to her and then ran back into her bedroom.

I imagined that she wanted to thank Rainey. I pulled a black garment bag from a hanger and draped it on the bed. I opened it and sure enough there was a deep green paisley dress inside adorned with an avocado shawl and a sea green brooch. I sat down on the bed and waited.

Tanny came back and picked up Lili's package. "Do you need me Mom? Rainey said he would help you if I dress Lili."

"Yes Dear, I can manage. Make sure you wash up before you put on your new dress."

"I will. Hmm," she said feeling my dress, "so this is paisley… very funny feathers."

I read the card that was attached to the top of the hanger:

To my beloved…I saw you admiring dresses in the catalogue from Paisley. I hope I made the right choice. The hand woven shawl seemed to be the perfect accomplishment. I tried to match the color of the brooch with the teardrop I gave you so many years ago. This is not a Christmas present because I know we agreed not to exchange gifts… it is just a token of my never ending love for you.

Rainey

I wiped a silent tear from my eye just as my husband walked in still dripping wet from the shower. I stood up and not saying a word I turned around and he undid the frock I was wearing and he helped me out of it.

"I think maybe someone should wash their hands before they get all dressed up." He suggested.

I glanced at them; they were a familiar blue color. I laughed and went to the chest of drawers and pulled out a large carton and placed it on the bed next to my new outfit. "As long as we are not exchanging gifts you may as well open this." I picked up my dress and went into the bathroom to bathe. When I came out Rainey was dressed in his new duds. I wasn't sure how he would react to the light grey trousers and over-shirt that I had bought him. He was smiling.

"You will be the Belle of the ball as usual my dear. Does your husband have exquisite taste or what? Are you sending me a message by saying that my clothes are dull? I hope the Grey Lady won't take a liking to me."

"I think you are safe my dear, from her anyhow and Lauren isn't here so there is only me to contend with. Grey isn't a very bold color so it isn't that much of a change. You look good in whatever you are wearing or not wearing, and the grey brings out the blue in your eyes."

I sat at my dressing table noticing my green teardrop lying on an overturned mirror. Rainey had bought it for me at the gift shop at Avastavalley where we had spent our first night together twenty two years ago. I picked it up and he placed it around my neck.

"I'm glad that you took this with you when you ran away from me…it gave me hope that you took a little part of me with you."

I patted his hand. "As it was, I took a very big part of you."

He smiled. "Do I need a tie?"

I straightened his collar. "No, you do not. I know how you hate them and that is why I bought this shirt." I ran my hands over the silky paisley. "You do have exquisite taste and I shall be ever so careful as not to spill cranberries down it. Thank you for my non Christmas gift."

"And thank you for mine."

"Now what shall I wear on my feet?"

He replied by reaching under the bed and producing a box which contained green ballet slippers. I sat on the bed and he put them on me. I pulled him to my bosom and kissed the top of his head. "I love you Rainey Quinn."

He looked up at me. "And I love **you** Vienna LaFontaine."

The dinner was superb. Chandler made no more incendiary remarks and even Tanny and Lili were on their best behavior. After dessert the men retreated to the smoking room in the Harem room so that Uncle John could smoke his pipe and the rest could partake in the Cuban cigars that Gray had somehow managed to procure. Rainey treated them to a very expensive bottle of cognac. Zoe took the little girls upstairs and we ladies remained and enjoyed coffee and chit-chat. Rosy filled us in on some of her more notable moments on her trip to the Green Sea. She assured us all that she and Evan were never in any danger and that they were treated well in all the little Indian villages. The natives were all grateful for the trinkets and cloths and tools that she and Evan had gifted to them and they were treated to ceremonial festivities every night. They were in awe of her long red hair. She said she was lucky to come home with as much hair as she did and that only once did she fear she may lose it all to one besotted chief. However, he was content just to have a few locks to hang from his spear. I cringed as everyone else laughed.

Rainey made an entrance at eight thirty asking if anyone minded if he stole me away. I was more than ready for bed and so was Aunt Jannie. We took the lift and walked her to the LB suite where she and Uncle John always stayed when they visited. At first I had been reluctant to let anyone stay in the rooms that had once been sealed off since the apparent drowning death of Jeremy's little sister, LizBeth. Once it was revealed that she was still alive but living the life of a five year old in an institution in the Netherlands we had her brought back to a facility close to home where she had lived out her final years. With Ash's permission, Rainey had torn down the wall that the senior McAllister had built to conceal her rooms and we modernised them somewhat. I had lived in the castle for twenty years never knowing that her rooms were behind that wall. I had often wondered upon discovering the rooms if they were indeed one of the secret rooms that Jeremy had said existed. Rainey had discovered two and maybe these were the third. Technically, I guess that isn't right because I knew about the Corinthia/Avaleena room long before he did. I just hadn't remembered until last autumn that I did. Anyhow, Rainey convinced me that LizBeth had been kept in the dark too long and it was time to let the sun shine in. No one had encountered her spirit, so that was a good thing. I had wondered at times why the spirit of Jeremy's grandmother, Miss Mary had never appeared to anyone at the castle. If anyone had just cause to do so it was her having died horrendously after falling through the conservatory windows. She had never visited me as I searched through her closets for something to wear. Maybe she liked that I had restored the conservatory and was adorning myself in her ageless costumes. I had talked a lot to her when I was at odds with Rainey last fall…I should say "at odds with myself." I shook these thoughts out of my head as Rainey quietly opened our young daughter's bedroom door hoping they were asleep. The door squeaked a little and Lili squealed, "Daddy, Mommy!"

"I will have you know that I just got her to sleep; now look what you have done!" Tanny said annoyingly. "Well, one of you is going to have to tell her another story 'cause I am plain tuckered out." She crossed her arms and looked at us crossly.

"Don't get your knickers in a knot young lady; it is Christmas Eve after all." Rainey scolded.

"What does that have to do with anything?" She wanted to know.

Rainey sighed and pulled her down on his knee as he sat on Lili's little bed. "It has everything to do with Christmas Eve as it is a night for miracles and I am going to tell you a story about a miracle that happened many, many years ago."

"Oh Rainey, can't Mommy tell us? She's a much better story teller."

"I know she is but mommy is tired and going to bed and your old dad is your only option for tonight…what do you say?"

Tanny laughed and said that Rainey wasn't old. I kissed them all and said that I would see them bright and early the next morning.

I wanted to wear something for Rainey that would flatter my expanding body…as if anything could do that. I pulled my lingerie drawer open and found something wrapped in white tissue paper. I carefully undid the yellow ribbon and discovered a long white satin nightie and peignoir and a little note that said: "Will you wear this for me tonight Vienna? This is our very first Christmas Eve together…I want it to be perfect…R."

When that man had managed to purchase this gown and the dress and hide them away until tonight was a complete mystery to me. I took no time changing and anticipated Rainey seeing me in it.

I sat down at the dressing table and brushed my hair until it shone wishing someone else was here to do so. I heard a voice coming from far away.

"Mama, can you hear me? I have something to tell you…"

I jumped up calling out my missing daughter's name. "Ava, is that you? Where are you Honey?" I felt a cool breeze coming from the glass doors of the balcony… one was partly opened. I drifted over that way and slid through the partial opening still calling Ava's name. It was snowing. I barely felt the cold wet flakes on my face as I searched and called out my daughter's name. She did not answer. I was jolted out of my dreamlike state by Rainey calling my name.

"Vienna, where are you Sweetie…why is this door open? Oh my God…Maveryn?"

I turned away from the railing wondering why Rainey was calling Maveryn's name. In an instant he crossed the terrace and picked me up and carried me inside and sat me down on the divan ordering me to stay there while he closed the door.

"What in the name of God were you doing out there Vienna? I need to get you warmed up; your feet are turning blue. Here, let me get you out of these wet clothes."

"But Rainey, you wanted me to wear this."

"Yeah, well it will have to be another night now won't it?"

He undressed me, pulled another gown from the dresser and slipped it over my head and told me to stand up. He picked me up again and placed me in bed tucking the blankets firmly around.

"Its flannelette Rainey, you know I hate flannelette."

"Well, you should have thought of that before you went traipsing off into the snow barefoot and in a floor length gown. I'm going to get some towels so don't move."

He came back and wrapped my wet head in one of the towels and wound another one around one of my feet while he massaged the other one. "Are you going to tell me what you were doing out there Missy?"

"Ava called me."

He stopped rubbing and looked at me anxiously. "Honey, it's been a long day and I know you are tired…"

"She told me she had something to tell me, but she didn't say what. I thought she was outside because the door was partly open. I heard her Rainey, I heard her calling me. I think she wanted to tell me that she was alive and that we shouldn't give up on her."

Rainey let go of my foot and took me in his arms and stroked my face. "You always said she was Honey and we will go on believing that she is. How did she sound?"

"She was happy…I thought she sounded, I don't know, maybe elated. Why did you call out Maveryn's name Rainey?"

"Well, you were standing at the balustrade in your silvery gown with your hands outstretched to the heavens and white snowflakes covering your head…I guess I just had a moment. Lie back down and I'll attempt to get the circulation back in your feet again."

"I'm all right, honest I am."

He looked upwards and attempted a little humor. "Help me Lord to make it through another day with this woman. I fear she will be the death of me one way or the other. I try, I really try but the minute she is out of my sight…well, you know and one man can only do so much."

I smacked him a little. "Yes, and if he knows what is good for him, he will get me out of this woolen gown before I break out in hives or die sweating!"

"You are such a drama queen." He said flatly.

"I beg your pardon…a what?"

"Surely you know what a drama queen is?"

"I do not. I have never heard the term before."

"Well that's because you have been holed up here in this fortress for twenty years. You have absolutely no idea what goes on in the outside world or what is making the rounds as clichés."

I objected to his thinking that I was out of touch with the world. He mumbled something as he rummaged through my night-attire drawer. I He approached me holding a sheer nylon nightie.

"Will this do my Ladyship?" He asked cheekily.

"It will not! Can you not find something that isn't see-through? Lili and Tanny will be crawling into bed with us in the morning and I don't want them to see their mother naked."

"You've shown them your tummy before…"

"Yes," I interrupted, "I have, but just a little, not the ugly parts."

"Honey, you don't have any ugly parts."

He slipped a cotton nightdress over my head and I squirmed to have it fall into place. "Well maybe not to you, but little girls don't have to see what is in store for them when they get tangled up with a man and he scars them for life. These stretch marks will be with me forever."

He laughed crawling into bed. "Are you complaining?"

"Yes and no. Don't get too comfortable because you may not want to stay when you hear what I have to tell you." I warned him.

"I doubt that, but go ahead. Dare I ask what you have done that I don't already know about?"

"Ava has my bracelets." I answered glumly.

"**THE** bracelets?"

"Yes, and I am afraid they may be the reason that the plane crashed." I turned my back to him and pulled the quilt over my head.

He uncovered me and rolled me over gently. "Look at me Vienna; you don't really believe that do you?"

"You're the one who said they are cursed, so yes I do."

"I know I said that, but if I really believed it then I would have thrown them into the English Channel. Believe me I thought of it but the girls told me I couldn't. They reminded me that I had bought them out of love for you and held on to them even though I had no idea if I would ever see you again. They represent love, and they do not possess any supernatural powers. Why does Ava have them anyway?"

"Remember, just before she left for Vancouver she said that she'd forgotten to pack her toiletries? I said she could take my "holdall" bag because everything she'd need was in it."

"Yes, because I collected it for her. I didn't know your bracelets were in it."

"I forgot they were in with the rest of the jewellery too When I couldn't find them I realized that I had taken them to London and never unpacked them. I'm so sorry Rainey."

"Shh, you have nothing to be sorry for. You blaming them for Ava's plane crashing is as ludicrous as me blaming them for the earth-quake. Nothing has control over the weather and certainly not some little silver bracelets! You don't even know if Ava had them with her for sure do you? She was only going to be gone for one night, so why would she take an extra carry-on?"

"I don't know Rainey, but just the thought…"

"No more thinking tonight okay? By the way, when did you discover that they were missing?"

"Five days ago." I confessed.

"And you kept it to yourself because you thought I would blame you? Haven't I always told you that you can tell me anything?"

"Yes, I'm sorry; I just felt so guilty."

"No more Honey, no more of this nonsense. Promise me you won't dwell on this all night?"

"I wish I could take one of my "happy pills.""

"Do you mean the ones Dr. Jai prescribed for you?"

"Maybe."

"If it's not them, then what are you referring to?"

"Molly Magan made a potion for me that would help me sleep and calm my anxiety. I still have a vial but daren't take it because it may not be good for the babies."

"I suppose that depends on what all went into the making of the potion. Do you know?"

"Not really; she said it was natural ingredients from her garden."

"Well I have seen that garden and I am pretty sure she grew some hallucinogenic plants and probably those tall green ferny stalks are marijuana so thank God you haven't taken anything."

"She would not have given me something illegal or mind altering Rainey. Maybe Meggie knows what is in the tincture or we can ask Mrs.D. if she knows."

"Why would Mary know?"

"Mary knows everything. She has been taking tonics that Molly and Meggie have concocted for her for years to help with her rheumatism and her own sleep problems."

"Have you been self-administering this potion up until you discovered you were pregnant?"

"No, I haven't needed to take anything since you came back into my life. Your love has quelled my anxiety and I always feel safe with you. Falling asleep in your arms is a pleasure I look forward to every evening, but it is different now Rainey…our daughter is missing."

"I know Honey, I know and I feel your pain. It is no different from mine, but I say let's leave it alone for tonight. After the holiday we'll see if we can come up with something that is safe for you to take. Meggie is still coming here for dinner tomorrow is she not?"

I said that she was and Rainey said that Ava would be home soon and that would put an end to all of our anguish. For now we could only take consolation in each other's arms. I was very agreeable to that.

"Me hearing Ava's voice meant she's alive doesn't it? You don't think it means something else do you?"

"No Darling, it doesn't mean anything else."

I prayed that he was right.

CHAPTER 7

Uncle Bob's Cabin

Nash placed the scrumptious delicately browned turkey on the table in front of Ace and told him that as head of "our" newly formed family it was his job to carve the bird. He did so with expertise and along with surprisingly tasty mashed potatoes that came from a box, rich gravy, creamed corn, cranberries, sage dressing, and piping hot biscuits we feasted on our Christmas dinner in Uncle Bob's Cabin. Monty doled out the remainder of the wine and we drank to each other's health and happiness. Prior to dinner I had suggested that we all take a minute to pass wishes on to our families and pray that they knew we were safe. We said the Lord's Prayer as it seemed appropriate. We saved Evie's shortbread and colorful Christmas Trifle to have with coffee later as we were all stuffed from the delicious meal.

Earlier in the day we had all trekked along the ski-do path that Nash and Monty had carved out along the lake's edge. Evie recorded the occasion on her camera. Monty asked her when she was going to run out of film and she replied, "Not any time soon." We ended the walk with a snowball fight initiated by Nash.

A most enjoyable evening was spent sitting around the fireplace and reminiscing of holidays past and listening to Christmas music on the radio. When the generator shut down we lit our lamps and climbed the stairs to our respective rooms. I don't think I slept a wink all night because I couldn't stop thinking about my family at Avanloch.

After a simple breakfast of leftover biscuits and preserves the next morning Nash and Monty collected some fishing paraphernalia and set off to drill holes in the frozen lake. They were pretty sure that Bob Quinn Lake was home to trout, pike and other northern species. The weather had taken a turn for the worse again and the rest of us declined the invitation to join them on the ice and opted to remain inside the warm lodge and play cards.

I did try my hand at ice fishing a couple of times over the course of the next few weeks but was not successful at even catching a minnow. Standing around on frozen water trying to keep warm around a fire burning in an old oil drum was not my idea of recreation when I could be inside cozying up beside the fireplace. Nash had assured me that we would not stay in Akemantack for the winters as they were too long and that the temperature could reach as low as minus forty. I shivered at the thought. The average mean temperature for the winter months at Avanloch was a balmy thirty five to forty degrees above zero.

The morning of the twenty-seventh dawned free of clouds and fog. Nash had announced the evening before that he and Monty had plans to go hunting if the weather permitted. Nash spent an hour cleaning his rifle and cramming a backpack with binoculars, an assortment of knives, two whistles, small flashlights and whatever else he deemed necessary. Monty was in charge of fueling the snowmobiles and making sure the tools were on board in case of a break down. He had come into the kitchen where Evie and I were making a lunch of turkey sandwiches and holiday goodies for them. He was carrying two sets of snowshoes. I remarked that they appeared as though they could actually hold a man's weight unlike the ones he had constructed out of badminton racquets at the camp.

"No comments from the peanut gallery." He said grinning. "But just for you I am planning on bagging a nice plump bunny rabbit for you to make stew out of."

"Don't you dare Melton Montgomery!" Evie sputtered indignantly.

"Don't worry Honey, I'll get one for you too." Monty teased.

"You know exactly what I meant Monty; we are not eating helpless little bunnies!"

"There may be no big game and we need the protein so…"

Evie stopped him with her hand. "Then you will have to cook it and eat it yourself because Ava and I will have no part of it!"

She stormed out of the room. Monty looked at me. "Is she fricken serious?"

"I think so. My suggestion to you is that you do not come home with a rabbit, and if you don't come back with venison then you are going to have to do a lot more fishing! Now drop those snowshoes and go find Evie and tell her that you weren't serious." I advised him.

He saluted me. "Yes Ma'am," and cursed, "Women!"

He almost collided with Nash as he exited the kitchen.

"What the hell is going on here? What did Monty say to Evie that got her so steamed?"

"Just a little disagreement over rabbits." I answered.

"What?"

"Please see to it that no dead rabbits come back with you...we are not that hungry yet."

He nodded. "Got you. I'm all done so I have time for you now. What do you want to do?"

"You have time for me...how nice of you to fit me in between your chores."

"Sorry, that came out all wrong. You know I'll drop whatever I am doing at any time if you need me."

"I know, and I didn't mean to sound so snarky. I wouldn't be a bit surprised if we have lost Monty and Evie for the night so I guess we'll have a game of canasta with Ace and Sali; what do you say?"

"Sounds good, but just one game as I'd like to get to bed early." He winked and asked me if I thought things were going to develop between Evie and Monty.

"Darling, they already have and I think tonight is the turning point. No playing footsy with me under the card table you hear?" I cautioned.

"I can't promise any such thing." He said grinning from ear to ear.

I got up early the next morning to make coffee for Nash and Monty and to see them off on their hunt. Monty seemed anxious and

I could tell something was on his mind. Nash was at the door ready to go when Monty told him that he wanted to talk to me and could he have a minute. Nash looked at me curiously and said, "Sure, why not?"

As soon as the door closed Monty asked me if I would talk to Evie. I told him of course I would, but did he have something in particular he wanted me to talk to her about.

"Yeah, me; I don't think I came across as a stand-up fellow last night. I'm afraid my weaknesses outweigh my attributes, but I don't think she got the full picture of my failures."

"What weaknesses and failures are we talking about?"

"You know Ava, my lifestyle, my addictions, my debacles with women. I don't want to take advantage of her and our situation, but I don't think I can help myself. She's innocent Ava to the wickedness of man and his lustful ways. I'm not marriage material, especially to someone as pure and unspoiled as her. I can't avoid her and I don't want to but suppose she gets the wrong idea about us and I hurt her badly?"

"What happened with the two of you last night anyhow?"

"You'll have to ask her yourself, but let's just say I am not as noble as Nashman. I did not ask her to marry me. So, will you speak to her on my behalf?" He pleaded.

"I will, but you haven't made it clear whether you want me to build you up or tear you down?"

He frowned. "I don't know myself. You know my weaknesses so you do what you think is best for Evie. I got to go…"

I grabbed him by his coat tail. "Oh no you don't, you are not leaving your romantic future with Evie in my hands! Who do you think I am anyhow? You know perfectly well that I am a novice at this love thing myself so I am not qualified in any way to give advice to anyone, especially two people I am very fond of. You need to fight your own battles but I will be in your corner cheering you along. Have I made myself clear?"

"Sort of. Why was it so easy for you and Nash?"

"Who says it was? We did get rid of our excess baggage right away though and if you haven't come clean with Evie about your past maybe that's the first thing you should do. I am pretty sure it won't make any difference in the way she feels about you. The past is just that Monty and it should have no bearing on the future."

"Me thinks you are too wise my dear. Has Evie spoken favorably of me?"

"Her eyes sparkle when she says your name. She refers to you as a man for all seasons."

"What the hell does that mean?"

"Think about it… you have abilities that most men can only dream about. You can make something out of nothing, you always see a light at the darkest hour, and above all that, you are kind and appreciative."

"You know that you have just described Nash?"

"Well then, I guess you are both cut from the same cloth. Now all you have to do is be honest with yourself and Evie and let nature take its course. Now you best get going." I gave him a peck on the cheek and gave his ruddy whiskers a tug. "Have you ever thought of trimming this thing?"

Nash appeared at the door at that precise moment. "Do I even want to do what is going on here?" He tapped his watch. "Times a wastin man."

I blew him a kiss. "You just let Asta out and the cold air in, you know."

"Damn it; Asta get back in here!"

She came and sat down beside me, tail between her legs. "Don't pay any attention to that old grouch; Mama will take you for a long walk later."

"You'll have to keep her on her leash you know or else she will pick up our trail and follow?"

I bent down and petted her. "What makes you so sure that she wouldn't rather stay with me?"

He grinned. "You're probably right there. Don't get into any trouble okay?"

I waved them out and told them to have a good hunt.

"You have a good day Ava." Monty said winking.

I picked up our empty coffee cups and placed them in the sink. I suggested to Asta that we go back to bed. The swinging kitchen doors swung open.

"Have they gone?" Evie asked.

"Just barely; you can probably still catch Monty if you want to see him."

She went to the stove and poured herself a cup of coffee and asked me if I wanted a refill. I shook my head. She said there was no need as she had seen him earlier.

I glanced at the clock and wondered how much earlier she was talking about. She sat down.

"Did you talk to him? Did he tell you that we spent the night together?"

Her demeanour was out of character. Yesterday she would have been blushing and unable to look me in the eye, but today she was full of confidence and asked me what I thought about that.

"It doesn't matter what I think Evie, the question is what and how do you feel about it?"

"Do you want to know what happened?" She continued before I could answer. "He followed me to my room you know. He apologised profusely about the "rabbit thing" and asked me if I had thought he was serious. I said I didn't know and then I apologised telling him that I knew he was only thinking about feeding us. He sat next to me on the bed and asked if we could talk and we did for an hour or so. He told me about his ex-wives and son. You already know about them don't you?"

I nodded.

"He told me a lot of malarkey about himself. I think that he thought that by demeaning himself he could discourage me because he knew that I had feelings for him. He told me I shouldn't hang my star on him because he was no good for anyone, and especially me. Then he said that he was very fond of me but it would be best for me if we just be friends. He patted my head like I was a five year old child and said good night. I let him go without saying a word. I waited until you had all gone to bed and then I went to his room. I could see that his lamp was on so he was either still awake or had fallen asleep without turning it off. I didn't knock; I just turned the knob and walked in. He was sitting by the window with a glass in his hand. I got the distinct feeling that he was expecting me. He poured me a drink and I sat down across from him. We just sat there looking at each other and not saying a word until our glasses were empty. I asked him if I could stay the night with him and that I didn't expect anything afterwards. I said that I might regret it but I doubted it. I didn't wait for an answer but started to get undressed. He came to me then Ava and the rest is history. I hope he doesn't think I am a loose woman. I've never even thought of doing something like that. What do you think came over me?"

I tried not to laugh. "Oh Evie honey, that is not what he thinks of you at all. His exact words were that you were innocent and unspoiled and too good for him. He thinks you're an angel and I think what came over you was pure and simple good old fashioned desire."

"So he did tell you that we slept together?"

"Not in so many words, but I kind of got the gist of his rhetoric."

"Do you think he likes me Ava?"

"Oh, he likes you all right. He is kind of dancing on thin ice."

"What do you mean by that?"

I didn't get to answer her as Ace and Sali came in saying that there had better be coffee.

I was not so anxious about being rescued ever since I had the dream on Boxing Day. I wasn't even sure if it was a dream or if I'd had a premonition. I decided not to tell anyone because most people don't believe in such things and I didn't want to get their hopes up, and I didn't really believe it myself. Nash caught me however when the date just popped out when he asked me how our inventory had gone.

Monty and he had returned home from their hunt with a young two point moose and two grouse. I was glad that they hadn't bagged a Bambi. I had never eaten moose meat before but Sali said that it was better than any other meat if prepared properly and Nash certainly knew how to do that. The two of them had fresh liver for supper that night while the rest of us finished off the turkey. Monty promised us that we would have the best spaghetti sauce ever when he made it with the grouse the next day. I was looking forward to not having to cook.

I cautioned Ace and Sali and Nash that Monty's and Ava's relationship may have reached a new level and that they may be a little sensitive to remarks.

"Christ, now I've lost two good men to whatever's in this northern air!" Ace exclaimed.

Sali just laughed and said it was about time.

Nash chased them both out of the kitchen with a spatula saying he needed to spend a few minutes alone with me. While he was frying the floured liver in hot grease I badgered him about keeping his cooking skills a secret from me.

"I've been a bachelor for a very long time so I had no choice but to learn the basics or starve. Meat and potatoes are about all I can manage. I leave the rest up to Cajun Max."

"Max doesn't sound much like a Cajun name. I thought the Cajuns were of French heritage?"

"His full name is Maximilian Virgile and his family was originally from eastern Quebec and were known as Acadians. Some time ago they made their way south to Louisiana. I am not sure why, but Max makes it sound as though they were exiled. Anyhow, many drifted back to Canada and settled here and there. Cajun is the French pronunciation of Acadia; the name given to the lands in a portion of the French colonial empire. That's all I know. Max just appeared at my doorstep one day five or six years ago and said he needed a job and had heard that I was looking for a hired hand who was good with animals, could cook and was not afraid of hard work. How he had got wind of that I do not know as he had come directly from some little settlement in the Maritimes. He said he came upon my ad in the Free Press that I had posted and he wanted to come out to the northwest and so he hitchhiked his way to Vancouver and then took a bus to Ft. St. John. From there he caught rides with transport trucks until he ended up in Spring Valley where he paid someone to drop him off on my doorstep. He didn't write or send me his qualifications or anything; he just came. He arrived with the clothes on his back and one duffle bag. He has never told me much about himself and I don't ask. I am sure there is quite a story there but I respect his privacy. He was a little hard to understand at first but I have gotten use to his French dialect. He's fifty nine years old, stands six foot three and can wrestle a bear to the ground. When my cat died two days after giving birth to three kittens he became their surrogate mother. He sent me into town to get bottles and formula and to this day they follow him everywhere, so he is also a gentle giant. He's the chief cook and bottle washer and looks after the place like it is his own. I never have any qualms about leaving for the winter."

"How is he going to feel about you bringing a wife home?"

"He's always saying to me, "Why don't you go find yourself a nice comfortable woman Nash? She be good for you and there be less work for me but you got to look her over better than you did the last one." I told him that the same goes for him and he replied that once you've had the best there ain't no more lookin to do. That's as close as he has ever come to indicating that there was once someone in his life. He'll like you just fine Hon, but let's not put the cart before the horse as there is no guarantee that you will take to my way of life. You may not be able to live in Akemantack Ava."

"What would you do with me then?"

"I'd go wherever you want to go, Scotland, Vancouver, middle earth, anywhere."

"That's not how you reacted to Avery's refusal to live in your world."

"If it wasn't obvious then it is now, and that is that she didn't mean very much to me. Obviously I was not head over heels in love with her like I am with you. I will make whatever sacrifice I have to just to keep you in my life… is that clear?"

"Very, but it's not going to be necessary because I know I am going to love living with you in the backwoods of British Columbia and we get to come out every winter so what could be so horrible about that? Nash, suppose if you had of married Avery and then we met just as we did, what would have happened then? Have you ever thought about that?"

He shook his head. "Sweetie, only you would think of something like that. It didn't happen, so why go there?"

"I guess because I am my mother's daughter."

"Yeah, well that makes sense to no one but you. Now let's get off this morbid nonsense and tell me how you made out with your calculations of how long our provisions will last?"

"I think we will be good until February the second." I bit my tongue as soon as I said it.

"Why February second; are we out of staples by then?

"Oh, I just meant that we would do another inventory around that time, that's all."

"I don't think so Ava or else you would have said so. You named a specific day…why? Will we be out of food by then or do you know something that the rest of us don't?"

"Don't be silly; of course not! And now with the moose meat we will have no trouble holding on. Is the liver cooked? Come on then, let's eat."

He took hold of my arm. "I'm getting to know you pretty well Ava Lane Nash and you speak often of your mother and her friend Meggie and of prophesying and reading the future in cards. Have you done that… have you predicted when we'll be found?"

"I can't read tarot cards and I certainly don't have any. If you must know, I dreamt that we would be rescued on February the second, but it certainly doesn't mean that we will be. There, are you happy now and don't you dare mention it to anyone else!"

"Oh, I'm happy all right, my wife is a soothsayer. We are going to be rescued on Groundhog Day…sounds fitting."

I smacked him. "Very funny."

We celebrated New Year's Eve with a late supper of Nash's barbecued moose meat ribs, my baked beans, Monty's smoked trout, Sali's bannock and Evie's shortbread. Ace contributed his appetite. We played charades, danced and rang in the New Year with the countdown on an American television station. We all slept in the next day and awoke to Asta's loud barking. Nash dressed quickly and ran down stairs to see what all the commotion was about. He yelled for Monty and Ace. There was definitely a tone of panic in his voice.

Wondering what was going on I slipped into my housecoat and joined Evie and Sali who were standing near the top of the stairs holding on to each other. They were fixated on the men downstairs who were all holding rifles aimed towards the porch door. I asked what was going on. Evie whispered that it was a bear. Sali corrected her and said that it wasn't just any old bear but that it was a grizzly. He had broken down the outside door and was trying his best to do the same to the inside one. Luckily, it was made of solid fir and it would probably hold him back.

I watched in horror as the massive beast appeared at the lounge window and stood up. I gasped; he towered over the men by several feet. He opened his giant mouth and bellowed and the lodge shook. Asta had backed up but continued to growl ferociously. Nash was trying to send her away as the bear's focus seemed to be on her. I felt like disaster was about to strike and without giving it any thought I ran down the stairs and snatched her up. I think Nash yelled at me. I heard the window shatter the second I hit the first step and the retort of a dozen bullets echoing in my ears. Sali grabbed me and Asta as I screamed out Nash's name.

"It's all right Dumpling; the beast is down."

I collapsed on the stairs. Evie sat down beside me and told me to put my head between my legs and take some deep breaths. I did as I was told.

"I think your woman needs you Nash. Evie, you and Sal okay?" Monty yelled up at us.

Sali said they were coming down. Nash climbed the stairs and took me in his arms.

"You nearly gave me a bloody heart attack Ava. What were you thinking?"

All I could get out was, "Asta, Asta…"

"She's fine, we are all fine. Did you forget that she's a bear dog? I'm going to take her down and let her see that the bear is dead and then I want you to keep her in the kitchen while we come up with a way to get that critter out of here. Can you do that?"

"Of course I can. I'm sorry Nash; it's my fault that it crashed through the window isn't it?"

"He was coming through one way or the other so no, it's not your fault."

"Where did he come from? You would have told us if you had seen any signs of a bear hanging around wouldn't you? Suppose if we had of been out on one of our long walks along the lake? I'll probably never feel safe outside again." I shivered.

"No, there have been no signs and you can bet we'll be carrying guns with us from now on. This is a most unusual and isolated occurrence. I have never seen anything like it in all my years in the wilds or even heard of an attack as such. If we could do a post-mortem on it I am pretty sure we would find that the bear was literally starving to death for one reason or the other. He is pretty emaciated and he's missing teeth so I think he was one sick puppy." He tilted my head up. "I wasn't too worried as I knew we had the fire power to take him down. Now I know what Monty meant about you and the wolf. Promise me that this is your last act of bravery?"

"I can't promise you anything, but you are wrong, I was scared to death."

"Yeah, we all were. Take the girls and Asta and stay in the kitchen until we get the beast out of here. Do you think you can make a pot of coffee?"

"Of course and we can help you drag him out of here you know?"

"I do. There's going to be a lot of clean-up what with the broken window and door, not to mention blood so maybe get the cleaning supplies ready. If you gals can't handle the blood, don't worry, Monty and I can."

"As long as it is not yours or anyone else's, I can."

Nash laughed. "That's my girl. Come on, let's go down and see if Monty and Ace have devised a plan to haul that giant bruin out of here."

That was how we spent New Year's Day; having a most unpleasant visitation and cleaning up the aftermath. The guys had managed to get the critter out using a winch and the snowmobiles. They dragged it a safe distance from the lodge and left it for the scavengers to enjoy. The screen on the front porch was toast but the door itself was reparable. A piece of plastic and scrap lumber now occupied the space where the window had been. We were thankful that the beast had landed on the wood floor and not the carpet. We would have a lot of explaining to do to the owners.

I got another lecture from my husband that night when we finally made it to bed. I responded to it by asking him to give me a refresher course on firearms as it had been a long time since I had fired a gun and that it was only a twenty-two and that certainly wasn't the weapon needed up here. He hugged me and said that maybe that was a good idea. I asked him if there were a lot of grizzlies in Akemantack. He said that with the dozen or so dogs in the village and his three the area was bear free and that it was rare for him to see a grizzly even on his treks. I wasn't sure that I believed him but I wouldn't pursue the matter anymore tonight. I had found out that Nash had two other dogs beside Asta. They were black and tan German Shepherds, brother and sister and were five years old. Their names were Carter and Cash; named after June Carter and Johnny Cash. He also had three horses and the three cats. Three seemed to be his number. I asked him why he had brought Asta with him and what did he do with her when he went to Belize. He replied that his first stop last November had been to Quesnel where he left her with his parents. She was overdue for booster vaccines and the vet clinic in Spring Valley was temporary closed due to the owner's illness. His parents had delivered her to Vancouver for him and to have an early Christmas with him as he was pretty sure he wouldn't make it back to Quesnel because of the prox-imity for his outing with the "businessmen." He laughed and said he had not been looking forward to taking a bunch of green horns on a winter wilderness adventure but it was money in the bank so he had accepted. The plane crash took care of that and he hoped that they weren't sitting on his doorstep waiting for him.

A new Monty greeted us at the kitchen table the next morning. I liked what I saw. He winked at Evie and said that it was a new year and he had a new outlook on life so he had decided to take my advice and trim his beard. Trim was not the right word as it was completely gone. He was forty three and had definitely looked his age before. The transformation was astounding and I remarked that he looked ten years younger. He grinned and said that there had been a reason for his madness and we all knew that the reason was Evie. Nash told me later that he had never known Monty without the red beard and it was going to take some getting used to. I guessed that love made people do unusual things.

And so the days turned into weeks and nothing much changed. We continued with our walks along the lake paths. The only tracks we ever saw were deer, racoon and squirrel, but the guys always carried their rifles, just to be safe. Monty came across a fifty pound bag of bird seed tucked away in a corner of the basement. He didn't find any bird feeders in the sheds so he made one out of a sawn log and hung it up outside the dining room window. Dozens of chickadees arrived within minutes of filling it with the nutty mixture. Woodpeckers and two blue jays also came to visit along with a couple of squirrels. They gave us hours of pleasure watching and listening to their chatter.

"I hope it doesn't come down to us needing that birdseed one day when all the other food is gone." Ace had said gloomily one evening.

Monty said that as long as there was game in the woods and fish in the lake it was never going to come to that. Nash looked at me cheekily and asked if I had anything to add and. I ignored him and said it was time to get the coffee and pie.

"There's pie?" Ace asked with baited breath.

"Yes, Evie and I attempted to try our hands at making pastry. Don't get too excited as it may not taste as good as it looks. You have cherry or apple to choose from. I'm sure they would be better if we had made them with fresh fruit but beggars can't be choosy you know."

"Who cares, bring it on girls!"

The pie crust was no match for Mary McDuffs, but there were no complaints. My husband kept smiling at me after every bite and I wasn't sure whether he was complementing me with his eyes or if there was something entirely unrelated on his mind.

Sali usually accompanied Nash and Monty ice fishing. Evie and I would walk down with them but never stayed long as we would rather be back in a warm kitchen baking and planning supper. There were a lot of old things like coffee cans and utensils adorning the walls. I wouldn't call them antiques, but maybe they were as they had certainly seen better days. Monty and Nash thought they could clean a corroded grinder sufficiently so that they could make hamburger. They did, and we now had moose hamburger to experiment with. The guys were quite happy with barbecuing burgers with Nash's special sauce and eating them on fresh baked sourdough. That was our suppers at least twice a week.

The evenings were usually spent playing cards or watching a hockey game on television. Nash was stingy with the amount of time the generator could be run each night and so it was then that we would do laundry, run the deep freeze and watch an hour or two of T.V. We were usually in bed by ten o'clock. The weather remained unsettled. Most days started with a promise of sun but quickly escalated into cloud and light drizzle. Nash woke me up one evening at midnight and insisted that I come outside with him. I went, but I wasn't very enthusiastic about doing so. I changed my mind when I witnessed the spectacle that graced the sky. I had seen the Northern Lights many times back home, but here it was as if they were on a giant picture screen right in front of me. I was awe stuck and though I was near freezing I did not want to leave the picture show. Luckily the next three nights remained cold and clear and we were treated to the magnificent sight over and over again. The best viewing spot was down at the lake's edge. The guys would make a bonfire and we would sit and enjoy the phenomenon in comfort on benches that they had found in storage. Hours passed, our coffee or hot toddies would become icy but we were too engrossed with the entertainment to care. Evie used up a roll of film hoping that her camera was good enough to take night photos. I was pretty sure these colorful wonders of the north would remain with me forever… but wait, I reminded myself that I'd be living up here so I'd be seeing them whenever they chose to come out and dance.

Suddenly it was January the twenty eighth and we had not seen one full day of clear blue skies. It was evident that we were not in any flight path as we had never even heard the drone of an airplane. We had been separated from the rest of the world for forty two days. Ace was becoming more and more antsy every day. He was helping Nash and Monty with chores, but seemed to tire easily. I was worried that he had an undetected infection.

One night just before the cards were dealt, he uncharacteristically lifted up his shirt and said, "Look Doc, no scarring!"

I reached across the table and took a closer look as I hadn't inspected his wound site for some time. "Not so one would notice, but there is still an indentation where the cut was deepest."

"You should have stitched me up Doc."

"Yes, I should have." We looked at each other and broke out in laughter.

"I don't know what they find so funny Nash but I assume it is there little secret, just like her little chats with Monty. What do you make of it?" Sali smiled impishly.

Nash said that he hadn't noticed.

"Like hell you haven't!" Monty disagreed. "Every time Ava and I spend two minutes together you ask what is going on."

"Guilty as charged. I can't help it if my wife is charming and amicable to you two buffoons, can I? And, I think maybe you should stop trying to cause trouble Sal." Nash said good-humouredly. "And, by the way, I know exactly what is going on. If Monty's not seeking advice about Evie then Ace wants to talk about his wife."

"Not always Nash; sometimes we just want to ask her what's for supper." Ace disagreed.

"I wish you would stop considering **my** wife as your personal chef Ace."

I sat there twiddling my fingers amused by the conversation and asked if this was what cabin fever was. I was met with a resounding "No!" Evie suggested they quit talking about me as if I wasn't in the room and deal the cards. "And, to set the record straight, I am glad that Monty had Ava to bounce things off of because you all may not know, but if Monty had of rejected me I might have gone off the deep edge."

Monty patted her hand. "That was never going to happen girl. I may be a buffoon, as Nash so aptly pointed out, but I am not stupid and I'm going to state it here in front of you all that I love this gal and she's crazy enough to love me. We're planning to have a rosy future together."

Evie was crying quietly. Nash got up and shook Monty's hand and hugged Evie.

"I wish I could say something good about this man Evie but nothing is coming to mind so I will just say, "Good luck Honey; you're gonna need it."

Monty laughed. Sali congratulated them and said she had predicted it just as she had Nash and me. I got up and went into the den and came back with the last bottle of chardonnay; it was Evie's favorite. Nash collected some glasses and poured the wine. I made the first toast but only pretended to drink. I had my suspicions that I might be pregnant.

"To my two dear friends; you two are as opposite as night and day but your personalities have melded and you've become one. I love you and I hope you will find much happiness together and stay in my life forever." I was overcome with emotion.

"Do I have to say it again? Cupid apparently lives in this damn North Country. Thank the stars that Sali and I have our mates waiting for us back home. One more thing; Monty, this better not mean that our flying days are over? Evie, be gentle with him will you?" Ace raised his glass.

"I can't promise you anything Buddy. Let's get out of here first and then it will be day by day."

We all said, "Amen."

We awoke to a dense fog on January twenty ninth. Nash kept saying that it was going to burn off and the skies would clear. My husband was a very poor weather forecaster. It was by far the dreariest day since the little blizzard we had faced up at the camp. We couldn't even see as far as the bird feeder. At noon I stuck my head out the door and was immediately engulfed in what I could only describe as wet pea soup of which I was very familiar with. The bleakness of the day added to the despondency of our situation. I hoped that a nice hot meal at supper would perk everyone up a little. Nash cut up some moose meat into cubes and I browned them and made a broth and added barley and the last of the jar of minced onion and put it on the stove to cook slowly. We were almost out of canned vegetables. I figured by adding a can of corn and throwing in a handful or two of macaroni I could extend the stew to last a few days and I could try my hand at dumplings. Evie thought a chocolate cake would be the perfect dessert and I left her assembling it and keeping an eye on the soup. I had developed a slight headache and thought a little rest might make it go away. It wasn't long until Nash found me.

"How did you manage to sneak by me Ava? This isn't like you to lie down in the middle of the day. Are you feeling all right?" He felt my head.

"I wasn't sneaking. My head hurts and my stomach is a little upset, that's all."

"You work too hard. I'll get you an aspirin."

"I don't need one."

"Why not, you said you have a headache?"

"I'll be all right. Just cover me up and leave me for a half hour or so okay?" I think I fell asleep the minute he closed the door.

The thumping of the generator woke me up. I was alarmed to think that I had slept until dark. I jumped up and without even glancing at the clock dashed downstairs. Everyone was sitting at the dining room table playing cards. I asked Nash why he let me sleep so long. He said it had only been a couple of hours.

"So why is the generator running?"

"Because I thought the light might dispel some of the gloom. Is your headache gone?"

I said it was but for some reason I felt rather disoriented. I said that I was going to make a pot of tea and did anyone want any. Nash followed me into the kitchen and asked if I was ill because it was very unlike me to drink tea. I shrugged my shoulders and checked on the stew.

"It doesn't appear as though my dream is going to come true does it?"

"Is that what is bothering you? It's going to happen any day now Ava, we have to believe that." He put his arms around me and hugged me tightly.

I hugged him back and somehow managed not to cry.

It was the perfect night for ghost stories. We settled around the fireplace with our various choices of after dinner drinks; tea for us girls and whiskey for the guys. Nash remarked that it was the last of his stock and they would be reduced to brandy and cognac from then on.

Monty launched right into the subject of the night. "You've told us about your sister's mother haunting your castle Ava, and you've hinted that there are more, so out with it, are there anymore spirits hanging around? Surely there is at least one poltergeist?"

"We do not look on Maveryn's visits as a haunting Monty. I think I told you that before didn't I? She is the only spirit I have seen and as far as I know, there are no poltergeists. No one has ever mentioned things being disturbed, doors do not open and shut on their own and the piano doesn't start playing on its own." I stopped speaking but suddenly remembered something. I guess Nash could see that I was lost in thought because he asked me what had me perplexed. "There was this one incident that we never found an explanation for...I had forgotten about it until just now. It was shortly after my mother and father were married. Maveryn came to visit. I think she wanted my father see her."

"Really Ava, and what did he think about that?" Nash asked flippantly.

"Let her tell the story Nashman!" Monty implored.

I gave Nash the evil eye and he groaned. "Anyhow, as I was saying before I was interrupted; a strange notation in a journal in my mother's sitting room was pointed out to my mother and father by Maveryn. It warned that three strangers were going to come to the doors of Avanloch. One stranger would be invited and one would have a mission to fulfill, but the third would deliver a message of extreme peril and it should not be ignored or much grief would come upon the house. There were no other entries in the journal and my mother did not recognise the handwriting. My father thought someone in the house was playing a cruel trick and vowed to find out who the culprit was. No logical conclusion was ever determined, so maybe it was a poltergeist. According to my parents, the pages did appear magically when Maveryn took them into the sitting room."

"I just got goose bumps Ava. Do you think that the message was warning your mother not to travel to Andorra?" Evie shuddered.

"Oh, most certainly! After her disappearance we all wished that she had paid attention to the portent, and especially when it was reaffirmed by her friend Meggie who had foreseen danger in her travels."

"This Meggie is your mother's gypsy friend who tells fortunes and reads cards?"

"Yes Evie. She also predicted that my mother would be found alive and that green, water and lilies were a clue to her whereabouts. She may have never been found if it wasn't for my father's friend Stu running into her in Verde El Mar, which incidentally means green water. The reference to lilies no doubt refers to Mama naming my baby sister Liliana. So we concluded that Meggie was the third stranger as the other two were accounted for. Meggie was Molly Meagan's granddaughter and my mother's dear friend whom you've heard me speak of. Word had been sent to her after Molly's death informing her that she was the sole inheritor of her grandmother's estate, which by all means, was no great size, but still it was something. So, that is what we concluded because no one wanted to even entertain the idea that it was the Black Russian's doing." Oops, I said to myself, I shouldn't have mentioned her. I got up and asked if anyone wanted anything. Nash pulled me back down on the sofa.

"Whoa there young lady…where do you think you are going? Who are the other two strangers and who the hell is the black Russian?"

Everyone was staring at me waiting for my answer. "I should not have mentioned her but seeing I did, I will quell your curiosity. Her real name was Tatylyanna Speshiloff and she was once my adoptive father's fiancée. He broke it off with her when it was discovered that she planned on robbing him blind so that the coffers of her family could be refurbished. She did not take the rejection well and returned to Avanloch from her family home in Russia. Jeremy was away on one of his overseas business trips so the household had to deal with her and her insolence. She refused to leave and put them through a living hell. Aunt Jannie was in charge of the household then and was about to have her forcefully removed from the castle.

It never came to that as Taty mysteriously fell to her death down the grand stairway."

"Why would you say mysteriously Ava?" Nash queried.

I shrugged my shoulders. "There has been talk that she may have been pushed, that's all."

"By anyone we have heard of?"

"There is a mixed opinion on that. First, Aunt Jannie and Mary McDuff thought it was the ghost of LizBeth, but then she was found alive so it couldn't have been her. Second opinion was that it was Miss Mary. I'm going to quit talking now."

Nash laughed. "I think not my dear. You are not going to pull another Shahrazad on me and the others. I know who Miss Mary is, but maybe the others don't, and you still haven't told us who the other strangers in the warning are."

"Yes Ava, don't leave us in suspense, please." Evie pleaded.

"It is really not all that interesting you know. Miss Mary was Jeremy's grandmother and she met a most untimely and heartbreaking death by falling through the windows in the conservatory. As far as I know she has never presented herself in any way or form to anyone so it is most unlikely that she was the force behind Taty's death. Miss Mary's death was devastating to the family. Her husband destroyed the conservatory and it sat in a state of ruin until my mother restored it. Her room was left intact; the closets are still full of her stylish clothes which Jeremy insisted my mother make full use of and she does, that is when she isn't pregnant as Miss Mary was a very petite woman. Rosy and I were always allowed to dress-up in her jewels and high heels when we young just as Lili and Tanny are today. As for the other two strangers, one was Roberge Farradan, my mother's friend who was the invited one and Taty's daughter was the one who had a mission to fulfill and that was to take her mother home so she could be at peace."

Nash asked why her body had not been sent home to her family in Russia after her death.

"Who said it wasn't? Somehow her evil soul remained and Maveryn was tormented by it as she lay dying. She is the one who dubbed her the Black Russian and she insisted that Jeremy put locks on room six and promise that it would never be unlocked again. Unfortunately, it was opened again many years later which resulted in dire consequences. However, that is all in the past and room six has been reconstructed. Taty's daughter was able to capture her mother's soul and so freed Avanloch. Don't ask me how because I have no idea how it was done. Now I am through talking or else the night will go on and on with gibberish about the Grey Lady and white witches and séances and Avaleena's diaries. I have to leave something in the vault for another night, don't I? Are you coming to bed Nash?"

He said he would be up in a minute. I wished everyone sweet dreams. I did my nightly routine and was just crawling into bed when Nash came in. I had left the curtains open as I was hoping that the night would clear and the Aurora Borealis would come out to dance. Nash grinned mischievously and said, "Hi Sweetie." He undressed quickly and cuddled up to me and asked if I was going to keep my back turned on him. I told him that maybe I just wanted my backside warmed up and he said he could definitely do that. He rested his cheek on my shoulder.

"The Black Russian hey?"

"Yes, and don't you dare bring her up in front of my father!"

"I promise I won't even though I am pretty sure there is way more to the story. Turn over please Ava; I want to look at you one last time before I turn the lamp off. There's my beautiful girl. I love you Ava and I can't imagine life without you."

"Silly old goose, you never have to because I'm not going any-where without you."

"It can never get any better than it is right now, can it Ava?"

"We'll find out together now won't we?"

As if by some miracle, the fog dissipated and the sun broke through the very next day. Monty and Nash had spray painted an S.O.S. distress signal on the lake's frozen surface shortly after we had arrived at the lodge. Feeling hopeful that our day of salvation was imminent, they scurried off to give it a much needed new coat of red dye. After two days and no sight or sound of an aircraft, our hopes were diminished once more. We were running dangerously low on staples, the moose meat was almost gone and we were running out of fuel for the generator. Monty and Nash geared up for another hunt and to replenish the wood pile. Evie and I sifted through what was left in the pantries; it wasn't very promising. We still had six turkeys so decided to unthaw one. We had used up all of the milk but still had several pounds of butter, one dozen frozen eggs and a block of cheese left. Thank heavens we had flour and the sourdough culture. The canned fruit, vegetables and soup were all gone. We had a few tins of Spam left and enough pasta for three meals and there was plenty of coffee, tea, cocoa and peanut butter. If we had to live on bread and jam and peanut butter and moose meat, then so be it.

Half an hour ago we sent Monty and Nash off on their hunt with a thermos of coffee and another one full of leftover stew and some sourdough bread. I stood at the kitchen window and wondered why I hadn't heard the sleds leaving. Ace said he'd take a hike up to the shed and see what was happening. He returned saying that the air was pretty blue up there. Apparently one of the snowmobiles had sprung some sort of leak and the guys were attempting to repair it but so far had not had any luck in doing so. It wasn't long afterwards that Nash came up the basement steps covered from head to toe in oil. He asked me and none too politely, I might add, to get him a change of clothes. I did and I suggested that they shelve the hunt for another day. I did not like the look I saw in his eyes. His little fit of temper was most unsettling. He made me feel like I was responsible for the breakdown. He stormed out of the kitchen with his clean clothes and a few minutes later I heard the basement door slam. Evie came in and asked me what was going on. I said I had just witnessed a side of my husband that I hadn't known existed. I needed some air so I put on my coat and mukluks and headed down to the lake. Evie had wanted to come with me but I thanked her and said I needed some alone time and that Asta would keep me company. I sat on the bench and stared out across the frozen expanse. I tried to reason why Nash had reacted so angrily to my suggestion of postponing the hunt. It wasn't as if we were going to starve to death in the next two or three days. I felt tears sting my eyes but wiped them away quickly. The sun was delightfully warm and I decided to go for a little jog. I came to the end of the trail and without even considering the risk of running into a wild animal I ventured into the woods following Asta and some little tracks. They looked like those of a common house cat. Had the owners of the lodge left one behind? We hadn't gone very far when I heard a strange cry and rustling in the trees. No domestic cat I knew of sounded like that. My heart was beating rapidly and I scolded myself for being so stupid. Asta was growling and her hair was standing up on end. I daren't turn my back on whatever was lying in wait for us so I started walking slowly backwards. I tried to remember what Nash had told me about encountering wild animals…was it to make yourself as big as you could and yell? I raised my arms above my head just as my eyes caught a movement to the left of me. Sure enough, it was a cat…a very big cat. He was standing on the top of a large snow covered rock staring at us. His fierce yellow eyes penetrated into my soul. I didn't scream, maybe because I couldn't, but I did freeze in my tracks and all I could think of was if I survived this, I'd be dead anyhow as Nash was probably going to kill me. Asta was barking ferociously and the cat snarled and looked as if it was ready to pounce when it suddenly raised his head and looked beyond us.

"Drop to the ground Ava!" Nash ordered.

I didn't have to be told twice. I heard two shots ring out over my head. "Don't shoot him Nash, don't shoot him!"

Nash dropped his rifle and sunk to the ground pulling me into his arms. He was whispering something inaudible. I saw Monty behind us, gun still aimed where the cat had been perched. "Is he dead, did you kill him Monty? It was my fault; he shouldn't have to die because we ventured into his territory." I sobbed.

"He's not dead Ava; we aimed above his head just to scare him off. How about we get you out of here and then you can tell us what the hell you were doing out here all alone in the first place. It's me isn't it? It's the way I spoke to you isn't it? Well I can't take that back but I can apologise for taking my frustrations out on you. Thank God you had the sense to take Asta with you. Without her barking…I don't even want to think about it, but I'm definitely having second thoughts about you living in Akemantack."

I brushed his hands off me. "Then I guess you made a big mistake marrying me. I won't get in your way anymore, and you won't have to come looking for me ever again!" I stormed past him. Monty took hold of me and asked me where I thought I was going in such a huff.

"You've never struck me as the kind of girl who goes running off half-cocked or can't face up to her blunders. So Nash yelled at you a little; is it worth almost getting yourself killed?"

I wanted to hit him but I knew he was right. At the precise time I was apologizing an unexpected sound penetrated the silence of the skies. We all looked up and there it was…what we had been waiting seven weeks for…silver wings in the sky.

"Well, I'll be a son of a bitch!" Monty exclaimed. "Come on kids; get a move on!"

Nash took my hand. "You heard the man Babe; let's get out of here!"

We covered the distance back to the lodge in record time yelling and waving as we ran. The rest were waiting by the SOS signal on the lake gesturing to the small plane circling them. We arrived just as the pilot dipped his wings and sped off to the south. It was two P.M. on February the first, forty seven days after the day we had crashed.

We were all pretty giddy and Nash and I forgot our personal problems while we were celebrating. Apparently everyone was outside looking for me when the aircraft was heard up the hill. Ace said he figured the pilot had spotted our downed plane and realized that we had fled the camp and had the good sense to investigate further. He assured us that we would be rescued tomorrow and that we better get a move on righting Uncle Bob's Cabin.

Nash held me back as the rest made their way up to the lodge.

"Are we all right Ava? Are you going to forgive me?"

"I am on one condition and that being that you forgive me first for being so stupid."

"I thought we weren't going to use that word? You weren't stupid honey, you weren't thinking clearly and all because I yelled at you needlessly. When Evie came up to the shed and told us that you had been gone for two hours and that her and Sali couldn't find you and you weren't answering to their calling, I really lost it. Monty laid into me saying he had warned me many times before that my temper was going to get me into serious trouble one day and I was terrified that that day had come. If anything had of happened to you Ava…"

"It didn't Nash. I think that perhaps I scared myself sufficiently good this time. But in my defense, I was only following tiny tracks. I thought that a cat had been left behind so imagine my surprise when I came face to face with the mountain lion. I'm sorry I was so careless. Please say you will reconsider about taking me home with you, or do you want a divorce?"

He laughed. "Yeah, I want a divorce all right; a divorce from my temper maybe, but never from you. We are going to talk about where we are going to live another day, but not today. And in your defense, those tracks you saw were not those of a common house cat. They were made days ago while the snow was soft and are distorted from freezing and thawing. I'm sure Asta was more interested in them then you were, but you felt that you had to follow her, right? Okay, shall we join the others? This is a day for celebration and there is no one in the world I would rather be celebrating with than you."

"I really want to live with you in Akemantack Nash…"

He kissed me and said that we had lots of time to figure things out.

I asked him if he had been smoking.

"Sorry Babe, but when Sali came up and said that they couldn't find you I had a drag or two of Monty's cig hoping it would calm me down."

"Did it?"

"No."

"Did you enjoy it?"

"A little."

"Then you shouldn't give it up; life's too short not to do what you enjoy."

"I can live without it. Besides, it's a dirty habit and not good for one's health. Do you still love me Ava?"

"I do and I certainly don't want you dying prematurely on us so I'm good with your decision."

We walked in on a cleaning frenzy. Sali was scrubbing the sink and Evie was all set to wash the floor. Ace and Monty were on their way downstairs to straighten out the basement. Nash said he would help me in the other rooms as soon as he showered as he was still greasy. Monty said that they could handle it and that Nash and I needed to iron out our differences so "scat."

Nash said that we had already taken care of that. I wasn't too sure that we had. I sent him on his way and asked for the pail under the sink so that I could clean our bathroom. I did not follow him upstairs but went into the den and closed the door and started cleaning the mantle and the outside of the fireplace with full intentions of cleaning the upstairs bathroom, but the one in the den would get done first. Monty had started the generator and I thought that music would help get the jobs done faster so I put some records on the stereo and turned it down low. I didn't hear Nash come in until he snuck up behind me and encircled me in his arms. I jumped a little.

"Sorry Honey, I didn't mean to startle you. I thought you were going to join me upstairs?"

"There is work to be done down here and I want to do my share." I pulled away from him.

"Are you still pissed with me Ava?" He asked hesitantly.

"I don't like that word."

"Sorry, but If you want to live with the rough and tough men and women of the north then you had better learn to put up with their colorful language and unrefined ways. I know it's going to be hard for such a young and refined lady as you are but..."

I didn't let him finish his sentence. "You've changed your mind...I can come live with you?"

"Yes, my sweet. Was there ever any doubt? We will need to set a few ground rules though. Are you agreeable to that?"

"Yes, anything you say." I threw my arms around him. "I know I was wrong to venture off on my own; I could have killed us both."

"I was never in any danger Ava."

I backed up a little and placed my hands on my stomach. "I didn't mean you Nash; I meant me and our baby."

We didn't lose eye contact. He took my hands and sat me down on the sofa. "Is this why you have been off your oats… is it because you're pregnant?"

"Have I been cranky; I'm sorry I haven't meant to be."

"I wouldn't say cranky, just different and then you were ill yesterday, so maybe that's why?"

"I'm not positive that I am pregnant and yet, I am pretty sure. Are you all right with it if I am?"

"Well Honey, I'm pretty sure that you didn't get this way all on your own, so yes I am perfectly all right with knowing that we are going to have a baby. We talked about this remember? I would have liked you all to myself for a while longer, but my mother taught me how to share…so yeah, I'm good." He beamed radiantly.

"I suppose we could have postponed the inevitable for a while longer if we had been able to keep our hands off each other." I said smiling back at him.

He laughed. "Yeah, well from the minute I met you I pretty much knew that wasn't going to be an option."

I scolded him a little for being so brazen and made him promise not to utter a word to anyone.

He said he wouldn't and wondered if he was going to be in trouble with my dad because he was bringing his daughter home pregnant.

"I'm not fourteen Nash, and I seem to remember that we are married; at least we think we are."

"Well, if it's not legal, it will be soon enough."

Monty found us cuddled up on the couch an hour or so later. "I can't hold them off any longer. I told them you were up to no good in here but they made me call you in for the last supper."

I sat up. "Is it that time already?"

"Early supper, early to bed and early to rise; did you forget we are out of here tomorrow?"

We had not. We followed him into the dining room where a small feast had been set out.

"You cooked without me?" I asked jokingly.

"Yeah," Ace said holding my chair for me. "We've been watching you slice and dice and open cans. Think we got the hang of it just in time to give you a rest. Mind you, most of it is your creations anyhow. What we don't finish off tonight we'll feed to the vultures tomorrow."

Monty produced a bottle of wine that he had stashed away waiting for this very moment. I let him pour me a small glass knowing that I would pass it to Nash later. I asked everyone what one thing absent from our cuisine they had missed the most. Evie spoke first.

"French fries; you all know I lived on fast food and I have become very fond of a certain chain's fries. However, I must admit that the ones you made for us up at the camp Ava were far superior to any I have ever had."

"Yeah," Ace agreed, "they were delicious. Vera doesn't like to cook but she does make a mean chicken cacciatore, so I hope she has one waiting for me."

Sali said anything her husband cooks for her but she figured that everyone would be joining in on her return so there would be a food explosion ceremony.

Monty said he wanted lobster and Nash said, "Beer."

I told Nash that he may not like what passed for beer in Scotland and that I was with Monty on the lobster thing. We said our good nights and headed upstairs at eight o'clock. I doubted that anyone was going to get much sleep anticipating our rescue tomorrow.

"I don't mind telling you that I am going to miss this place." Nash confessed when we finished packing our meager belongings and nestled together in bed. "Will this be the end of the honeymoon Ava?"

"It doesn't have to be. We have some very nice rooms at Avanloch that will fit our needs quite nicely. I would suggest the south tower but that all depends on how much snow there is and how cold it is."

"Is this the same tower that you and your sixteen cats were going to spend the next sixty years of your life decaying in?"

"No, that was the north tower." I giggled. "And again, thank you for saving me from that lonely, lowly existence."

"Anytime my dear. Are we allowed to still be doing this?"

"Do you mean making love?"

"I'm afraid I'm naive on the subject of pregnancy."

"Me too Nash so we are going to have to learn together. I will feel better once I talk to my mother. I will tell you though that when I left home last November she was almost four months pregnant and her and my dad were still making out."

"Making out…how?"

"They have never minced their words or passion for each other in public. They hold hands and touch and kiss all the time…how do you say it…is it necking?"

"Really, they neck in front of you?"

"Yes, they are very amorous and they never apologise. You can't imagine the quiet that filled the castle last autumn when they weren't talking. It was like living in the fabled dungeon. We were all walking on eggs and dreaded when the two of them were in the same room together."

"Why didn't you confront them Ava?"

"Oh, we tried, we really tried." I lamented. "Daddy said he had no idea what was bothering her and she wouldn't talk to him so he was just biding his time until something broke. Mother said that nothing was wrong and clammed up. They promised us that they will never let things go so far ever again. It took my mother's disappearance to bring the whole sorry mess to a head."

"Are we talking about another disappearance other than the one where she ended up in Spain?"

"There is still much to tell you Nash, and it's a long trip to Scotland. Now I want to get back to you and me and the baby. Did your parents tell you about the birds and the bees?"

He laughed. "I guess I was about twelve or so when dad asked me if I knew what went on between a man and a woman when they were in love. I said I did, but I hadn't a clue. I was too embarrassed to ask and he was too embarrassed to explain. I guess when I started hanging around with girls a few years later we approached the subject again. I said I knew it all to let him off the hook but I still wasn't too sure about anything. It all came evidently clear to me when I lost my virginity to a girl in the back seat of my mother's car a few years later."

"Colton Nash!" I exclaimed pretending to sound appalled. "Are you telling me that you took advantage of a young girl to satisfy your boyish sexual curiosity?"

"Yeah Honey, I did. Actually though, she was the teacher and I was the student. God, that was awkward. I would never want to be sixteen ever again." He pulled me closer. "I like it just fine where I am. Did your mother give you the sermon?"

"Sort of. When Rosy was about eleven she asked mama why her and her dad had separate bedrooms. She told us because they weren't in love and that it was a marriage of convenience so that we could all stay together. It was then that I asked her if she had loved my father. It was one of the few times she spoke of him. She said she did and that she would never love like that again. When I started going out with what's his name…"

"You mean Randy?"

"Well, there wasn't anyone else. Anyhow, she asked me if I wanted to go on the birth control pill. We talked earnestly then and she made me promise that I wouldn't look on sex as a rite of passage. That short, unsatisfactory experience could have soured me on sex forever, but my mothers and fathers loving ways encouraged me not to give up on love. I regret that I didn't wait for you Nash."

"You said that I'm the only one you ever fell in love with, so in a way you did wait for me, and so we have to look on our past mistakes as experience. Thankfully when we found each other we were smart enough to realize that we had arrived at our destiny."

I was married to a very wise man.

CHAPTER 8

Bringing Ava Home

Nash woke me at five a. m. on February the second. I rolled over and told him to go away. He walked around the bed and pried open my eyes.

"You don't mean that do you Ava? Have you forgotten what today is? It's the day you predicted, the day we would be rescued. You take the first shower and I'll strip the bed okay?"

"I'm not dirty, I don't need a shower." I said slapping his hands a little. He pulled the covers off me. "Damn you Colton Nash! I'm going to get even with you in Scotland!"

"Yeah sure; now come on, get your lazy butt into the shower. Do you want me to carry you?"

"Only if you are coming with me…" I answered suggestively.

"We don't have time for that right now." He slapped my bottom and said that he would take me up on the offer later.

Reluctantly I climbed into the shower and came out to find Nash holding my journal.

"I was tempted to read it but my conscience wouldn't let me intrude on your private thoughts."

"There is nothing in there that isn't meant to be read. My mother always kept a diary. Hers was in the form of letters to my father. I know she would want a detailed account of my experiences up here so I wrote it mainly for her. You are welcome to read it anytime, but you might be embarrassed by my description of you and my feelings for you. Anyhow, this is not the time as we have things to do." I took the journal out of his hands and he pulled me down on the bed and said he had reconsidered and wanted to take me up on my proposal.

"Sorry, I like my men clean so get your grubby self into the shower. I'll go make coffee if someone hasn't beaten me to it. Bring the bedding down with you and you can start the generator so we can get the washing machine going."

"Yes Ma'am, but you don't know what you are missing."

"Matter of fact I do, but that is neither here nor there right now."

"Sometimes I don't understand you at all. What does that even mean…here or there?"

"It just means that it is not happening right now, I guess." I pulled up my slacks and vowed that all my clothing would be going in the trash the minute I got to the boys' house.

"Is that where we are going to be staying until we can get a flight to Scotland?"

"We will be on a plane tomorrow if my father has anything to say about it. You can make book on that so we will only be in Vancouver for one night. Is that all right with you? What about your parents; are you going to want to see them?"

"I think a telephone call will suffice. We'll visit them when we come back in the spring."

"Yes, and we are going to have to talk about that but we have lots of time." I blew him a kiss and made my way to the kitchen.

Monty was on his way out to start the generator. I had coffee with the girls and Ace. Nash joined us shortly throwing the sheets down the basement stairs before he sat down. No one wanted anything to eat. I guess we were all too hyped up and didn't want to take the chance of being sick before or during our flights. We had discussed that last night and everyone but Monty and Ace had different degrees of uneasiness about flying again. Nash had mixed feelings but was more worried about me. I assured him I would be all right and that I had a Gravol tablet for anyone who wanted one. I was pretty sure that I would be okay as long as I could sit with Nash.

We had the bedding and towels all done and hung on the clotheslines in the basement within two hours. We girls remade the beds with clean sheets from the linen closets and made sure the rooms looked better than the way we had found them. The guys were clearing the packed snow off the lake where it was anticipated that the aircraft would be landing. We collected our belongings and carried them down to the shore. It was a beautiful warm sunny day. We walked over to see if we could be of any assistance to the men. Nash was working on erecting a flag of sorts. We were told it was to denote wind direction. I thought that small planes could land in snow and wondered why they were working so hard to expose the ice. Ace said that they didn't know what kind of plane would be landing and so they wanted to be prepared for anything. He said if the craft was equipped with skis then ice was better than snow for landing; only trouble was there are no brakes on skis so they required a longer landing site. He said that there were many ultimate back country planes like the Piper Top Cub that could take off and land on ice or snow, but the trouble with them is that they only hold one crew member and two passengers as far as he knew. He mentioned other small aircraft that were popular in remote areas such as the Cessna and the Skyhawk. Then he made a joke saying that someone once said that flying was the second greatest thrill to man and that landing was the first. I didn't find it very funny.

At nine a.m. we heard the roar of the engines. A helicopter led the way. It circled and then landed in the snow on the beach.

"Well I'll be damned…looky there Monty; that be an armed forces heli!" Ace yelled.

It appeared that the Canadian government had sent one of their Search and Rescue {SAR} helicopters for us. Monty and Ace rushed over to it as the rest of us watched a small aircraft slide in on skis. Behind it a larger one touched down coming to a halt four meters behind the Cessna. It was bedecked with Royal Canadian Mounted Police SAR letters. In all, six people alit from the planes; two R.C.M.P. officers, one of whom was the pilot, two from the SAR heli and the pilot and a passenger from the last. There were handshakes and hugs before any introductions were made. One of the men from the helicopter pumped Ace's and then Monty's hand.

"Acerman, how are you, you old son of a gun? I always feared you'd bring that bucket of bolts to a crashing halt but come on, you could have picked a more hospitable place and time to do so don't you think? Is this the fabled Melton Montgomery? Pleased to meet you Sir." He moved on to Nash. "And this can't be anyone but the grandson of the legendary Lander Champion; Colton Nash, I presume. My pleasure Son. Your granddad and mine were buddies from another time. "Ladies," he said, removing his hat, "I'm very pleased to see that you all have survived the ordeal relatively well; Dick Bracken at your service. We will have you all out of here just as soon as possible, just a few details to check into. What say, you and Monty give us a tour of the crash site Ace?"

With that brief introduction the three of them along with the pilot and one R.C.M.P officer made their way back to the helicopter and were airborne before we even knew who Dick Bracken was. The other officer informed us that Mr. Bracken was from the Federal Aviation Office in Victoria and that he was the one in charge. I had a moment of panic. I whispered to Nash that I might be in big trouble. He asked me what I was talking about.

"I presume that the plane is going to be searched and it will be discovered that narcotics are missing. I was responsible for that shipment Nash…"

"Hush, you are worrying needlessly. It's not like your license can be revoked or anything."

"I guess you are right, but still the same."

"And who's to say that you are the one who doled out the meds anyway? There were others who could have done so, especially me, so quit fretting. I wonder who this fellow is coming towards us. Does he look official to you?"

He introduced himself as Al Jones, owner of the lodge.

"You are the last person on earth that we expected to see here." Rainey said to him pleased as punch. "It seems we won't have to contact you when we hit the city after all."

We chatted for a few minutes and then Nash said, "Come on, let's show you what we have done with the place…have we got a story to tell you. Unfortunately, it required a little remodelling."

Nash had introduced me as Ava Lane Quinn. I was a little hurt that he had not presented me as his wife. He hadn't forgotten we were married had he?

"Yes, Miss Quinn, I know exactly who you are. I am honored that my humble cabin was refuge for such a woman of your stature. I trust it met with your approval."

"Mr. Jones, my life or status is of no more value than any of my companions. But, to answer your question, your cabin is a four star resort and I would recommend it to anyone and I hope to return someday as a paying guest. That being said, we will be compensating your hospitality with a full reimbursement for all the goods that helped to save our lives. This place has been our haven and it was only by the grace of God that Nash was led here. Oh, I should give credit where credit is due and that is to his dog Asta who steered him in the right direction."

Nash laughed and took my hand as we walked up the little incline and into the kitchen. "And this here stove and work area is where this lady of mine performed her magic everyday feeding us with her wonderful creations." He opened the cooler. "Here is one of her experiments, sourdough, and let me tell you, it makes the best bread this side of San Francisco!"

Mr. Al Jones looked a little puzzled when Nash called me his lady. "Oh, did I forget to mention that a wedding also took place here? Ava Lane did me the honor of becoming my wife and we will forever hold this place in our hearts as it is where we have been honeymooning for five weeks. Now can I hold you to this confidence as we would really like to tell her parents in person? Good, now how often do you get bears knocking on your door?"

He pulled me along with him into the lounge. "What's wrong Honey? Are you crying?"

"Maybe a little. Thank-you for saying what you did."

"Anytime my love."

Mr. Jones had a good laugh regarding the grizzly incident and said that his insurance would pay for a new window. He declined reimbursement of any kind but Nash made it very clear that we were indebted to him and his wife and that we needed to make restitution. They hashed it out for a while before Mr. Jones finally threw up his hands and agreed to a small amount. I asked him if he would accept a cheque from the Royal bank of Scotland because I would like to get the matter over and done with. I added that the cheque was in my maiden name.

"That is not a problem Miss Quinn, or should I say Mrs. Nash?"

I handed him the bank-draft for an amount that my companions had agreed upon the night before. I had met with great resistance from my fellow cohorts when I had asked them to let me foot the bill. They were all well aware of the fact that my family had "money to burn" so to speak, but insisted that they wanted to pay their share. Nash convinced them that they would not win the argument with me as he had already squabbled with me over the matter until he was blue in the face, so please let me have my way. Monty said that they would accept my generous offer but that they would get even with me one way or the other.

"You already have." I declared. "You have all rewarded me with your friendship and your participation in the happiest day of my life which I am sure you all know was my marriage to Nash. That is worth more than any paltry sum of money. I am thank-full to have you all in my life. Perhaps I thought that our situation was bleak at first but it turned into being the most wonderful adventure of my life and if I had to do it all over again I would…as long as it was with you all."

"I think I speak for all of us Ava," Ace said, "when I say that we are glad that you were aboard our ill-fated flight. You kept us fed and entertained young lady and moreover, you doctored me so I owe you a debt of gratitude. This experience has not soured me on flying but it has restored my faith in mankind. I'm glad to be going home but I'm going with a new outlook on life. You know the saying, "If you're given lemons, then make lemonade." Well we made the best lemonade that we possibly could and it was all because of this troop!"

"Amen to that!" Sali concurred.

And so our separation from the outside world came to a close. Mr. Jones had attempted to rip my cheque in half as in his words; "It was ten times too much!" I convinced him that one could not put a value on life and that the lodge probably saved ours so was worth every penny to us. It was not just to cover the cost of foodstuff, but for the gas and propane and firewood that had kept us comfortable. I told him he could donate some to charity if he wished. He seemed satisfied with that and gave us all an open invitation to visit the lodge at any time as his guests and suggested that we may want to have a reunion of sorts here at some time in the future. We all agreed that was a wonderful idea.

Ace was asked to fly with Al Jones and the lone pilot who stated that he could use a co-pilot. Sali rode with Monty and Evie on the helicopter. Nash and I were guests on the R.C.M.P. plane. I hesitated slightly before I boarded looking wistfully back at Uncle Bob's Cabin. Mr. Jones had told us that originally only a cabin sat where the lodge is today. It was owned by his late Uncle Bob so hence the alternate name of the lodge. It had nothing whatsoever to do with Bob Quinn Lake. We had a chuckle over the Quinn name. We had also learned that our plane had landed between the boundaries of Spatsizi and Tatlatui Parks, just as the boys thought. We would have had one hell of a trek to reach any road or civilization. The only access was by plane. Our downed aircraft had been spotted by a Conservation Officer, one Connor Lewis who was out tracking the movement of an elk herd. He was stationed in Stewart and had been unable to fly due to the unusual stormy weather until yesterday. He did not find the elk herd but instead came upon a pack of wolves. He followed them right to the plane where he said the alpha male wolf sat on a ledge above the plane and howled. Mr. Lewis immediately knew that it was a recent crash site and radioed the position. The camp looked deserted and he followed his gut to the lodge in hopes that there were survivors. No one could comprehend how Flight 296 could have veered so far off course. We were living proof that it had.

Nash asked me if I was all right. I replied that I was just saying good-bye to our honeymoon home. He reminded me that we could revisit anytime we wanted.

We were all flown to Fort Nelson where we were taken to the police station where we placed our first telephone calls to our families. I managed to get out a few words to my mother and father before I broke down. Nash rescued the phone from me and assured them I was well and that he would be accompanying me to Vancouver and that we would call them from there. I heard him say that it was not all his doing and that we survived because it was a group effort.

"Thank-you Sir; I look forward to meeting you all too. Ah, I believe our lass has recovered enough to talk." He passed me the phone.

I was still sniveling. I smiled at my husband and managed to get out "I love you." to my parents and tell them that I was in good hands.

Sali was leaving us here as she was going north and the rest of us were going south. We had a tearful good-bye. Asta was going home with her. How do you tell a dog that you will see her in a few months? I hoped she somehow understood that we were not deserting her. We watched until the small plane was out of site. The rest of us were flown to Dawson Creek where we boarded a chartered flight to Vancouver. We had been warned by the police officers that we were going to be greeted by hoards of reporters so we might want to prepare a statement. Security would protect us as best they could. However, it would not stop the cameras from flashing and questions from being yelled in our direction, especially since there was a celebrity involved. Nash had told me not to worry and that he would protect me.

"You don't think I am the celebrity do you? That is just plain ridiculous!" I groaned.

"The paparazzi can make a mountain out of a molehill Doc and to them you are fresh meat. They don't get to interview a royal every day and that's what you are to them." Ace said. "Nash can get you away from the vultures and Monty and I will handle them, so not to worry."

"I am not in the least bit worried Ace but me being royalty is about the silliest thing I have ever heard. It must be a slow news day if I am the lead story…all of us maybe, but not just me."

"How was your mother's homecoming handled?"

"With the utmost discretion. My Uncle John prepared a statement for her to sign about her captivity and rescue and it was released to the press. No reporters were allowed on the property. The gates were closed and round the clock volunteers from the village manned the perimeter for several weeks."

Nash suggested that I should prepare a statement also. It was all so ridiculously bothersome. I hoped my brother's had not been hounded and that Nash and I would not be followed. That worry was for naught because we were greeted by an entourage from Malcolm Dean's Pharmaceutical Company and Lloyd Becker's Outfitters and my father's Architect family. They surrounded us and escorted us to a waiting limo where two security guards ushered us into a limousine driven by my mom and dad's long-time friend and chauffer, Manuel Demarco. Although I was jubilant at the reception we were getting I felt an icy finger creeping up my spine. Had anyone made this connection before? Could Manuel Demarco be related to Anton DeMarco? Dare I mention it when I get home? I told myself that I was just being skitterish; there were probably a million variations to the name and none of them were even remotely related…right? It was just a coincidence wasn't it? Lord, don't let me be a portal for a detrimental discovery. If I mention it at all it will just be to my father. Nash and I said good-bye to Evie, Monty and Ace with promises to keep in touch as we entered the driveway of my brother's home. Morgan and Mason ran out to meet us. We took a few minutes to introduce them to our fellow castaways before they were whisked off to resume their lives. Ace was going home to his wife and Monty was going with Evie to her apartment as he didn't really have a place of his own. They had a lot to figure out and I hoped they would stay together. I was wondering if Nash and I could make it in the outside world ourselves. I informed my brothers that Nash was coming home with me. They did not question that until we were in the house. They wanted to know everything about our weeks of isolation in the northern wilds.

Laughing I said, "Give me a minute will you? The first thing I want to do is get out of these rags that I have been living in for six weeks! Your new brother-in-law has been dying for a beer so will you get him one while I change please Morg?"

"Sure," Morgan said, "what, what did you call him?"

"Oh, did I forget to mention that Nash and I got married? You fill them in Honey; be back in two shakes of a lamb's tail." I flashed a big smile in my husband's direction.

"You better make it quick Ava. Your sister is a very funny girl, boys."

I had only brought one dress with me from Scotland and it made me look like a haus-frau so I tossed it aside. I sighed deeply as I slipped into my blue silk lounging pyjamas. I hadn't realized that I had missed the feel of comfort so much. I ran a comb through my hair and dabbed on a light bronzy lipstick. Already I felt rejuvenated.

I found the three of them sitting side by side on the chesterfield waiting impatiently for me.

"What do you say boys?" I directed my questions at my brothers.

"Well, we are waiting to hear the details from you." Morgan said.

"Didn't you tell them anything Nash?"

"Only that we fell in love and got married. I left the details up to you Dear."

"Well they are going to have to wait as I need to call Mom and Dad." Mason handed me the portable phone and asked if I was hungry.

"I don't suppose you have any fried chicken do you?" I asked not expecting the answer I got.

"As a matter of fact we do. Dad told us to have a variety of your favorites on hand so we got the chicken and pizza and salads and four flavors of ice cream." Mason said grinning.

I told him to bring it on and I would nibble as I talked and that a diet Pepsi would be nice. I dialed the castle and put the speaker phone on. Daddy picked up on the second ring.

"We've been waiting for your call Honey; it's so good to hear your voice. I suppose you are dead tired?"

"As a matter of fact I'm not. I'm sorry it's so late Daddy." I motioned Nash to come and sit beside me. "How is Mama? I hope she is sleeping."

"We weren't going to get any sleep until we heard from you. Your mother is wide awake and wrestling the phone out of my hands so here she is." He said laughing.

Mama came on the line and we cried a little again. I managed to assure her that I was in perfect health and that our misadventure was not the nightmare that she had envisioned. I told her about the wonderful friends I had made and one in particular. Then I told her that Nash was coming home with me. She said that they had already surmised that he was from the earlier conversation with him and that they couldn't wait to meet him. I said he felt the same way about them. Daddy came on the line again and said that our flight home had already been arranged. He had booked us to fly directly into Edinburgh, and depending on the weather Evan would meet us and fly us home. If it was stormy we would have to take the train to Waverly, but one way or the other Rosy and Evan would be there to meet us and take us to Avanloch. Our flight was scheduled to leave at six p.m. tomorrow evening February 4th. Ten and one half hours later we would be touching down in Edinburgh and factoring the time difference, we should be at Avanloch by two on the afternoon of February 5th.

My father had to convince my mother to let me go and get some sleep so I could be rested for the long flight. She said she was probably going to drive herself and everyone else in the house crazy waiting for me. I heard my dad say before she hung up that it would just be a normal day then wouldn't it. Nash asked what he meant by that. I said he was just joking. I wanted to call Rosy but didn't have the energy and I was already hoarse from talking so much. We went to bed telling the boys that we would finish our story where we had left off in the morning. I said goodnight and made them promise not to tell dad that I was married.

Just before Nash crawled into bed I told him that this was the last chance he had to change his mind. He asked me about what and I said about coming to Scotland with me and staying married.

He asked me to repeat what I had said and I did. He turned and went into the bathroom and came out with a wet face cloth and a bar of soap and stood over me threatening to wash my mouth out if he didn't like my answers to his questions. I grimaced and asked what the question was.

"Do you love me?"

"Yes."

"Do you believe that I love you?"

"Yes."

"Then why in hell would you ask me such ridiculous questions?"

"Because I do love you; I love you more and more every day, but I don't want you to feel obligated to me. Maybe our marriage isn't even legal and if it's not, I will set you free if you have any doubts. I mean, there we were, two people pushed together by circumstance and both lonesome in our own ways…"

"I'm going to stop you right there Ava." He put the soap down and sat on the edge of the bed and took my hands. "Okay, so let's say that I was lonesome and ripe for a lustful fling and you just happened to fit the bill, so why in the world did I ask you to marry me then? I needn't because you accepted all my flirtatious advances and were more than willing to share your bed with me. I wanted to marry you because as I said before, I wanted the whole marriage experience, not just the sexual part. I wanted a woman to share my life with and raise a family with and you were it, you are it…everything I have ever wanted but had given up on finding. So my dear, the answer is no, I do not want to be released from you, not today or tomorrow or fifty years from now. Are you clear on that?"

"I want to be, but Nash you have to see my side. You are the catch of a lifetime. You could walk down any street and there would be a dozen beautiful women running after you and vying for your attention but you would be stuck with this plain Jane ingénue lass…"

"Why are you always running yourself done Ava? Do you not know how beautiful you are and just not on the outside, but the inside too? And why do you make me out to be some Don Juan? I am just an ordinary man. Tthere is nothing special about me except in your eyes and that is the way I like and want it. There is a reason I am thirty-one and single. I am very particular and up until six weeks ago no one ever met my expectations. So if you think I am going to let that one in a lifetime girl get away, you are plum crazy!"

"Maybe I am for I am my mother's daughter after all." I responded smiling a little.

"Of course you are, but is there a hidden meaning in there somewhere? Now I have to ask you if you still want me coming home with you to meet your family…maybe you have come to realize that I am not worthy of your love and that I am incapable of living up to your standards? Is that it Ava?"

"Talk about being crazy! I cannot imagine my life without you. I never thought I would have someone that I could call mine and who would hold me in his arms every night and tell me how much he loved me and wake me every day saying, "Good morning Sunshine." I just wanted you to be sure Nash. I never had any intentions of letting you off the hook and you can believe me when I say that I would fight for you tooth and nail!"

"That's my girl. I don't want to hear another negative thing out of your mouth, do you hear?"

"Yes, and now I think we should try and get some sleep for it is a very long way home."

"Yes, we should **try**."

We were up at nine a.m. and with coffee in hand Nash put a call through to his parents. According to his mother our rescue had already been documented and there were pictures of us scattered all over the television. I switched it on and found a news channel. I frowned. Nash had done his best to shield me from the reporter's cameras but they had managed to take some pretty unflattering pictures. Nash winked at me as he asked his mother if she got a good luck at the woman he was trying to protect. She asked if I was indeed Ava Quinn, and what in the world was a young woman of my stature doing on a cargo plane to Spring Valley. Nash said it was a long story and he would go into great details in May when we got back from Scotland. She wanted to know what he meant by "we" and why was he going to Scotland.

"Well Mom, it's like this; I found the woman of my dreams on that fateful flight and she did me the honor of becoming my wife. Yes, you heard me right; Ava and I are married. How, well Ace had a license to marry us. Yes, another story. I promise you that you will all love her just as I do. I am going to take her home to Scotland.

Yes, I know it is a castle. There are a few things going on there so that is why we will be there three months. We will be stopping off in Quesnel to visit with you and Dad and Ruby on our way home to Akemantack…yes Mom, Ava is coming to live with me there. She is quite the woman and she knows just what she is in for." He smiled and asked me to get him a refill as his mother was asking a thousand questions. "Of course you have your doubts that she will be able to adjust and we have a few ourselves, but it doesn't matter because if things don't work out up there, we will leave. It doesn't matter where we live as long as we are together. Here, Ava would like to say hello."

He passed me the phone even though I was shaking my head "no." I took a deep breath. "Hello Mrs. Nash. I guess this a real shock for you to hear that your son has gone and got himself married off to a foreigner? My parents are going to be just as surprised, but they will love him just as I do. I pinch myself regularly because I think I am in this unbelievable dream that just goes on and on. This whole thing has been one incredible adventure and the reason we all survived was because of your son and then he went and fell in love with me…" I started to cry but managed to blubber that I was the luckiest girl in the world.

Nash took the phone from me and said that now he had two weepy women to tend with. He promised his mother that he would call her from Scotland. He hung up said, "Let's go shopping."

It was not one of my favorite things to do but he wanted to look "half decent", as he put it, for my parents. Morgan and Mason had taken the day off from their studies and offered to drive us to the mall. I helped Nash pick out six new casual shirts and left him with Morgan while Mason escorted me to a dress shop. Nash had asked me if he needed to buy ties. I told him that my dad abhorred ties and we did not overly dress for dinner.

"In fact," I said, "my mother is nearly always barefoot and quite frequently comes down for dinner in her lounging clothes and especially more so now that she is pregnant." I think that put him at ease.

We finished filling the boys in on our adventures in the north without mentioning my encounter with the wolf or the cougar over a nice luncheon. Then Nash told me he had some business to conduct with me. He took my hand and led me to a very classy jewellery store. I knew what he was up to and told him it wasn't necessary.

"I beg your pardon my Lady, but it is absolutely necessary! How will anyone know that you are already taken if you are not wearing rings, and besides, I want to."

We picked out a beautiful yet simple set, and then learned that it was called Kismet. How fitting for two people that were brought together by providence. There was even a matching band for Nash. We didn't have time to wait until they were engraved so we would have that done in Scotland. We would wear them until just before the plane landed and then we would wear them on chains around our necks until we announced our marriage to my family.

Manuel picked us up at four and drove us to the airport. We managed to convince the boys that it wasn't necessary to accompany us as it would be a two hour wait before we boarded our flight. Of course I had to stir the pot a little and asked Manuel if there was an alternate spelling to his last name. He said that he thought that it was originally DeMarco but didn't know when or why it was converted to Demarco. That was not the answer I wanted to hear.

Soon after we were air bound Nash ordered me a club soda and a beer for himself. He settled back and asked if I felt like talking, or did I want to have a little nap. I said that I wasn't sleepy.

"Okay then. I'm curious if there is some significance to the question you asked Manuel about the spelling of his surname. Are you trying to connect some inconsequential dots?"

"What do you mean?"

"It was not lost on me Ava that your mother's abductor's surname was the same as Manuel's. Are you suggesting that they may know each other?"

"Of course not! For some reason it just hit on me that it was a strange coincidence. I am surprised that you even remembered Anton's last name." I answered innocently.

"I remember everything you have ever told me Ava. I trust this is not going to play on your mind all the way to Scotland or that you plan on investigating it further?"

I didn't want to lie so I said that I was pretty sure that I wouldn't because it would accomplish nothing. So why did I have the nagging fear that Manuel was somehow involved with my mother's disappearance two and a half years ago? I knew that she kept in touch with him and wondered if she had mentioned that she was going to Nazeth to try and find the rightful heir to the Infinity Bracelets. Did he somehow know that Anton was going to be there also looking for clues to their existence and would he have passed the information on, but for what purpose? Could they perhaps be cousins? No, that was just plain silly! But yet, Anton had a replica of the bracelets made for my mother…did he know she possessed the real ones? Of course not or else he would have found a way to get his hands on them wouldn't he? What was the matter with me; why was I so unnerved by this similarity in the names? What I was thinking was ludicrous. Had my mother even thought about it? I promised myself that I would never bring the correlation in the names up…at least not to her.

"Speaking of my mother," I said, "I should tell you a little bit about the history of Avanloch so that if certain things and people are mentioned you won't be totally in the dark, and as I said before, it's a long flight. Are you up to another saga?"

"I am indeed and as usual, you have my full attention." Nash promised.

I started with, "Just before we rescued mama from Anton's clutches, my dad found a diary that was supposedly penned by Avaleena McAllister in 1847, courtesy of the Grey Lady…"

CHAPTER 9

Celebrations

Rainey was dancing in jubilation and asking me to dance with him. It didn't matter that it was two o'clock in the morning; we had just got word via the telephone that Ava was alive. It was the news we had been waiting for what seemed like forever. Rainey pulled me out of bed and danced me around the room. We were laughing and crying at the same time. He kept kissing me and thanking me. I told him that I had done nothing that required thanks.

"You waited for me for twenty years, you never stopped loving me, you gave me Ava and Liliana and now you are going to give me two more children…I think I have plenty to thank you for. I could never have gotten through these last two months if it wasn't for you Vienna. I thank my lucky stars that it was only two months and not two years like it was with you. Honest to God I am still amazed that I made it through that agonizing time. I still have this recurring nightmare that you're still gone…Ava's disappearance brought it all back in living color."

"It's over Darling; it's all over. I'm here and I am never going anywhere without you and our baby will be home soon. There are no more tears Rain, no more tears."

I felt the tension easing out of his body as he danced me over to the stereo and dropped a long play record down unto the turn table.

The first song out was "Smoke Gets in Your Eyes" by the Platters. He said that he loved that song as it reminded him of our love.

"I like it too Honey," I said, "but it is sad because she leaves him at the end. Is that why it reminds you of us because I left you?"

"Maybe I never really listened to the lyrics before but it doesn't matter does it because you are never going to leave me again are you?"

I told him that I was not and then I suggested that he should go down stairs as surely the phone had awakened the Duffys' and they would be wondering and worrying that perhaps it was bad news. He was back in less than five minutes and said that Mary was making coffee and that he was going to join her because he was too wound up to go back to sleep. He told me to get back in bed and I told him he was crazy if he thought I was going to do that. Zoe had heard Rainey running up and down the hallway and met us at her doorway anticipating that something had happened to me. We told her the good news and asked her to keep an ear open for Tanny and Lili. Hopefully they had not been awakened.

I guess it was a day for dancing as Mary D. was flitting around the kitchen from cupboard to stove and back again. I laughed saying that her lumbago must have abandoned her today.

"Oh Miss Vienna, say it's so, say it be so, say Miss Ava is coming home!"

I hugged her and Duffy who had just entered the kitchen. "It's so Mary, it's so." I assured her.

"Oh Luv, that is the best news these old ears ever heard. We must get busy; we must have a big homecoming! So much to do, so much to do. Oh just wait 'til Miss Rosalyn here the news…did ye be calling her yet?"

Rainey escorted her to a chair. "There is lots of time for that Mary as she isn't even out of the bush yet. We'll know more later on in the day."

"What do you mean that she ain't out of the bush yet?"

"That was a phone call from the R.C.M.P. to inform us that she and five others had been spotted by a conservational officer near their downed plane. It appears as though they took refuge in a remote lodge. It is already late in the day in Canada and so the rescue will be taking place tomorrow. We will be informed as soon as they are picked up. They will be flown to Vancouver and then we can make plans for her homecoming, okay? I think we will keep it on the down-low though just as we did Vienna's. What do you think Hon?"

"Yes, just family. That is how she will want it."

Rainey insisted that I go back to bed and get some sleep as it was going to be a long day and we had no way of knowing when Ava and the rest of the castaways would actually be rescued. I surprised myself and fell asleep almost immediately and didn't awaken until noon. We got our first call from Ava at seven in the evening. They had been flown to Fort Nelson and would be taking another flight to Dawson Creek and then finally to Vancouver. We were both too emotional to talk so our conversation was very brief, but I did manage to blubber that I loved her before passing the phone to Rainey. He found himself talking to Colton Nash as Ava was crying too much to talk also. He assured Rainey that Ava was in perfect health and that he would have her calmed down by the time of their next phone call which would be from her brother's house. He added that Ava had advised him of the time difference so it would probably be in the early hours of the morning. Rainey said he didn't care and to tell Ava we loved her and couldn't wait to see her. When he hung up the phone he said that he had gotten the distinct feeling that something was going on between our daughter and this Colton Nash. That impression became fact when we next talked to Ava and she informed us that Nash was coming home with her.

The hours ticked by slowly as we awaited their arrival. I don't know who was more excited, Rainey, Tanny or me. We were sitting on the divan in the downstairs parlour when Rainey announced that the helicopter was in view. Thankfully, the day had dawned bright and clear. Tanny and I were ordered by my husband to stay put at the front entrance with Amma and Johnny because the driveway was wet and he didn't want me falling. I was becoming weary of being treated like an invalid. I smiled and said that I wouldn't follow him. Tanny had scolded me again earlier.

"You know this has to stop don't you Vienna?"

I asked her what she meant and she said in a very grown up voice that we had to stop getting lost. "First, you go away for almost two years and we don't know where you are and then Rosy runs off to the jungle and now Ava has been in some frozen country for months…why can't you all just stay home?"

I told her that I would have a talk with the girls and she told me to have one with myself too. I wondered how she would react when we tell her that we were moving to Canada. She may be a bigger force to contend with than Rosy.

I watched the helicopter land and a minute later Rainey had Ava in his arms and was swinging her around. They were laughing jubilantly. She waved and grabbed the hand of the man who had alighted with her and they ran up the drive to my waiting arms.

We had a few teary moments and then she stepped back and looked at me. "Oh Mama," she laughed, "How you have grown!"

Rainey arrived with Rosy in tow and he said that he finally had me where he liked me, "Plump and sassy and happy."

Tanny was gushing all over Ava as she was introducing Nash to us. Rainey shook his hand and thanked him for looking after our daughter.

"That has been my greatest pleasure Sir." He turned to me and with a twinkle in his eyes he took my hand. "Lady Vienna, I would know you anywhere; it is indeed an honor to meet you and your husband. I feel I already know you as I have been on many a journey with Ava as she has taken me on the roller coaster that has been your lives."

He kissed my hand and I laughed a little. "It has been that Nash, but I would do it all over again if the outcome would be the same."

Rainey put his arm around me and concurred. Johnny and Amma were introduced to Nash. It was mentioned that we had understood that his first name was Colton. Ava explained that he was just "Nash." I liked either name.

We all toddled off down the hallway to the kitchen where the Duffys' were waiting. There were more tears shed. Mary remarked on how healthy Ava looked as she had expected her to come home nothing but skin and bones.

Nash had an answer for that. He put his arm around Ava. "This young lady here kept us all fed Mary, and she credits everything she knew to watching you in the kitchen since childhood. We all came out five or six pounds heavier thanks to her."

Mary was touched. "You mean you have been paying attention all this time child?

"You cooked Ava? What, what could you possibly cook up there and how?" Rosy asked.

"To be sure, there are tales to tell. Let us take a seat in the family room as tea is all laid out. Mr. Nash, is this to be your first "high tea"? Has Ava told you of the tradition?"

"She has Mary and I am looking forward to learning all your customs."

"We are not very formal here Nash. Mary is joshing when she calls it "high tea." It is merely a light luncheon to tide us through until dinner." I explained.

Mary took her designated place at the head of the table with Duffy on her left and then Rosy and Evan. Johnny and Amma sat at the far end as usual and then Tanny, Rainey and me. Ava sat next to me and Nash was on her other side next to Mary. Zoe was still upstairs as Liliana was sleeping. This was the seating arrangement that I preferred and there was still lots of room for more when the occasion arouse as it would for dinner. Amma's and Johnny's girls, Zoe and Caron and Jeanette would be joining us. We never knew where Lily would choose to sit. She usually preferred being next to her father or in his lap. She was like her mother that way.

Ava and Nash were still standing. I told her to sit down. She squeezed my hand.

"In a moment Mama; Nash and I have something to tell you all." She smiled up at him and he winked at her. "Mama, Daddy, everyone, Nash isn't just Nash; he's my husband. We are married and I hope you will all be happy for us because we are very, very happy."

"Oh Darling…" I started to speak but Rosy interrupted me.

"Married, how is that even possible? You've been in isolation for weeks and weeks and you don't even know each other…"

Rainey stopped her and said sternly, "Rosy, how about you let your sister talk; it is hers and Nash's story to tell, all right?"

She blushed and said she was sorry.

The newlyweds sat down still holding hands. Nash said he would like to answer Rosy's questions because he was sure that everyone was wondering the same thing. He asked her if it was all right with her and she said that it was.

"I will start at the beginning. Ava and I met, so to speak, fifteen minutes after the plane crashed. I was stationed at the rear with my dog Asta and the cargo was behind me. The Piper Navajo is one of the smaller freight planes and has a small payload, but it is the preferred aircraft of our pilots, Ace and Monty. Ace admitted that we were a little overloaded but didn't think it contributed to the crash. We were lucky that none of the cargo shifted too far forward which was a miracle in itself as the plane landed on its belly. The nose somehow dug into the snow and remained upright. I appeared to be unscathed and made my way down to the cockpit. I was the last to board and didn't pay much attention to the other passenger, but I did notice that there were four others. My friend and neighbor Sali, was one of them. I said a quick hello and waved to the pilots and took my seat. It was very unusual to have more than two passengers on a cargo run and at the time I didn't know what circumstances had brought them all aboard. I was ten minutes late and believe me I struggled with that wondering if my tardiness had put us right in the middle of the storm's fury just as Ava did with the bracelets…"

Rosy interrupted Nash again. "What, what did you say about the bracelets?"

Evan reminded her that she was supposed to sit and be quiet. She shot him a dirty look.

Ava told her sister that she may ask questions whenever she wanted to and she hoped that we would all feel free to do so also. She said they would explain the bracelet thing later okay I told them to continue. Nash took up where he had left off.

"I didn't pay much attention to any of the other passengers right away as I could see that Ace was lying on the floor of the cockpit. He was bleeding profusely. Sali and I managed to get him off the cold hard floor and unto one of the sleeping bags from my newly acquired purchases. Sal gave him something to hold over his wound to curtail the bleeding. Monty was also injured but he said it was only a dislocated shoulder. Then Sal and I went to get the nurse and that is how I first laid eyes on Ava. She thought she was dead and had gone to hell and that I was the devil."

We all grimaced. I said, "Oh Honey; did you really?"

"Well, I was just sitting there not feeling anything and thinking that I must be dead when I heard someone call my name. I was hoping I was in heaven because you had always told me that there was no hell Mama, and then this strange man put his hand on my shoulder and asked if I was all right. He was calling my name. I looked into his big black eyes and knew exactly where I was…hell. He assured me that we were not dead and he was not the devil. He said they needed my help as the pilot was injured. He was not pleased that I was not a nurse and stormed away saying he was going to break into the medical supplies with or without my permission. I thought he was very rude."

Nash laughed. "And I thought that she was very haughty. A nurse always accompanies the medical shipment so I admit I was very annoyed with her even after she explained how she had come to be with the supplies. At the same time, I was also mesmerized by the fire in those deep blue eyes and I had a strange feeling in the bottom of my gut. I attributed it to stress at the time but before long I knew it was something else. She asked me to help her as she doctored Ace and that was the beginning. Before the day was over I knew I was in trouble."

Rosalyn raised her hand and said she had another question if it was all right with everyone.

"I have a few questions of my own." I concurred.

Rainey stood up. "Before we start cross-questioning these two, we should be congratulating them. I, for one want to welcome Nash into the family and hug my daughter."

He helped me to my feet and we enclosed our daughter and her new husband in our embrace. Nash thanked us for accepting him and for raising such an amazing daughter. Rainey pointed out that he had not had the pleasure of having a hand in that and that it was all my doing. He immediately apologised to me expecting me to take exception to his remark. His eyes were sad.

"Sorry Honey, I didn't mean it to sound accusatory; forgive me?"

"I think we are way beyond blaming each other aren't we? Let's make Nash comfortable with us before we reveal our confusing and painful relationship, okay?"

He hugged me. "You are right as usual. Now, how about a toast? Mary, do I have to go to the den or do you still have a bottle under the sink?"

"I do Mr. Rainey, only it be in the top cupboard now 'cause of the wee ones you know."

Johnny retrieved it and Amma passed us all a glass. Evan was shaking hands with Evan and hugging Ava. He told Nash that he had married into one hell of a family. Rosy almost reluctantly shook Nash's hand and said that she was reserving judgement for a while. Nash laughed and pulled her into his arms and jokingly said that he was doing the same thing. Ava told her sister that she would come to love Nash just as she did and asked her if she was angry with her because she had gotten married before her. Rosy appeared to be dumbfounded and said that the thought never crossed her mind but that she was sorry that she wasn't at the wedding and was sad that Ava was all alone.

"Oh, but I wasn't Sis! I had my new family beside me and our little wedding ceremony was incredible…just you wait, you will see what I mean."

I wanted to cry for not being with my daughter on the most magical day of her life, but I wouldn't. Anyone could see the love that poured out from them when they looked at each other and that was all the magic I needed.

Rainey raised his glass after everyone else had congratulated Ava and Nash.

"My daughter once asked me how it felt to fall in love and how would she know that it was real. That was at a most difficult time in my life…" He smiled at me but his eyes were sad again. "My Vienna was missing and I wasn't sure if I would ever see her again…"

No one uttered so much as a sigh while he took a few moments to compose himself. His anguish tugged at my heart strings. All I could do was squeeze his hand and whisper that I was right beside him and that I wasn't going anywhere.

"I know that Honey. Sorry people, I got lost there a little. Anyhow, I told Ava how I had missed all the signs at first and hadn't listened to my heart, but that I did now. I told her that her heart would sing and that she would eat, sleep and breathe with his name on her lips. She would know a joy that surpassed anything else she had ever experienced. I am so happy that I can see joy flowing out of her eyes and I know that it is love that put it there...to our daughter and our new son-in-law...may the joy and love they share today last forever."

Nash stood up. "Thank-you Sir; I only hope and pray that our love will last through the ages as yours and Vienna's has."

"None of this "Sir" stuff you hear?" Rainey asserted. "Rosy, what did you want to ask them?"

"I want to know why there were so many passengers on board if it was essentially a cargo plane and why they couldn't radio for help immediately to start with."

Ava said she would let Nash answer and he did to everyone's satisfaction. It was the first time that we had heard that there was a casualty and that the instrument panel and radio had been damaged beyond repair and that there was no black box on board. It was somewhat of a miracle he said that the pilots had not been killed as there wasn't much of the cockpit left. The windshield was completely shattered and the instrument panel was left hanging by its wires. Monty and Ace had been thrown to the floor and that was what probably saved their lives. He laughed a little saying there wasn't much left of the geese either.

"I want you all to know that Ava was a trooper. She was a little laid back the first day but the next day she took charge. Sali's skills in the kitchen were very limited and Evie lived on fast food and Monty and I were too busy with wood gathering to worry about food. We would have been satisfied with canned soup and crackers but Ava stepped in. She rescued the vegetables from freezing and made soup. She made potato salad and French fries and desserts with the fruit. Who would have thought that so much could be done with what we had and with only a small camp stove and an open fire? And that was just at camp! Once we were settled in at the lodge her expertise really excelled."

Mary clapped her hands. "That's my girl!"

"I can't believe you learned how to cook Sis. This doesn't sound like you at all." Rosy said.

"Don't get too excited everyone, I remembered how Mary did some things but mostly I read cookbooks as there were lots to choose from. Evie was a big help and the guys did the cooking of the wild game. Who are you to talk Rosy…I know you and Evan cook."

Rosy laughed. "You can't count what we do as cooking. I make salad and bake a few potatoes and open a can of beans. Evan barbecues steak and burgers, but we eat out a lot or else we are here and don't worry about our next meal. No, I am not a cook nor do I want to be."

"Well, the days were long and it was something to do and I enjoyed it." Ava confessed.

"What did you do at night and how did you keep warm?" Amma asked.

"The girls kept the fire burning while Monty and I were in the woods. If it was too cold they spent time in their sleeping bags in the tent reading or whatever. We ran the kerosene heater when it was needed, but fuel was a precious commodity so we were vigilant about its use. Ava was Ace's nurse so she had a lot to tend with there also."

"He wasn't any trouble Nash." Ava asserted.

"Says you now, but I am sure there were times he taxed even your patience Hon. This girl did everything without complaining…"

"I complained about the cold Nash. Stop making me out to be a saint please."

"Sounds just like her mother." Rainey teased.

"To answer your question Amma, we played cards at night and we talked. I learned a lot about live in northern Canada and about all the people I was stranded with, especially Nash. I am afraid I bent his ear a little too much the first night, but I was so worried about you Mama that I just blurted everything out about you and Daddy. I'm afraid there isn't much that Nash doesn't know." Ava professed.

"That's all right Dear; we wouldn't want him to arrive here totally unprepared would we?"

Nash laughed heartily. "You don't know how close that is to the truth, but I deviate. As I was saying, Ava was a trooper. She even had a bout with the Chinook fever…does everyone know what that is?" Nash asked.

Only Rainey knew of it but he was not aware of the consequences it can have on someone's mood and health until Nash explained what happened to Ava.

"Not only did she become ill but she had an experience of déjà vu which brings me to tell you of this most unusual coincidence. It appears as if this was not the first time that I had pulled Ava out from a snow bank…"

"Oh my God Nash," I stammered, "it was you, you're the boy who rescued her in Bern!"

"Snow bank, Bern, what's going on here Vienna, Ava?

"It's all good Rain." I reassured him. "This is not the first time that Nash's and Ava's paths have crossed. It was a long time ago wasn't it Nash, and yet when Ava first introduced you, I had the sensation that I had looked into those eyes before."

"My wife, the clairvoyant…"

"That's not fair Daddy. Mama cannot see into the future; she is just overly sensitive to such things and what about me? I'm the one who had the déjà vu memory?" Ava defended my sixth sense though there was no need to.

"You are right Ava, it seems as this is a day for me to put my foot in my mouth over and over again." He was asking for my forgiveness again with his eyes.

I said that I knew I was weird and that strange things happen to me and that everyone here knew that and I wasn't ashamed to admit it and that he was free to joke about it all he wanted. He grimaced and asked what happened in Switzerland. After my explanation, Nash told Rainey that this was not the first time that they had met either. Talk about the ribbing that went on then. Rainey relaxed a little when Nash explained the circumstances of their meeting. He apologised for not remembering and asked for Nash's forgiveness saying he definitely had other things on his mind at that particular time. He clutched my hand to his heart. I wondered what kind of an impression we were making on our new son-in-law with all of our faux pas. As it turned out, Ava had already alerted him to our fragile relationship that dated back almost twenty four years.

Rainey asked Nash and Ava to continue on with their adventures in the wilderness.

"Well Sir, everything was going along relatively well and I thought Ava and I were getting closer day by day and then I told her I was leaving for a few days to look for help. She was not pleased and went so far as to unzip her sleeping bag from mine that night…"

Rosy violently interrupted him. "What, you were already sleeping together?"

Evan's chair made a scraping sound as he rose and told Rosy to follow him into the kitchen.

She hesitated for a few seconds. Evan pulled her chair back, and then with a huff, she rose and followed her fiancée. Had Rosy always been this blunt? I wanted to apologise for her outburst but Rainey beat me to it.

"Sorry kids; I think Rosy has forgotten that you are a grown woman Ava."

"She has always been so protective of you, and I guess that will never change no matter how old you are." I added.

"I don't think that's it at all Mama. She never once opposed my hapless relationship with Randy. In fact, she encouraged me to accept his proposal even when I confided in her that I didn't think he was the "one." Now I am three years older and a whole lot wiser, and if she can't tell the difference between a silly teenage fling and the ardent love I have for Nash then her eyes and ears need readjusting. No, there is something more going on with her then just concern over Nash and me sleeping together. She has been cool towards Nash from the minute she met him. In the backseat of the helicopter she asked me if something was going on between him and me. I told her there was and she said she hoped it wasn't a case of Stockholm syndrome which was plain silly as I was not Nash's captive. I was shocked by her assumption but laughed it off. I am not laughing anymore."

Nash told her not to be too hard on her sister and that he would have her eating out of the palm of his hand before the night was over. "You know, maybe she wasn't too far off with that Stockholm thing. Maybe you did develop an emotional attachment to me because you were fearful and anxious. Maybe it was your way of coping."

"Yes, sure that is it Nash and love has nothing to do with it." Ava said defensively.

"I don't mean now Sweetie… but maybe in the first few days."

"That's a bunch of "you know what." I can't believe you said that."

Rainey chimed in. "Hey you two, we will have none of that second guessing each other. Vienna and I have enough to go around for everyone, don't we Honey?"

I tried to make light of it. "I suppose we do, but that is not the heart of the matter. Rosy has been rude and I apologise for her discourtesy Nash."

"There is no need Vienna, but thank-you. I understand where she is coming from though." He put his arm around Ava and said he was sorry and that he knew she loved him.

Did this sound familiar to me? Could they be the mirror image of Rainey and me? No, of course not; they didn't have a two decade history that could drag them down to our level.

Rosy looked a little sheepish when she and Evan returned. "I'm sorry Ava, Nash…I seem to have jumped to conclusions again without hearing the full story. It really is none of my business anyhow, and as Evan so wisely pointed out, I have absolutely no idea what you had to contend with up there. I am thankful that you had each other."

Ava reached across the table and took her sister's hand. "It's okay Sis. I suppose that you are all wondering the same thing about Nash and me sharing sleeping bags. It was very cold up there and Nash made me change into dry clothes before I went to bed that very first night. He warmed a pair of long-johns up for me over the bonfire and sent me inside to change. That did not go well as I started hyperventilating the second I undressed. He came in and found me shivering uncontrollably in my sleeping bag. It didn't matter that the bag was good for minus forty degree weather, I could not warm up.

He zipped our bags together and started the process of massaging my body back to life. I was a little resistant at first, wasn't I Honey?"

"Umm, resistant is not the word I would use; you were downright defiant! I persevered and within five minutes or so she quit struggling and started to relax. You know about the benefits of body heat don't you Rosy? That's all it was; a survival tactic. Ava was even able to joke about it saying that it was not her motive operandi to sleep with a man on a first date. We just seemed to evolve from there and all was well until I told her that I had to venture out and look for help. I thought that she had come to terms with it, but obviously she hadn't. She woke up in a mood the next morning saying that she was living a bloody live nightmare and that nothing was real. I attributed it to the Chinook fever. When she wouldn't even look at me or wish me good luck when I was leaving, I figured that I had read her all wrong. I left hoping that I would find a way off the mountain and get her home to her family. I was pretty sure then that I had met the girl I wanted to spend the rest of my life with but she didn't feel the same way, so my heart was very heavy. I didn't look back and within minutes I would be out of sight from her and the others when I heard her calling my name. I turned and there she was running after me following in my footsteps and falling down every few feet with Asta on top of her. She asked me if I would wear her tartan scarf and she presented me with a little flag that she had made for me. She said it was to keep me safe. I have never in all my life received a more precious gift."

We were all tearing up a little…well at least the women were. Rainey cleared his throat a couple of times and squeezed my hand extra hard. Nash stood up and produced the little flag from out of his wallet. Ava was amazed that he still had it.

"Of course I do." he declared. "I only had to call upon its' magic once so it still has power."

"You used it once…you never told me you were in any danger so when and why?"

"It wasn't for me Ava. I don't think this is the time for your parents to hear about your little escapade do you?"

Ava said, "Good God, no!"

The cat was partly out of the bag and we all demanded to know what she had done. Nash told us that we had a very brave daughter and reiterated her run-in with the cougar. Rainey told her that wasn't being brave, but rather reckless. She said that she knew it and was very thankful that Asta was with her and that her barking had led Nash and Monty to her. She thought that maybe there really were some magical powers in the flag after all. The two of them continued on with their story after Ava explained the legend behind the flag. I had heard it before but never really put any stock in it. Finally, it was time to talk about the wedding. Rosy wanted to know why they had decided to get married and how did it come about. Nash took over. He told us that he had spent the whole of Christmas Eve day getting up the nerve to ask Ava if she would marry him. He knew they may be found anytime and then what would happen? Would they go their separate ways never to meet again? No, he wasn't going to let her get away on him. He knew the time was right after he calmed her down upon the discovery of my bracelets.

"Yes," Ava admitted, "I was pretty shook up. Nash convinced me that they or me were no way responsible for the plane crash or Grandfather Little Crow's death."

"Oh Darling," I said regretfully, "I am so sorry that you had to find them like that. I didn't even discover they were missing until weeks later which was very unusual because I always know where they are. Your dad tried to convince me that you probably didn't even have them with you at the time of the crash."

"It's okay Mama because without them Nash may never have asked me to marry him."

He laughed. "I doubt that very much hon. It seemed like a good time for me to pop the question though and so I went for it and was met by a very resounding "NO.""

"Why, why did you refuse him Ava?" Rosy asked.

"Because he didn't know who I was." Ava said flatly.

I asked her what she meant.

She explained how she had kept her true identity a secret because she was afraid everyone would think she was some noblewoman and they would treat her differently. She was worried that Nash would feel uncomfortable with her when he found out that she was an heiress. Rainey asked her if at that time she had plans to bring him home with her. She said she did.

"So, you were just going to march him up to the front door and hope he didn't notice that Avanloch was a castle?"

"I hadn't thought that far ahead Daddy."

"Funny because I asked her the same question and she had the same response. I have a question for you Sir, and you too Evan? How did you react when you discovered that the women you loved were women of means and home to them was a medieval castle?"

Rainey told Evan to go first. "It wasn't a shock Nash because I already knew Vienna and Rosy's dad, Jeremy. I was a worn out bush pilot in Australia and thinking of relocating to a more hospitable climate when I came upon an ad posted by Lands' End Airlines in London. They required not only a pilot, but a mechanic also. I fit the bill and gave them a call. I came up for an interview on my own dime and thankfully I was hired in the spring of nineteen seventy five. I met Vienna and Rosy's father, Jeremy McAllister, shortly after and have been the company's and family's personal pilot ever since. I still work as a mechanic at the hangar, but am available at a moment's notice if I am called upon by the family. I met Rosalyn later in the summer. She was fifteen to my twenty three. I was attracted to her, but she was too young for me to do anything about it. To her I was just someone who worked for the company."

"That's not so Evan. You know I had a crush on you." Rosy interjected.

He laughed. "Yeah, a teenage crush; every older man's dream and terror."

Ava asked him what he meant by that and he said to ask her father and he did.

"I knew when I met your mother that she was way too young for me in age. Yet, she was so much more mature and sophisticated then women I had previously known who were twice her age. I was drawn to her innocent charm and devil may care attitude and I knew that it might mean trouble, but I couldn't help myself. I did not back off as Evan did."

"I'm very grateful that you didn't Dear." I said and told Evan to continue.

"Rosalyn's father passed away the following year and I was there to offer support to the family. Rosy and Ava had one of their rare quarrels after the funeral and I somehow ended up in the middle. I thought Rosy was a little too hard on her sister and I suppose I took Ava's side. Well, I am pleased to say that I lived to tell the story as I certainly heard it from Rose later on. I suppose that was the start of it all. We didn't start dating until she was seventeen. Now here it is six years late, and we are still only engaged. Anyhow Nash, back to your original question. I always knew Rosy lived in a castle and that her family was loaded so it didn't bother me. Hell, maybe that's why I hung around so long waiting for her…for the moolah."

"You don't give one iota about the money Evan so don't give Nash the wrong idea." Rosy jabbed her fiancée in the ribs.

He laughed and said, "What about you Rain? What did you think when you found out that Vienna was royalty and that she controlled an empire?"

I answered before Rainey had the chance to. "Evan Govern, you know perfectly well that I have no royal blood in me and as far as I know neither do any of the McAllister's. I did not earn one single dollar of the wealth that has been accumulated…I just married into it. I certainly do not control an empire!"

"He's just pulling your chain Mama; you know he loves you." Rosy came to Evan's defence.

"I know." I smiled at Evan and he winked at me and pretended to bow. I picked up a bagel and was going to throw it at him but Rainey caught my arm.

"Whoa there my love, these things can be lethal."

We all had a laugh, and then Rainey answered Nash's question.

"It was a very cold day in January when I first saw Vienna for the first time in twenty years. I did not think the day could get any colder…but it did. She did not seem pleased to see me and she ran away from me…again. I got pretty sloshed that night and kicked around a few good friends because they hadn't informed me that

Vienna made frequent trips back to Bridge Falls. They didn't want to stir anything up as they thought I was long over her. All they had to do was ask and I would have told them that I was never going to be over her. I was pretty cynical back then so I really couldn't blame then. I couldn't let her get away without confronting her. The rest is history and here we are today, and I think more in love than ever. So, hell no, the money or her status was never a problem. I would have loved her if she had been penniless and lived on a mountaintop in Timbuktu."

I could have cried but I just whispered that I loved him too.

"So Nash," Johnny said, "you've heard how Evan and Rainey handled it so what was your take on finding out that Ava was an heiress and had lived in a castle all her life?

"I was initially amused. You see, Ava told me that she had been lying to me about who she really was. I don't know about you guys, but my first reaction was that she was already engaged or worse yet, married. I certainly didn't expect the answer I got so I imagined that she thought I wasn't good enough for her. I'd be all right to have a little fling with but marriage was out of the question because I wouldn't be able to live up to her standards. She put me at ease over that immediately. We had fallen in love living in a tent in a frozen waste land so a castle was just a step up, right?" He laughed. "Lucky for me, she agreed to become engaged, but I had a surprise for her and that was that we were going to be married that very evening. It was Christmas Eve and the perfect night for a wedding. I will let her tell you about it. So, we had to deal with some crazy photographers at the airport because of who she is and I got to ride first class for the first time in my life so I'd say I am okay with her being somewhat of a celebrity. Money could, but will not jeopardize our marriage. If Ava wants or needs something that I cannot provide her with, I have no problem with her dipping into the family coffers. So nope, I am good with it. I loved her before I knew she was rich so that changes nothing."

Rainey stood up holding an empty glass. "To our sons-in-law… well said boys. We could not have chosen better for our daughters. Welcome to the family Nash!"

Ava told us about the wedding then and how beautiful it was. She said that Evie had it all documented on film and we would see for ourselves how lovely it had been. Nash had picked out a song for them to dance to from the owner's large collection of albums. It was the same one Rainey had chosen for our wedding song. She had us in tears again and then she laughed.

"Funny thing is that we don't know if we are actually legally married…Ace's licence may have expired. Nash is going to call him tomorrow."

"Suppose it isn't," Rosy wanted to know, "will you do it all over again?"

"You betcha," Nash said, "and the sooner the better!"

"I think you should definitely have another wedding whether the first one was legal or not and I think, no, I want you to get married a long side of Evan and me…let's have a double wedding; what do you think Sis, Nash? Is that all right with you Evan?" Rosy said excitedly.

Evan said he thought it was the best idea that she'd had ever had. Ava and Nash asked what we thought and we were in full agreement that a double wedding would truly be the icing on the cake. So, it was done, our grown up girls were to be married on the same day, May the seventh. The twins would be three weeks old by then so all was well. Amma got up and said she was going home as she had to leave some tears for the weddings. Evan and Johnny left for some undisclosed job at the workshop. I asked Rainey and Nash if they would mind if I had a little time alone with my daughters. Ava suggested that perhaps Rainey could show Nash the lay of the land. He said he would be delighted. Nash said that Ava had painted a picture for him of all the rooms, the visible ones and the secret ones so he was looking forward to seeing them in person…especially where the Black Russian and The Grey Lady hung out.

"Ava Quinn, excuse me, Ava Nash, have you been filling his ears with nonsense?" Rainey scolded her.

"Yes, factual nonsense…just in case, well you know…"

Ava laughed and kissed both her father and her husband and told them to have fun. It seemed like forever since I had spent any time with my two oldest daughters and soon we would all be separated so I best make the most of these special times. I had suggested to Rainey that he should advertise in the Waverly and Edinburgh papers that he was available for small architectural jobs and so he had. The replies were more than he had bargained for but he was up for the challenge as long as it didn't interfere with his most important job which was keeping an eye on me. He did most of his work in the downstairs office but also worked on them upstairs in the parlour when I was resting. We had moved the large settee and an oversize armchair from it into our spacious bedroom to make room for Rainey's drafting table. Of course Liliana liked to draw and colour and be with her father so he had built a small table just for her. She chattered incessantly so I don't think he got much work done when she was with him.

Ava and Rosy sat side by side on the settee and I sat in the armchair facing them. We talked for an hour or so about the weddings to be and reminisced about the "good old days." Rosy asked Ava if Nash would be able to adapt to life at the castle.

"Did you think we were going to live here Sis? I thought that Nash had made it clear that we were going to live in Akemantack? Our plans have always been to stay here until the twins were born and for your wedding…which is now mine also, and then we will be going back to Canada and to Nash's home."

"You have to be kidding! Surely you don't plan on living in the sticks in that frozen wasteland where bears and lions run free! Why on earth would you even consider such a thing?"

"Because he is my husband and we need to make a life for ourselves. Sure, there is a possibility that I may not like it at first, but I am pretty sure that I will adjust. It is not as uncivilized as you think Rosy and besides, we will only be living there for seven or eight months of the year as we will be coming "out" for the winter months. I think it will be the perfect place to raise a family."

"Oh sure, away from schools and hospitals or any kind of medical care. Hopefully you will come to your senses before you become pregnant!"

Ava had a peculiar little smile on her face and it dawned on me what it was. She had only had water at lunch; no alcohol and not even a sip of coffee. She was already pregnant.

I came to her defense. "That is uncalled for Rosy. It is your sister's life and what she chooses to do with it is none of your concern. Where else would she be if not by Nash's side? Now suppose you tell us what is really bothering you because I don't think it has anything to do with where your sister lives."

She said coldly and bluntly that Evan wanted to move. I was a little startled and asked her where he wanted to move to.

"A farm, can you believe it? He wants to buy a farm. He says he wants to get out of London and quit his job with Lands' End. Can you believe it?"

"Yes, I can. Evan is not a city person and that little three room flat the two of you reside in is hardly what I would call a home."

"Maybe you are right; we should get a bigger place, but moving out of town is not an option."

"Why not Dear?"

"Because of my job Mama; I don't want to be commuting every day to work."

"Then you should quit your job." I said offering her the solution.

"What? I can't quit my job! Why would you even suggest that I could?"

"Because you can; the company can and will exist without you being there ten hours a day, but your husband may not. You need to think of his needs. Evan loves it here so you should move back home and take your place as the Mistress of Avanloch."

"What are you talking about? That is your job and I am not…"

I didn't let her finish speaking. "I am giving up that title and so it is vacant. I only want to be known as Mrs. Quinn and that is why Rainey and I and the children are moving back to Canada."

Rosy sprang up out of her seat. "What did you just say?"

"You heard me right Rosy. We are moving back home after the babies are born so you need to take your place here as the lady of the house with Evan by your side. The title is rightfully yours and you need to acknowledge it. Times are changing. There really is no need for all this Lady and Laird nonsense, but you and Evan can keep it or dispense with it, that is up to you. I'm not suggesting that you completely retire from McAllister Enterprises, but you certainly don't need to be there every day. You do plan on starting a family soon don't you?"

Rosy hadn't heard a word I said. "He put you up to it didn't he? He says he loves me like a daughter, but what father would take his daughter away from her mother…or is it because Ava will be living over there too. I'm not really family am I so my feelings don't count, do they?"

"That's not so and you know it. You are every bit my daughter as is Ava and now thanks to Avaleena's diary, we share the same bloodline. That however has no meaning to me for I have raised you and I have loved you and I always will. I am going to miss you something crazy and it is not like we are never going to see each other again. I will come back and I hope you and Evan will come and visit us in Bridge Falls. This was not Rainey's idea; it was mine. I asked him to take me home last fall way before I even knew Ava would be moving to Canada. She will be just as far away from me as you will be."

"How can you call it home? This is your home; you have been here forever. If you go, then I am going too!"

"Avanloch is your rightful place and you will come to see that. You and Evan will be the perfect caretakers, I am positive of that. Besides, your mother is here. You couldn't leave Maveryn now could you?"

Rosy headed for the door just as Rainey and Nash arrived. "You're my mother, but you seem to have forgotten that!"

Rainey stopped her. "Hey, hey, what's going on here? Where are you going in such a hurry and in a huff young lady?"

"You should know as you are taking my mother and moving away!"

Rainey looked at me disapprovingly. "I thought we were going to do this together Vienna?"

Defensively I told him that the opportunity arose and it had seemed like the perfect time.

"Yeah, well I can see that went swimmingly well." He shook his head and went through the door he had just come through calling Rosy's name.

Nash sat down next to Ava and took her hand. "I take it that she didn't take the news well?"

"This is the first I heard of it, how do you know?" Ava asked.

"Your dad told me but said it was hush-hush until your mom and he could tell Rosy. I told him that it would make you very happy and that it is a heck of a lot closer to visit you in Bridge Falls then coming all the way over here to Scotland. I'm sorry that it has made Rosy unhappy."

"Hopefully Rainey can placate her. If not then Evan will. It's going to happen so she will just have to accept it. How did your tour of the house go Nash?"

"Exceedingly well. I am looking forward to discovering more intimate details in the days to come as one cannot appreciate the magnificence of the décor in just one walk through. The ornate chandeliers and elaborate ceilings alone took by breath away. Ava has told me that you remodeled most of the rooms?"

"It kept me busy as I had not much else to do besides care for the girls for some twenty years. Now, I believe that you two may have something to tell me?"

Ava blushed a little. "I'm not sure Mama, but I think I may be pregnant."

I reached out and took hers and Nash's hands. "I thought as much. I am very happy for you and for me and Rainey too. The first thing we have to do is get your hunch confirmed. It's a wondrous thing to be pregnant and I want you to enjoy every minute of it. Does Nash know about "you know what?"

He laughed. "Do you mean about the "girl" thing? No problem as I'm rather looking forward to a little doll that looks exactly like her mother and grandmother."

I smiled and said that it was an age old hex. "I just accepted what my mother and Aunt Jannie told me. I have wondered if there was some way to reverse it as I would have liked to give Rainey a son, but thanks to my great, great, great grandmother, we Lafontaine women have to pay for her indiscretion."

"What do you mean by a hex Mama? I thought it was just a hereditary issue."

"Have I never told you about Magyar?"

"No you have not; I have never even heard that name before."

Rainey reappeared just as I was about to speak. He pulled up a stool and sat down beside me.

I asked him how Rosy was. He shrugged his shoulders and said that it was hard to tell. She said that we were mean. He left her crying in Evan's arms and asked me who Magyar was.

"Vienna was about to tell us how the spell that was cast upon her great, great, great grandmother came to be that has prevented the women in her family from having male children." Nash explained to Rainey.

"My wife lives this enchanting life…you know, gypsies, fairies and magic, so don't put too much stock in some of the yarns she spins. This is a new one to me though…when did you come up with this romantic notion that your family was cursed Hon?"

"It's not my story." I replied a little too sharply. "I shall tell it for Ava's and Nash's benefit. You can believe it or not, makes no difference to me."

"This took place in seventeenth century England. I'm not sure of the actual date or place; I would have to ask Aunt Jannie again. Anyhow, Magyar… she was known by May; fell in love with an Earl who was already married. His wife was a bit of a sorceress and barren herself. She put a hex on May saying that she and all her descendants would never bear a male child. So far it is true as no LaFontaine woman has ever bore a son. The Earl never got the son he wanted to carry on his name and soon left May and their three daughters. That's all I know. Now if you will all excuse me I think I am going to have a little rest before dinner."

Rainey looked a little sheepish and said that was a good idea. I hugged the kids and went into the bathroom. Rainey asked if I needed his help and I said that I didn't and that I would see him at dinner. He said he'd leave me to rest then and that he was going to track down Tanny and Liliana and see what they were up to.

I heard the door shut behind him. I needed some fresh air so I opened the patio doors and felt invigorated by the balmy winter breeze. I wandered the deck paying homage to all the statues that Rainey had erected in my absence last year. I stopped at the sculpture of Diana. Rainey had told Tanny that it reminded him of me because

I was graceful, yet slightly wild and liked to dance in the moonlight. I smiled and laid my hands on my stomach voicing that I was anything but graceful right now. I thought I would like to go for a walk and wondered if I could maneuver the back steps. I reached up and found the key in the alcove above the gate and unlocked it. The steps were dry. I decided to change my footwear for some decent walking shoes. I grabbed a cloak and a small flashlight…just in case. I descended the stairs slowly holding on to the railing as I went. When I reached the bottom I looked back up and complimented myself for my victory. It was time I got out of the fishbowl…I knew everyone was just looking out for my well-being but they needed to give me some credit for being able to look after myself. I would be back before anyone even knew I was gone.

The pavilion seemed like a safe choice. I had expected the walkway to be wet but it wasn't. I was about to descend down the six steps into the pavilion but stopped at the top and surveyed the vistas that surrounded the castle. I was going to miss the grandeur of these Scottish moorlands, the marshes, the endless valleys and the snow-capped pinnacles of Widow's Peak. I best get my fill of it over the next six months. My eyes came to a halt when they reached the crypt. Did I think I could manoeuvre the grassy path to have a visit with Maveryn? I stepped off the paved sidewalk unto the lawn and was pleasantly surprised that I didn't sink in too deeply. I turned and looked back towards my bedroom window half expecting to see my husband peering down at me. I shrugged my shoulders and said, "Here goes."

I made my way gingerly over the embankments until I was on the pathway to the mausoleum. It was clear sailing now and I picked up my pace a little. I reached the entry and pulled the door open. As always, I placed the rock against the door to hold it open. I knew perfectly well that the door could be opened from the inside but… well, that was just my little paranoia. I walked directly to the south wall where Maveryn's niche was.

"Hello my dear friend; I am sorry I haven't visited for a while, but I am here now." I removed the dead flowers from her vase and apologized for not bringing fresh ones. "Perhaps I will gather some greens from the trees before I leave. I can't stay too long as Rainey will be checking on me soon." I sat down on the concrete bench in front of the stained glass window and commenced with my chat beginning with the news that both Rosy and Ava were home safe and sound after their adventures. "But of course you knew that, didn't you Mave?"

I felt a twinge in my belly and laughed saying that the twins were objecting to my sitting on the cold bench. The cramp intensified when I stood up and I knew it was time to head for home. I said my goodbye quickly and made my way slowly to the door holding on to the wall as I went. Once outside I bent down to remove the rock and was immediately met with resistance in the form of painful spasms. I felt liquid running down my leg. I cursed myself for not peeing before I left the castle. I managed to right myself and headed for home. I pulled my little flashlight out of my cloak as darkness began creeping in. Another barrage of pain hit. I made my way to a large yew tree and leaned on it for support. I felt between my legs. I was pretty sure that my water had broken. I panicked when I pulled my hand away and discovered that the wet, gooey liquid was blood. I had to get home, I had to get home. I somehow managed to get back on the path before I collapsed. I pulled my knees up to my chest and screamed. I tried to fight off the blackness that was enveloping me. "Rainey…Rainey." I would die with his name on my lips.

CHAPTER 10

The Last Dance

"All right girls, that's enough dancing for one day. You've plum tuckered me out. Turn the music off Tanny and let's go see if your mom needs help getting ready for dinner." I bent down and let Lili crawl up onto my shoulders. Tanny opened the door into the great hall where we met Rosy, Ava and Nash. Rosy asked me if I had heard it too.

"I'm afraid I didn't hear anything; the girls had the stereo cranked up full blast."

"It sounded as though the helicopter just took off." Rosy said as she walked towards the entrance. She opened the door and we watched Evan's heli disappear from sight. "That's odd; he never said anything about going anywhere. I wonder…"

She never managed to finish her sentence as we all turned when we heard the back door slam and saw Amma running towards us yelling something about Vienna. She reached us laboring to get her breath.

"Where is she Rainey, where's Vienna?" She finally managed.

"She's upstairs in her room Amma…why are you so panicky?"

"Because I just got a call from Jake at the stables saying that Johnny told him to call me because Vienna was in trouble."

I felt an icy chill run up my spine. "Take Lili, Rosy"

I heard the child guard at the bottom of the steps snap as I slammed it open. I took the stairs two, three at a time, kicking the guard at the top open as I sprung through it. Ava was yelling behind me but I was oblivious to anything she was saying. I was met with a cool gust of wind as I opened our bedroom door. "Not again, not again Vienna!" I shouted as I realized that she was not on the balcony. I peered in every direction over the railings; she was nowhere to be seen. The gate was open; the key was still in the lock.

"Where is she Daddy, where's Mama?"

I told Nash to look after Ava as I bolted down the steps. Where could she be, where would she go…the mausoleum of course. I was winded when I reached the crypt. I inhaled and took a deep breath because the rock was still holding the door open so that meant she was still inside. I entered calling her name. I could see immediately that my girl was not in this chamber of the dead. Ava was calling me. I stumbled blindly towards her voice. A light was showing me the way. Nash took my arm and shone the flashlight to a puddle on the path.

"Over there Daddy, there's another one by that tree…its' blood, its' blood…" Ava cried.

Nash was the voice of reason. "Let's not speculate as to what happened or if that is even Vienna's blood. The good thing here is that it appears as if Evan found her and got her into the helicopter and maybe Johnny is with them too. They wouldn't have had time to contact the house…"

"No," I interjected, "the intercom to the house is down, but the one to the stables and shops isn't." I took off racing towards the house with Ava and Nash following. We rounded the corner of the garage and met Rosy and Amma running down the driveway.

"We have to get to the hospital, hurry, hurry." Amma said passing me some keys. "I don't even know which car they are for, I just grabbed a set."

I took them from her. "They are for the sedan; get in everyone."

Nash took the keys out of my hand. "I think not Rainey."

Ava and Rosy pulled me into the backseat and sat me between them holding onto me for dear life. Amma sat in the front with Nash. He said it might take him a minute or two to adjust to having the wheel opposite of what he was used to. She told him that he may feel compelled to cross over to the other side of the road but he must resist the urge to do so. She said she would warn him if he started to drift. He thanked her.

"What has happened to Mama; do you know Amma??" Ava pleaded.

"Johnny phoned and told us to get to the hospital in Waverly as fast as we could. He said that Evan had found Vienna on the path to the crypt and that she was haemorrhaging. He managed to get her to the garage and called Johnny and the two of them got her into the helicopter. They didn't feel that they had a minute to lose. He said she was still in emergency and they were waiting for word on her condition. I'm sorry, but he said her condition was grave."

Ava and Rosy were weeping. I was numb. I knew it was my fault that Vienna was in the state she was. I had left her alone too long and I had chastised her several times over the course of the day. She had sought refuge from me again and in doing so I had put her life in jeopardy. She was this special flower that I adored and loved more than anything else in the world. I had plucked another petal from her spirited persona, and now she was paying for my insensitivity. I felt a tear slide down my face as I cradled our two girls. I would not let them suffer anymore by proclaiming my guilt once again. Nash was driving as fast as it was safe to do so, but Waverly had never seemed so far away.

Amma instructed Nash to drop us off at the front door of the hospital and they would park the car and meet us inside. There was no one manning the front desk. I cursed. Rosy seemed to know her way around and led us around a corner where there was several nurses sitting at a counter behind a glass partition. Rosy explained who we were and asked where her mother was. One nurse picked up a phone and the other came around to us and said they were expecting us and would we please follow her to the second floor. We met Johnny coming down the hall as we alit from the elevator. He was wearing hospital "scrubs" and there was a bandage on his right arm.

I grabbed his left arm begging him to tell me where Vienna was. "Tell me she's all right Johnny, tell me she's alive! My God, what happened…there was so much blood…"

"Thank God you're here." Johnny said fervently. "She's in surgery Rain. She was haemorrhaging something awful…thank God

Evan found her when he did. We didn't have time for anything; we knew we had to get her to the hospital and fast. What was she doing out there in the dark anyhow?"

All I heard was the word "surgery" and I asked him why she was in surgery.

"They are trying to save her life." He said bluntly.

I felt my legs give out from under me. Johnny and the nurse caught me and walked me and the girls to a private family room. The nurse left saying she would see if she could get us an update of how the surgery was going. Ava encouraged me to sit down and promised me that her mother was going to make it.

"She just has to Daddy, she just has to."

I couldn't comfort her because I had the sinking feeling in my gut that I had seen the last of the queen of my heart. I couldn't tell my daughter that I feared her mother was dead. I heard them talking but I couldn't make any sense of what anyone was saying. Johnny was pacing back and forth. I wanted to join him, but I had no feeling in my legs. The door opened; Amma, Nash and Evan walked in.

Johnny and Evan had given blood. Ava asked if it was for her mother. Evan said it was a precaution in case she required more blood then was on hand. He said they were going to put a rush on testing it. Even though they were both Vienna's type there was a protocol that had to be followed. Nash asked where he could donate. I found myself standing up and said I would go with him just as the nurse came in smiling. She said that there was good news and that Dr. Macintosh would be with us in a few minutes.

"Did you hear that Daddy? Mama's going to be all right..." Ava said through tears.

"We knew she would make it didn't we Daddy?" Rosy tried her best to sound positive but there was anxiety in her voice.

We were all holding hands when Mac walked in. He was wearing a beanie on his head and cloth slippers on his feet. He came over to me and shook my hand.

"She gave us quite a scare Rainey." He said acknowledging the girls. "I don't mind telling you that if it wasn't for the fast action of these two men," he nodded to Evan and Johnny, "there would be a much different ending to this story. I'm more than thrilled to tell you all that Vienna came through the surgery with flying colors and we expect her to make a full recovery."

I felt like I could breathe again. "Did you perform the surgery Doc?"

"I'm thankful that I didn't have to." He let out a long sigh. "Thankfully, Vienna's gynecologist,

Dr. Beatty was still on the premises after conducting a seminar earlier. I credit her expertise with saving Vienna and the twins…" He saw the shocked look on our faces and laughed. He shook my hand again. "I'm pleased to tell you that you are the proud father of two, and here's the kicker…one's a boy."

I had to sit down. It didn't even register with me at first when he said the twins were born. All I could think of was that Vienna was alive. Everyone was congratulating me. Ava was laughing and saying that the curse was broken. Numbly I asked her what she was talking about.

"The curse Daddy; the curse that says that LaFontaine woman can't have a male child. Didn't you hear what Mac said? The twins are born and one's a boy, one's a boy."

"They are born? But it's too early Mac…how?"

"It was determined that Vienna had a placenta abruption. This means that her placenta had prematurely separated from the uterine wall which caused the excessive bleeding and a decreased supply of oxygen to the babies. The bleeding could not be controlled and so an emergency caesarean was performed. The babies were extracted successfully but Vienna was not out of the woods as the bleeding did not cease. The only way to stop this was if her uterus was removed. I'm sorry Rainey; we tried to contact you for permission but were unable to. The surgery was necessary to save her life. There was no time for a local anesthetic or epidural to take hold and so she had to be put under general anesthesia."

"You know I would have consented to anything Mac, anything that would have saved Vienna's life. I need to see her, I need to see my wife Mac." I pleaded.

"They were just finishing up with her when I left the operating room. Let's just give them a few more minutes to transfer her to recovery, okay? Do you think you can answer a few questions for me first?"

"Can't it wait? Surely nothing is of any importance right now."

"Maybe we can answer your questions Mac. I don't think Daddy is thinking too straight right now. What is it you would like to know?" Ava volunteered.

"The causes for a placenta abruption vary. I know Vienna didn't smoke or use drugs and she did not have high blood pressure. Did she complain about discomfort and tenderness in her abdomen? Did she have any swelling in her legs lately?"

Ava said she couldn't answer that as she had been away for three months and just arrived home today. She asked him if her mother's anxiety over her was in some way responsible for what had happened.

"Yes my dear," Mac said to Ava, "I am well aware of your absence and am very happy that you made it home safe and sound. Of course stress plays a big role in our health, but seeing you were home when this happened I doubt very much if it had anything to do with her abruption. Does anyone else have anything to add?"

Rosy and Amma said that Vienna had not complained to either of them of any pain or discomfort. I concurred and kept my guilty tongue to myself.

"So it appears as if our girl was just out for a walk by herself when she got into trouble. Evan, can you elaborate a little more on how you came to find her?"

"I was just about to close up the garage when I heard something. At first I thought it was an owl screeching and was about to dismiss it as such when I saw an erratic flashing of light. It was not very bright but was darting from side to side. Suddenly, it arched straight up into the sky and I swear something touched my shoulder. I looked around, but no one was there. I guess curiosity got the best of me and I thought that I had better check the light out."

Rosy hugged him fiercely and said thank God he did. He smiled. "I'm glad I did too Honey. Don't laugh; but I honestly thought that the shape I saw crumbling to the ground was the fabled Grey Lady. It took me a second or two to steady my nerves before I checked it out. I practically had a heart attack when I saw that it was Vienna lying under the grey cloak. She still had the flashlight in her hand and it was still aiming skyward. As I took it from her, a vapour, will-o-the-wisp, shadow…call it what you may, appeared, rose, and then just vanished. There is no doubt in my mind that it was your mother Rosy." Evan choked up as we all did. "It would stand to reason wouldn't it that Maveryn had followed her and stayed with her until help arrived…you tell me because I have no other explanation as to what happened. Was it her hand I felt on my shoulder? I know strange things go on at the castle, but this is all new to me…"

"Just go with it Evan. If I have learned anything living here, it's that it is best to except the paranormal as just another fascinating aspect of living in a centuries old castle." I suggested.

Evan shrugged as if to say he would deal with it another time. "I didn't have time to dwell on the mystifying vapour because I realized that Vienna was lying in a pool of blood. I picked her up and ran as quickly as I could back to the garage. I didn't think I could get her into the copter by myself and started yelling for help. Of course no one heard me. I put her down on the bench and called the shop; Johnny wasn't there so I tried the stable. Luckily he had his motorbike there and within two minutes we had Vienna loaded. I daren't take the time to go to the house Rainey…I'm so sorry for that."

I pulled him into my embrace and patted his back. I would be eternally grateful that he hadn't as it was his quick decision that saved Vienna's life.

"And, I will be forever sorry that I didn't get that intercom to the castle repaired. You should know Rainey that she uttered your name before she lost consciousness. I promised her I would get you to her, but there was no time…there was no time. I have never been more scared in all my days. All I could do was cradle her and hoped that by elevating her legs that I was somehow curtailing the blood flow and we prayed. Lord, how we prayed." Johnny offered.

"All our prayers were answered today guys." I turned to Mac. "I need to see my wife **now!**"

Ava asked if we weren't forgetting something; namely the babies. Mac said they were in the neonatal intensive care unit, {NICU} and to prepare themselves because they were very tiny. He called a nurse to escort them to the unit and took me to where Vienna was recovering. The matronly nurse there was not pleased to see me but Mac smoothed it over with her saying that they didn't want to be responsible for keeping us apart any longer.

I sat down next to the bed and reached under the blankets and found her hand.

"I'm here Baby, I'm here."

I haven't a clue as to how much time elapsed before Vienna started to stir. I alerted the nurse. She put her magazine down and encouraged Vienna to open her eyes.

"There, that's it luv, it's time to wake up. Don't you want to say hello to your hubby?"

She nodded in my direction and Vienna turned her head and attempted a little smile.

"Hi Gorgeous." I smiled back.

"You haven't called me that in a long time." She said groggily.

"Well shame on me for not voicing what is so." I stood up and stroked her face. "You are the most beautiful girl in the world and I love you so very, very much."

"I love you too Rainey." She looked around. "I don't know where we are though. I am so very tired and my shoulders hurt something fiercely and I have a headache. What's wrong with me?"

The nurse informed us that she was calling for assistance in getting Vienna to her room.

"What does she mean…my room?"

"Honey, you are in the hospital. You had an accident and you had to have surgery."

She was quite insistent that she didn't have an accident. I wished the doctor was here to explain to her what happened. I held her hand as the crew moved her and the bed into an elevator and down to the intensive care unit. I had asked for her to have a private room so wasn't sure as to why she was being put in the ICU. I stood back as two new nurses rushed in and attended to her checking her vitals and her IVS. All the while Vienna was watching them eagle eyed. It was unnerving to see the statistics of her life blipping on the monitor.

"There you go Mrs. Quinn, you are all set. The doctor will be in to see you shortly."

Vienna was very calm, but there were tears in her eyes as she told me that she had figured out why she was in the hospital. She put her hands on top of the blanket and touched her stomach. "They are gone aren't they Rainey? I lost our babies didn't I?"

"You did not Sweetheart. The twins are born and you are just recovering from a surgery that was necessary to save your life." I squeezed her hands. "They are just down the hall sleeping in their little beds."

The tears were flowing freely as she asked me if I was telling the truth. I told her I would not lie about such a thing. Dr. Macintosh walked in flanked by Ava and Rosy. The girls rushed to their mother crying how wonderful it was to see her. I told them to remember that Vienna had just had surgery and to be gentle. They both looked at me and said, "Really Dad?"

Mac laughed. "I don't mind admitting that you gave me the biggest scare of my lifetime young lady. If it hadn't of been for Evan and Johnny's quick actions, it would be a whole different story, and that Dr. Beatty was here was a stroke of sheer luck."

Vienna asked him what he meant. He explained from start to finish what had transpired and Evan's and Johnny's involvement in saving her life. He apologised about the hysterectomy saying that she probably wouldn't be here if they hadn't performed it.

She thanked him and said that we had not been planning on having any more children anyhow. I squeezed her hand and she asked if she could see the babies.

"Well my dear," Mac explained, "tomorrow will be soon enough for that. You just need to know that they are resting comfortably in their incubators…they are very tiny you know."

"How tiny?" She asked hesitantly. "Are they too small to live?"

"No, not at all. The little girl, Novia, is that her name Rainey? She is 1.418 kilograms, 3 pounds, 2 ounces."

Her eyes sparkled. "You named her Novia? That is so beautiful Rainey."

"Novia Vienne," I said, "after her beautiful mother."

"And the other baby girl, what about her?" She questioned Mac.

"Haven't you told her yet Rainey?"

"What, or my God, she didn't make it did she?" Vienna cried.

"No, my dear, that's not it at all." Mac said patting her hand. "I'll let Rainey do the honors."

"Sweetheart, we do not have another daughter. We have a son; you gave birth to a little girl and a little boy. I know it's quite a shock and he has no name…"

She didn't even hesitate. "Yes he does, his name is Zander."

"Zander?" We all echoed.

"Mama, did you know you were having a boy?" Ava asked laughing.

"I suspected as much because no well-mannered LaFontaine lassie would dare to kick me as much as a boisterous lad would. His name is Alexzander, after your grandfather Rainey, and Paul after your father. I want him to be called Zander. I suppose I best make an amendment to his name. Alexzander Paul Evander Johnathan Quinn…what do you say Rainey?"

"Yes, yes, that is just perfect darling, just perfect." I smiled. "I don't want Novia to feel left out with only two names so I think she will be known as Novia Josephine Patricia Vienne…in honour of your dad and my mom."

"Oh, you two!" Rosy moaned. "Are you sure you don't want to add a few more names?"

"I think that is sufficient. Now is anyone going to tell me why I can't see the babies today and you never did tell us Zander's weight Mac?"

"He is a little smaller than his sister. He weighed in at 1.332 kilograms; 2 lbs,15 ozs."

"Oh, that is so tiny!" Vienna exclaimed.

"Some preemie twins can weigh less than 2 pounds, so not to worry. We are going to take very good care of them."

"I know you will but I need to hold them, I need to feed them."

"And you will my dear, all in due time. They need to remain in the incubators and be monitored for twenty four hours for any signs of distress. In the meantime the nurses will help you pump your milk that can be given to the babies through a nasogastric tube. You don't produce much milk for the first four days anyhow, but what there is will be beneficial to them. You can handle that can't you Vienna? Rainey and the girls can be your eyes. I know you are impatient but we have to keep you healthy also. I need you to rest comfortably for a few days and the way you will manage that is through pain medications…"

Vienna interrupted him. "Certainly not! I will not poison the babies with narcotics!"

Mac nodded. "I understand your concern, but they are a necessary evil. The anesthesia administered to you to control pain during your surgery should be leaving your body anytime now. You are going to need regular meds to ease the pain and discomfort so you may as well get used to it." He put his hand up to stop Vienna from objecting again. "Who's the doctor here? Good, now listen to me. The drugs do not enter the breast milk directly from the mother's blood like say asthma meds do, so you will be administered them after you have pumped milk. Now I am hoping that you will only need to be on these meds for 4 or 5 days and then we will switch you to something milder, all right?"

Vienna nodded, but not very enthusiastically.

"Good. Now we are going to be watching you very closely for the first few days for any side effects that may occur from the anesthesia or the other meds. No matter how small the complaint is I want you to inform the nursing staff, do you hear?"

I asked him what some of the concerns were. He passed me a list and I read it out loud for everyone to hear. It included severe headache, vomiting or nausea, stomach, back or leg pain, fever, trouble breathing or dizziness or fainting. Vienna remarked that since she was bedridden there was no chance of her fainting. Mac laughed.

"You think not do you My Lady? You lost one hell of a lot of blood and even though it has been replaced, you may still have light headiness."

She asked if she had Evan's and Johnny's blood in her. He told her it was on reserve and hopefully she would not require any more transfusions. He left us then. Vienna asked me what the twins looked like. I had to admit that I hadn't seen them yet. She asked me why.

"I had to be with you when you woke up. Ava and Rosy have been keeping watch."

"Well, they are here so who is watching them now?"

"I don't think they are going anywhere Honey, but I'm on my way." I kissed her and told the girls to make sure she didn't get into any trouble.

I found Nash sitting on a chair outside the viewing room to the NICU. I touched Nash's shoulder and asked him what he was doing.

"Just keeping vigil Rainey, just keeping vigil."

"Thanks, but as I told Vienna, they aren't going anywhere. God, they are so tiny."

A voice behind me asked if I was the father. I turned and was introduced to Barbara, the twin's nurse for the day. She asked me if I would like to take a closer look. I wasn't sure if I wanted to but I knew I had to for Vienna's sake. She gave me a gown and a mask and I followed her into the unit. I stood over their incubators and wondered how anything so small could survive. I had a lump in my throat the size of an orange. I wanted to reach in and pick them up and take them to their mother. Barbara said we would be able to hold them in a few days. She said they were breathing on their own and weren't showing any signs of distress. They were being monitored very closely and we were to feel free to ask for an update at any time of the day or night. I thanked her.

"They are going to be just fine Mr. Quinn; you can assure your wife of that." Barbara promised. "We are going to take very good care of them. Before you know it they will be 4 pounds and you will be able to take them home."

"How long will that take?"

"It varies, but it is usually four to six weeks. Smaller preemies can take up to eight weeks."

"What; that seems so long?" I asked flabbergasted that it would take so long to gain a pound.

She smiled and patted my hand. "It's an uphill battle and they will probably drop a few ounces before they start to gain. Soon they will be on a steady feeding schedule and then we will start to see things happen. One day at a time Mr. Quinn, one day at a time."

I nodded knowing Vienna would not be thrilled with the news. I asked Nash where Amma and the guys were. He said that the suite that the family had at the Inn was not big enough for them all so she was booking more rooms and then she had to go shopping for clothes for Evan and Johnny. He wasn't sure where they were. I tried not to visualize their stained clothing but it didn't work, and the guilt rose up to greet me again. I best get rid of the negativity as I could not have Vienna hear it in my voice.

I shuffled off to her room and found out that she had required her first dose of pain medication. Ava said that Vienna had become very agitated so the nurse had administered a mild sedative also. I told the girls that they should collect Nash and get something to eat. The fridge and the pantry at the family suite had already been stocked and they would make me a sandwich and be right back. I told them I wasn't hungry. It was then that I found out that it was midnight.

I sat by Vienna's bed and watched her sleep. She woke up briefly and smiled at me before falling back into a deep restful slumber. Nash arrived with a pint of milk and a ham and cheese sandwich. I settled in for the night in a recliner that had been brought in for my comfort. I had made it quite clear to the nursing staff that I was not leaving my wife's side. To my amazement, I fell asleep and awoke to see Vienna sitting up in bed smiling at me.

"Hi Rainey."

"Hi V." I smiled back.

"Why did you call me that; that's' two or three times now in the last few months? I was never "V" to you, so why now?" She asked curiously.

I got up and walked over to her. "I don't really know." I pushed her hair back from her face and kissed her. "You are and were always Vienna to me; sometimes "V" just comes out. I've been reminiscing a lot about how we met and all the good times we had… that's when

I wasn't being a jerk. I'm looking forward to returning to all our old haunts and our old friends."

"I am too Rainey. I'm really going to miss Avanloch and everyone, but Bridge Falls is calling to me to come back. I know not what awaits us there but I'm sure it is all good."

"I'm going to miss Avanloch too Honey. I'm going to miss lying on the knoll with you and Tanny and watching the clouds as they rise over Widow's Range and seeing them transform into dragons and unicorns and angels."

"We have clouds in Canada too you know. I can't believe I haven't asked you about our babies yet…have you seen them this morning?"

"Wait right here okay? I'll go and see what they are up to."

She grabbed my shirttail. "You are so funny Rain. Before you go I need to tell you that I am so sorry that I had the twins without you…it wasn't supposed to happen that way."

I wiped a little tear from her eye. "I know it wasn't and I am sorry that I was the reason that you had to suffer because of what I said to Nash about you living in a fairy-tale world."

"Oh my darling," she said softly, patting my hand, "that has nothing to do with my going for my little walk. And that is all it was supposed to be, just a little walk. I'm pretty used to your little remarks about the fantasy world that I sometimes live in so it had absolutely nothing to do with me venturing out on my own, do you understand?"

I told her that I would never be sure but she could rest easy as I was going to run everything past my brain before I ever opened my mouth again. She said, "Good luck with that and see what you can do about getting me out of this bed so that I can see our babies."

CHAPTER 11

Vienna

Because I was not allowed out of bed, I was taken in my bed that afternoon to the NICU. A nurse inclined the twin's incubators so I could get a good look at them. They were so very tiny. I shed a few tears marveling that these precious little beings could even survive. The next day I was able to get out of bed and be seated in a wheelchair for half an hour at a time. Rainey would wheel me down to the NICU and we would sit hand and hand and talk to our babies through the window. On the third day, we gowned up and visited with them up close. On the fourth day, I held and fed Novia for the first time. Rainey was right; she had my coloring and brown eyes. Both Ava and Lili had Rainey's electric blue eyes so I doubted very much that Novia's eyes would remain brown. Zander was finally strong enough to be removed from the incubator for more than five minutes three days later so I could nurse him. Whereas Novia was content and wide eyed, Zander was fidgety and only wanted to sleep. What could I say; he was a boy. He had blue eyes like his father.

I was moved to a private room near the NICU when I no longer needed to be monitored. Rainey never left my side except when I would kick him out after the twin's last feeding of the evening. He was determined to not miss one minute of their early days as he had not been privy to do so with Ava and Liliana. We would sit together for hours just holding our little miracles and telling them stories. I would watch Rainey as he talked lovingly to them telling them how they were going to love Canada and all the things he was going to do with them. He was going to teach them how to ride bicycles and horses and he was going to take them fishing along with their older sisters. I was so very thankful that he was with me this time from the get-go.

One day he arrived with a package for me from a department store. In it was a bright teal blue coat with a fake fur collar and a tam that went with it, a pair of mittens and ankle boots. He helped me get dressed and made me sit in the wheelchair even though I was quite capable of walking. He took me outside for a jaunt and some badly needed fresh air. This became a daily ritual. Some days we would pop into a little restaurant for lunch, but usually we would go up to his room at the inn where we would lie on the bed and cuddle.

Ava and Nash stayed for the first five days. I convinced them that Lili and Tanny needed them more than I did and so they should resume their lives back at the castle. They returned every few days bringing the girls with them for a visit and would spend the night with Rainey periodically.

Rosalyn and Evan were in the process of moving to Avanloch. Evan was ecstatic that Rosy had decided to reduce her days at McAllister Enterprises from five days to one a week. We had a long heart to heart one day. She was still not happy that Rainey's and I were leaving her and Avanloch, but she had come to terms with it and respected our decision.

Aunt Jannie and Uncle John visited once a week as did Ash and Gray. One day Roberge and Lauren showed up with gifts galore for the twins. I was so very pleased to see them in their new roles as husband and wife and to hear that they were going to be parents in seven months. They were both glowing and wanted us to be Godparents. I did not burst their bubble and tell them that we were moving back to Canada. Roberge's father had not returned from Brazil yet so there was no news of his lineage.

Zander was finally discharged from the hospital on March seventh, four weeks and three days after his birth. Novia had reached four pounds weeks earlier.

I was very happy to be home. Avanloch would always be my home away from home and I would leave with a heavy heart. It was time to move on however, and we would just as soon as the twins were old enough for the journey.

In two short months we would see our eldest daughters married to the men they loved. I was so very happy for them, yet I was sad that I would be so far away from both of them.

Rainey and I had a renewed love for each other even though that seemed impossible that we could love each other anymore than we already did. I guess tragedies do bring people closer.

Shortly after we were resuming life back at Avanloch, I had a very unsettling vision. I was sitting in the downstairs parlour with the twins in their bassinettes beside me. I had closed my eyes and there before me were thirteen figures in dark, hooded robes holding hands and dancing in a circle formation. They were chanting, "Alleluia, alleluia, the witch is dead. Rejoice; the wicked witch is dead." They parted and there on the ground was a woman lying motionless in front of them. I could not see her face but she had long flowing golden hair. I shivered. Had I just had a premonition? Lord, I hoped not. I would not let this image unnerve me as soon I would be leaving this mystical realm and all the ghosts that inhabited its walls behind. No, there would be nothing but reality and sunbeams in Bridge Falls for Rainey and me.

≈≈≈≈≈≈≈≈

Recipes from Uncle Bob's Cabin

Sali's Bannock: Oven 375-400 degrees F

Melt 1 tablespoon of shortening in baking pan
Dissolve ¼ teaspoon baking soda, ½ tablespoon sugar, ¼ teaspoon salt, 1 ½ teaspoons baking powder in 2/3 cups of water.
Approximately 3 cups of flour.

Make a well in the flour and pour in the liquid mixture. Blend quickly with your hands, adding more flour if needed to make a soft dough.
Lift it to the prepared pan and spread.
Bake for 20 to 30 minutes.

May also bake in a covered frying pan on top of the stove turning when 2/3 done or browned on one side. Eat while warm.
Add fruit to batter when in season such as Saskatoons or huckleberries.

Monty's Wild Game Spaghetti Sauce:

    1 pound grouse meat or venison cut in cubes or 1 pound lean
        ground beef
    ¼ pound of butter (only if using wild game)
    1 chopped onion or ¼ cup minced onion flakes
    Few cloves of garlic or pinch of garlic salt
    2-4 teaspoons Italian spices
    Salt and pepper
    1 large tin whole tomatoes
    1 small tin tomato paste
    1-4 tablespoons brown sugar (personal taste)
    1 pinch cinnamon
    1 tin mushrooms (optional)

Brown meat. Add onions and mushrooms. Sprinkle with salts and pepper.

Add tomatoes and tomato paste breaking up tomatoes as they cook.
Add ½ cup water.
Add Italian spices, a little more salt, brown sugar and cinnamon.
Heat to boiling and add 1 tablespoon butter.
Cover and simmer on low. If too thick add mushroom juice or a little more water.
Serve over pasta.

Nash's Moose Ribs   Oven 275-325 F

3-4 pounds spareribs or short ribs
Rub 1 tsp. salt, ¼ tsp. pepper into ribs. Brown meat in hot oil.
Mix: 1 minced onion
     2 tbsps. Brown sugar
     ½ tsp. dry mustard
     3 tbsps. Flour
     1 tbsp. Worcestershire Sauce
     ¼ cup cider vinegar
     1 – 1 ½ cups ketchup
     1 cup water
Pour over ribs. Cover and bake until tender; basting periodically with liquid in pan.
May add ½ cup celery OR Crushed Pineapple.

Evie's Christmas Trifle

     1 pkg. strawberry or raspberry jelly powder
     1 pkg. lime jelly powder
     Prepare as directed
     1 pound cake or white cake
     1 pkg. instant vanilla pudding prepared reducing milk to 1½ cups.
     4 cups whipped cream, cool whip or 1 envelope prepared Dream
         Whip
     1 can of mandarin oranges, pineapple chunks or any canned
         fruit, drained

Break cake into mouth size cubes and place in a glass bowl. Pour prepared jelly over and toss until absorbed. Fold in pudding and ½ of the whipped topping. Cool until set or make day before. Top with remaining topping.

Ava's Sourdough Starter

Combine ¾ cup +2 tablespoons all-purpose flour with ½ cup non-chlorinated water in a glass container. Stir vigorously until batter is smooth; it will look thick and be sticky.
Scrape down the sides, cover and store at room temperature 70-75 degrees F.
Let sit for 24-36 hours or until bubbling. Feed (with above mixture) every day or weekly if refrigerated.
To use: Take out amount needed for recipe and replace amount used to the starter.

Sourdough Bread (2 loaves) Oven 425 F

    1 cup sourdough starter
    1 ½ cups lukewarm water
    5-6 cups all-purpose flour
    1 tablespoon salt
    1 tablespoon sugar (optional)

Add water and 3 cups of the flour to the starter in a large bowl. Beat vigorously. Cover and let it work for 2 hours or more.
After it has doubled, add sugar and remaining flour.
Let rest 15 minutes.
Knead until smooth and elastic…add more flour if needed.
Cover and let rise until doubled—1-2 hours.
Form into loaves. Let rise 2 hours
Score loaves and bake 20-25 minutes — golden brown and sounds hollow when tapped on bottom.